George N. Rumanes

THE MAN
WITH THE BLACK
WORRYBEADS

PUBLISHED BY POCKET BOOKS NEW YORK

THE MAN WITH THE BLACK WORRYBEADS

Arthur Fields edition published 1973

POCKET BOOK edition published June, 1974

L

This POCKET BOOK edition includes every word contained in the original, higher-priced edition. It is printed from brand-new plates made from completely reset, clear, easy-to-read type. POCKET BOOK editions are published by POCKET BOOKS, a division of Simon & Schuster, Inc., 630 Fifth Avenue, New York, N.Y. 10020. Trademarks registered in the United States and other countries.

THE MAN WITH THE BLACK WORRYBEADS was originally published by Arthur Fields Books, Inc.

This book is dedicated to my wife, Maria
to my son, Nicholas
to my daughter, Sophia
and to the brave people of Piraeus.

AUTHOR'S NOTE

This is a story set in the ancient port city of Piraeus, Greece, during the dark days of the Nazi occupation of 1941–42. Although it is fiction, that occupation was all too real, as was the suffering of the Greek people. The German conquerors were determined to break the spirit of the conquered Greeks, and no weapon was more effective than enforced hunger. While their produce was shipped to Germany to feed the fatherland, Greeks fainted in the streets from hunger; by early 1942, in Athens and Piraeus alone, nearly two thousand men, women and children a day were dying of starvation and disease. The cemeteries could not contain all the bodies.

During the first year of occupation, the port of Piraeus was employed by the Germans primarily as the embarkation point for troops and materiel for the Greek islands. But when the island of Malta was reactivated by the British, the German high command, blocked from Italian ports, turned Piraeus into a major staging area for Rommel in Africa. Many ships such as the Bulgarian tankers mentioned in the first portion of the book carried precious oil to fuel the Panzerkorps. It was in the snug harbor of Piraeus that vast German supply fleets were provisioned with men and munitions, safe from attack by the RAF, which had its hands full trying to cover the British retreating before the savage onslaughts of the Desert Fox. A few daylight raids were attempted, but damage was insignificant and the German convoys continued to operate in and out of the port virtually undisturbed.

The events described in this novel are based on these historic facts. This is the story of the people of Piraeus at a strange and terrible time in their lives. I know the story. I am one of the people. I was there.

George N. Rumanes

Los Angeles, California

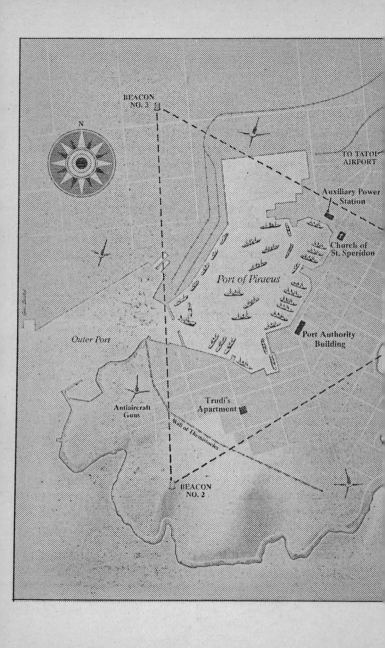

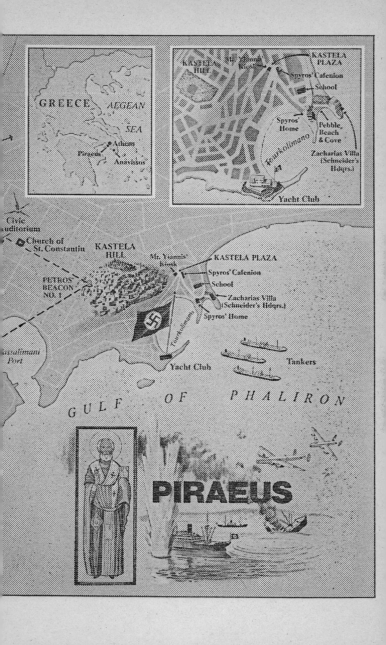

GREECE

AEGEAN
SEA

Athens
Piraeus
Anavissos

KASTELA
HILL

Mr. Yiannis'
Kiosk

KASTELA
PLAZA

Spyros' Cafenion

School

Spyros'
Home

Pebble
Beach
& Cove

Tourkolimano

Zacharias Villa
(Schneider's
Hdqrs.)

Yacht Club

Civic
Auditorium

Church of
St. Constantin

KASTELA
HILL

Mr. Yiannis'
Kiosk

KASTELA PLAZA

Spyros' Cafenion

School

Zacharias Villa
(Schneider's Hdqrs.)

PETROS'
BEACON
NO. 1

Tourkolimano

Spyros' Home

Passalimani
Port

Yacht Club

Tankers

GULF   OF   PHALIRON

PIRAEUS

BOOK I

DECEMBER, 1941

1

Aeschylus, writing in 490 B.C., called the little port city of Piraeus the "jewel in the diadem of Athens." But the father of ancient Greek dramatists carefully surrounded the phrase with quotation marks, so probably he borrowed it from some anonymous poet. The city had changed, of course, over the last twenty-five hundred years. It was larger; its population in excess of ten thousand, five times its size in ancient days. Its streets were now paved, power plants provided electricity, the port facilities were among the best in the world; but the qualities of Piraeus that had inspired Aeschylus remained virtually unchanged.

Her rocky, inhospitable soil and benign climate helped form her character. Men had clawed away rough, gray-brown earth to build their homes and schools, their hospitals, and open-air arenas; along the waterfront and beaches the buildings clustered together, but immediately behind the harbor the land soared to the sharp, jagged cliff of Kastela Hill, which overlooked the plains sweeping inland toward Athens, seven miles away.

The frugal crops that grew in the stubborn earth had to be nurtured, tended with love, but nature rewarded such attention with abundant yields. Almonds and olives and pistachio nuts dotted the small, gnarled trees, and beyond the city limits were lush groves of orange and lemon, accented with lime. When the breeze blew down to the sea it sometimes carried the hint of sharp citron, the delicate fragrance of almond, the light but rich scent of olive. This bouquet mingled with the stronger spices of saffron, oregano, and thyme. Figs flourished in the valleys, and everywhere the sun was kind to the grape vines, which, like the determined local farmers, somehow managed to survive in the dry, chalky soil.

The impression Piraeus created was one of dazzling,

3

almost unbearably bright whiteness. The buildings, most of them simple, were painted white—not an ordinary white, not a white that smudged or turned gray, but a white so pure that in bright sunlight it could bring tears to the eyes. Ports in other Mediterranean countries, nations like Italy and Spain, relieved their whiteness with splashes of pastel, but since antiquity Piraeus had remained white only, with a clarity unmatched elsewhere.

But even more than its sparse, dry soil, even more than its whiteness, Piraeus was shaped by the sea, and if the land was her heart, the sea was her soul. Her harbor, consisting of inner and outer portions like the chambers of some exotic seashell, was deep, and for thousands of years had provided ships of all nations with shelter from the raging storms that swept out of Asia Minor and Africa. The Phoenicians had found refuge there, as had the Carthaginians, the sailors of the Pharaohs, the Israelites. Alexander the Great had mounted his fleet in Piraeus when he had set out to conquer the known world, and both Julius Caesar and Mark Anthony had cast anchor there. She had been a major base for the warships of the Ottoman Empire, Great Britain, and France. Horatio Nelson had gone ashore from his flagship, and Napoleon Bonaparte had gazed from his quarterdeck at its rugged shoreline.

The water itself, Sophocles had written, was unlike the water anywhere else in the world. It was transparent, and shipboard arrivals marveled that they could peer from the decks of their vessels thirty to forty feet to the ocean floor. And as with the white buildings, those who saw the sparkling clarity of the water never forgot it. That water and the exceptional harbor attracted the ships of scores of nations to Piraeus, making her an unusually cosmopolitan city for her size. She had been called one of the most wicked, too; and for centuries seamen, stoked with beer and ouzo, would roar out of her tavernas to quench their passions in the brothels, whose doors remained open day and night.

The white warehouses that lined the harbor, the houses

on the steep, rising hill, the merchant vessels that rode at anchor in the placid waters of her harbor, all reflected the many facets of light striking the water. No wonder Aeschylus had called Piraeus a jewel. But what sort of gem was she? An emerald, perhaps. At some hours of the day her waters were deep, pure green. A sapphire, some said, because at other times the water turned a serene blue. On clear nights, when the moon shone and the heavens were filled with stars, the waters of Piraeus turned silver; and when clouds darkened the sky, as if to warn his mortals that Zeus was displeased with them, Piraeus' waters turned black, like the precious black pearls worth the ransom of a tyrant in the ages when Athens had been the most powerful, cultured, and influential city-state on earth.

Mostly the sea was tranquil. The sons of Piraeus found sustenance there, providing their families with fish of infinite varieties. For every merchant ship to drop anchor at Piraeus there were countless fishing vessels that made the port their home. These ranged from tiny one-man craft with small, ragged sails to ships of eight and nine hundred tons that required a full crew. Poseidon, the god of the sea, was the city's patron; and the people of Piraeus, almost all members of the Greek Orthodox Church, still nourished the superstition that his trident continued to watch over them.

Practically every man and boy in Piraeus could swim, and the sea held no terrors for them. In many families small children learned to swim before they could walk, but few regarded the accomplishment as anything out of the ordinary. The men of Piraeus always could swim, handle a boat, gauge the weather at sea, cast and mend nets, and manage a haul unaided. They could slice the water with speed, cavort like dolphins, causing those from other Greek cities to remark with amusement that the native of Piraeus was only part-human, the better part of him fish.

Piraeus had remained unchanged and changeless through her long, turbulent history. She had been a thriving commercial port in the days long before Homer, more than two thousand years before the coming of Christ, when the plains of Attica that would become Athens had pastured the sheep Euripides had called Attica's gift from the gods. Gradually the city-state had come into being, and in 493 B.C. Themistocles fortified Piraeus and made her the official port of Athens. All who came to Athens by sea, and they came by the thousands, disembarked at the port of Piraeus. When the Persian invaders, the first of many foreign masters, were driven out, Athens joined the Peloponnesian League of Greek city-states, and her great age of glory began.

Piraeus' sons fought in the Persian wars in their own phalanxes; they died at Marathon and at Thermopylae, and her seamen took the lead in the campaigns that smashed the supposedly invincible fleets of the Persians and Egyptians. Even the Phoenicians, long regarded as the most accomplished sailors in the Mediterranean, paid the seamen of Piraeus the supreme compliment, refusing to take up arms against them.

Piraeus first tasted the joys of democracy in 445 B.C. when Pericles, perhaps the greatest of all Athenian statesmen, gave the city-state this novel form of government, in which every freeman was his own master and participated fully in the affairs of government. Piraeus shared, too, in the culture of Athens' golden age, the time of Aeschylus and Sophocles, Euripides and Aristophanes, Socrates and Plato and Aristotle. Piraeus was advanced when Britons painted their naked bodies blue, Paris was a miserable village on the bank of the river Seine, and Rome was showing the first sign of active life.

The decline of Athens began about 360 B.C., at the time the most remote of Greek kingdoms, Macedonia, rose to prominence. The hard-driving Philip, the man who united the Greek city-states, was succeeded by his son, Alexander. Alexander was a military genius who conquered virtually all the known world at the time; and Athens, the capital of the empire, knew a new period of prominence and power.

When the Romans invaded around 150 B.C., the Greek states lost their liberties. Greece became a dependency of Rome, but her schools remained unrivaled; her philosophers and writers and sculptors continued to influence the world. Barbarian hordes began to invade Greece in 395 A.D., and thereafter, for fifteen hundred years, Athens and Piraeus knew a long, dreary succession of foreign masters —Roman, barbarian, Crusader—but they remained Greek above all else, and the foreign invaders could neither assimilate them nor drive them out. The long, harsh Ottoman rule that began in 1453 lasted almost five hundred years, yet all that time the Greeks continued to speak their own tongue, follow their own customs, cling to their ancient beliefs and traditions.

A rising spirit of nationalism caused the long-oppressed people to revolt in 1820. George I was placed on the Greek throne, and during his reign modern Greece attained a greater degree of independence than she had known since her fall to the Romans more than two thousand years earlier.

When World War II broke out, Greece managed to remain neutral, in spite of her alliance with the British. But on October 28, 1940, the Italians invaded her territory from Albania. Although hard-pressed, Britain sent a number of warships to Piraeus as well as several regiments of troops to help the Greek army. But the Greeks needed no assistance in their fight against Mussolini. The defenders, fighting under the command of General Alexander Papagos, counterattacked with such fury that they not only drove the Italians out of Greece but managed to occupy more than one quarter of Albania.

The beleaguered nations of the West laughed at Mussolini, but Hitler was not amused. The success of the Greeks gave the Allies an unexpected foothold, threatening his entire southern flank, and Hitler was compelled to act. The British, subject to an overwhelming Nazi air attack at home and threatened by the German Wehrmacht in North Africa, realized that Hitler could not afford to remain idle; they knew he would have to attend to Greece before concentrating on the Russian invasion, and any delay would be costly for him. In March, 1941, they augmented their small force in Greece. It was in Piraeus that the reinforcements debarked for Athens.

The Wehrmacht struck in April, 1941, and its invasion of Greece was a model of German military planning and efficiency. The Greeks were hopelessly outnumbered by the better armed, superbly trained Wehrmacht. The main Greek army was smashed, small pockets of desperate, heroic resistance were wiped out, and the German tidal wave moved across Greece. Athens and Piraeus braced themselves for the inevitable, and the king escaped with his government into exile. Over a century of Greek independence came to an abrupt end.

The people of Piraeus, for so many centuries accustomed to the vicissitudes of history, were compelled to witness the humiliation of the British expeditionary force. Totally lacking air cover, and with only token artillery support, the fewer than ten thousand men were overwhelmed by the onrushing Germans and retreated in disarray to Athens, then to Piraeus. The increasingly confused withdrawal became transformed into a headlong flight, and even seasoned troops lost their composure when they reached the harbor and found an inadequate number of transports awaiting them. The men crowded onto the ships, and under the fire of the Stuka bombers managed to escape to Crete, which they were forced to evacuate a few weeks later, in May.

Once again Piraeus, Aeschylus' jewel, was occupied by a foreign conqueror. Above the Yacht Club on the cliff, on the highest flagpole in the city, a huge red and black swastika banner snapped and fluttered in the stiff December wind.

2

Lela made the sign of the cross in front of the waterfront church and splashed through a puddle, spraying water on the men who stopped to let her pass.

The longshoremen knew her. When she was in a hurry, all that mattered to Lela was her destination. She could not see to her right, her left, or in front. Though it was early evening—an hour she rarely permitted herself to be seen outside—she was combing taverna after taverna in search of Hans, her German lover. She knew he was drinking ouzo somewhere around the port. That in itself did not concern her—it made him easier to handle. But if he drank too much, he would begin to feel the need for companionship, and she knew those tavernas where he hung out. There was always a girl only too eager to listen to a soldier's story, especially if he paid for her drink. And this Lela did mind.

For the saints had smiled on Lela Lellos at last. Hans was the best of all possible lovers—six feet three and strong as an ox. But give him enough ouzo, and there was no telling what he might do. Lela had too much invested in him to take a chance. The Wehrmacht had consigned him to washing cars in the motor pool with the rank of private when Lela had found him. Not only was he now Colonel Schneider's personal driver, which gave him freedom to travel anywhere, but he provided her with food, and these days food was far more precious than anything she could earn on the waterfront. Everyone Lela knew was hungry, many were starving. And though at times she felt guilty, she was still careful to hide the choice rations Hans brought her—tins of meat and soup, bread made in Colonel Schneider's own kitchen, fresh fish. Yes, the saints were watching over her, and let those who believed the saints were indifferent to a waterfront girl go straight to hell.

Lela was not a standard five-thousand-drachma girl. She was an artist and had the credentials to prove it. Good thing, too, for only an artist could have violated the one rule a madam makes sure a new girl understands—collect in advance. Not only had she refused to do that, but on a memorable Easter Sunday eleven years ago she had refused to be paid at all for thirteen consecutive hours of work!

Lela had been awakened that morning by ringing church bells joyously commemorating the advent of Easter. The bells of the distant churches had subsided—as a rule they started services before seven, since their families went to bed early the night before—but around the port of Piraeus the people stayed up late and services didn't begin until after nine.

The bells of a nearby church had started to ring, two small bells that chimed rapidly because they were light and the bell ringer did not have to pull too hard. By using one hand for each bell, he was able to orchestrate his own cadence. The bell ringer was an old man; he would drop the ropes of the two small bells, let them swing three times, and then yank the rope of a third, heavy bell and let it ring four times lightly. The fifth and final ring would produce a rich and heavy sound of low frequency, as if to say that the bell ringer was tired and, besides, most of the people had left the church anyway.

That last low rich note was the one to decide Lela. She had turned over on her stomach, put her arms around the pillow, and smiled. She knew that every Easter the boys of the orphanage held a picnic on Kastela Hill, only a mile away. Today, to celebrate the resurrection of Our Lord Jesus Christ, she would perform an act to win the saints' favor.

So it was that on Easter Sunday, behind a boulder and in the shade of a bushy pine tree located on the south slope of the Kastela Hill, Lela Lellos, then nineteen, did contribute to the delinquency of one hundred eighty-seven minors between the ages of twelve and eighteen. Ac-

10

cording to the sworn statement of fourteen-year-old Petros Zervas, who kept count, Lela engaged in sexual intercourse without a stop from ten in the morning to eleven at night. Petros Zervas was thorough; not only did he compile the total, but he kept track of the virgin boys she turned to men, a figure that reached an awesome record never approximated in the past and certain never to be broken in the future. In recognition of her achievement Lela had these figures tattooed on her left breast, while across her stomach another tattoo read: "Thank you, Miss Lela." It was signed: "Petros Zervas—14."

It was hard to believe that eleven years had passed since that memorable day. Eleven years of many changes. For one, she finally decided to pay good money to erase the statistics from her body—it was too time-consuming to have to explain her feat to all her clients, and in her business, time was money. For another, Lela had started to bulge in the wrong places and her face showed the strain of trying to keep awake for the sailors who never seemed to seek her services until the early hours of morning.

With the German occupation competition grew tough, and she had to draw on all her experience to compete with some of the young, fresh amateurs who crowded the streets, parading their beautiful legs and firm breasts in broad daylight. Recognizing her limitations Lela became the Lady of the Dark. At that hour her clients, hard-up German replacements, did not mind about her looks.

Lela was getting old and knew it. The young ones told her as much to her face, called her one of nature's left-overs, and every time she passed a plate glass window she could see it. But at least she had Hans. Never mind that he was a German and the enemy; never mind that he was a drunk—her greatest fear was that some day he might sober up and take a good look at her and then what would she do? Where could she go? He was her meal ticket. He knew where to get food, and he gave it to her liberally.

She knew that all occupied countries had their conquerors and their slaves. Like a dutiful slave, she hurried to the next taverna, trying to find Hans.

3

At first glance the house, located about five city blocks from the Piraeus waterfront, resembled scores of other homes. It was white, stood two stories high, and was solidly built, with a walled garden in the rear. Grape vines grew on the southern side, there was a small fig tree, a spindly almond tree, and a variety of herbs were cultivated at the back. Vegetables were growing in every available foot of space, the flowers having disappeared, and this, too, was typical of any house in Piraeus in December, 1941. Food shortages, which had been acute for months, were becoming more severe, and every home owner added to his larder with the products he could grow himself.

The place was occupied by three men, one of them a servant. The master of the household was young, perhaps in his mid-twenties, and taller than most Greeks. He had black hair and an old-fashioned walrus mustache like those worn by many Greeks at the turn of the century. He wore a sober black business suit and was courteous and dignified, as befitted a man of stature. A framed diploma in the library certified that he was a notary, but he had no discernible practice. He was also part owner of a warehouse on the waterfront, and had been given a neatly typed receipt, duly signed by the Wehrmacht commandant of Piraeus, when the Germans appropriated the facility for their own use. So he had little to occupy his time.

The second man, who was in his early twenties and looked even younger, was almost as tall, slender, with an eye for the girls of the town. He owned a small fishing boat equipped with a fairly new engine, but gasoline was so scarce that when he went out on his almost daily trips he relied on his neatly patched sail. He was an accomplished fisherman, and because he carefully obeyed the Nazis' regulations, turning over half his catch to them, they allowed him to take out his boat unmolested.

The middle-aged manservant, who walked with a slight limp, appeared to be a Macedonian, and like so many mountain people was surly, taciturn, and suspicious of all strangers. He never joined others for a cup of coffee at a cafenion, and left the house only to buy cigarettes on the infrequent occasions they were available. He seemed to possess a sixth sense and always knew when a pack could be purchased. The neighbors found him lazy and slovenly, and looking down from their own second-floor windows, they often saw him dozing in the sun, his back propped against the garden wall.

The neighbors knew a great many other things about the occupants of the house, but kept the facts and their conjectures to themselves. An active, organized underground had not yet been developed in Piraeus, but the residents hated their conquerors so passionately that there were few informers in the city. Besides, people who became involved with the Germans, even innocently, sometimes vanished, and no one ever heard of them again. Long before the invasion, stories had circulated about the concentration camps the Nazis had set up in conquered lands, and there were rumors now that such an establishment was under construction somewhere in Thessaly. Whether or not the stories were true, the residents of Piraeus, no strangers to enemy occupations, kept a respectful distance between themselves and their conquerors.

The neighbors could have told the Germans many things about the house and its occupants. The place had been purchased soon after the British had first come to Piraeus, and shortly after that the two young men and their servant had moved in. Some of the neighbors had expected them to depart when the British fled; a few, who were particularly observant, noticed that on the night before the British escaped, a full colonel, wearing the red

13

tabs of the General Staff, paid a long visit to the house. They also knew that before the arrival of the Germans and their Italian satellites, they had occasionally heard the men speaking English. Since spring, however, the three had addressed each other exclusively in Greek, at least in public. The neighbors were aware of other unusual comings-and-goings: two guests had made repeated visits for a few months. They, too, appeared to be Greeks; they always arrived by fishing boat, after dark to avoid the German and Italian curfew patrols; they never ventured out by day and departed as mysteriously as they had come.

But there was much about the occupants of the house that the neighbors could not have possibly known. All three had been carefully selected for a difficult and dangerous mission for which they had undergone arduous training, all knew Greece and her people, and spoke the language fluently. The "servant" in reality was Sergeant-Major Peters of the Royal Corps of Signals, a native of Lincolnshire and a professional soldier who had served for more than twenty years in the British army. He was a crack wireless operator, an expert in communications. His surly nature was not feigned, nor was his laziness, but the theater of operations high command in Cairo had unlimited faith in his ability to send and receive coded messages under the most trying conditions.

The younger man was Lieutenant the Honorable Robert Ashley-Cole, the younger son of a baron. Recruited in the summer of 1939, soon after his graduation from Cambridge and before the actual outbreak of World War II, by M.I.-6, the operational branch of British Military Intelligence, he had received a full year of specialized training for his present assignment, that of second-in-command of an espionage-sabotage unit stationed behind enemy lines. He had at first regarded the task as something of a sport, but he had been shocked by the conditions in Piraeus. The people were starving, those questioned by the Gestapo disappeared without a trace, and the bodies of those arrested for petty offenses were thrown into the public squares, there to remain until hauled away by grieving relatives.

The man known as Georgios, who commanded the outpost and was also in direct charge of several field agents—only he and his own chief in Cairo knew the precise number—was the most mysterious of the group. Major David Cunningham of M.I.-6 had spent fifteen months in training for his volunteer assignment, and his superior, Brigadier Ian Campbell, was somewhat reluctant to admit that the man he regarded as his best qualified field agent wasn't in fact British at all, but American. Cunningham was twenty-six years old, a Rhodes scholar who had taken a degree in modern Greek, and had spent several summers in Piraeus and Athens, a native of Bloomington, Indiana, who had joined the British army when he had seen the war approaching. At the moment he was also furious.

Cunningham stared at the slip of treated rice paper containing the message that Sergeant Peters had decoded a quarter of an hour earlier. It contained only two words:

REQUEST DENIED

Cunningham cursed under his breath. He damned military red tape, British stupidity, and his own predicament. Yesterday, December 7, the Japanese had launched a surprise attack on the United States Pacific Fleet at Pearl Harbor. The German-controlled radio had been jubilant all day, announcing details, and for once there had been no need for Propaganda Minister Joseph Goebbels to lie or exaggerate. The Americans had taken a frightful beating, and the entry of the United States into the war was assured.

Ever since he had been granted his commission in M.I.-6, Cunningham had enjoyed a private understanding with Brigadier Campbell, or so he had thought: if and when the United States entered the war he would be permitted to transfer to American Military Intelligence.

Well, he had submitted his request last night, less than an hour after Sergeant Peters had confirmed the news of Pearl Harbor via the B.B.C.'s regional broadcast from Cairo. And now he had his answer, a flat turndown.

In all justice to the brigadier, Cunningham really couldn't blame him for taking such a stand. Cunningham had been given a complicated, tricky job, and two years of preparation had gone into laying in an underground apparatus. Now his first real test was at hand.

Three freighters carrying oil for General Rommel's Afrika Korps, which was threatening the British position in North Africa, were riding at anchor in the harbor of Piraeus, perfect targets for sabotage. The ships also carried provisions and other supplies for the German and Italian garrisons in Greece. Cunningham knew the brigadier wouldn't even consider his transfer request until those ships were destroyed.

A light tap sounded at the door.

Ashley-Cole simply would not or could not learn that under the circumstances in which they lived it was absurd to go around the house knocking on doors. "Come in."

The lieutenant entered the library, and at least refrained from saluting. "Sorry to hear the news, sir," he said.

"Pearl Harbor?" Cunningham snorted. "You may have a lot of faults, Robert, but I never thought you were a hypocrite. At long last your prayers have been answered— America is in the war."

Ashley-Cole's expression remained unchanged. "I meant your own situation, sir, your transfer request."

Cunningham crumpled the rice paper into an ash tray, and touched a lighted match to it. He watched it burn. "There goes my war, pal—and I'm left stuck with yours."

"But, sir—" the lieutenant protested.

"Don't 'sir' me, Robert. There's nothing you and everybody else around here would like to see more than me piling my Yankee ass aboard a U.S. sub."

"I assure you, sir—"

16

"Save your breath," Cunningham said. "Well, now that we know where we stand, is that why you came in—to express your heart-felt condolences?"

"No, sir," he said. "The Bulgarian tanker has shifted her position."

Cunningham looked up with interest. "Just as we thought."

"She's moved in to the Krysoupolis wharf, and looks as though she's going to discharge her cargo before she sets sail for Africa. I saw crates of tinned goods and fresh fruit and produce, but couldn't get close enough to make a complete surveillance, but I knew you'd want to attend to that yourself."

Cunningham pulled up his black tie, slipped on his jacket and an old overcoat, then settled a slightly battered homburg on his head, transforming himself into a somewhat threadbare, once prosperous Greek businessman. "Cover for me, Robert."

"Yes, sir."

Cunningham did not look around when he left the house and started toward the waterfront at a leisurely pace. He knew that Ashley-Cole would be following behind at a safe distance.

The air was bracing, and the salt scent cleared Cunningham's mind. He heard the hubbub of the waterfront before he saw it. The tanker, tied to the wharf, was directly ahead. He joined a small group of Greeks watching the scene, careful to stand slightly apart from them. Italian *carabinieri* were directing the preliminary unloading operations—a half dozen were shouting simultaneously, each issuing contradictory orders as he stalked up and down the wharf—and the Greek longshoremen didn't know whom to obey.

Cunningham immediately spotted two Wehrmacht officers, a captain and a lieutenant, who stood alone at the foot of the dock, observing the scene. Should it become necessary they would intervene, but at present they seemed to enjoy watching the growing chaos.

Ashley-Cole had been right about the cargo. On board

ship were crates of oranges, bags of flour—hundreds of them—and high piles of canned goods. It wasn't surprising to find that many of them were of American manufacture; the United States shipped her products to neutral nations in the Middle East, and more often than not they were diverted en route to feed the Wehrmacht.

As Cunningham watched, the confusion increased. About ten yards from the foot of the dock a platoon of Wehrmacht troops, armed with automatic rifles and commanded by a lieutenant, stood guard over a number of large sealed crates and boxes. Some were marked *Gefahr!*—danger—and the American knew at once that these were explosives, perhaps shells for Rommel's Afrika Korps. Others bore the stamp of the Krupp and I.G. Farben companies, and it was not difficult for a trained operative to determine they contained spare parts for Rommel's mechanized army.

Greek farmers, some driving carts, others pushing wheelbarrows, had begun to arrive with vast quantities of melons, figs, olives, and other produce. Piraeus and the rest of Greece might be hungry, with starvation imminent, but the Gestapo had commandeered all the wares of the farmers of Attica for Rommel. Crates were being loaded and unloaded in a huge net suspended from a winch, the operator in charge sitting high above the main deck of the freighter.

A group of young Greeks caught Cunningham's attention. They appeared to be under the direction of a slender young man whom the others addressed in shouts as Nico, and for every crate they handled they managed to take tribute, stealing a melon here, a can of soup there, a handful of figs. The Italians were too busy to notice, and Cunningham thought it typical of the Greeks to engage in such petty pilferage.

Cunningham couldn't blame them for stuffing food into their pockets and under their shirts. Hungry men stole food; that was natural. But their operation was so small-time! If he had any hope of carrying out the assignment Cairo had in mind, he would need the active cooperation of Greek nationals—men very much like these—but if this was the caliber of potential recruits, his task seemed all the more formidable. They were totally disorganized—look at that one chase an orange that had rolled from his jacket!—they were like children. Something Brigadier Campbell had conveniently neglected to mention in his long elaborate briefings.

Cunningham turned to examine the ship. She flew the Bulgarian flag, and a number of Bulgarian merchant seamen stood on her starboard deck, leaning on the rail and watching the scene below. Her narrow bow, exceptionally high bridge, squat amidships, and spreading fantail identified her as a tanker that had been made in Holland at least thirty years earlier, probably to bring the oil of the Dutch East Indies to Rotterdam and Amsterdam. Certainly she looked a wreck. Her hull was rusting and hadn't been painted for a year, her deck was littered with refuse and even from this distance her bridge looked filthy.

Far more important was her vulnerability to explosives, and Cunningham, the demolition expert, studied her carefully. Her bridge was so high that a bomb would do relatively little damage; and explosives planted on her deck would cripple her but might not sink her. Then Cunningham noticed she must be carrying oil in two holds, the smaller one forward and the larger aft. She was thin-skinned, as were so many of the old Dutch vessels built for the East India trade, and her hull was no more than an inch to an inch and a half thick, simplifying his task even further. A charge of only a few pounds of TNT or its equivalent, planted and detonated against the hull anywhere in the vicinity of the after hold, would blow the damned ship clean out of the water. The job should be simple, barring complications, but he realized it would not be as easy as it first appeared. The Italians might be sloppy, but the Germans took no chances, particularly with such precious cargo vital to Rommel.

An idea began to form in Cunningham's mind. His concern was not one tanker but three. As nearly as he could judge from this distance, the other two vessels in the harbor were sister ships of the tanker tied to the wharf, but he'd make certain by having Ashley-Cole take detailed photographs of all three through the telescopic lens. The success of any demolition effort depended on precise planning and execution, and after waiting and hiding through all these months of Nazi occupation for an opportunity of this magnitude, he had no intention of bungling.

A screeching metallic wail called Cunningham's attention to the winch, which had halted in midair, halfway between the ship's superstructure and the dock. The operator shouted helplessly to his shipmates who shouted down to the Italians; the bedlam immediately intensified. The Bulgarian deck officer began to gesticulate at the man, who only shrugged; the Italians issued instructions at the top of their voices. The young Greek onlookers came to life, chattering and gesturing.

The Wehrmacht captain looked annoyed and called up to the deck officer, ordering him to get back to work.

The mate leaned over the rail. "The winch seems to be broken." He seemed to be more concerned with speaking an articulate German than with the problem of the winch. "Only one member of our crew knows how to repair it, and he has gone ashore."

Everyone started shouting again, and it was all Cunningham could do not to laugh. The German captain was conferring angrily with his lieutenant. It might take hours to search the whorehouses of Piraeus for the missing sailor, and by then the schedule would be knocked cockeyed. All of them—Greeks, Bulgarians, Italians—were hopeless, Cunningham thought with disgust. Now, if something like this had occurred in the States, nine Americans out of ten could fix the damned winch, blindfolded.

Suddenly he heard a steadily clicking sound almost at his elbow. Startled, Cunningham, whose survival depended upon his alertness, turned and saw that a Greek had materialized out of nowhere.

The clicking sound came from a string of beads he was methodically working through his fingers, as if in tempo to some difficult deliberation. Then, his mind apparently made up, he slipped the beads in his pocket, brushed past Cunningham, and started toward the ship.

The dark-haired Greek, who was slender and somewhat taller than most of his countrymen, appeared to be in his mid-twenties and walked with the spring of an athlete; he called attention to himself principally because of his manner, which Cunningham recognized as one of supreme self-confidence. Certainly his audacity was breathtaking. If one of the German sharpshooters didn't gun him down, an excitable Italian *caribiniere* might, but he seemed totally oblivious to personal danger.

Heading straight for the Wehrmacht captain, he said a few words to him and without waiting for a reply pushed past him onto the dock. Cunningham pressed forward to see what happened next.

The young Greeks recognized the newcomer and called out loud greetings to him, but he had no time for them. Leaping onto the gangplank, he made his way to the deck of the freighter, and gesturing curtly to the man stranded on the winch, ordered him to come down. The Bulgarian reacted instantly to the authority in the Greek's tone—or perhaps he was just pleased to find someone to relieve him.

As soon as he reached the deck the Greek pulled himself onto the stalled machinery, climbing the chain hand-over-hand with easy grace. He studied the winch, and it was obvious to Cunningham that he understood machinery. He ran his hands over it gently, expertly, then reached into his hip pocket for an instrument that appeared to be a wrench at one end and a screwdriver at the other. With deft motions he began to work, concentrating his entire attention on the task and ignoring the tumult below, the many eyes on him. All at once the winch squealed, began to move again, and the crates of produce in the net inched higher.

Though he had achieved a considerable triumph, the

21

Greek's expression remained unchanged; and Cunningham, watching him closely, realized he had never
seen a Greek with such distinctive eyes—unlike most of
his countrymen's, this young man's were a deep, piercing
blue.

4

The six-story apartment building, towering on the heights
above the ancient, crumbling Wall of Themistocles, overlooked the main harbor and the outer port. This aberra-
tion had been the dream of a Piraeus native who had
migrated to America, made his fortune, and then returned
home so filled with gratitude to his adopted land that he
paid it architectural tribute by building Piraeus' only skyscraper.

Unfortunately he died before he could move into the
penthouse apartment he had reserved for himself; and
shortly after the first handful of tenants had occupied
their apartments the war broke out. Because of its unob-
structed view of harbor shipping, the Germans had de-
creed that no Greeks could live there; they ousted the
occupants and gave the apartments to their own higher-
ranking civil servants. Colonel Johann Schneider, the
Wehrmacht commandant of Piraeus, had wanted the penthouse for himself, but his own headquarters were located
in the official military compound near Kastela Plaza, on
the opposite, eastern side of the city, and military necessi-
ty required that he live there. So he had done the next
best thing and given the penthouse to his mistress.

Trudi Richter, ignoring the cold, wrapped herself in her
absurdly frilly black silk peignoir and looked down from
her terrace at the harbor of Piraeus. She hated the miserable place as only a sophisticated Viennese could hate a
little Greek port. She loathed the sight of the tankers she
could see in the harbor because they reminded her of

Johann Schneider, whom she also loathed. No, for Schneider she felt mere contempt, and on occasion she even was sorry for him; he meant well enough in his way and he provided her with the protection that, God knew, she so desperately needed. So she couldn't afford the luxury of hating him. But his chauffeur was another matter.

Damn Hans. The colonel's driver was too good-looking —all the girls of Piraeus made a fuss over him—no doubt he was with one of them right now, which explained his phone call: "Forgive me, Fräulein, but I've been held up. I'll be a little late." He knew she was due at headquarters —and that Johann was punctual to a fault and expected everyone else to be. He would be furious if she didn't arrive on time. He also knew she had a very important errand en route to headquarters. It was urgent, and Hans should know it better than anyone else—he stood to gain enough from it himself.

Shivering slightly from the cold, Trudi went inside, closing the glass terrace doors behind her, and looked around the living room. The apartment was hideous. Someone, presumably the builder of the skyscraper, had furnished the penthouse with cheap but functional chairs, tables, lamps, and decorations imported from the United States. The divan and easy chairs, with their cushions of bright green and scarlet tweed, were made of bleached maple and vaguely resembled the Scandinavian furniture she remembered from shortly before the outbreak of the war. The lamps were stark, the tables blond boards mounted on slightly tapering, blond legs, the carpeting was thick—although it shed furiously—and on the walls were prints of the Parthenon and the skyscrapers of New York.

Everything in the place was tasteless. The chinaware, glasses, and silverware in the kitchen, as well as the cooking utensils, were utilitarian, thick and ugly and indestructible. Trudi's own bedroom resembled a whore's— appropriate enough under the circumstances, although it hadn't been intended for that purpose. The enormous bed was canopied, the pink shades on the lamps actually had

23

deep flounces on them, and the Mediterranean-style dressing table and chests of drawers were decorated with frilled runners.

To an Austrian, bred to one of Europe's oldest, finest, and most exquisite cultures, it was intolerable. But then so was everything nowadays. Who could imagine she would have to take a succession of high-placed Germans as lovers just to survive. And her situation wasn't unique: Austria wasn't the only country Hitler had occupied, and she couldn't even begin to guess how many tens of thousands—or was it millions?—were being forced to use their wits or their bodies for survival. All that mattered *was* survival, she knew, in as much comfort and safety as possible.

Wandering into the kitchen, she poured herself a cup of the coffee she always kept on the stove, good, strong Viennese coffee, and then lit one of the American cigarettes that Johann procured for her. She supposed she should begin to hoard her supply, but she would worry about that when she ran out. Johann would find some way to obtain American cigarettes if she demanded them.

Strolling back into the living room she found herself thinking of Kurt, and was surprised. Why, after all this time should he creep into her mind now? Perhaps it was those tankers in the harbor—they must have reminded her of the honeymoon cruise they had taken in the Mediterranean on a freighter. Poor Kurt. She had met him in the hospital where she was working as a nurse, and she could still remember her excitement that morning as she had helped him scrub. Kurt Richter had been one of Vienna's outstanding young surgeons with a brilliant career ahead; he was a favorite of the chief of surgery and worshiped by his associates. If only he hadn't combined all that with an equal dedication to liberal principles which, everyone could see, were fast becoming obsolete.

But if Kurt had been foolish, what excuse was there for Trudi? How easily she had been taken in by his ideals. Six months after they had met, they got married. Just like

24

that. Trudi had known little about politics in those days; Kurt had been an enthusiastic follower of the martyred Chancellor Engelbert Dollfuss, killed in a Nazi raid on his office in 1934. How impossibly naïve she had been then, at eighteen, and how much wiser she was now at twenty-five. It had been a costly education. Kurt had belonged in the gentle world of the Emperor Franz Josef and had been unable to cope with the age of the swastika. He had paid for that failure with his life. She had survived.

When Kurt had transferred his political allegiance from the martyred Dollfuss to the new chancellor, she had been only vaguely aware of his beliefs; all that had mattered to her had been their love for each other. But she had learned better in March, 1938, when the Germans marched into Austria, conquering her homeland in a bloodless coup. Chancellor Kurt von Schuschnigg had been made a captive, and was even now still languishing in a concentration camp. Kurt Richter had been less fortunate. Certainly Trudi's own nightmare had begun when Kurt had been hauled off to a concentration camp, where he died a few months later. She had never learned the details and didn't want to know them.

Only her own total innocence, her complete lack of interest in politics, had saved her own life. As the wife of an Austrian patriot she had been interrogated at length, but eventually convinced the Nazis that she was as ingenuous as she appeared. Besides, the Nazis had better use for a young, exceptionally attractive woman. Long before she had received word of Kurt's death, she had been seduced and then handed from German officer to German officer, so many she couldn't remember them all. Not that she had cared, really. Her will to survive had made it possible for her to endure anything; only the strong survived today, and she had learned how to be strong.

Colonel Müller had been her first real protector, and had taught her to attach herself to one man of prominence and power, as befitted a woman who enjoyed the good things life had to offer. The next had been Willy Streck, whose memory still sent chills through her. Willy had brought her to Athens two years ago, and they had posed as husband and wife while pretending to engage in research. They were so efficient, those Nazis! Willy's real assignment had been to establish a hard core of collaborators in high administrative posts in Athens.

Then, eight months ago, he had been sent off on a new, secret mission, and since there was no place for Trudi, he had presented her to Colonel Johann Schneider as a special gift. She had felt no shame at being passed from man to man—what the hell, she was still alive, still enjoying luxuries beyond the grasp of most people.

It was the only life she knew now, and she entertained no false illusions about her fate if she protested or rebelled. She was still the widow of an Austrian liberal, and her failure to play the role that had been assigned to her would lead straight to a concentration camp. In her present situation one German was much the same as another, and the identity of her lovers was less important than the perquisites they could provide.

The squat, ugly American clock on the mantel behind Trudi chimed. She drained her coffee, lit another cigarette, and went into her bedroom to prepare for her appointment with Schneider. And if Hans showed up too late to attend to her own business en route to headquarters, he would regret it. One word to Johann would send his chauffeur back to the motor pool—it would serve him right.

Poor Johann, the most inept of lovers, who was so pathetically anxious to please her while preserving his self-image as an attractive, virile man. What he didn't know wouldn't hurt him—that she was no longer capable of responding, either physically or emotionally, to any man. It wasn't Johann's fault. This isolation, this wall that had grown around her was her only protection, and under no circumstances would she permit herself to be made vulnerable again. Never again would she make the mistake of loving any man as she had loved Kurt, and it wasn't accidental that she could scarcely remember how she had once felt toward him. Why dredge up yesterday when all that mattered was today?

Trudi vigorously brushed her long, red hair, the shade known in Austria as "Vienna gold," and then busied herself with mascara, rouge, eyeshadow, and lipstick. The use of such lavish cosmetics had been a game to her only a few years ago, but now they were tools, and she worked with them slowly, using infinite care. She darkened the thin line of her eyebrows, used a shadow of an even deeper shade of green than that of her eyes to bring out their color, and heavily applied her rouge and the blue-black lipstick that had been popular in Berlin even in pre-Nazi days. The results were dramatic, and it didn't matter that she looked like a high-class whore. That was what she was, a damned attractive one, and she had never yet met a German officer who wanted his mistress to look like the idealized wholesome plump blondes pictured in Nazi propaganda.

Throwing aside the ridiculous, frilly peignoir, Trudi glanced at her reflection in the full-length mirror and was satisfied. Her stomach was still flat, her legs and thighs long and lean, her waist tiny and her breasts high and firm. In spite of all the wear and tear, her body looked as fresh and desirable as it had when she was eighteen.

Knowing that the mere sight of silk next to a woman's body acted like an aphrodisiac on Schneider, Trudi began to dress for the day's liaison. She chose a black silk bra and panties, then carefully pulled on the black silk stockings Johann always managed to obtain for her from some mysterious source. She fixed them in place with a red garter belt that reminded her of an Offenbach operetta, then stepped into high-heeled black pumps. She pushed a button for her Greek maid.

The middle-aged woman, drab, gray-haired, and meek in her black uniform and white apron, avoided meeting the girl's glance as she entered the room. Trudi considered her a drone, and the maid encouraged the relationship. Her wages were better than most, she could steal precious food from the larder and icebox, and she was determined

27

that nothing should disturb such a profitable arrangement.

"Yes, Fräulein?"

"What's happened to that car and chauffeur? Doesn't Hans know he's late?"

"I can't say, Fräulein."

Irritably Trudi tugged at a bra strap. "Let me know the instant he gets here."

The maid murmured acquiescence and hurried out of the bedroom.

Furiously, Trudi searched through her extensive wardrobe for an appropriate dress. She discarded a red gown with a low neckline as too flamboyant for the time of day, and finally settled on a sleeveless, black frock of clinging silk. It was almost too subtle for Johann, but it showed every line of her supple body. Slathering on French perfume Schneider had obtained for her specially, she made a final critical examination of herself in the long mirror. Smiling humorlessly, Trudi Richter, mistress, could no longer find any trace of Trudi Richter, nurse. The Greeks called her "the German whore," and she resented the mistake. At least let these stupid peasants get it right: she was the *Austrian* whore.

The maid reappeared. "The car and driver are here now, Fräulein."

Trudi threw a cashmere polo coat over her shoulders and swept out of the apartment.

The engine of the enormous, American-made limousine was running, its heater keeping the interior warm, and Hans raced around the car, saluted, and opened the door. Hans was good-looking in a rugged, blond way; but now that he was in his late thirties he was developing a paunch. Though he worked only a few hours a day, his job had its drawbacks. He never knew when Colonel Schneider might want to drive into Athens or otherwise interfere with his personal plans. And this imperious Austrian bitch wasn't easy to handle, either, although he had learned to deal with her by treating her with a casual blend of good humor and politeness. If she weren't the colonel's woman he'd tame her fast enough in the only way she understood, but that was out of the question, so he let her know in indirect ways that he wanted her, while at the same time never speaking out of turn.

"Good afternoon, Fräulein Richter."

Trudi's green eyes were stormy, and she refused to return the man's flirtatious gaze as he tucked the lap robe around her. "You were due here three quarters of an hour ago."

He waited until he had seated himself behind the wheel before replying. "I had unexpected business, Fräulein."

"Woman business, I'm sure."

She sounded irritated and, glancing in the rear-view mirror, he wondered if it was possible that she was jealous. "It was unavoidable business, Fräulein," he said tonelessly.

She glanced at the ruby and gold watch that Willy had given her, a gift whose origins she had been careful never to question since high-ranking Gestapo officers had their own means of obtaining valuable property. "Colonel Schneider expects me on the hour," she said sharply.

"I'll have you there with time to spare, Fräulein Richter. You have my solemn word."

"Is there time enough for me to attend to some business of my own before we go to headquarters?" Trudi demanded.

So that was what had upset the bitch. "Of course. In fact," Hans said smoothly, "I had an idea that was in your mind and have allowed ample time for it."

The girl sat back as Hans started across Piraeus. She had grown so accustomed to the piercing sound of the car's siren that she was usually barely conscious of its wail, but today she found herself noticing the scramble of pedestrians, donkey carts, and other impediments in the driver's path.

The sight of so many pinched faces was depressing. As a girl in Vienna she had heard that the women of Greece, like those of Budapest, were among the great beauties of

29

Europe, that they were smart and chic. One more myth exploded. Once, in the days when she had been a nurse—damn Kurt for bringing all that back today!—she would have been torn with pity for the Greeks.

She remembered nervously pacing the floor of the German field hospital, awaiting her first war wounded. Hand grenades, artillery shells, and hot steel from exploding bombs had torn the flesh and shattered the bones of the first soldier she saw. The ugly irregular, bloody cuts—the leg bones, half white and half pink, jutting out over the soldier's high boot; the bloody face of another with his jaw and half the upper teeth hanging by the flesh—horrified her.

Where were the handsome soldiers? She saw mostly ugly, short men, some crying in pain and disgust. The tired family men wearied with boasts and promises held back their tears, the young soldiers wept.

So it was with the Greeks. They were so poor, so exhausted, their faces showing no animation. On visits to Paris, Brussels, and other German-occupied cities, first with Colonel Müller and later with Willy, Trudi had grown accustomed to the hostility of the people who stared back at her. But the Greeks were unnerving because they looked at her without expression of any kind. They seemed too exhausted, too empty of hope, even to hate.

Yet she couldn't feel sorry for the Greeks—as she had soon learned not to feel sorry for the war wounded. Her own situation would have been as bad as theirs, perhaps even worse, if she hadn't done something to improve her lot. She had physical assets that were lacking in these skeletons, of course, but where was their spirit, their *desire* for life? If the slavelike Greeks were typical of conquered people everywhere, perhaps the Aryan race deserved to rule Europe for the next thousand years.

The swift-moving car slowed down when it reached the Wall of Phalares in a working-class district on the eastern side of the city. Built by the ancients, the wall at one time had been the bulwark that had protected Piraeus from invaders. Originally it had been about twelve feet high, but several rows of stones had been removed from the top by householders who had used the chiseled blocks to build their homes. Now the wall was a symbol of Piraeus' decay. In places it was eight feet high, in others only four; the once-handsome stones had been chipped, some were crumbling, and weeds choked the base for the better part of its length. Trudi, who had learned something about the Wall of Phalares when she and Willy had posed as researchers, couldn't blame the Greeks for neglecting this relic of their past. Hungry people desperate for food didn't have time to repair an ancient wall that served no utilitarian purpose.

Hans slowed the car to a crawl, turned into a street so narrow it could just accommodate the vehicle, and made his way down the cobblestones between white-walled houses whose second-floor balconies, each with its pot of plants and flowers, leaned forward until they almost touched.

Hans pulled up outside an old warehouse, and after a moment a wooden double door creaked open a foot or two. Two Greeks of indeterminate age appeared in the alleyway; they were dressed in baggy trousers and shapeless coats, and both had hats pulled low over their foreheads, concealing their faces.

Hans spoke with slow deliberation. "If the Fräulein will permit," he said, "I would like to buy a package of cigarettes. I seem to have acquired a taste for Greek tobacco."

It was not the first time they had played this scene, and Trudi spoke her own lines with equal assurance. "Of course, Hans," she said. "I don't share your taste, but go right ahead."

He walked off down the alleyway, a burly Wehrmacht sergeant preoccupied by his errand, and not once did he glance in the direction of the two Greeks who stood in the shadow of the half-open door.

Trudi ignored them, too, but lowered the car window a few inches.

31

One of the men started to saunter past the car, pausing just long enough to say a few words as he reached the window. "The usual?" he asked.

The Austrian girl's nod was almost imperceptible, and she paid no attention when she heard the cap of the gas tank being removed. Instead she took a tiny container of bright red polish from her handbag and concentrated on painting her nails.

When the man was finished siphoning out the gasoline, he carefully replaced the cap, then strolled past the car again and dropped a thick wad of folded paper money onto the seat beside Trudi.

She closed the window, carefully counted the money— a task that took quite some time since gasoline fetched an inordinately high price on the black market. Then, after concealing one quarter of it in the leather upholstery where Hans would find it, she stuffed the rest into her handbag.

"Gnädige Fräulein, we have been expecting you."

At the sound of the voice Trudi felt herself tremble, as she always did whenever she confronted Colonel Schneider's secretary, Ilse Brugger.

There was little chance of avoiding her. She occupied the outer office of the colonel's personal suite on the second floor of the German headquarters, a villa that once belonged to a prosperous Greek named Zacharias and commanded a full view of the Gulf of Phaliron. It featured a high-domed formal entrance hall, with a fountain in the center of a floor paved with mosaic marble tile—the envy of the Wehrmacht commander in Athens, who could scarcely conceal his jealousy whenever he paid Colonel Schneider a visit.

But the heart of the complex was the large, opulent second-floor quarters in which Colonel Schneider worked and lived. It was here that Brugger, the only woman on the staff, had her office—one plainly furnished room, directly outside the colonel's, with nothing but her desk and a number of locked filing cabinets, so that visitors were obliged to stand. The floor of old oak was bare, a large map of Piraeus occupied one wall, and opposite it stood the chamber's only decoration, a large felt swastika. Many Wehrmacht officers were surprised to see it there, but kept their feelings to themselves. Even general officers and colonels knew better than to antagonize a dedicated Nazi.

Schneider's office-bedroom, which commanded an imposing view of the gulf, had been the master bedchamber and looked it. A balcony opened out over the sea, the furniture was massive, expensive, and had been imported from France; two Gobelin tapestries and a Greek frieze decorated the walls, and only the bed, which converted into a sofa in daylight hours, was utilitarian. But Schneider rarely slept in his office. Instead he used the inner chamber that had been the dressing room of the former mistress of the house, and he had not changed the feminine furnishings, almost absurdly frilly. A visiting Wehrmacht inspector general had remarked that the room reminded him of a Munich bordello, and he was not too far wide of the mark. It was here Schneider most frequently entertained Trudi Richter, a fact known to both his superiors in Athens and his subordinates in Piraeus. Adjoining the bedroom was his private dining room, where he ate most of his meals, and when Trudi was not present in the villa he usually invited his staff chief or some other officer to share his table with him.

Staff members and visitors were strictly forbidden to enter the suite without permission, and even during the colonel's absence no one broke his unwritten rule. Ilse Brugger, a cold, snarling tigress, would tolerate no trespassing; but if anyone managed to get past her, they would surely be stopped by Schneider's huge mastiffs, Churchill and Mussolini, one-man dogs who had been trained to tear intruders to shreds.

While it was true the dogs recognized only one master, there was a single exception—and whenever Trudi Richter entered the outer office of the suite, not bothering to knock on the door that bore the brass plate, *Kommand-*

ant, Churchill and Mussolini went wild with joy. Yelping with pleasure, their tails beating a furious tattoo, they leaped on her, licked her and slathered over her, drenching her with their saliva.

And so it was today. Laughing, ineffectually brushing their paws from her polo coat, her haughty arrogance vanished as she dropped to her knees to embrace the ecstatic dogs, Trudi hugged the animals and her eyes became soft and tender.

Gently disentangling herself from the frolicking mastiffs, she finally pulled herself to her feet and, looking across the room, met the disapproving glare of Colonel Schneider's secretary.

Ilse Brugger, a tall, rawboned and ungainly woman, had long been a misfit who had found her niche among the military. Her thick legs and fleshy feet were almost unobtrusive in sensible lisle stockings and heavy shoes, her tight-fitting tunic compressed her overly ample bosom, and her unruly hair was kept cut short. She had a rasping voice that some who spoke to her on the telephone mistook for a man's, and she had learned to walk like a man, too. When Trudi had asked Johann, who so admired beauty, why he tolerated someone like Brugger, he had replied she was the most competent secretary available. But Trudi wondered what price he was willing to pay for efficiency. Ilse Brugger not only was unattractive and unappealing—but there was a suggestion of cruelty about her, a sickness that made Trudi's flesh crawl. She had no social grace; finesse was simply beyond her. Authoritarian, demanding instant and total obedience, she displayed similar deference in the presence of her superiors.

Trudi was the one exception. While obviously aware of her relationship with Schneider—and she made it her business to know everything about the colonel—Ilse Brugger could not help resenting the girl in any number of ways. Her easy assurance, her ill-concealed sense of superiority—superiority from an Austrian!—but most of all her beauty. Ilse Brugger could not deny the girl's dazzling looks, her graceful carriage, the way she seemed *accus-*

tomed to the admiration of men. Brugger would never forget the first time she had seen the girl; Colonel Schneider had brought her to a staff meeting and introduced her, like some hard-won prize, to his assembled officers. They had fawned over her like the colonel's mastiffs. One major had blushed like a schoolboy when presented to her—an officer, who only weeks before had been decorated for outstanding valor in defense of the Fatherland on the Eastern Front!

Yes, the girl's acknowledged beauty was the one quality that most obsessed Brugger. Late at night on her spare cot, she would fantasize herself to sleep with delicious thoughts of raking great welts in that translucent skin, twisting those lovely limbs until the perfect red lips stretched ugly in piercing screams. Yet at other times she had quite opposite reactions. She would see herself—not that clumsy fool Schneider—caressing the girl, fondling her long hair, cradling her soft shoulders against her body, tracing her fingers along the down of her long curving back. . . .

Brugger showed large, yellow teeth in an unctuous smile.

As Trudi started toward the inner office-bedroom without pausing, the dogs at her heels, Brugger fell in beside her.

"The Herr Colonel is attending a meeting at the Port Authority building with the captains of the tankers, but is always prompt. So you needn't worry, he won't keep you waiting for long." She laughed hoarsely, suggestively.

The secretary took Trudi's coat from her shoulders with a familiarity that made Trudi pull away. She inspected the girl with interest. "A charming dress, and it shows your—you—off to such advantage. Tell me, Fräulein, is it new?"

"I've only worn it once or twice," said Trudi matter-of-factly. And then she added: "Johann brought it back for me when he went to that meeting of area commanders in Paris last month."

"The colonel brought it, and from Paris." Brugger

35

reached out to finger the fabric, and Trudi forced herself to submit to the other woman's touch.

"Real silk, ah yes." Brugger's eyes were bright. "Perhaps you'll permit me to visit your apartment some day and see your wardrobe."

Trudi could think of nothing less appealing than playing hostess to this grotesque creature, but habitual caution caused her to watch her words. "I'd be delighted, but I suggest we wait until the Herr Colonel next travels to Berlin. As you know, I must be available when Johann wants to see me."

Again Brugger showed her oversized teeth. "But of course, Fräulein Richter, we all have our duties and obligations."

Ilse Brugger and Trudi Richter, two servants of the Third Reich, awaited the return of Colonel Johann Schneider.

5

The German army truck moved unnoticed along the Piraeus waterfront, and even Cunningham—like everyone else admiringly watching the blue-eyed young Greek expertly hoist the cargo from the wharf, swing it high into the air, and deposit it gently on deck—was scarcely aware of it. The vehicle inched into an open space between two warehouses, then began to back toward the dock adjacent to the Bulgarian tanker, apparently maneuvering into position to discharge its load for transfer to the ship.

Cunningham's attention was called to the truck when the driver, shifting into reverse with a gnashing of gears, suddenly increased his speed. The vehicle seemed to leap backward, and it was only moments before the inevitable happened: the driver crashed into a Greek farmer's donkey cart, smashing it to kindling, squashing its load of melons.

The donkey fell to its knees, its high-pitched bray sounding like the shriek of a child.

The attention of everyone—the German sentries, the Italian *carabinieri,* the crowd of Greek onlookers, and the Bulgarian sailors on the deck of the tanker—was drawn to the accident. The truck driver belatedly honked his horn, the donkey screamed, and the shouts of men added to the bedlam. The Italians, waving imperiously, tried to restore order, but only made matters worse. The Wehrmacht captain and his lieutenant ran to the site of the accident, as did the German officer in command of the munitions detail. Only the German sentries guarding the cases of war supplies held their places, but they, too, craned to see what was happening.

The Greek farmer tried to haul the donkey to its feet, but the cobblestones underfoot had been transformed into a wet morass of melon meat and juice, and the animal went down again. Its terrified cry could be heard above the strident sound of the truck's horn, which had become stuck. Several of the other Greeks hurried forward to the farmer's assistance, and between them they managed to set the struggling, kicking donkey on its feet again. The farmer examined the beast closely, and then, apparently deciding it was more frightened than hurt, dashed to the cab of the truck and slammed his fist angrily on the metal door.

The Wehrmacht captain, paying no attention to the irate Greek, pushed him aside and, his own temper out of control, lashed out at the driver at the top of his voice. Several small boys darted in and out of the crowd, trying to gather up what they could of the spilled melons, and the Italians made matters still worse by attempting to stop them.

Cunningham, biting back a smile at all the commotion, nearly missed what happened next. The blue-eyed Greek was paying no attention whatever to the scene below, but continued to operate the winch throughout the commotion. And Cunningham was startled to realize that he was doing something very much out of the ordinary: instead of unloading on the deck of the Bulgarian tanker the net bulging with cases of supplies—auto parts, explosives, some ammunition—he had quietly swung it across the deck and over to the far side of the tanker.

Evidently no one besides Cunningham noticed what the Greek was doing, not even the Bulgarian sailors who lined the starboard rail to watch the confusion taking place on the dock below.

The Greek pulled a lever, one end of the net fell away, and the cases of cargo dropped into the water. The noise on the dock masked any splash.

The blue-eyed man sprang to his feet, and in a single effortless motion, hoisted himself to the top of the winch, poised there for a moment until he was balanced, and then executed a graceful dive into the water on the port side of the tanker, out of sight.

The tanker blocked Cunningham's view. Cautioning himself not to run, and thus call attention to himself, he made his way as rapidly as possible toward the port side of the vessel, trying as he went to assimilate the significance of the Greek's actions. The man's audacity, his reckless disregard of the heavily armed German and Italian troops, was impossible to believe.

Reaching the far side of the tanker, Cunningham was even more astonished to see a fishing boat, a craft about twenty feet long with a patched sail, looking so nondescript it was indistinguishable from scores of others in the harbor, snugly anchored just below where the net had disgorged its cargo.

The whole thing had been planned from the very beginning!

As Cunningham watched in mounting excitement, the Greek climbed into the fishing boat, and methodically began to haul in the large heavy crates bobbing in the water. Anyone else would have had a crew of men to help him, but this man worked all alone. He used a grappling hook with the same expertise he had handled the winch, and although he seemed to be unhurried, taking his time, he salvaged five crates in the span of a few minutes.

38

What made his performance so stunning was the meticulousness of his planning, his coolness under danger. Only the tanker shielded him from Wehrmacht marksmen, and the Germans, Cunningham knew, were merciless in their treatment of black market operators; still, he refused to be rushed. The only indication he was aware of his danger was the expression on his face; instead of the wooden businesslike mask he had maintained aboard ship, his whole face had come alive in a dazzling impish smile. No wonder the young Greeks on the dock had been so pleased to see him: men would follow that kind of grin loyally, devotedly.

The Germans at last became aware of what had happened. Cunningham could hear the Wehrmacht captain shout an order—he was that close—and then saw a half dozen run toward the port side of the tanker, closely followed by the Italians. Cunningham wanted to shout a warning, but the Greek apparently was endowed with a sixth sense when it came to impending danger. His timing exquisite, he dropped to one knee in the stern and started an engine concealed beneath a camouflage of fishing nets.

The machine responded to his touch, the "fishing boat" seemed to leap through the water, and he was well across the harbor, heading on a zigzag course, before the Germans could reach the port side of the tanker and open fire on him.

Cunningham watched until the little boat swept around a bend and disappeared from sight, leaving only a churning wake behind.

6

When Spyros Kanares' wife passed away before the war, he opened the cafenion on the north side of Kastela Plaza just to keep busy. He gave it the same name as that of his country and his ship, "Hellas." And when the Germans commandeered his home—a mansion two "decks" high with a magnificent view of the sea—he had accepted it and understood. The Germans were the conquerors and he the slave.

But what Old Spyros could not accept, nor even understand, was the loss of his icon. It was a magnificent icon of Saint Nicholas, patron saint of sailors, and he had bought it from an African in Madagascar and mounted it on board the *Hellas* all the years he was captain. But the icon, a black Saint Nicholas, was treasured not only by Old Spyros; the three German chaplains who had appropriated Spyros' mansion felt it a fitting addition to their own quarters. Old Spyros had appealed to them in German, tried to make them understand the sentimental value of Black Saint Nicholas. He had even gone so far as to offer to buy it back from them in return for keeping up their garden. All in vain. The chaplains replied only in classic Greek, a language Spyros could not understand; smiling, they asked him to sit down and lunch with them, drink Greek wine, smoke their pipe tobacco. But nothing was mentioned about returning the icon. Slamming his huge hands on his own table in disgust, Old Spyros stormed out of his home. Very well, if he could not rescue his saint by honest means he would find someone to steal him back, and never mind whether Black Saint Nicholas approved or not.

But who?

The cafenion on Kastela Plaza was only a block and a half from the mansion, and from that day Spyros kept a detailed log of the chaplains daily habits. One afternoon, while awaiting the return of the chaplains from their daily constitutional, Old Spyros saw just the man for the job run into the empty grade school above the boulevard. Even from that brief glance—one moment there he was in the school courtyard and the next he had disappeared inside—there was no mistaking him: Spyros never thought he would see Petros Zervas again. What could account for the young man's sudden appearance in the Kastela area? Why was he running so furtively into the empty school?

Petros Zervas, Spyros knew, was a man marked from birth. Conceived and born inside an orphanage, Petros had never met his mother, the maid Miss Magdi, or his father, the accused seventeen-year-old orphanage boy named Dinos Zervas. The day before his appointed wedding with Miss Magdi, Dinos disappeared from the orphanage. Miss Magdi followed soon thereafter, leaving behind on the empty bunk on which his father had slept, her four-month-old son, Petros.

Being born and raised within the very walls where he was conceived had some advantages, however. As other children were brought to the orphanage, Petros demanded more rights; since he had seniority over all the other children, he became their undisputed leader, and it didn't matter whether they were younger or older. Thus on that Easter picnic years ago, Lela had to ask Petros' permission to make her mark in history, permission Petros had readily granted on one condition: that he went first. So at the age of fourteen not only was Petros lord of the orphanage, but for years afterward his was the only name which could be read by a large segment of the male population of Piraeus when engaged in a very, very private affair. And should any of them express any curiosity upon finding Petros' tattooed inscription across Lela's stomach, Lela would be only too happy to enlighten them with her own embellished version of the story.

Yes Spyros thought, Petros Zervas had always been a man marked by history. At the age of eighteen he had won the advanced studies' scholarship and was accepted at law school. But he became an electrical engineer instead: the engineering school was located near the teachers' college for women. Petros never had the chance to use his degree. By the time he had finished his studies Greece was occupied. Petros, as well as others, felt the weight of the enemy boot on his neck, but unlike the others Petros saw this as a new opportunity. His methodical mind had fastened on the vulnerability of the German supply depots. Within months Petros Zervas was a wealthy man. He had filled warehouses with stolen German trucks, gasoline, automobile tires, ammunition, guns —all of which he sold at the highest price he could get.

His operations, marked by their unexpectedness and originality, defied German counter-measures. The Germans tripled their guards, they trained their patrols to detect possible suspects and even to shake down their own vehicles. But inventories still ran short.

But all good things must come to an end. Petros had rented an apartment in Athens. It was a simple apartment, nothing ostentatious to give any indication of his material wealth. Petros' landlord had a daughter, a beautiful girl named Maria Asprou who moved in with Petros and there she could have remained forever, for all Petros cared. But one day she made a mistake. Maria began to feel that sharing Petros' home also gave her the right to share Petros' life. Petros, who preferred to be his own master, responded by bringing somebody else's beautiful daughter to the apartment to impress just that point. Maria first threatened suicide, but when that failed to move Petros, she remembered he was doing something— she didn't know what—at the German supply depot. She told the Gestapo all about Petros, but they were a fraction of a minute too late to make the arrest. Penniless and a wanted man, Petros had escaped from Athens and fled to Piraeus, where he could circulate in only a very circumscribed area and for only a short period of time. The rest he spent in hiding.

Spyros ran a big hand over his face. Reviewing all the remarkable accomplishments of the young man—those he himself had observed, those he had learned from Lela and others—Spyros was all the more certain that Petros Zervas was the right man to rescue the icon from those stupid German chaplains, who saw it only as a quaint religious relic, who would never understand its beauty, never appreciate its power. Yes, only Petros could perform the miracle.

Old Spyros gave Petros a few hours, and then decided to pay him a visit. At about seven in the evening, with a small tray on his outstretched right hand, the old man turned east on Phaliron Boulevard. When he reached the bottom of the seven flights of concrete steps, he looked around to make sure that no one was following him. The plaza was deserted as usual, except for Mr. Yiannis, the veteran of the 1922 war, who was sweeping the area around his newspaper kiosk, not because there was any debris but because it was habit and gave him something to do.

Spyros looked at the steps and for the first time they seemed three times as high. The old man's back wasn't straight as before; his shoulders drooped low and forward and his steps were no longer easy. They were short and jerky, and with each step his legs broke at the hips, not at the knees. The old man no longer climbed stairs in the center as he had before; and now, as he balanced the tray with his right hand, he clung to the rail and slowly pulled himself up with his left. At the end of each flight he stopped to rest, and it took him ten full minutes to reach the fine gravel of the street above.

There he stopped, turned around, and looked across and over the rooftops below, toward the Yacht Club where the large German flag was waving lazily in the cool afternoon breeze. The sun was setting; it lighted the Church of the Prophet Elias and the acacia trees and cast long shadows on the plaza and on the asphalt of the boulevard below. The war had not touched the east side of the hill. Everything was the same as before, but it was quiet.

Where are the people? Spyros wondered. Where are the shouts of the mothers calling for their children? Where is the donkey? Where are the fine screams of the youngsters going home from school? Where is the fisherman with the basket on his head peddling his catch to the noisy housewives? Where is the loud cry of the chestnut vendor? Where are the people?

He put down the tray with the garbanzo-bean coffee, the slice of dark bread, and the chunk of goat cheese. The old man felt the small cup and it was cold. With a sigh, he lifted the tray and continued toward the Sixth Piraean Grade School. Looking around before entering the gate and closing it behind him, he hurried through the empty yard. He looked into the classrooms one after another, and finding all of them deserted, tried the door to the storeroom. As he had anticipated, Petros Zervas was curled up in a corner under a blanket on a makeshift bed. He appeared to be sleeping soundly.

The old man started to cross the room, but had moved only a few feet when he witnessed a remarkable sight. Petros had awakened in a split second, coming fully alert instantaneously. Just as instinctively his stiletto was in his hand, and he was ready to spring.

"You don't want to kill Old Spyros, boy."

For an instant the younger man blinked in the light—obviously he had no idea who had awakened him—and then grinning as he recognized the old captain, jumped to his feet in the sign of respect every Greek showed his elders. "I don't like to take unnecessary chances, Mister Spyros," he said. "I thrive on risks, but only when they mean something to me."

"Sit down, boy. Here. Drink some coffee." He put the cup in Petros' hand. "It isn't very hot. I brought some bread and cheese, too."

Petros ate ravenously. "I never thought food would taste so good. Thank you, old man."

Spyros did not reply. He was studying Petros' young face and slender body. Suddenly his eyes flashed with anger. "Don't ever let the Germans get hold of you, boy. Don't you ever let them touch you."

"Don't you worry about me," Petros said, and drank some coffee. "They need five times as many hounds to find me, let alone catch me. I am the invisible Greek."

Nobody sought him out and presented him with food without a reason, so he knew the old man wanted something. As he waited, he reached in his pocket and brought out his black worrybeads.

Nodding to the steady clicking of the beads Spyros

44

hesitantly explained his dilemma and the sad case of the Black Saint Nicholas.

Petros dropped the worrybeads into his pocket. It was all he could do not to burst out laughing. "Look, Mister Spyros," he said at last, "stealing saints is a little bit out of my line. Stealing food, guns, gasoline, tires, fine. But saints?"

"Petros—"

"Look here, Mister Spyros. How do I know the Black Saint is not the type that can perform miracles? Suppose he doesn't care to be stolen? I am up to my neck with the Germans as is, no sense adding a black saint to my troubles. Suppose I reached for it—"

"Him."

"Him. Suppose I reached for him and he paralyzed my hand. Or struck me with green lightning. Then what?"

"As far as miracles go," Spyros said seriously, "Black Saint Nicholas has nothing to do with them. Not that he doesn't want to perform miracles." He leaned closer to Petros so even the saint couldn't hear. "Confidentially, I don't think he can perform any."

Petros had been baptized in the Greek Orthodox Church and given the name of an apostle, but had not been inside a church for the last five years. Still he considered himself a good Christian—he believed that people must have faith in the unseen power, though he questioned the variations of worship, the frustrated singers who had become lay readers, changing the tempos of the chants at no one's request. But having no clear-cut evidence to the contrary, his mind remained open and icons such as Saint Nicholas, black or green or yellow, *might* have the power to create unpleasant situations for sinners, especially if the thief were to commit his sin in the presence of the saint's icon. A paradox within a dilemma is a paradox, Petros thought, and made up his mind.

"Mister Spyros, the answer is no. I will not steal the Black Saint Nicholas. Not for you, not even for my own, unwed mother."

"Who asked you to steal?" Spyros said, in astonishment. "I don't want you to steal. What I want is to have you *move* my saint. From my mansion to my cafenion. Don't you see?"

"No, I don't."

"You won't be a thief," Old Spyros reassured him, "you would be a . . . saint mover. You will move a saint."

"And who is going to explain to your saint that all I am doing is moving him?"

Old Spyros pointed above.

"But isn't the saint supposed to protect you? If you have to protect him he isn't much of a saint. Personally, I don't think he's worth all this."

"Damn young people," Old Spyros mumbled to himself, "twisting things around. All right," he said aloud, "maybe he's nothing more than a piece of old wood and a slap of black paint. But I want you to know that I bought him as the icon of Saint Nicholas. Maybe he isn't Saint Nicholas at all. Maybe he's Saint Christopher or Saint John the Baptist, maybe not even a saint. For all I know he could be the face of his Abyssinian painter or the face of his cousin who sold him to me, but the important thing is that to *me* he is Saint Nicholas. I protected him all these years and I intend to protect him now, even if he may not have the power to protect me."

Spyros crossed his arms over his bony chest and stared at Petros, who no longer could contain himself. "Go ahead, laugh at me. But I warn you that you are not going to change my mind about my Black Saint Nicholas. So—are you or are you not going to steal him?"

"I wish you didn't have to use the word steal," Petros said, slightly offended.

"What do you say, boy?"

"I'm not a boy," Petros said.

"The only thing I can offer you in payment is coffee. All the coffee you can drink."

"I don't want you to pay me," Petros said, rubbing his face with both hands. "I don't even want your coffee. Don't you know I have a price on my head? Don't you realize the Germans are likely to come into your cafenion and arrest you just because you happen to know me?"

"Saint Nicholas is my protector and—"

"Saint Nicholas, Saint Nicholas," he dismissed the old man and his saint with an irritated gesture. "By the way, of all people why did you come to me?"

The old man slowly picked up the coffee cup. "I knew you from the time you used to come for coffee with that other boy, Nico. I thought you might understand an old man. That's all."

Petros looked into bright eyes that stared back at him, clear and free of questions, inhibitions, clear of the flicker of indecision. "My problem is, old man, that I do understand you. That's my problem number one. My problem number two is that I am going to get you your Black Saint Nicholas and my third problem is that you are likely to stick the icon outside your front door for everyone to see, and before you know it, we're both going to end up in a concentration camp."

"If you get him for me, boy."

"I am not a boy any more," Petros said, and smiled.

"Very well, Petros," Spyros said and stood up. "And I promise you I will hide him so well that no one will ever dream my Black Saint Nicholas is back where he belongs. And that is a promise from an old man, boy."

7

The great city of Cairo, capital of Egypt and headquarters of the British Middle East Theater of Operations, was not very old, having been founded in 1000 B.C. or thereabouts; but its predecessors, Memphis and Babylon, both of which no longer existed, stretched back to the earliest periods of recorded time. The two million inhabitants of Cairo were relatively untouched by World War II, their government having established one of the most extraordinary forms of so-called neutrality known in the war. In spite of this supposed status, Egypt was the nerve center, staging area, training ground, and vast supply depot for Great Britain, whose continued hold on the Suez Canal was vital to the war effort. Prime Minister Winston Churchill knew, as did Adolf Hitler, that Britain had to keep Suez at all costs. Its loss would be a blow so crippling that Britain well might be knocked out of the war.

Consequently no theater of operations was more important; and the ultimate success or failure of Great Britain and her allies, including her newest ally of a few days, the United States of America, depended in large part on the grim tug-of-war being waged in the deserts of North Africa. Britain had scored first, months earlier, driving the enemy back and following him into Libya. Then the Germans had come into the area, and General Erwin Rommel had proved himself a genius in the handling of tanks. His Panzerkorps had scored a series of brilliant successes, but the British had managed to fight back tenaciously, and the lines were stabilized, temporarily, in the vicinity of Tobruk, a British stronghold about three hundred and fifty miles to the west across the desert.

The continuing threat of a Nazi invasion of England and the commitments of Empire around the world—in the Far East, India, and the Pacific as well as Europe and Africa—placed an almost intolerable strain on Britain's resources, but Suez still remained her single most important communications and supply link with her vast domain in the East, so she concentrated all of the power she could muster in Egypt.

The Royal Navy made one of its primary bases at Alexandria, where Admiral Sir Horatio Nelson had won one of his greatest victories over the massed sea might of Napoleon Bonaparte. A reserve, mobile land force of approximately seven hundred tanks was massed at Tobruk and to its east. Huge supply depots for arms, munitions, food, uniforms, hospital equipment, oil, gasoline, and the thousands of other items needed by modern armies were spotted throughout northern Egypt. And the

Royal Air Force had accumulated three hundred fighter planes stationed at a number of camouflaged fields, stripping other areas of needed air support.

All the same, the British in Egypt suffered from severe shortages. One was in manpower, and London had repeatedly informed the tough, able theater commander, Sir Claude Auchinleck, that no additional troops could be spared. The entry of the United States into the war was responsible for another, curious shortage. Thanks to supplies from the world's wealthiest and most productive industrial nation, the long-run prospects of the Allies had grown brighter; and Prime Minister Churchill, deciding to conserve his bomber strength for a later, massive effort against Germany, had withdrawn all of General Auchinleck's bombers and flown them back to England, thereby robbing him of his air striking power.

In spite of these deficiencies, Britain continued to prepare for an ultimate showdown with Germany in North Africa, and it was said that The Auk kept photographs of Rommel, Stuka bombers, and Panzer tanks in his bedroom as constant reminders of the struggle that still lay ahead. Eventually the industrial might and military manpower of the United States could tip the scales in the Allies' favor; but America, crippled at Pearl Harbor, needed time to mobilize. In the meantime Britain had no alternative: she had to fight for survival.

Between modern Cairo and the Al Mokkatam Hills lay the old Arab city, much of it built between the eleventh and sixteenth centuries. The hub of this area was the vast Salah al Din Square, where, from the twelfth century to the nineteenth, military forces had paraded, public executions had been held and, in recent decades, British officers had played polo. On one side of the square stood the Mosque of Sultan Hasan, one of Islam's architectural gems, built in 1361, and opposite it was a modern mosque, Al Rifa'i, completed in 1912, where members of the reigning Egyptian royal family were buried.

Between them, and dominating the area, was a great Ottoman mosque built in the nineteenth century by one of the rulers of the Turkish empire, Mohammed Ali. But even this mammoth house of worship was dwarfed by the complex in which it stood—the Citadel, a fortress whose original bastions had been erected in the twelfth century by Saladin the Great. Frequently enlarged since that time, the Citadel had been the headquarters of Egypt's military rulers, foreign and domestic, for more than eight hundred years.

A portion of the huge complex had been "borrowed" by the British, and it was there General Auchinleck made his headquarters. The members of his staff had ample reason to hate the ancient structure, whose stone walls and floors, they claimed, had been cunningly devised to trap the heat during daylight hours and to intensify the cold at night. The outside temperature rose to a comfortable 75 to 80 degrees in the afternoons, but inside the Citadel it was sweltering, and when the cold winds swept in from the desert at night and the outside temperature sometimes fell below freezing, the Citadel was a refrigerator. It was small wonder that men who worked there from twelve to twenty-two hours per day, seven days a week, longed to be stationed elsewhere.

On the second floor were located the offices of the commander-in-chief, his chief of staff, and his deputies in charge of the theater Royal Navy, Royal Air Force, and Eighth Army. Only those who had legitimate business there and could prove it to the aides-de-camp to the various general officers were permitted to pass the lines of the heavily armed, very polite grenadier guards who stood sentry duty.

Even more secure was the third floor, where the assistant chiefs of staff for Operations and Intelligence and their immediate subordinates made their offices. This area, to which no outsiders were admitted at any time, was guarded by Royal Marines in combat dress, all of them men who had undergone commando training. Here could be found all the secret war plans of the three major services, and no enemy agent, no neutral observer, and, indeed, few British personnel had ever set foot in its sacred precincts.

The heart of the third floor was the war room, where enlarged maps of the entire theater covered all four walls. Brightly colored pins studded the maps, giving the daily situation at a glance, and these were kept up to date by a lieutenant-colonel and two assistants who kept abreast of all changes and developments.

To the right of the war room stood the office of the Operations chief, to the left was that of the Intelligence chief, and down the long, gloomy corridors were the cubicles occupied by their subordinates. At the end of one corridor was a corner office with cross-ventilation, which alleviated neither the heat of day nor the cold of night, and now, in mid-afternoon, it was sweltering. On a wall a map of the theater was taped, and in it stood clusters of pins showing the stations occupied by various M.I.-6 operatives.

A huge four-bladed fan turned slowly from the ceiling, creating a slight stir in the hot, dry air, and swarms of flies from the great square below flew in and out the open windows. No one in Egypt believed in keeping out the insects with screens, which were said to hamper circulation. An old Turkish rug covered the floor, a long, leather sofa with cracked cushions occupied one wall, and several visitors' chairs were scattered around a scarred conference table. The room was dominated by a huge desk littered with documents, reports and plans, all of them marked *Secret,* and slumped in the swivel chair behind the desk was a balding, square-faced man in his early fifties wearing the tropical field uniform of a general staff officer.

At first glance Brigadier Ian Campbell appeared to be dozing, which was scarcely surprising since he rarely got more than three hours' sleep on any given night. But in truth he had closed his eyes because he was suffering the discomfort caused by indigestion contracted at general officers' mess. Contrary to the conviction of troops in the field, General Auchinleck and his staff subsisted on meager fare; precious shipping had far higher priorities than the officers' mess. Brigadier Campbell was sick of tinned bully beef, experience had taught him to be wary of the fish, supposedly caught near Alexandria the previous day, and only the chicken and rice were safe to eat. Or so he had thought until today.

Brigadier Campbell, his eyes still closed, wondered whether to run the risk of lighting his pipe. The odors rising from Salah al Din Square were pungent reminders that he was not in Leicester Square; only in Bombay and Port Said had he ever encountered a stench more foul. He tried hard to recapture a cold, clear little lake in the highlands of Scotland where he liked to fish; the air there was bracing and pine-scented, and at that moment the brigadier would have given a month's salary for a breath of it.

An aide-de-camp appeared in the open door, and even though his superior's eyes were closed he did not hesitate to interrupt. "Sir," he said, "an urgent message from Cunningham in Piraeus is just starting to come in to Signals."

His indigestion forgotten, Brigadier Campbell hurried into the corridor, where his deputy, Wing Commander Ross, was already on his way. Together they entered a tiny room whose four walls were filled with high-powered radio receiver and transmitter sets. Sitting at a bare table were two sergeants in short-sleeved shirts, headphones clamped to their ears, and both were transcribing the message being transmitted to Cairo. Behind them stood a young lieutenant, who stiffened when he saw the two senior officers.

"Well," Brigadier Campbell snapped, "what does Cunningham say?"

"The message is still coming in, sir," the lieutenant said, gently clearing his throat. "And then it will have to be decoded."

Campbell turned to his aide, who had followed him. "Take the message in sentences, phrases, even individual words," he ordered, "and have it brought to me at once!"

He stalked back to his office, Wing Commander Ross at his side.

Neither spoke until they reached the corner room, and Ross closed the door. "Why the excitement, Ian?"

"You know Cunningham doesn't use 'Urgent' unless he really means it, Pudge."

The lean RAF officer's face creased in a bloodless smile. "You're assuming, I take it, he knows our meaning of 'Urgent.' "

The brigadier hooked his thumbs in his Sam Browne belt. "Come, come, Pudge. I'll grant you he's not my favorite officer. He's direct—like most Americans—says what he thinks, and he's so cold-blooded he sometimes makes me uneasy. But he's still the best man of any nationality we could have put on the job."

Wing Commander Ross nodded grudgingly.

Campbell viciously punched a buzzer on his desk. "Where in the devil is that message?"

A captain hurried into the office and handed him a sheet of paper. "Here's the first part, sir. We'll have the rest in a moment."

Campbell stared at the paper, Ross looking over his shoulder, and together they read: THREE BULGARIAN TANKERS, OIL AND OTHER SUPPLIES ROMMEL, NOW HERE. PRESUMABLY FOR FEW DAYS.

"Well," the brigadier said. "Oil for Rommel. The Auk will want to know about this."

The wing commander scratched his chin. "It could be the beginning of a new Panzer buildup. Whatever it is, Rommel is desperate for oil, and tankers are his only source of supply."

A lieutenant came into the room with another sheet of paper. Campbell snatched it from him. The brigadier and his deputy read the rest of the message: REQUEST AUTHORITY TO DESTROY TARGETS. ALSO REQUEST IMMEDIATE DELIVERY OF TWO DOZEN LIMPETS.

"Why the devil does he want limpets?" Campbell asked

rhetorically. "He knows we have smaller explosive devices."

The wing commander smiled, but made no comment.

"On the other hand," Campbell said, "the new devices can be set only by trained frogmen, and I assume he's hoping to use local talent, although he doesn't say."

He scribbled on a pad of paper, then handed his reply to Ross.

The deputy scanned the message: AUTHORITY GRANTED. GOOD HUNTING. LIMPETS WILL BE SENT USUAL CHANNELS. EXPECT DELIVERY EARLY TOMORROW.

"That should cover it," the deputy said.

The aide-de-camp came into the office in response to his superior's summons. "Sir?"

"Send this off to Major Cunningham at once. We can just catch the BBC musical hour from Cairo, so you'll have to hurry to put this into code. You have only a quarter of an hour."

The aide was unperturbed. "Very good, sir."

"Well, Pudge," the brigadier said to his deputy, "the next step is up to you. Arrange to fly in the limpets to Captain Devlin. He can take them to Piraeus in his boat."

Ross smiled. "He'll be carrying a larger catch of fish than usual this trip."

"Cunningham will need quite a few men to carry that many limpets. I hope he realizes it."

"Amend your order to him, Ian. You know how stubborn these Americans can be. Tell him to use no fewer than nine men, which is the absolute minimum for three tankers, I should think."

Brigadier Campbell brooded as he straightened his uniform. "He certainly doesn't tell us details, does he? On the other hand, I dare say he's wise not to become too chatty when there's always the chance the Gestapo may be listening in. Attend to the amendment, will you, Pudge? I'm going downstairs. The Auk will be enormously pleased."

8

Running downhill, Petros passed Old Spyros' cafenion and entered the small triangular Kastela Plaza. Hesitating momentarily, he proceeded toward the plaza's small island with its anemic acacia tree in the center, glancing about cautiously for patrols and the slits of car headlights. Satisfied that the Germans were only going to spot-check the area tonight, he started out through the empty lots and back streets for the pine grove on top of Kastela Hill.

The Hill of Kastela towered four hundred meters above the port of Piraeus. Before the war its foothills and steep slopes had been heavily populated by citizens whose social and financial positions could be determined by the elevation of their homes. Just above the water, on the northeast foothills overlooking the harbor of Turkolimano, was the spot picked by members of Piraeus society to build their dwellings. The southeast foothills had been claimed by the wealthy, who found that money and possessions did not necessarily buy their owners' way into society. Midway up the western slope of the hill, which overlooked the harbor of Turkolimano, dwelt the upper middle class, retail shop owners and civil servants; above them came the homes of those of indifferent wealth. But all were topped by the working classes whose homes perched above, high on the steep sides of the hill, just below the large groves of cypress and pine trees.

Such distinctions of elevation may have been observed by day; but at night the young from all walks of life, no matter where they lived on the Hill of Kastela, would climb up to the pine grove to breathe in the resin-scented air. Overwhelmed by the beauty of the countryside, inspired by the benign spirit of the Prophet Elias, who had also fled to the hills to escape oppression, the young people, restless and curious, seeking the cool of evening, gave themselves to each other in the age-old ritual of Mediterranean love.

It is doubtful whether the spirit of the Prophet Elias would have appreciated being selected to sponsor such uninhibitedness, but since he himself had turned away from man-made rules he wasn't exactly in a position to object.

From the southern edge of the grove by day one could see the small harbor of Passalimani below with its wide streets and plaza, its theaters and expensive dwellings. To the east below Phaliron Boulevard, the cliff dropped to a sandy beach, in the middle of which was the square cement dance floor of the nightclub situated inside the cliff's large, natural cave. Overlooking the sea were the large stately homes of the shipowners and the bright foreign consulates with flags flying from their roofs, and long, black limousines lining their driveways.

Directly below the grove sparkled the bright waters of the oval-shaped harbor of Turkolimano with its small red-white-and-blue fishing boats lined in rows, while on the beach their nets were spread over poles to dry. Gently rising and falling from their moorings in the harbor were a few remaining yachts, protected from the force of the ocean by a breakwater of boulders. Across from the breakwater, the other jaw of the harbor's mouth began— on a small rocky peninsula, green with seaweed, with the coast guard's lookout perched low on its spine. From the tavernas the ceaseless twanging of bouzouki music—the contagious beat that sent graceful zembekico dancers twisting, leaping, wildly snapping fingers—seemed to mix with the twirling columns of white smoke pouring from stoves where sardines were always frying.

A stone's throw from the noisy Pan-Kastela Swim Club, a narrow stairway climbed steep cliffs to the backyard of Spyros' mansion. Petros had asked him where in the house he kept the saint.

"On the roof," Spyros had told him. "I have a small replica of my ship's bridge on top of the roof. You reach it by means of a long spiral staircase. As soon as you step inside the wheelhouse you'll see him. He is right above the compass to the left of my telescope."

He had then given Petros the log he'd kept, the daily record of the chaplains' habits and activities.

Petros didn't bother to look at it. Instead he asked how well Spyros knew the chaplains.

Spyros looked at him uncomfortably.

"You know . . . what sort of people are they . . . what do they like or dislike? . . . things like that."

"How should I know?" the old man said, slightly offended.

"Don't you know anything about them?"

Spyros pointed to the log. "It's all in there."

"What about there?" asked Petros, tapping his own forehead. "Look, these are the things I have to know if I'm to get back your precious icon."

"Well, then never mind."

Petros stared at the old man.

"You don't have to know anything." The old man's face started to get angry and the blood rushed upward.

"All right," Petros said, "I'll find out myself. And I'll read your damn log."

"I don't want you to go for my Black Saint Nicholas."

"It's too late for that. I've promised."

"I don't care," Spyros said, "I don't want you to go after him."

"But why not, old man?"

"I have my reasons, you dirty little bastard." Spyros grabbed Petros by the collar of his shirt and pulled him close.

Petros looked at Spyros' trembling hands. The anger faded momentarily from the old man's face, but then he started to shake Petros viciously.

"Spyros . . ." Petros said, raising both arms in surrender. "Spyros?" he said, puzzled.

"Don't 'Spyros' me, you little animal," he said and pulled harder. "Don't 'Spyros' me," he added in a loud voice, falling backward as his hand slipped from the collar.

Petros reached out and caught him before he fell.

"I can take care of you with my right hand tied around me," the old man cried, grabbing for Petros' collar again. "No one gets Saint Nicholas out of there. . . . Do you hear me, you little bastard?"

Petros stared bewildered at this man who commanded such respect, even as Spyros continued to shake him as only an old man would—first with force and then with weak tugs. And Petros helped him by falling into the rhythm so the old man wouldn't have to pull so hard, for he could see he was exhausted.

"Stop it, old man," Petros shouted at last and pried the old man's arms apart.

Spyros' arms dropped to his side. He was still swaying to the rhythm of his tugs, but his face was white and trickles of perspiration cut paths across the deep triangular wrinkles, the hash marks of the sea.

"Old man," Petros said, steadying him. "Are you all right?"

Spyros did not reply, but slowly eased himself to the floor.

"Can I do something? Just a minute. Let me give you a hand."

"I'll make it," Spyros whispered and sat down again.

"Stay as long as you want, old man," Petros said and sat down next to him.

He saw the old man wipe tears from his eyes and looked away. "What have I done to you?" Petros said.

"Nothing."

"Spyros . . ." Petros shook his head. "I thought you liked me. I like you, old man."

Spyros broke into uncontrollably loud sobbing and the tears streamed down his cheeks. "I didn't want to hurt you . . ." he mumbled at last. "Why should I hurt you? I love you, boy," he shouted. "I don't want you to go and get shot to pieces for an old chunk of wood."

"Were you trying to make me mad at you, Mister Spyros?"

The old man nodded.

"Why in hell did you have to go through all that?" Petros cried. "You could have had a heart attack, trying to shake my head loose."

"I'm nothing but a selfish old fool," Spyros said through his tears. "Trying to send you over there to get all shot up."

"You're not sending me. Nobody can send me anywhere unless I want to go. You can't tell me to go somewhere unless I want to go. Do you understand?"

"Yes," Spyros said, nodding.

"Well . . . I want to go."

"No!" Spyros jerked to his feet. "You can't do it!" He started for Petros again.

"Wait . . . wait . . . wait, old man," Petros said, spreading opened palms in front of him. "I don't want to fight with you again. I've had enough of that."

"Don't you see," the old man said, "for days I've been saying to myself, Spyros, you're a selfish old man. Spyros, you're a slave. Your Black Saint Nicholas is a slave. Why do you endanger a young man's life to move your saint from one jail to another?"

"There is no danger involved," Petros assured him.

"For you," he said, "maybe. What about me? From the day I asked you to help me, my whole life has changed. My nerves are jiggling me out of my mind. At night I can't sleep. Five or six times a day I pick fights with my customers. Three yesterday, five today, and only Black Saint Nicholas knows how many tomorrow." He paused in thought. "Maybe he is against it. Maybe he likes it there. After all these years, maybe he got sick and tired of me."

"Mister Spyros," Petros said and smiled, "I will not take the icon out of there because of you. I would like to take him out for myself. And if you don't want him, I'll return him to the Germans."

"Boy," Spyros said, coming closer to Petros, "Black

59

Saint Nicholas is worth more to me than anything else I have. My home, my cafenion, everything. Someday, when the war is over and if I am still alive, I'll get him back. But if you go there and something happens to you, what am I going to do?" He grabbed Petros by the arm. "I've changed my mind now," he said sadly. "I don't want you to go there and steal him. You have to promise me that." The old man paused for Petros' answer but Petros remained silent. "Someday," Spyros said, "I'll figure a way to get him out of there myself. But not you."

"Is this what you really want?"

"Yes. I love my saint, but I don't want to see you hurt. You must promise me you won't steal him."

Petros studied his face and trembling lips. His eyes no longer sparkled; they looked tired and gray.

"This is a promise, old man. I won't steal it."

"Him."

"Him," Petros repeated.

"Thank you," the old man said. "You promise."

"I promise," said Petros. "You're a good old man, Spyros."

Spyros thought for a moment and then agreed. "Yes, maybe I am."

Petros watched his friend's tired body cross the schoolyard.

"Good luck," Petros yelled after him. "I hope you live a million years."

So it was that Petros found himself approaching Spyros' former mansion. He came the long way—up the long narrow stairway leading from the pebbled beach below to the rear entrance. Otherwise he would have had to check in at the gate to the German compound. The extreme eastern corner of Kastela had always been the most silent portion of Piraeus, and he had always wondered whether the wives of the wealthy who lived in its large houses ever had children. Probably not. As nearly as he could tell, they bore their sons and daughters full-grown; the first time they made an appearance they were already conservative ladies and gentlemen, to whom speaking out loud was even more unpardonable than nodding a public greeting to the chestnut peddler.

Now, of course, the houses were occupied by the officers of the conquerors, mature and sober men who, come to think of it, resembled the Greek industrialists, merchants, and shipowners they had displaced. But the quiet was deceptive, and Petros realized that at any moment a patrol might appear.

He slipped through an alleyway and onto the street. He looked up and down, but no one was in sight, not a sound, although nothing could be heard anyway over the hollow cough of the waves that crashed against the rocks below.

Petros inspected the ground floor of Spyros' mansion and tried to see into the windows of the second floor. They were all closed, and he tried the front door. The shining brass knob did not turn and he shook the door lightly as the German guard in front of German headquarters in the Zacharias villa directly opposite looked on curiously, unseen by the young Greek. Petros backed into the middle of the street, his eyes on the ledge of the second-floor windows.

Impossible, he thought; the only way to remove Black Saint Nicholas was through a ground-floor window or door like a gentleman, or else to jump out a window higher up, no easy task since the back of the house dropped straight to the sea.

He saw a flash of light turned on high in a second-floor room, and immediately someone pulled the heavy drapes together.

Petros looked toward the Kastela Plaza for patrol cars and wandering civilians who might recognize him. Satisfied he was unobserved, he decided to investigate the rear of the house when he heard the metallic thrum of coasting bicycles behind him. Instinctively he ducked under the bare branches of a young acacia tree.

Realizing the trunk of the tree was too slender to

conceal his body, he stepped out and boldly sauntered toward Spyros' mansion.

Their machine pistols hanging loosely under their arms, the two Germans rolled their bikes to an easy stop in front of Petros. One soldier checked his luminous watch as the other blocked Petros' way.

Petros was not prepared for this. Now he had to improvise quickly. One of the soldiers ordered Petros to halt.

"Good evening," Petros said, greeting the German with a smile.

"Let me see your papers."

Petros found himself staring into the muzzle of an automatic rifle. "You'll find them in my right hip pocket," he said.

The soldier frisked him expertly, an experience to which Petros had become accustomed, then removed the identity card and stared at it in the glare of the flashlight. "Petros Zervas," he read. "Engineer at the power plant."

"Correct." All at once Petros saw a chance. "We had a report of a power failure, and I came to investigate."

The two Germans were joined by the soldier who had been watching him from the Zacharias villa. "I've had my eye on this one for a quarter of an hour," he said. "He's been moving up and down the street, studying the windows."

"So I have," Petros said. "The best way to pinpoint a power failure is to see whether lights are flickering, or go off very suddenly."

"How do you check lights during a blackout?"

Petros pointed to the sliver of light shining through the drapes of the second floor of Spyros' former home.

"That's against regulations!" one of the soldiers said. "All lights must be covered after dark."

"You know chaplains," Petros said. "Military regulations mean nothing to them."

The soldier was still suspicious. "How did you know that chaplains are billeted here?"

There was no legitimate way Petros could have known, and he tried to make his reply sound convincing. "We have lists, naturally."

A chauffeur-driven car pulled to a halt and the man in the back seat rolled down his window. "What's going on?"

One of the soldiers approached the car and saluted.

A sudden dread filled Petros. The passenger was wearing civilian clothes, which could only mean he was an officer in the Gestapo.

The man listened to the soldier's account, then took Petros' identity card. "This is simple enough to check," he said. "If this Zervas is here on legitimate business, he had to check in at the sentry gate and they'll have his name on the list. Wait here until I return." He started to roll up the window.

"If you please, sir," Petros called after him. "I have reason to believe there's a severe power drain in the chaplains' house, and if our information at the power station is correct, it could knock out all the electricity on this street."

The Gestapo officer hesitated. Colonel Schneider had a notorious temper, which wouldn't be helped if his power went out. "What do you propose to do about it, Zervas?"

"I beg permission, sir, to go into the house and investigate. I'm sure you'll be back with my clearance before I'm finished."

The suggestion sounded reasonable. Anyone who wanted to cause trouble would pick a more likely target than the chaplains. Now if it was German headquarters. . . .
"Very well," the officer said. "You men, station yourselves outside, and if he tries to leave before I return, stop him."

The soldiers saluted, and the car moved off down the street.

It would take approximately ten minutes, Petros estimated, for the Gestapo officer to determine that his name wasn't entered on the duty roster and return to place him under arrest. With luck he might have just enough time.

He rapped on the door, and when an orderly in shirt-sleeves opened it, he explained he'd come from the power plant to investigate a possible power leak.

"There's nothing wrong with our light." The orderly was an inoffensive man in his late thirties.

"I have my orders," Petros said, and pushed past him.

The little orderly was upset. "Be good enough to wait here while I report to Chaplain Heindorf and Chaplain Stroop."

Petros fidgeted in the entrance hall, the precious seconds ticking away in his mind. He still had his stiletto, which no German had ever found when frisking him, but it wouldn't do him much good when the Gestapo officer sent in the soldiers after him.

Two chaplains, one in a major's uniform the other wearing a captain's insignia, appeared from an inner room. "What can we do for you?" the one he assumed to be Major Heindorf asked.

Petros explained he had been sent from the power plant to check a possible power failure, and since he could see there was no trouble downstairs—"You haven't noticed any flickering, have you?"—he'd like to look upstairs.

"But there's nothing up there except bedrooms, and above that the roof with some sort of wheelhouse." And Major Heindorf sounded embarrassed as he explained that the former owner was a ship captain who used the place—well, to be truthful, he wasn't exactly sure *what* he used it for . . . signals, beacons of some sort?

"Beacons," Petros repeated, nodding. "Yes, that would drain power quickly enough."

"But I thought I explained," the chaplain said. "It's been virtually sealed off since we took over. No one goes up there."

"So they'd have no way of knowing whether there was a short circuit bleeding the line?"

64

The major shrugged. "I doubt it. As I say, no one uses the place. Still . . ."

"It will take only a few minutes," Petros said.

"August," the chaplain said to the orderly, "take this man upstairs so he can check out the power."

Petros found it almost impossible to hide his exultation as the orderly led the way. They climbed to the second floor which, from Spyros' log, he knew contained the bedrooms of the three chaplains. He wondered idly where the third chaplain might be. So far his luck was holding.

The third floor was the attic, and in one corner was the small set of stairs that led to the roof. Petros let his knife-hilt slide down into his hand, and when he pressed the release the stiletto slid open.

The orderly unlocked a trapdoor and indicated Petros should go up the spiral staircase to the roof. "I wouldn't know what you're looking for," the orderly said. "When you finish, call me and I'll show you the way down."

Petros waited until he could no longer hear the man's feet on the metal stairs.

"Saint Nicholas," he whispered, pushing the stiletto blade back into the ivory handle, "if you haven't performed a miracle before, you better start thinking of one now." He looked over to where Spyros' wheelhouse stood. He could see its black, square outline, the mast extending straight up with the crow's nest on top, the supporting cables anchored to steel hooks in the concrete. The lanyard ran along the mast to the deck, and the old man had used it to hoist the international code pennants on national holidays and whenever he wanted to communicate with the captains of foreign liners that had once anchored in the Gulf of Phaliron.

The cold north winds were beginning to come alive tonight, as they had done every night this past week. In weather like this, Petros could imagine, Old Spyros must have remained in the wheelhouse all night long, sending messages by blinker light to the fishermen, their red and green lanterns appearing and disappearing as they fought the storm, trying to steer their wobbling boats straight into the mouth of the Turkolimano.

Petros looked down over the parapet. It jutted out over the land and dropped straight down to the pebbled beach below. From beneath it doesn't look too high but from above . . . !

What will you do now, Zervas? he asked himself as he saw one of the soldiers looking up at him from the street side, automatic rifle in hand.

"Freedom or death," he said aloud and smiled in recollection of the words of Greek women who danced to their death off a mountain cliff, rather than be captured alive by the Turks. "Freedom or death," he repeated. If the Germans suddenly start upstairs, would I jump?

"No, I wouldn't," he answered aloud. "I don't know what I am going to do, but I am not going to jump," he added and kicked aside a roll of twine old Spyros had used to mend the Samoan fishing net still hanging on the side of the wheelhouse. "Well, Saint Nicholas," he said and opened the door to the wheelhouse. "Let's see what's so special about you."

Old Spyros' sanctuary was an exact replica of the S. S. *Hellas,* except that the only windows were in front, facing the sea. Spyros must have been self-conscious and did not want anyone on land to see him trying to fight the storms; but the sailors who saw him fighting the helm would understand.

Petros looked past the compass to the telescope, but could find no trace of the icon. The old man had told him the Black Saint Nicholas was above his compass and to the left of the telescope, hadn't he? Petros looked around and felt the walls, just in case the chaplains had moved him. No icon.

"Poor Spyros," Petros said. "They sent the icon to Germany after all. Well, at least they had the decency not to tell you."

Petros closed the door to the wheelhouse. Across in the Zacharias villa, he could see the Germans opening the top-floor windows and tossing wooden crates into the water below. The light was bright inside, and Petros could see the soldiers but not what they were doing. He returned to the wheelhouse for the telescope to focus it on the villa. Through it he could make out a supply room and the soldiers filling shelves with provisions.

He reached up to replace the telescope on its cradle when his eye was caught by an impossible sight. He wanted to weep, but instead began to laugh aloud. Directly above his head, hanging from wire across the ceiling, was the icon. It was just as Old Spyros had said. It was painted black on a wood mounting. It was above the compass and to the left of the telescope. But one thing Spyros had neglected to mention: the icon of Black Saint Nicholas was lifesize!

"Old man," he said, laughing nervously, "you must pick your garbanzo beans off the grape vines. How can I possibly get out with a monster like that?"

He appealed to the icon, even as he climbed onto the compass. "Forgive me for talking to you this way, but Saint Nicholas, you'd better do something, because you are the biggest saint I ever laid my eyes on."

Petros pulled down the nearest end of the icon, breaking the wire, then let down the icon slowly. He rested the icon on the floor in front of him. They were both the same height, six feet one! Fortunately the wood backing of the icon was light enough so that Petros could lift him with one hand.

"I came here to sneak you out, Saint Nicholas," Petros said, looking the saint straight in the eyes. "At least do me a favor and don't get stuck in the spiral staircase on our way down. If I know the Germans they're rounding up a regiment for us." He looked at the saint. "Maybe I'm crazy," he said and raised the icon's face close to his, "but talking with you somehow makes me feel better. And something tells me you have something to do with it. I certainly hope so, because I just happen to know what the odds are against us."

Petros waited for the saint to reply. "All right, say

nothing . . . but at least help me, help us, get out of here."

The sea was slapping viciously against the rocks. The northern winds whipped the branches of the lemon and orange trees against the villa; overhead the clouds were black and running low.

Petros steadied Saint Nicholas against his hip and started for the door. Just then the wind blew it open, revealing August the orderly blinking up into the darkness.

"Please hurry down," he called out, "there's a big storm coming up."

Petros dropped the icon quickly, and the wind picked it up and sent it crashing against the south parapet.

August stepped onto the roof and stared in disbelief. "What is happening here? You said you wanted to check the power lines. You said nothing about removing the icon."

Petros stepped closer as the man backed off in sudden fright.

"Don't be afraid. I'm not going to hurt you," said Petros, moving closer.

"Don't get near me," the orderly screamed and tore open the door halfway. Petros kicked it shut and leaned against it.

"I told you I am not going to hurt you," Petros said. "I just want you to keep quite. Will you do that for me?"

"Who are you?" the man asked, shaking. "Where are you going with Saint Nicholas?"

"There's nothing to be alarmed about," Petros said calmly. "Nothing will happen if you do as I say. Now, take your jacket off," Petros said, in the same calm voice. "Then your shirt and belt."

The orderly reached for the buttons on his shirt. Petros backed up to give him room, but the moment he did the man dashed for the door again.

"Help!" he shouted. "Major Heindorf!" Petros slammed the door shut, jamming August's body. "Captain Stroop . . ." he shouted again. Petros muffled his mouth with one hand and grabbed him by his belt with the other.

68

"I told you to keep quiet," Petros snapped, one ear listening for footsteps on the stairs. He was about to unbuckle August's belt and tie him up when he heard auto tires careening around the corner, the motors racing as gearshifts were thrown into low.

"Do you know who's out there?"

The terrified orderly shook his head.

"Let's go," Petros said and started for the south parapet, dragging the orderly behind him. There were more sounds of screeching tires, and voices began to rise.

Petros leaned over the parapet, keeping the man at arm's length, and saw below that six cars filled with German soldiers had pulled up and the men were fanning out along the street in front of the house.

The orderly pulled himself free of Petros' grip and started to run. Petros gave chase but the man gained and had started for the stairs before Petros could catch him.

"Help!" the man screamed, trying to free himself. "Chaplain . . ." And then his voice faded as the slim stiletto blade pierced his chest and entered his lungs. He jerked backwards. Downstairs the Germans were pounding on the front door.

"I am sorry, little German," Petros said and laid the man on his back. Then he ran to the parapet, picked up Saint Nicholas, and started for the door. Suddenly he changed his mind and ran to the other side of the wheelhouse. Laying the icon on the deck and holding it down with his knee to prevent the wind from carrying it away again, Petros searched around the base of the wheelhouse until he found the ball of twine he had kicked earlier. I hope it's strong enough, he thought, as he tied a knot around the middle of the icon and slipped it over the parapet. The wind banged the icon against the wall and Saint Nicholas flew past two windows and finally touched ground near the back door.

Petros ran back to the stairs and listened intently. No voices were coming from inside and he could not hear the knocking at the front door. He started to climb down the metal steps to the hall.

He could now hear the Germans slamming the car doors outside, as he ran to the end of the upstairs hall, the bleeding stiletto held high in front of him. So far so good! He tip-toed down the stairs to the ground floor when a door opened and he saw Heindorf talking to an officer. From the rear Stroop and the other chaplain were slowly approaching. Bending low, Petros cut past the two chaplains into the kitchen and out the back door. A dozen machine pistols cut loose, making the pots in the kitchen clatter and shattering the glass in the back door.

Petros scooped up the saint and started down the long, narrow stairway leading to the rocky shore. The windows of the Zacharias villa flew open, flooding the water below with light. Some of the troops were racing down the stairway after him, while others tried to catch him in their flashlights. The second volley came just as Petros' feet touched the ground below. The Germans were trying to pin him down until their comrades could reach him or until patrol cars could come around from the Turkolimano side.

Petros waited until the shooting stopped, then picked himself up from the ground and started to edge along the cliff to the pebbled beach, beyond the direct line of fire.

The soldiers advanced to the bottom steps, firing their automatics downward, scattering dust from the yellow cliff out over the waters of Turkolimano. The Germans on top were firing long bursts over their heads, the bullets ricocheting shrilly from the rocks.

Holding Saint Nicholas tightly, Petros ran along the path between the rocks, against the wind, trying not to get cut by the sharp, rocky points or fall into the water.

The Germans reached the bottom of the cliff and the firing stopped.

High above on the boulevard, the troops pulled their patrol cars near the ledge and with spotlights began to comb the white beach and the rocks along the side of the cliff. Whenever a bright spot crept near, Petros held the backside of the icon in front of him and remained motionless behind it as it blended against the yellow cliff.

At the bottom of the steps, the soldiers split into two groups, one started out for the Turkolimano side, the other for the pebbled beach.

"Saint Nicholas," Petros said, "we are locked in tight."

The Germans were close and Petros could see their shining helmets against the roving spotlights as they waded through the spray kicked high into the wind by the sea. The water thundered against the boulders and drowned out the wails of the sirens of the patrol cars.

The Germans had to have found the orderly's body, for directly behind Petros from the roof of Spyros' house came a shower of small-arms fire.

"Black Saint Nicholas," Petros said looking up at the flashes, "We're not doing so well on land." He waited for the spotlights to pass by. "Let's go," he said, and sliding down the rocks, against the barnacles and the slippery seaweed, he fell into the water.

The waves crashed hard, pinning him against the rock. When the water started to recede and the foam thickened, Petros anchored the saint to the rock like a pole and vaulted himself into the deep water. Digging the six-foot saint into the bottom rocks, he again propelled his body forward, under the oncoming wave, and wrapping his arm around a rock on the reef, waited for the backwash.

When the boulders had taken the full brunt of the sea, and as the foam boiled over, Petros bobbed up to the surface for a deep breath. Holding Saint Nicholas with one hand, he dug hard into the water with the other, kicking his legs viciously. Cutting through the crest of the wave, he swam past the last critical mass of water into a wet dale of calm, and pushing harder, slipped by the sharp edges of the boulder. Twenty-five meters out from shore he stopped and looked back.

The Germans had already passed the spot where he had last hidden, and all lights were now concentrated on the ground in front of them and around the base of the cliff. The German officer on Spyros' roof continued to spray the area in front of the patrol with short bursts of bullets and the Germans from the Zacharias villa, who couldn't see anything and who didn't know what was happening anyway, joined in the wild target practice by scattering rusty tin cans along the pebbled beach. Soon the small beach became a burning inferno of copper and hot lead.

Petros, who could see the flashes but could not feel the bullets whistling past him, ducked under a floating grocery crate and, resting on the icon, swam around to the other side of the small peninsula. The Germans did not stop shooting at the beach until they had exhausted their ammunition, and then they started to pelt the beach and water with their billy-clublike hand grenades.

Puzzled by the explosions, Petros pulled himself up on the icon and rode the waves to the shore.

The gale had grown fierce. He ran across the beach and crawled under the overhang of ice-plant-covered cliff, where, protected from the wind and salt spray, he stripped and wrung the water out of his clothes.

The Germans, out of explosives at last, reported back to their superiors that the suspect had been sighted, fired upon, fallen into the sea, and was presumed dead.

It was past midnight and the storm had reached its peak when Petros climbed up the dirt path to Phaliron Boulevard. With the Black Saint Nicholas under his arm, he dashed across the street, through backyards, for the safety of the schoolyard and storage room.

There he changed into dry clothes, gently wiped the sand off Saint Nicholas and finally had the chance for a long leisurely look at his black face. "Saint Nicholas," he said, thoughtfully rubbing his chin, "maybe you can perform miracles and maybe you can't. But knowing the Germans as I do, I wouldn't want to bet on it either way."

Then he lay down on his mattress and a moment later was fast asleep.

The wind grew stronger, heavy drops of rain began to fall, grew heavier in a deep, inviting rhythm. Major David

Cunningham, his coat collar upturned, a slouch hat pulled low over his forehead, smiled in quiet satisfaction. Then he moved away from the shadow of the schoolyard wall and started back through the deserted streets to his own quarters.

9

All night and all day the storm continued to lash Attica. The angry waters of the Saronic Gulf pounded the shores; and not until morning of the following day did the wrath of the elements burn out. The sun slid past the last white clouds hanging over Cape Sounion, its light raked the calm waters of the gulf and bathed the whitewashed homes, the eastern slope of the Kastala Hill, with morning red.

In the triangular plaza in front of Old Spyros' cafenion, the housewives hauled precious firewood and broken tree branches from the ankle-deep mud covering the boulevard, while Spyros spread his on the marble tables in his cafenion's veranda to dry. On the Turkolimano the Germans aboard the commandeered yawls and schooners loosened the sails from the booms and set them high on the masts to dry. The fishermen spread their nets over the beached varkas and poles and set to bailing the rainwater from their boats.

By eight o'clock all the sails were up at Turkolimano and from a distance its mood looked festive. The hot sun relaxed the fishermen's muscles, tense from two days' confinement and tightened by the cold wind. As they worked they sang. They sang of love, of the sea, of the Arab women on the North African coast and the wild love of the gypsy girls on the shores of southern Spain. They sang and the sun went higher, but without realizing it the rhythm of their singing betrayed their feelings, fell into the steady monotone of a lament, a dirge. They spread their nets and mended their nets, and sang happy songs so they would not weep, songs to keep their spirits up; but every once in a while they would raise their eyes to the mast of the Yacht Club, where the huge swastika was flying.

It was eleven o'clock. The sun was beating down and it was hot. The asphalt in the streets had dried and the tiled roofs, the nets, the sails, and the yacht decks began to steam. Some of the fishing boats began to file out of the harbor with their German escorts.

On the hillside and in the homes around the harbor, the housewives hung their blankets out of the windows or on their clotheslines to air, and Old Spyros turned the dry side of the firewood down and wet side up. In the garden of the Zacharias villa, two Greek prisoners were sweeping the path to the front door clear of fallen leaves, while two others trimmed broken and dislocated limbs from the orange and lemon trees.

On the roof of Old Spyros' home the German flag was flying at half mast.

Spyros fixed a cup of coffee and served himself in the veranda at the table nearest the sidewalk. Mr. Yiannis, who was sunning himself outside his kiosk, threw up both hands to indicate that he, too, had had no customers all morning. Old Spyros shrugged his bony shoulders in reply and sipped his coffee, his eyes staring at the white sails at Turkolimano. He smacked his lips in displeasure at the taste of the garbanzo beans, closed his eyes, and leaned back so the sun could fall on his face and neck. He sunned himself contentedly; then his ears picked up the steady sound of boots. He opened his eyes and saw the three German chaplains walking toward him.

"Good day," he said, and stood.

"Good day. We would like to talk to you," Chaplain Heindorf said. "Inside, please."

The three chaplains filed through the door into Spyros' establishment. The old man tightened his lower lip and his eyebrows arched in puzzlement. He took two deliberate slow sips of coffee and then followed the chaplains inside.

74

The severe-looking faces of his visitors puzzled him even more. "Can I fix you some coffee?" he said, showing them to a table.

"It is not coffee we need from you," Chaplain Roehm said. "Coffee is not the reason we are here."

So they *could* speak modern Greek; why didn't they say so the last time they talked! "Why don't you sit down anyway?" Spyros said and pulled two chairs aside.

"No, thank you," Major Heindorf said. "I just have a question or two for you. It won't take long. The shooting, the explosions which I am sure you and everyone else heard the other night," the chaplain said. "All that rifle firing. Could you possibly have an explanation for it?"

Spyros smiled as though he thought the question ridiculous. "If there's no shooting here, there'll be shooting someplace else."

"No." Heindorf raised his index finger. "I'm talking about this particular night. Do you know a reason for it?"

"I can think of many reasons," Spyros said. "But you are asking me to tell you something I don't know. If I had fired those guns, I'm sure I would have known the reason."

"Aren't you Greeks curious?" Heindorf asked. "Don't you ask one another what could cause all that noise?"

"Of course we do," Old Spyros said. "First thing we do is try to find out which one of our friends is missing. Shooting means killing, doesn't it?"

"Did someone get killed? A friend?" Heindorf asked in sudden interest.

"Not that I know of," Spyros said, his eyes narrowing. "But if someone is dead I'm sure he had a friend or two."

"We can assure you he did," Heindorf said, exchanging glances with his companions.

"I guess you're trying to find out from me something you seem to know already," Old Spyros said, his face turning serious. "Is it someone I know?" he asked.

"We believe you do," Chaplain Heindorf said and glanced at Stroop.

"Whoever it is . . . would you please tell me?" the old man said, his hands gripping the back of a chair.

"August, our orderly, was murdered the other night."

"Oh, no," Spyros said. "But he was a good fellow."

"We thought so, too," Heindorf said. "He was the kindest of human beings, Mister Spyros. He could not fire a rifle in anger. That's why I kept him out of the ranks . . . because he loved his fellow man so dearly he could not bear to kill him."

Heindorf looked at the old man, who was shaking his head sadly. "Nothing could change his mind," the chaplain continued. "Not the army, not the threat of punishment, nothing. He loved the Greeks, not because they were Greeks but because they were humans, and yet another human, a Greek, stabbed him to death."

"Who would do a thing like that to the poor fellow?" Spyros said. And then he stopped shaking his head and his eyes turned sideways and low as if something had awakened his memory. "Who would do a thing like that?" he mumbled and then fell silent.

"A Greek, Mister Spyros. A Greek stabbed him to death," Heindorf said again, a sting in his voice.

"I'm sorry to hear that," the old man said without lifting his eyes from the floor.

"August is dead because he tried to stop a Greek from stealing your Black Saint Nicholas."

"No!" Spyros shouted.

"Yes!" Heindorf shouted back. "August died because he tried to protect something you loved, old man."

"No . . . no," Spyros mumbled, shaking his head and reaching for the chair.

"No?" Heindorf asked, and stepped closer. "No? Mister Spyros?" Heindorf lifted the old man's chin so he could see into his face. "We buried that innocent human being yesterday," Heindorf said and pulled his hand from Spyros' chin in disgust.

"I am sorry," Spyros mumbled. "I am very sorry," he

76

added trying to lift his eyes to see the chaplains, but fearing what he would see there—that his beloved Black Saint Nicholas not only had cost the orderly's life but the life of the boy he had sent to rescue his saint as well.

He slumped in the chair, head low on his chest, hands hanging by his sides, legs spread apart. The chaplains looked down and they knew.

"Do you want to know about the shooting?"

The old man regained his senses. He sprang to his feet. "Yes! What about those shots?" he cried and started to walk away. "Tell me about the shots."

"You are interested, aren't you?" Chaplain Heindorf asked with a satisfied smile.

"Yes . . . I am," Old Spyros replied. "I am very interested," he said over his shoulder. The old man stopped and turned. His face was twisted and his breath short. "All those shots . . . all that shooting . . . who was it for?"

"The shots," Chaplain Heindorf said, "were aimed at the man you sent over to steal your icon."

"Oh . . . yes?" Old Spyros said aloud.

"And this young man is, I'm afraid, also dead."

"Saint Nicholas?" Spyros asked.

"Both were shot and fell into the sea."

"Dead," Spyros said to himself as his lower lip started to quiver. But I told him not to go, he said to himself. I told him not to do it. He appealed to the chaplains. "I went there and told him I don't want my Black Saint Nicholas."

"Where is 'there'?" Chaplain Roehm asked.

"Over there," Old Spyros said vaguely, pointing toward Turkolimano. "He was a good boy," he reassured Heindorf. "One of the best," he said. "Never seen a nicer young man," he added, blinking his eyes and smiling to make them believe he was telling the truth.

The chaplains remained silent. Heindorf took Spyros by the arm and sat him in a chair. Stroop went behind the coffee counter and brought a glass of water. "Drink," Stroop said.

Spyros drained the glass and returned it to the chaplain for more. He ran his tongue over his wet lips. "More water," he said, as he struggled for breath.

Chaplain Heindorf felt the old man's pulse, then let the hand drop. "I leave you with your conscience," he said and started out the door, the other two following.

"Yes . . . with my conscience . . ." Spyros said.

The old man walked out in the street and started down toward Turkolimano. The fishermen mending their nets greeted him, but Old Spyros didn't reply. Old Spyros' body was functioning, but his mind was not. A fixed smile had suddenly appeared on his face. Old Spyros smiled at the German guard in front of the marine gasoline station, and when the German smiled back he continued happily along the Turkolimano waterfront, where he threw pebbles over the water, tried to scoop shrimp from the water with his hands.

Shortly after nine P.M. Spyros was apprehended by a German patrol for violating the curfew, but the desk sergeant at the station released him after he had given him all the water he could drink and after tying a paper tag on his shirt on which he had written "Insane." Later it got cold, and the old man entered the Church of Saint Constantin, where he slept in a center pew. He was awakened the next morning by the bells. He volunteered to help the priest ring them, but when he started to yank the heavy rope he spoiled the melody of the archdiocese's regulation chimes, and the priest kicked the old man away.

That day was the happiest in Old Spyros' life. He visited all parts of the city, smiled at everybody, and everybody smiled back. He played in the park, watched the Germans exercise, rang the bells at the Saint Triada, and was chased away by the priest. But when the priest saw his smile he understood and returned to his church.

At night Old Spyros returned to his cafenion, filled himself with water, closed the front door, and slept. Next morning he made free coffee for all who passed. Word got around, and soon there were fifty people drinking his coffee and smiling at Spyros. When the coffee was gone Spyros went down to the pebbled beach. He looked up and waved at the chaplains in his mansion above, but they did not wave back.

Darkness fell and he returned to his empty cafenion. All the glasses and cups and coffeepots he had given away to his customers. The tables and chairs he had not given away, but his customers had read the tag and had helped themselves.

Spyros was tired and sat down in the middle of his cafenion. It was a cold evening and the old man shivered. Three days had passed since he had last eaten, and his cheeks were hollow, his face white from exertion, his lower lip blue and trembling. His heart was pounding rapidly and his stomach was aching from hunger. The old man got up to drink more water and then lay down in a corner and feel asleep.

At nine-thirty in the morning Spyros opened his eyes. The low sun coming through the large front windows and open door had barely had time to warm the cafenion. He tried to orient himself. His senses began to return, he felt the coolness of the tiles on his back and slowly rose to a sitting position. When he saw that the tables and chairs were not stacked in the back, he pressed his hands against the floor and tried to get up, but his legs started to shake and he decided to wait before trying again.

Outside he saw Mr. Yiannis sunning himself in front of his newspaper kiosk; Spyros saw the firewood he had picked strewn on the veranda floor. He looked down, saw his dirty pants and shoes, and when his eyes caught the tag on his chest he pulled it off and read it. Without trying to think any more, he pressed his bare hands against the floor and this time his legs held and he brought himself erect. He put the tag in his pocket. He walked slowly toward the door, holding himself upright by clinging to both sides of the door. Mr. Yiannis had his face turned to the sun and could not see Old Spyros. The old man hoped he could remain unnoticed, as he stepped down on his veranda and bent over to pick up a pine branch to use as a cane. When he tried to straighten up, his legs trembled at the knees and he sat down just as a German sedan sped past. Mr. Yiannis didn't look up as Old Spyros dragged himself to the veranda steps and with the help of the cane began to walk.

As on every morning, the plaza was deserted and Spyros was thankful for he didn't want to be seen like this. He did not know what day it was, he could not remember what had happened to his cafenion, to himself. The last thing he could remember was talking with the three chaplains, and the next thing he saw was the ceiling of his establishment.

Old Spyros did remember the tag in his pocket, however. Four days ago his body was functioning but not his mind; today, his mind was functioning but not his body. He stopped at the end of the plaza and leaned against the wall of the closed pharmacy to rest. Where can I go? he thought and his eyes scanned Phaliron Boulevard and his home. Where can I go? he thought again and his eyes stopped at the seven flights of steps next to his cafenion. Old Spyros knew all at once that the only person in the world he wanted to see now was the boy. He remembered the chaplain had said something about him, but could not recall just what. He would have to ask the boy when he saw him. He knew he could never make it up the steps so he continued on, taking the long way to school. It took Old Spyros forty minutes to walk three and a half blocks.

When he entered the schoolyard he thought of calling out to Petros for help, but he decided to save his energy to reach the door of the storeroom. Leaning with all his weight on the stick, Old Spyros dragged himself to the center of the yard before stopping to catch his breath.

Up above, the Italian flying boat from the Island of Crete made its weekly pass and began its low gliding approach toward the aircraft harbor across the gulf. Now Old Spyros knew it was Friday. He squinted toward the sky, trying to bring his thoughts back to Tuesday.

Where have I been for the past four days? What did I do? . . . What happened to me? he asked himself silently. But his mind could not produce the answer.

Pressing down on his makeshift cane, Spyros crossed the rest of the schoolyard, twisted his legs around, and leaned back against the door jamb.

"Boy . . ." Spyros called in a throaty voice. "Boy . . ."

He looked at the door and waited to hear the bolt slide back. With the heavy end of the stick he jabbed at the door four times. He waited for Petros' answer, but when he heard nothing he swung the stick back and cracked it against the door.

He felt like sliding down to the gravel, but held on; if the boy had left the place for good the ground by the storeroom door could be his deathbed. Spyros cleared his throat and tried to make his voice sound normal. "Boy . . ."

"Why in hell don't you knock like a human being instead of trying to break the door in half?" Petros cried, opening the door. His eyes squinted in the bright sunlight. "You scared the wits out of me," he added, pushing the stiletto's blade back into the ivory handle. "Come on in; I have a surprise for you."

Old Spyros tried to follow him, but his legs wouldn't move and he slid to the ground.

"You know what?" Petros said from inside. "I took my life in my hands the other day and came down to see you before closing time. The door was wide open but nobody was inside. . . . Did you find yourself a girl?" He listened for the old man. "Spyros?" Petros said again. "Come on in. Your surprise is all set up and ready for you. Come on in . . . and be ready to kiss him . . . and me."

"Just a minute," the old man mumbled, struggling to lift himself.

Petros heard Spyros' voice but he didn't catch the words. He waited a bit longer, and when the old man didn't appear he went to the door.

Petros looked down to see eyes gaping up in shame,

blue lips forcing a defiant smile, while the hands gestured for time to compose himself.

"My God," Petros whispered and turned his eyes away, but couldn't help seeing his friend's legs folded under him or avoid hearing his grunts. "My God," Petros repeated, kneeling beside him. Putting both arms under the old man he lifted him up and carried him inside.

Spyros looked up at Petros. "Sick," he mumbled and closed his eyes so the tears would not show.

Petros kicked the door shut, looked down at the old man's white face, and then slowly let the old man's feet touch the floor because he did not want him to think he looked entirely helpless.

Spyros nodded thanks and tried to balance himself.

Petros put his arm around the old man, helped him stand up, and then, forcing a smile, tried to appear unconcerned.

"There he is," Petros said, making a sweeping gesture toward the icon. "Yours again," he added, and smiled at his old friend.

Spyros looked at the icon and squeezed Petros' hand, but his face did not show surprise or happiness. His eyes remained fixed on the saint, and he lowered them as in prayer.

Petros looked down as though he, too, were praying, but he was trying to figure out what was ailing the old man.

Petros steered him toward the mattress where he helped him lie down. "I still can't understand why you worried so much about me going after him," he said, indicating the icon. "I walked in and out as if I owned the place."

"The orderly?" the old man whispered, his memory beginning to return.

Petros froze. He turned and stared hard at the old man. "Did the Germans get you?"

Spyros shook his head and spoke the orderly's name.

Petros shrugged. "There's a war going on, people get killed."

"Death because of an icon?"

"It has happened before," Petros said and covered his friend with a blanket. "Now you take it easy."

Spyros stared at Petros with wide eyes. "Am I alive?" he asked in a whisper, putting his hand on Petros' arm.

"Of course you are."

"Are you?" He started to feel Petros' arm and face. "Are you?" he asked again and started to cry.

"Yes, I'm alive," Petros said, raising his voice, "and Black Saint Nicholas is here with us."

"My God," Old Spyros said, as the four-day gap began to close. "My God . . . forgive me," he added and made the sign of the cross. "Forgive me too, boy," he pleaded.

"There's nothing to forgive," Petros said and pressed the old man down. "You rest now, and I'll go get us something to eat."

"No, not for me," Spyros said, trying to raise himself again.

"Fine," Petros said, pulling the blanket over the old man's shoulders again. "I'll just bring something for myself then." He felt heat radiating from Spyros' body, and knew he would need a great deal of money, enough to purchase medicines that would kill the fever.

"Good," the old man whispered. "I don't want you to kill somebody on my account."

"Don't worry," Petros said. "Why should I bring anything for you? You are not hungry," he added, "you are just a healthy fat man with big bones sticking out your sides."

The old man turned over and did not reply.

10

Although Johann Schneider was a fumbling lover he was persistent, and Trudi Richter was usually exhausted after a long session with him. Particularly when he came to her penthouse apartment, where his conduct was less inhibited than at his own headquarters. As soon as she heard him close the front door behind him she dropped off to sleep and did not stir until she was awakened by her maid, who had been sent away during Schneider's visit.

Trudi sat up with a start and saw that two hours had passed. She had not intended to take so long a nap, and had to hurry; but first she had to make a telephone call. Picking up the instrument at her bedside she told the operator to connect her with German headquarters, and her call went through immediately. She asked for Colonel Schneider's office and the next sound she heard was the grating voice of Ilse Brugger.

"This is Fräulein Richt—"

"I recognized you at once, Fräulein. The Herr Colonel is attending a meeting."

"I'm very well aware of the colonel's schedule, thank you," she said sharply. "I don't happen to be calling him."

There was a long, hostile silence at the other end of the line. Trudi prolonged the moment, relishing Brugger's curiosity.

"Are you still there?" Brugger demanded.

"Oh, yes. Be good enough to send Hans to me at once with the car."

"I'm afraid that will be impossible, Fräulein Richter. Hans has gone off duty for the day."

Trudi's mind worked rapidly. "Then send someone else."

Ilse Brugger was at heart a bureaucrat who was

shocked by any departures from normal routines. "But this is highly irregular."

"Must I demand to be put through to Colonel Schneider?"

Brugger's voice stiffened. "Tell me what you want," she said, "and I'll see if it can be arranged."

"Send over the car and have the driver leave the keys with the sentry downstairs. Since you're evidently short of personnel, I'll drive over myself."

"It will be necessary, Fräulein, for you to sign three forms. One required by the motor pool, another by—"

"Put me through to Colonel Schneider," Trudi interrupted.

The other woman called her bluff. "If you insist, although he said he wanted no one to disturb him."

"Very well," said Trudi, tiring of the game. "I'll sign the forms when I arrive at headquarters. How soon may I expect the car?"

"The car will arrive in thirty minutes, Fräulein. Does that suit you?"

"Perfectly," Trudi said sweetly, and replaced the receiver in its cradle.

There was no time to bathe and do a complete new makeup job, so she worked with eye shadow, mascara, and lipstick, sprayed herself with French perfume, and dressed in the striped woolen suit that a tailor in Berlin had made for her. Though glamor was not required for her evening's plans, she knew she had a position to maintain. For the sake of Johann's insufferable male vanity she had to look desirable and exotic at all times. Fair enough; the life of a kept woman wasn't all that difficult. She lived in luxury, her conscience rarely troubled her anymore, and she had only one aim, to survive in comfort and without fear. As long as she had to be a whore, she might as well be the best—and the best dressed—in the business.

Her preparations completed, Trudi entered the living room and stopped short, surveying the shambles. Empty schnapps glasses were everywhere, a bottle had been

85

overturned on the supposedly stain-proof coffee table, and the contents of two ash trays, including a couple of Johann's foul-smelling cigar butts, had spilled onto the floor. Squashed cushions were scattered around the room, Johann having decided to experiment with a new position, and one of the lamps had been overturned, smashed fragments of its bulb littering the rug.

Let the maid clean up the mess, thought Trudi, and turned away in disgust. Just then the house telephone rang, and the sentry, addressing her with the deference she had come to expect, told her that Colonel Schneider's car had been delivered. She donned her coat, tucked a stray lock of her long, red hair in place and, after another application of purple lipstick, went downstairs.

Sitting behind the wheel of the American-made car, Trudi felt a sudden, unexpected sense of freedom. This wasn't the first time she had driven herself to the high command compound, and she wished Hans would take more evenings off. Driving the limousine gave her some sense of control over her own destiny; she could forget Johann, Willy, and all the others, and pretend she was living in a postwar world in which she was no one's mistress but her own.

Trudi avoided the working-class districts, which were dangerous, and kept to portions of Piraeus which, thanks to the curfew, were virtually deserted. Occasionally a dog or a cat appeared out of the shadows, quickly vanishing again, and sometimes she caught a glimpse of a shrouded human figure. But the Greeks knew the long, black car belonged to a German of importance, so they took no chances and kept out of sight. The girl drove at relatively high speeds through the twisting, narrow streets, and her sense of exhilaration increased.

The gasoline gauge indicated that the fuel tank was almost full, thanks to the foresight of Hans, who must have guessed what she had in mind this evening. She hated to share the proceeds of the black market with him, but their unspoken agreement made it impossible for her to cheat him. Not that it really mattered; there was more than enough for both of them, and the system they employed was foolproof. Hans would have the tank refilled at the motor pool in the morning and, since not even the pool commander had the authority to check the gasoline consumption of Colonel Schneider's car, no one would be the wiser.

Trudi had never before driven to the alleyway alone; she slowed the car to a crawl so she wouldn't lose her way. The headlights were dimmed by the blue glass required by blackout precautions, and she had to roll down the window to peer at various landmarks. Johann had warned her never to leave the car windows open, particularly at night, but she was not afraid. Germans so often worried needlessly: they might think Austrians carefree, but at least Viennese knew how to enjoy life.

Johann expected her to join him at headquarters for supper after his meeting, which was certain to drag on for another hour or two, so she was in no hurry. At least she would not be subjected to more of his lovemaking tonight, not after this afternoon's tiring session. That was one of the advantages of being associated with a man of middle years.

The girl reached the eastern part of the city, and feeling her first twinge of apprehension, found the street that led to the alleyway. It would be foolish to totally disregard Johann's warning, and when she saw the alleyway ahead she closed her window again. She struggled with the steering wheel as she forced the oversized car into the narrow lane, and wondered how Hans always made the task appear so easy. Driving halfway up the block, she pulled to a halt outside the double wooden doors of the old warehouse, but left her engine running. This was the ticklish moment, and she always felt a slight thrill of fear; tonight, alone, that fear was much sharper.

After a wait that seemed interminable, the door creaked open a few inches, and two men appeared. One was the middle-aged Greek who was usually in charge at the supposedly abandoned warehouse, but his companion was someone new, and Trudi inspected him covertly.

It was obvious he was unlike any other Greek she had seen in Piraeus, and it took her a moment to determine why. His clothes were of good material and cut, showing off a physique that was trim and powerful, and he carried himself with confidence. His boots were in better condition than any Greek shoes she had seen in Piraeus, and even his hair was neatly trimmed. It was strange that a man of such seeming stature should be engaged in the grubby black-market operation of siphoning gasoline.

Then the man looked at her, and Trudi felt a sudden excitement. His eyes were a deep blue, and so penetrating that he seemed to be looking through her.

He continued to stare at her, inspecting her with the bold self-assurance of a male who was rarely rebuffed by a woman.

Trudi felt uncomfortable under his unblinking scrutiny, but determined not to let this brazen Greek gain the upper hand, she returned his gaze, hoping her own eyes were veiled enough to hide her thoughts. No man had ever indicated so much to her with a look, and she was outraged, yet at the same time strangely flattered. She had no idea whether this Greek knew her identity, but it had to be obvious that she was no ordinary person. Not only was she dressed exquisitely, but her mere presence behind the wheel of such an extravagant automobile indicated she was someone of importance. Then she remembered why she was here, and she flushed.

Petros Zervas continued to stare at the girl, aware of his rudeness but unable to stop. She was no prettier than a score of others, but she had an air about her—the way she raised her head, tilting her chin and flinging back her red hair, showed she was a woman of spirit. No, it was more than that. In spite of the heavy makeup and flashy clothes, she was probably someone of breeding. A strange and fascinating combination.

Earlier that evening when he'd heard that one of the men who ran this operation had taken sick he quickly offered to take his place. It seemed a quick clean way to pick up some easy money, but now he needed that money for Old Spyros—a gallon of gas was worth thousands of inflationary drachmas, and readily converted to cash. The girl was an extra dividend he had never expected.

He had no doubts about the girl's identity. She was Colonel Schneider's woman, the notorious German whore, but how in the world could anyone so lovely tolerate such an old goat? What she needed was a real man to tame the fire he could see in her eyes.

The task of siphoning off the gas seemed to take longer than usual tonight, but Trudi restrained a desire to fidget. Under no circumstances would she permit this disturbing young Greek to realize his mere presence had rattled her.

Suddenly a pair of small lights appeared at the end of the alleyway, and Petros gestured frantically, trying to signal the girl to extinguish the car's headlights.

Too late she understood. Two figures in uniform appeared in the distance, members of a German bicycle patrol.

The men dismounted and peered up the alleyway, squinting and shading their eyes.

Trudi felt a stab of terror.

The soldiers locked their bicycles, then started up the alley, unslinging their rifles as one moved to the left and the other to the right of the narrow passageway.

Instinctively, without pausing to think, Petros approached the limousine, smiled at the girl—a reassuring, somewhat arrogant smile, as if to say she had nothing to fear, he was giving her ample time to get away—and then slowly sauntered toward the Germans.

He could sense them stiffen, and all at once he forgot the possible consequences of what he was doing and began to relish the little game he was playing with them. No time to speculate why he was helping the girl, he needed to concentrate, his timing had to be perfect. He waited until he was no more than one hundred and fifty feet from the Germans, then broke into a run and vaulted over a low stone fence.

One of the soldiers shouted, and then he and his companion gave chase.

Petros bent low as he raced across an open yard, squeezed between two buildings, and darted into the next street. He could hear the soldiers pounding behind him, then he heard the roar of the limousine and knew the girl had escaped. Now he could think only of saving his own skin, and that would prove absurdly easy for someone who knew Piraeus so well. He enjoyed the chase, knowing he would make the pursuing Germans look ridiculous.

He dashed a short distance up the street, then ducked into a narrow pedestrian walk adjacent to an old church he had sometimes visited when he lived in the orphanage. The Germans, who didn't even know of the walk's existence, probably would rush past, but he preferred to take no undue risks now, realizing the whole garrison would be alerted if they began to fire at him. So he climbed up a drainpipe, then flattened himself on the slanting roof as he watched the heavy-booted soldiers thundering down the cobblestones.

Grinning softly to himself in the dark, Petros waited, knowing the soldiers would retrace their steps the moment they realized they had lost him. He wished he could smoke, he felt hungry, and then, with a sharpness that surprised him, he felt an acute desire for the redheaded German whore. She had class, real style; she would put up a lively fight, but she had no more chance of winning than did these stupid Germans.

The pair came back down the street, both breathing hard, their footsteps lagging in hesitation. Petros waited until they vanished again, then forced himself to remain on the roof for an additional ten minutes. Sure at last that he was safe, he decided to return to the abandoned warehouse to pick up his share from the gasoline siphoned from the German commandant's car.

Hand over hand, he let himself down the drainpipe. Just as his feet touched the walk Petros felt his right hand twisted behind his back, and a pistol was jabbed into his ribs with such force that it expelled the air from his lungs.

A man stood on his left, another on his right, and he saw they were wearing civilian clothes, dark, belted trench-coats and broad-brimmed hats low over their fore-heads. Gestapo!

Neither of the hard-faced men spoke. One gestured toward the end of the street, and they started in that direction, the man behind Petros holding his arm so high behind his back that the young Greek felt certain his bones would crack.

Parked in an alleyway at the end of the street was a small German-made automobile; a man in civilian clothes sat behind the wheel, and when he saw them approach nodded in satisfaction and started the engine.

Petros felt a pair of handcuffs snapped onto his wrist behind his back, and then he was pushed into the rear of the car. The man with the pistol climbed in beside him, crowding him so far into the corner that it was impossible for him to move his legs, much less to kick any of his captors, in the cramped space.

The car leaped forward and still no one spoke. Petros, badly frightened, became a trifle less panicky. At least they hadn't killed him yet, and he tried to memorize the route they were taking, noting every turn every street on which they drove.

The man sitting beside the driver became aware of his interest and produced a length of thick black felt with which he covered the prisoner's eyes.

Total darkness enveloped Petros. Combined with the eerie, continuing silence, it contributed to a feeling of absolute isolation, and his fears increased again. The Gestapo were masters in the fine art of creating psycholog-ical terror, and he heard it was even worse than the physical torture they inflicted on their victims. Although the night was chilly and there was no heater in the car, Petros found himself sweating.

For the first time in longer than he cared to remember, he began to pray. Maybe it was too late, maybe he would end up another body dumped outside Gestapo headquarters awaiting pickup by anonymous-looking trucks, but at least he could beg forgiveness for his sins. But even he could scarcely remember the long list of Petros Zervas' misdeeds.

The car pulled to an abrupt halt and Petros, still blindfolded, was led across a cobblestone walk and up three steps. The prisoner was half pushed, half led, then his blindfold was removed. Blinking in the unaccustomed light, he found himself in a drab, nondescript living room that might have belonged to any middle-class Greek with a few thousand drachmas in savings. It contained a faded Turkish rug, two overstuffed chairs and a sofa, all made in Athens, as well as two locally made tables and a number of straight-backed chairs. The lamps came from Athens, too, as did the icon that rested in a corner wall niche. Anyone entering the house would have known it was a male household. Several large, lacquered shells sat on the mantel, and religious scenes were depicted in the room's two paintings. The hearth was empty of firewood; this was a strictly utilitarian chamber, devoid of frills. There was nothing to indicate this was a place where people lived. Perhaps it wasn't; perhaps it was just a place where men died.

Petros' captors, flanking him, both stiffened to attention when another man, also in nondescript attire, entered the room. The newcomer was surprisingly youthful, but he carried himself with an air of authority, and Petros wondered how someone so young could have become a Gestapo officer.

The young man looked at the captive with obvious satisfaction, and then turned to the silent pair. "I assume you frisked him." It wasn't a question.

Seeing their stricken expression, the young man gave them a sharp look and then ran experienced hands up and down Petros' body. When he found no firearms, he indicated he wanted the handcuffs removed, and then spoke to the prisoner for the first time.

"Undress," he ordered.

Petros started to protest, but the officer cut him short, cuffing him across the side of the head with such force that he staggered and almost crashed into the wall.

A deep, pure hatred welled up in Petros, and for an instant he wanted to strike back. But all three men were watching him, just waiting for him to make one belligerent move, so he fought down his anger. Besides, he had heard the Gestapo always stripped their prisoners, so reluctantly he began to remove his clothes.

A gleam appeared in the young officer's eyes when he saw the stiletto strapped to the inner side of the prisoner's right arm. He removed it, tested it in the palm of his hand, and his half-smile indicated he appreciated its superb balance.

Petros felt truly helpless without his knife and, as he stood naked before the trio, braced himself for the beating and torture he felt certain would begin at any moment.

But the young officer nudged the pile of clothes with his toe, and his curt gesture indicated he wanted the prisoner to dress again.

Petros was happy to climb into his clothes, no matter how clammy they were, but the unorthodox tactics puzzled him. Maybe that was part of the Gestapo system, he thought. They tried to stay one jump ahead of their captives, bewildering them so it would be easier to force them to talk.

The young officer left the room without another glance and his two subordinates relaxed somewhat, but continued to watch the prisoner closely as he donned his clothes. One kept a snubnosed pistol ready for instant use.

Petros noted that it was equipped with a silencer, and wondered why the Gestapo would bother to keep their murders secret.

Petros shoved his hands deep into the pockets of his trousers to calm his nervousness, and his fingers brushed against a row of smooth, cool stones. Scarcely aware of what he was doing, he took out his string of worrybeads. The black beads clicked reassuringly in his fingers, and he hefted them as he stroked them steadily. The familiar feel restored the sense of self-confidence he had nearly lost in the car.

The two men paid no attention.

The young officer returned and led the prisoner upstairs. Petros stuffed the worrybeads into his pocket and entered a library, its shelves filled with hundreds of books, most of them works of the ancients written in classical Greek. On the floor was another Turkish rug, which appeared to be in better shape than the one downstairs. Seated behind a hand-carved desk was a man who appeared to be only a year or two his senior. It was difficult to see his face because his features were concealed behind a squat pipe, on which he was puffing.

But his eyes, dark and even more penetrating than Petros', seemed to bore into the young Greek, measuring him.

Here, Petros realized, was the man who would determine his fate—if it was not already settled. He tried to return the other's cold, appraising stare, but could not. Once again he automatically reached for the worrybeads.

The man behind the desk gave no sign that he had seen the beads before, and now, in the light, he noted the worrybeads were black in color instead of the customary amber. "You are Petros Zervas," he said.

He made it a flat statement rather than a question, so Petros did not reply. Obviously the Gestapo knew who he was, so it would be futile to deny it.

The man took a thick manila folder from a desk drawer and began to leaf through it, taking his time. "Your dossier," he said at last.

It was apparent from its size that the Germans knew a great deal about him, and Petros' temples pounded.

"Just this week," the man said, "you stole several crates of valuable merchandise from a Bulgarian tanker in the harbor."

Petros began to protest, but the man cut him short.

"I saw you myself," he said. "Tonight you were observed siphoning gasoline from a German command car."

His tone indicated that he regarded such an operation with contempt.

Petros felt the need to justify himself. "I haven't been paid for the tanker haul. I needed the money."

"But you helped Colonel Schneider's mistress escape! Why?"

That was a question Petros was incapable of answering, even if his life depended on it, and his shrug indicated far more than he was able to put into words.

The man's scorn had a sting. "Trying to win Schneider's favor, no doubt."

"No!" Petros shouted the word, then abruptly fell silent again. It wouldn't do to explain that under no circumstances would he collaborate with the Nazis. Such an admission would seal his fate.

The man turned another page. "I see that until recently you were one of the biggest black market operators in Athens."

Petros' smile intended to look self-deprecating, as if such stories were always exaggerated. "Maria Asprou talks. My God, how she talks!"

It was hardly news that the bitch had given him away, but there was no need for him to mention her by name. Suddenly Petros' mind began to work furiously, and several little oddities fell into place. First was the matter of this man's accent. His Greek was almost too pure, making it plain to a real Greek that he was a foreigner. But there was no hint of German in the accent. If anything, it was British. But not quite. If the United States hadn't entered the war less than a week ago, Petros would have sworn he was American.

Maybe he hadn't fallen into the hands of the Gestapo after all. In that event, who were his captors, and why had they taken him prisoner? His hopes soared, even as his face remained expressionless. If cunning could extricate him, he was as good as free. "What do you want from me?" he asked.

Major David Cunningham instantly recognized the change in the young Greek's attitude, but he still held the upper hand and wasn't ready to reveal anything. "You must know," he said, "that your life is worthless. There are posters everywhere with your name and photograph. You're wanted on so many charges that you'll be shot on sight."

Petros was positive now that no one in this house was German. "Who are you?" he demanded.

Cunningham leaned back in his chair, seemingly relaxing, but there was no humor in his smile. His eyes were as cold as those of a Gestapo inquisitor as he knocked the ashes from his pipe. Taking his time, he stuffed another pipe, lighted it, and appeared to be testing the quality of his tobacco.

Petros remained silent, too. The attitudes of the others in the house indicated that all of them were members of a military organization of some kind, and if not Germans he and his confederates in all probability were spies. If so. . . . Life loomed large and sweet again, and Petros regained complete self-control. Flipping the worrybeads in the air, he caught them and stuffed them back in his pocket.

Cunningham, still taking time, puffed repeatedly on his pipe until his face was almost concealed by the blue-gray smoke.

"Who are you?" Petros asked again.

"Your new boss." Cunningham's tone was icy. "You'll take orders from me. And you'll obey them."

"Suppose I don't want—"

"The Gestapo," Cunningham interrupted, "will pay a fancy price for your head. I know many people who could use the money."

Regardless of the identity of this man and his associates, Petros knew he was trapped. He was furious. He hated working for anyone else; he loved the feeling that he was his own man, that his future lay exclusively in his own hands. On the other hand, if his surmise was right, this was his chance to move into really big assignments with even bigger payoffs. No more small-time operations like black market gas!

"You not only stole an icon, which was stupid," Cunningham said, "but you also killed a German. So you'll work for me, Zervas."

These people, whoever they might be, were thorough. Petros took a deep breath. "What will I be paid?"

"What you're worth." Cunningham had no intention of revealing the Greek was worth any price he asked.

Petros remembered Old Spyros' desperate need for food and medicine. So far, tonight, he had come up empty-handed. "When will I be paid?"

"When you finish your first job."

"What do you want me to do?"

Cunningham asked if Petros had happened to notice there were some tankers anchored in the gulf.

11

Corporal Dieter Dietrich had joined the Reichswehr in 1934, just in time to take part in Hitler's march into the Rhineland, and since then he had been enjoying the mounting glories accumulating to the Third Reich. Some of his army companions from the early days had risen in rank, some were even officers, but Corporal Dietrich had no complaints. He had plenty to eat and drink, he was accustomed to the disciplines of military life, and he had an easy assignment in Greece. The officers were freezing in Russia this winter; and even though Germany's victories were growing, so, word had it, were the casualties. No, Corporal Dietrich was eminently satisfied with his present assignment.

But it was a deeply troubled Dietrich who now sat outside his sergeant's office where he had been told to wait after relating the strange events of the night's patrol.

The German headquarters compound consisted of a number of outbuildings, surrounded by a high, barbed-wire fence. Sentries patrolled the barrier day and night, and an entrance gate and sentry box had been erected at one end of the street.

Contrary to the belief of the Greeks and even of some German and Italian military personnel, the Gestapo maintained no headquarters of its own in Piraeus. A small headquarters detachment, wearing the customary black uniforms with death's head insignia, lived and worked in a wing of Colonel Schneider's villa. They had virtually nothing to do with any of the other military in the city, and everyone gave them a wide berth. When they needed men they obtained them on loan from the large Gestapo command in Athens, a quarter of an hour's drive away, and consequently were able to maintain a low profile in Piraeus, which suited both Colonel Schneider and the Gestapo commander in the capital. Experience had proved that civilians in a conquered country were inclined to become careless when they thought the Gestapo wasn't operating in the vicinity.

But Dietrich knew about the Gestapo—he was one of those soldiers who seemed to know everything before it happened—and his concern increased when instead of the sergeant a lieutenant came out to tell him the captain wanted him to deliver his message personally to Colonel Schneider. When a mere corporal is told to report directly to the commanding officer, particularly in regard to a very delicate matter, the eastern front loomed large on the horizon.

As he and Private Weiss approached the headquarters building, he reminded the private not to open his mouth. Let him, Dietrich, do all the talking. Carefully they cleaned their boots, made certain their uniforms were buttoned before presenting their special passes, signed by the captain, to the sentry outside.

The soldier looked at them curiously, but merely directed them to an auxiliary parlor. This and two other rooms had been stripped of furniture and transformed into file cabinet chambers, and a warrant officer directed the activities of the soldiers trained as clerks. They were thorough, as befitted competent Germans, and took pride in the knowledge that they could provide Colonel Schneider or his superiors in Athens with any required data within a few moments.

A soldier called their names and told them to go upstairs. At the top of the broad staircase that led to the second floor, a small bedroom had been transformed into the so-called communications center maintained by a signal corps detachment. Its equipment included a large switchboard and wireless sending and receiving sets with extraordinary power and range. Two men were stationed at the receivers at all times.

Various former bedrooms housed Schneider's chief of staff and department heads. These officers came to work each day from their billets elsewhere in the compound and, barring an emergency that kept them at their desks after ordinary business hours, ate only their noon meal at headquarters. The chief of staff and the others were dedicated professional reserve soldiers, and were somewhat older than officers of comparable rank in combat units. Like their counterparts in France and the low countries, Austria and Czechoslovakia, Denmark, Norway, and all the other lands occupied by Hitler—with the exception of Poland, which still was regarded as a combat-zone—these officers were specialists in the problems of governing, controlling, and subjugating occupied nations.

In marked contrast to their quarters was the bare office occupied by the commander's secretary. Ilse Brugger often remained late at her desk, Dietrich knew, and it was just his luck she had to be there tonight.

Dietrich tapped diffidently on the door, and when bidden to enter he did so and stood stiffly at attention. Brugger glanced up from a pile of documents she was sorting.

"Heil Hitler!" she said.

"Heil Hitler," said Dietrich with surprise. No one had warned him that the Herr Colonel's secretary was a Nazi. He would have to be doubly careful.

Brugger pushed aside the papers. "Your captain said you wanted to report on a private matter."

"Yes, Fräulein," said Dietrich, "but we were told it was a matter for Colonel Schneider personally."

She encouraged them with a smile; her lopsided grin only made Dietrich even more nervous.

"To tell the truth," he said in confusion, "there seems little point now. Because the Herr Colonel's automobile is parked right outside the building."

Mention of the car made Brugger tense imperceptibly. She had felt out of sorts ever since that Richter bitch had insisted on driving herself here tonight. Perhaps the girl had suffered an accident or worse? "What about the Herr Colonel's car?" she prompted.

Dietrich was relieved at the chance to unburden himself. Speaking haltingly, he related in detail the incident in the alleyway. Brugger listened so intently the corporal found himself faltering repeatedly.

"The man escaped," he concluded at last. "We chased him for a block or two, but he vanished. He really must know Piraeus."

"Would you recognize him if you saw him again?" Brugger pressed him.

"It was very dark, Fräulein."

"And the driver of the car?" She spoke in a voice so low it was barely audible. "Would you be able to identify the driver?'

The corporal shook his head lamely.

"Take your time, Corporal," she said in the same low voice.

"By the time we got back to the alleyway, the car was gone." He brightened. "Maybe we were mistaken. Maybe it was another car we saw."

Brugger dismissed the suggestion impatiently, then scribbled at length on a pad of paper while Dietrich tensed apprehensively for the reprimand he was certain would follow.

Instead, the woman finished making her notes and looked up with a smile. "You've done well." Seeing their astonishment, she assured them she would say nothing to the Herr Colonel about the strange incident, but told them

100

to keep a closer watch on the alleyway in the future and report at once to her directly and in secret if ever again they encountered anything out of the ordinary.

The pair were so glad to escape that Dietrich even remembered to make the Nazi salute on his way out of the office.

After they left, Ilse Brugger sat motionless for a long time, staring venomously into space. Behind the closed door of the inner room she heard the sound of the Richter girl's carefree laughter.

Brugger made another brief note on the pad, and then assembled her notes in a folder which she put in the steel cabinet.

She locked the file, and picked up the phone and dialed the Gestapo.

12

"Feel any better?" Petros asked, striking a match and lighting the candle. The flickering yellow light sent the shadows of the map stands and the chemistry bottles galloping around the storeroom. He set the candle in the inkwell of a student's desk-chair.

Spyros nodded, his eyes still heavy with sleep.

Petros came closer and peered into his face. Apparently it confirmed what he had expected, for he turned away and took out his stiletto.

"What poor creature are you planning to kill tonight?" the old man said bitterly.

Petros shook his head resignedly. "Nobody, unless it's unavoidable, as it was with that orderly," he said. "I never kill unless I have to, I want you to understand that. I'm not bloodthirsty. I fight my battles fair, even with the Germans, who do not deserve such courtesy. I should do what some others do, sneak behind them and slice them to pieces before they have a chance. This they've got

101

coming, old man, because if you don't get as many as you can now, there'll just be more of them left alive to try to shoot you down later. And not for any good reason either, but for something trivial like running instead of walking. You know that. But I'm not like the others," Petros said. "I always give a German a chance. I don't take advantage of people, even when they're enemies."

"I guess so," the old man said and rolled over on his side.

"Good," Petros said and smiled. "Let me make a suggestion, Captain. Why don't you go along with me for a while, without argument, just for the present. As soon as you're up again and running around you can give me all the arguments you want. Agreed?"

"I guess so," Spyros said again. He nodded vigorously to underscore his part of the bargain, and suddenly he reached for his forehead with both hands.

"What's the matter?" Petros asked in concern. "A little dizzy?"

"No, it's nothing," Spyros said. "It goes away by itself."

"You sure?"

"Yes, yes, I told you."

Petros helped Spyros lie back. Just as he thought, the old man's flesh was now burning with fever. "I shouldn't wonder you're dizzy," he said easily, to mask his apprehension. "You've scarcely had a thing to eat. I'd hoped to fix that by now, but something unexpected came up."

He rose. "Well, I wanted to see how you were feeling before going out again. I'll be away for about . . . well, a few hours . . . but when I get back prepare yourself for a big feed, old man. I want you to be fit enough to handle it, so you'll need all the rest you can get. Do you want me to blow out the candle?"

"Please."

Petros spoke into the darkness. "I'll be back before you know it, so don't start worrying about me. All right?"

Old Spyros listened to the sound of Petros' footsteps until they faded. He tried to stand, but his dizziness forced him to the mattress. He rolled over to face the icon, but the room was too dark to see, so he closed his eyes and formed an image in his mind of the kindly black face.

"Saint Nicholas, have mercy on the boy," Spyros whispered. "He is doing all this for me, and you know why. Like me, he too never saw his family."

Spyros remembered himself as a four-year-old running in terror along the shores of Gulf Volos in Thessaly, after the Turks had killed the uncle with whom he had lived and left young Spyros for dead.

"At least let him have a family of his own. Look out for him, Saint Nicholas, and I'll give him my home," Spyros said and rolled over on his back, as a fine thought came to him.

Maybe it would be possible to adopt Petros and call him "Son" and he could call Spyros "Father," and both of them could utter a word they had never spoken in their lives.

13

The main part of Piraeus, the oldest section of the city, is situated on a peninsula jutting out into the Mediterranean like a large, bent thumb. The crumbling stone Walls of Conon from which the ancestors of the sons of Piraeus had watched the triremes of the Greeks, the sailing ships of the Phoenicians, and the galleys of the Romans, had been built and rebuilt time and again, but still performed their original function, that of preventing the sea from washing ashore and flooding the city.

Such history was of no concern to the Germans, however, who had emplaced four powerful anti-aircraft batteries behind the walls. The guns and the huge searchlights that stood beside them were manned around the clock by Wehrmacht troops who were sealed off from the rest of the town by an inner barrier, the Wall of Themistocles. The Germans also had taken possession of the Naval Cadets School as a barracks for their coast artillerymen, so the entire area was off limits to all Greeks.

On the other side of the Wall of Themistocles, life went on much as it had for centuries, at least on the surface. Old men with deeply lined faces sat on battered stoops to soak up the sun. Housewives cleaned their steps and the streets in front of their dwellings with brooms made of bundles of sticks tied together. Children played an old Greek version of stickball, their shouts mingling with the even shriller cries of the gulls that came in from the sea and circled overhead.

But even the gulls must have realized that times had changed: crumbs of food were hard to obtain now, and very little garbage tumbled from the donkey carts that made their way from house to house. The people left their homes every evening, just as they had always done, but they no longer went out to pay visits, drink ouzo or coffee, or engage in other customary pursuits. Their nocturnal walks were conducted for only one purpose: they were hungry, and they went out in search of food. They could find little in the usual sources. The Metroupolis bakery, which had been owned and operated by the same family for five generations, suffered a shortage of flour, and bread was available only on Mondays and Tuesdays, when long lines formed before the establishment opened its doors. The rest of the week the shops once filled with loaves and twists of warm, fresh bread and moist cakes were bare, the shelves inside the dusty plate-glass windows empty.

Virtually every butcher shop in the city was closed, its shutters drawn. Lamb had become virtually nonexistent. Flocks had been seized by the Germans, and the relatively few sheepherders who had escaped into the mountains had no way of sending meat into Piraeus. Beef, always scarce in the city, had vanished completely.

The greengrocers, many of whom had sold their wares from pushcarts in the streets, were nowhere to be seen.

The few residents with kitchen gardens had already consumed the last of their vegetables, and no supplies were coming in from the countryside. Orange and lemon trees never bore fruit at this season. Those who had hoarded dried figs and prunes guarded their prizes zealously.

In the taverns, where even the supplies of ouzo were short, the peddlers who sold pistachio nuts were gone too.

Families who owned goats were able to give milk to their children, but an adult armed with a knife or club—the Germans had confiscated all firearms—was required to stand constant sentry duty over his precious animals.

Those chickens that had been raised in backyards had long disappeared, and so had the omnipresent dogs of Piraeus. It was not considered good manners to ask a friend what had become of his household pets.

The people believed they were being systematically, deliberately starved by the Germans, but this was only partly true. Germany was conquering the world, and Berlin had more important matters on its mind than thinking about feeding the Greeks. Besides, a nation struggling with starvation was too weak to rebel, so crack Wehrmacht troops, which might have been tied down maintaining order in Greece, could be freed for more important duty—such as Rommel's drive across North Africa.

Piraeus lived with hunger. It was stamped in the faces of weary men who searched in vain for work. It was always there in the eyes of the women who combed shop after shop in search of a little flour, a cup of rice, a small bottle of olive oil. And it was evident most of all in the distended bellies of the children who no longer played energetically in the streets, but sat on curbs and balconies, staring lethargically into space, their young-old faces lined and drawn.

Lela made her way along the main port waterfront, where she hoped to find a few customers before meeting Hans. A few customers—she would be overjoyed with one! Only on the waterfront would she find a man, either a merchant seaman or a soldier off duty, who would pay the ten thousand drachmas she still insisted on charging. Some of the other girls, all younger, thought she was stupid to charge more than the standard price. But then they had no reputation—Lela Lellos was no five-thousand-drachma whore.

Suddenly someone caromed into her, almost knocking her to the ground, and she had to clutch his threadbare coat to avoid falling. He was slender and in his mid-twenties, with dark hair and huge, dark brown eyes; his clothes were worn, his shoes cracked and dusty; there was a hint of stubble on his chin and his face was an unhealthy shade of yellow. In all, Lela thought, cursing him in a voice that drowned his stammered apology, she had never seen anyone more insignificant. But he looked vaguely familiar, and as she stared at him in the dark she felt memory stir. "Aren't you Nico Andreades?"

He was pleased she remembered him after all these years, and all those men. "Yes, I am, Miss Lela."

How long had it been since he had seen the number 187 tattooed on Lela's left breast and Petros' message across her stomach? He had first read the inscriptions at the age of fifteen, and he had been seventeen the last time he had seen her. It was then, his curiosity finally overcoming his shyness, that he had asked her the meaning of the tattoo.

"Some other time," she had told him brusquely. "When I'm not so busy."

"When will that—"

"When you're older, a lot older."

Two days later, Nico's water polo team, the Olympics, the champions of Pireaus, had been playing a second-rate pick-up team from Kalithea, the Ethnics, composed mostly of kids from the local orphanage.

The popularity of the Olympics had brought out a large crowd, their cheering lubricated by beer and ouzo. The match had been nothing more than a practice game for the Olympics, and at first Nico had regarded it as such.

106

But the Ethnics had tied the score early and shut out their opponents thereafter, thus winning the enthusiastic sympathy of the crowd. Nico knew how it felt to be the underdog, but the fickleness of the crowd had enraged him. No matter how inadequate he was in most things, he was the best swimmer and the best water polo player in Piraeus.

So he had been exultant, with the score still tied and only a few seconds left to play, to find himself alone with the ball. The Ethnics' goal tender, thinking Nico intended to pass, was guarding the side where the highest scorer on the Olympics was waiting to receive the ball. Realizing that the goalie had fallen into the trap, Nico kicked his legs hard, rose and stretched halfway out of the water—but never got off the winning shot. Instead a fist caught him in the soft spot above the pelvis, doubling him over, and the game ended with the teams tied, two to two.

Nico dressed quickly, determined to hunt down his new enemy, but didn't have much of a search. The player who had hit him, a youth of his own age with deep blue eyes, approached him. The boy's smile was as broad as it was infectious; shaking Nico's hand vigorously, he apologized at length and introduced himself as Petros Zervas.

Nico, still seething, had already reared back, and as his fist sped toward its target, a thought crossed his mind. There, about to have his clean, white teeth rammed down his throat, stood his hero "Petros—14." By then it was too late, and the punch sent Petros reeling; and had not Nico put his arms around him and apologized in return, there would have been the bloodiest fight in the after-match history of Greek water polo teams.

So Petros himself had told Nico the story behind his encounter with Lela at the age of fourteen, and the two boys—turned "men" by the same woman—had gone on to become the closest of friends.

"Well, Nico," said Lela. "You've grown into quite a young man."

He knew that she was flattering him outrageously, that

he was ordinary and looked it. But he knew, too, that she meant well and thanked her politely.

"I often think of you and your friend, Petros Zervas, but I haven't seen him in a long time, either. I heard that he was no longer in Piraeus." She asked if he kept in touch with him.

"As a matter of fact," Nico confided, "I saw him just recently. I thought he was in Athens, but he showed up out of nowhere." Eagerly he told her about the incident at the docks.

Lela questioned him closely, and though she continued to smile, her eyes became shrewd and thoughtful. "You mean the Germans never caught him?"

"Not Petros, Miss Lela," said Nico proudly.

"Remarkable," the woman said, and tucked away the information in the back of her mind. Lela had heard of Greeks who informed to the Germans. The very idea offended her—Lela considered herself patriotic in her own way—but one of these days Hans might grow tired of her and find someone else, and she knew how difficult it would be to survive the occupation all alone. So in case of dire need, but only then, she might find such information useful, and Hans would be grateful until the end of the war. As for the incident with Petros, that was gone, like the markings on her stomach. She owed him nothing.

"What about you, Nico?" she asked. "What are you doing these days?"

He tried to make his shrug appear casual. "What are any of us doing these days? Looking for work that isn't to be found. Taking on odd jobs here and there to pick up a few drachmas. Like everyone else I hunt for a job by day and food by night."

Well, what did she expect? That was the trouble with talking to Greeks; they all had such pathetic stories. And the men, especially, seemed shamed by poverty, as if it were a reflection on their personal honor. "Your family is well?"

He looked away. "My little brother is sick, so my mother and sister must take turns nursing him."

So Nico had become his family's only provider. "When is the last time you had anything decent to eat?" she asked softly.

"Last night," he lied and then told her of a fine supper of meat and soup, so filling they couldn't finish it. Well, part of it was true. There still were some scraps left from the cans he had stolen at the docks. And they *couldn't* finish it; he told them to save the rest for supper tonight.

Lela would be a poor whore if she didn't know when a man was lying to her. "Come with me, Nico," she said. "Maybe I can turn up some food for you and your family. And something else for you just for old times' sake." She gave his arm a playful squeeze.

But he shook his head stubbornly. "I can't accept your charity!"

She pressed close to him. "Since when is it charity when a woman shows her feeling for a man she likes?"

No Greek male, she knew, could resist an appeal to his masculinity, and to make sure Nico would not back off she took a firm grip on his arm and started toward her home. They had walked a block or two when she realized that Nico had fallen strangely silent. When she glanced at him she saw tears in his eyes.

"To what miserable depths we have sunk," he said at last, "when a man must depend on the kindness of a woman to feed his family. I'm young, I'm healthy, but I can find no work, no way to earn a living. I am good for only one thing—fighting the Germans."

"Don't even think such a thing," Lela said sharply. "One of these days the Germans will overhear, and that will be the end of you."

"All of us—Petros, I, many others—are going to fight them, I promise you."

It made far more sense to agree with him, soothe him, but she could not allow this innocent to be slaughtered. "I

109

know the Germans," she said, "and I meant what I said. They really will kill you."

"Then I will have died for a reason."

He spoke so calmly that Lela stared at him, wondering for a moment if she had misjudged this young man.

"All this talk of dying makes me very cross," she said, tugging him along. "Come, Nicolaki, let's see if I can't give you a reason to live."

14

It was nearly one A.M. when Petros halted on the pebbled beach to survey the handsome Zacharias villa across the water that served as German headquarters. The very thought of entering the German compound once again filled him with dread, yet he knew it was one place he was certain to find food, perhaps even medicine. And Spyros' condition was worsening by the hour.

The Attica night was clear, intensifying the bright stars overhead; the water in the gulf was smooth as oil as it rose to its mark on the rocks and hung there, still, before receding in an easy flow without breaking and coughing. Petros waited until he heard the church bells ring one o'clock, then eased off his jacket and folded it neatly. The cool soft sirocco breeze made him shiver; he rubbed his hands over his arms and chest rapidly, and stepped between the rocks, thigh-deep into the cold water. Tightening his chattering teeth and drawing in his stomach, he waded out until he was waist deep.

Three times he tried and failed to submerge, but the fourth time he made it. A violent shiver shook his entire body, and he started to swim slowly toward the villa's peninsula. When he reached the familiar reef, his legs kicked out to avoid it, and the sound broke the stillness of the night. The two watchdogs on the peninsula came alive and barked immediately. Petros stopped swimming, waiting for the dogs to appear on the rock to investigate. He heard a half-bark and, realizing the dogs weren't really serious, took up his stroke again.

Five meters off the rocks he stopped and listened for the dogs again. Then, raising himself waist-high out of the water, he let fly a package he had been holding in his hand. It landed near the villa's back gate; for a second the mastiffs remained mute, then they jarred the night with their wild barks. They charged the package, he could hear the growls as they tore it apart, and then just as suddenly the barking stopped.

The peninsula was quiet; he saw no German sentries, heard no doors or windows opening. He vaulted the sea wall and crawled to the gate. The dogs were lying by their pens, and when they saw Petros all they could manage was a low, barely audible whine.

"Sleep well," Petros whispered, opened the back gate and slipped inside.

The back door was locked. So was the first kitchen window he tried. He jumped down from a small iron balustrade and worked the stiletto blade between the double doors pressing in steadily until the spring gave.

The long hall to the kitchen was dark except for one weak light. It was one forty-five now, and the German clerks should be fast asleep. Even the cook would not be up for another three hours. With the stiletto tightly clenched in his right hand he listened for sounds, but all was still.

In the bright moonlight he made his way quickly to the kitchen. He waited until his eyes had adjusted to the dark, turned on all the gas burners of the oven for warmth, and wiped himself dry with the cook's apron. When the shivering stopped, he turned off the burners and went to the refrigerator, from which he took the remains of a large roast of pork, half a cake, and a bottle of milk.

The first few bites of meat he bolted, but then he slowed down; he hadn't eaten for two days and wanted to be careful not to overtax himself. Petros ate the pork, washed it down with milk. The warmth of the kitchen relaxed his body, making him feel snug, secure.

The door flew open.

Stiletto blade in hand, Petros charged forward and before the intruder could find his voice, Petros had clamped a palm tight over his mouth and spun him around, slamming the door shut with a single motion. The figure struggled, clawing at his hand, trying to get free.

Petros waved the stiletto blade back and forth until he was sure it had been seen and then pressed it against the intruder's throat.

"One sound, one single sound, and you're a dead man. Understand?"

The German's hands dropped.

"That's better. Cry out, and I'll slice you into fishbait," he said. "Now, turn around."

The figure did as told, and Petros found himself face to face with Trudi Richter.

For a moment they stared at each other without a word. Evidently Trudi was the more astonished, for she drew her plain housecoat close about her, feeling suddenly exposed.

Petros was annoyed with himself. Had he stopped to think, he should have guessed he might run into her here. Where else would he expect to find Schneider's woman but in Schneider's quarters? For reasons he couldn't explain, her presence disturbed him. It was one thing to realize she belonged here, another to actually *see* her in German headquarters, wandering into the kitchen as she would in her own home.

She looked far different without makeup, Petros thought, softer, more vulnerable. Still she was an enemy—and mistress of the arch-enemy.

"The German whore," he said aloud.

"The gasoline thief," she said automatically in return.

Her voice softened. "I shouldn't have said that. I'm deeply grateful for what you did earlier tonight. I never expected to have the chance to thank you in person."

112

What was the matter with her? Clearly the man had broken in. She should watch for the chance, and cry for help. But how could she? Even now, the consequences of her capture in the alley made her tremble. . . . "But I still don't understand. Why did you go to all that trouble for"—she shrugged—"a German whore?"

Petros felt himself reddening, and brandished the knife. "This is no time to discuss such things. Remember my warning. One scream—and that will be the end of you."

To his astonishment she smiled at him. "I can't believe that the same man who risked his life for me a few hours ago would kill me now. Then, all you had to do was stand by and *I* was certain to be apprehended; while now you are in considerable danger yourself. All the same, you have my word I shall not betray you. There, does that satisfy you?"

He could see she wasn't taking his threat seriously. "I'm not sure. What are you doing in the kitchen?"

"I was restless, so I came down for a glass of milk." Far from sexually exhausting Colonel Schneider this afternoon, Trudi had only whetted his appetite. Johann had been insatiable tonight; and, now that he was finally asleep, she felt a sudden craving for a midnight snack.

"You sure you didn't hear me moving around downstairs?"

Now she knew what was troubling him. "No, and neither did anyone else, I'm sure. Or your life wouldn't be worth a thing."

"Very well. Help yourself," he said, pointing to the bottle with his stiletto.

Trudi saw that his teeth were chattering, and for the first time noticed that his shirt and trousers were damp and that small pools of water had formed around his shoes. That explained how he had made his way here, even though she found it difficult to believe that anyone could swim the bay at this time of year. "You need something stronger than milk," she said, and started across the room.

"Where are you going!"

She continued toward the liquor cabinet.

"Stop!" he cried. "I warned you once—"

Trudi thought his behavior childish, but did as he said. "All right, have it your own way. The second cabinet from the left contains medical supplies. Among them is a bottle of brandy."

Keeping an eye on her, he crossed the room and found the bottle. He gulped a substantial quantity of the fiery liquor, then incongruously wiped off the mouth of the bottle and offered it to her.

The gesture was so unexpected that Trudi heard herself laugh aloud.

"Better for restlessness than milk," Petros said as he, too, laughed.

"I prefer the milk." She poured herself some, and was amazed at the steadiness of her hand. "If it isn't too much to ask, why have you risked your life by coming here tonight? If you've come to kill Colonel Schneider," she said, her tone astonishingly conversational, "you'll never get away with it. He's arranged certain safeguards for his protection, and you'd be dead yourself before you left his bedroom. Assuming you could get into it in the first place."

"I'm not a murderer."

She glanced at the knife. "I'm very relieved to hear it."

The sight of her in her nightclothes, calmly taking a midnight snack, suddenly was too much for Petros to bear. Anger welled up in him, he felt his voice rising. "People all over Greece are starving, which is something a German like you wouldn't know—"

"I am Austrian!" Trudi interrupted sharply.

He paid no attention. "Right now an old man is clinging to life, hanging on by his fingertips until I return. He is starving and needs food. He is ill and without medicine he may die. So I came to the one place in Piraeus where I was sure to find food and medicine. And now that you're here," he said, "you're going to help me."

114

Taking down from a shelf a deep aluminum kettle, he dumped into it the medicines from the cabinet, including the bottle of brandy. He added the pork and the cake, opened the refrigerator and found some cheese, hard-boiled eggs, fruit. "I can't cook where I'm staying," Petros said. "Everything has to be cooked already."

Trudi showed him where the canned goods were kept and she handed him two large loaves of bread.

"Don't you think it's time we introduce ourselves?" she said half smiling. "I am Trudi Richter."

"Thank you very much, Miss Richter," Petros said.

"And what do I call you?"

Petros stared at her a moment. "Let's go," he said, holding the pot against his body and waving the stiletto with his free hand.

"Where are you taking me?"

"Just do as I say," Petros said harshly, indicating she should precede him through the back door.

When she saw the sleeping dogs she gave an involuntary gasp. She ran to them, crying, "Babies, babies," kissing them. "What did you do to my dogs?" She turned on him accusingly. "You killed my poor babies. Why did you have to kill them?"

"No. They're just drugged. See for yourself."

They wagged their tails drowsily, but their barks of greeting sounded like empty wheezes.

"What did you do to them?" she demanded angrily.

"Don't worry. They'll be fine in an hour. Let's go."

"Not until you tell me what you did to my dogs."

"It's nothing. I just gave them a little sleeping powder. I didn't want every German in the place shooting at me. Now will you get moving, or do I really have to do something to them?"

He handed her the kettle and, flashing the stiletto, indicated she should walk ahead of him. But when they reached the edge of the rocks, and she saw the black water below, she whirled in horror.

"Where are you taking me?" she cried. "They'll shoot me," she said desperately, looking toward the villa. "Surely you don't expect me to get in that water! It's freezing. Where are we going? I'd never get there anyway——" And she began to run back toward the villa.

Effortlessly, Petros blocked her way. He was amused to see she still clung to the kettle.

"And what do you think would happen to me if I left you behind?" he said. "I'd be dead the minute I hit the water. One shout from you, and——"

"I told you I'm not going to shout," Trudi said. "You have my word."

He laughed shortly.

"You can trust me."

"A Nazi?"

She must have realized how ludicrous she looked, hugging her stew pot, like some Viennese servant girl. "I am not a member of the National Socialist party, in spite of what you may think."

Slowly Petros removed his shoes and tied them together.

The events of the long night finally had overwhelmed her, and Trudi felt her control nearing the breaking point. "I was married once, but my husband is dead." She knew she was saying too much, but the man's disdain was infuriating. "He died in a German concentration camp for the one crime the Nazis would never forgive—he loved his country."

Petros slung the shoes around his neck. "Everything you say may be so," he said at last. "But everyone in Piraeus knows that you and Colonel Schneider——"

"What would you do if you were a woman?" she demanded fiercely.

"We have an old proverb in Greece," he said. "Choose the best life, habit makes it pleasant."

She wondered if he had meant it as an insult. She looked past him at the black waters of the sea, as dark as the cloud-covered sky above. "Don't send me in there," she said simply. "I want to live."

She had expressed his own feelings so exactly that, for a moment, he didn't know what to say. He took the kettle

116

from her hands and placed it on the ground. With a click, he dropped the stiletto blade back into its handle. Reaching out, he pulled her to him and kissed her.

Trudi was surprised at the intensity with which she returned his embrace.

Reluctantly, Petros released her. The taste of her lips lingered on his, but he knew his luck would not last indefinitely. "Once I am in the water," he said, "lower the kettle after me. It will float and I can push it ahead of me."

All at once Trudi felt tears come to her eyes. "Tell me, Greek, will I ever see you again?"

The familiar arrogance returned with Petros' laugh. "Why, Miss Trudi, I thought you wanted to live—"

"Tell me!" she said fiercely. "I don't even know your name."

That is true, he thought, but such knowledge would endanger her far more than him. She was caught up in the emotion of the moment, as she would be the first to realize in the cold light of morning. And there was only one way to show her.

"All right, I'll tell you where I live. That way you can return this call whenever you want."

He had expected her to stop him, but instead, like a dutiful schoolgirl, she waited to hear what he would say next.

He gave her one last chance: "Your German friends would pay a fat reward to find me, I can tell you. One hell of a lot more than you can make by selling a tank of gas."

Even as he told her in detail how to reach the schoolhouse, he tried to rationalize his actions. All she had to do was cry out and the Germans could forget about a search. They'd find him dead right in their back yard. But he knew there was some other reason he was telling her all this. A simpler reason: he wanted to see her again.

He plunged soundlessly into the bay and Trudi eased the aluminum kettle into the water and floated it gently toward him. Guiding it in front of him with one hand, Petros began to swim across the peninsula.

Trudi returned to the kitchen, opened the window, and as the moon lit the water she watched Petros until he had safely reached the other side. She watched him pick up his jacket and, holding the kettle with both hands, disappear around the cliff.

The church bells rang the hour. It was four o'clock in the morning.

Shivering from the cold, Trudi picked up the apron with which Petros had dried his body earlier. All at once she pressed the apron against her breast and began to cry. She cried silently, the tears streaming down her face.

The moon dipped behind Old Spyros' house. Trudi closed the window and after pulling down the shades turned on the light. She cleared the kitchen table of plates and glasses and scrubbed it clean so that no one would know anyone had been there.

15

Spyros awoke at dawn and felt so much better he insisted on reopening his cafenion. At first Petros would have none of it. "Wait until you're strong and well rested again." Petros had fed him early that morning upon returning from German headquarters, but the old man was still weak. "What's your hurry?" he asked. "In a couple of days, you will be able to leap walls and chew girders again. But right now you are my one concern because I love you, and I want to see you well enough to cut Petros Zervas down to knee height where he belongs." But the old man was adamant. He promised only to return to the abandoned school each day for a meal, as long as the food lasted. And he agreed to leave the Black Saint Nicholas in the storeroom, which he said he would use as a chapel.

Petros watched with misgivings as he departed, but made no further attempt to halt him. Now that Spyros was recovering, no man less than half his age could give him orders.

So, on a cold morning, with the rain falling steadily, Spyros returned to his cafenion. To his surprise, he found the place swarming with people, carrying marble tables high over their heads, dragging chairs, carting boxes filled with glasses and crockery.

"He is fine. He is fine," Mr. Yiannis had kept telling friends and neighbors who turned up at his kiosk to inquire about Spyros. When Spyros opened the doors to the cafenion, it attracted an even greater crowd. Among them was a young German soldier. The moment they saw him the Greeks melted away.

"Tell me," the German said to Mr. Yiannis, who started rearranging his newspapers uncomfortably. "What are all those people doing over there?"

"They're taking everything back."

"I don't understand."

"A friend of ours was sick, but now he is well and he needs his things."

"Did he sell everything before he became ill?"

"No," Mr. Yiannis said, stepping out of his kiosk to sweep the ground.

"Did he give everything away?"

"Not exactly . . ." Yiannis said. He never liked talking to German soldiers, even when they seemed sympathetic as this young one—a boy, really. He had fuzz on his cheeks and his eyes were a clear blue. My God, they were drafting babies into this war!

"I don't understand," the soldier repeated.

"What would a dead man do with chairs and tables?" Mr. Yiannis said irritably. "Somebody was going to take them. So when the people saw he looked bad . . . and sick too . . ."

"Did anybody try to help him?" the boy asked.

"No," Mr. Yiannis said, shaking his head. "Because nobody can help anybody. People have to help them-

119

selves. That's why," and Mr. Yiannis went back into his kiosk.

"Well, it looks like somebody helped him."

"I guess so," Mr. Yiannis answered coldly.

"So all the people are not bad. Are they?"

"I guess not," said Yiannis.

"Not even all Germans?"

Mr. Yiannis felt the fright in his chest, but the young-ster was looking at him with clear innocent eyes, as if earnestly trying to understand. "Look, Your Honor," Mr. Yiannis said, with a flash of anger, "none of these people are bad. They are all friends of one another . . . just like a pack of sharks."

"You mean vultures."

"No, sharks. The sharks play and love each other but they are always hungry. When a shark is wounded, the other sharks finish him off. It is the same with us these days."

"Are you all sharks?" asked the German, and still there was no menace in his voice, just curiosity.

Mr. Yiannis knew there was no going back. And sud-denly he didn't care. Suddenly he felt a great strength, strength enough to speak his mind to the very face of the hated enemy. "Yes, Your Honor, every one of us. All those people there are sharks . . . ready to cut one another to pieces when the time comes for someone to drop to his knees. But they are friends. Good friends. Each and every one of them. You see . . ." he said angrily and came out of his kiosk, "take a good look at me. You may not believe this, but I am a shark too. Bum leg and all, I am just as good a shark as any of them. I was not made to be one, nor were they. It was you who made us this way. You and your friends."

Mr. Yiannis stood before the soldier, his eyes blazing, his chest out. "Now you can arrest me for all I care."

When the German said nothing, Mr. Yiannis started to close his kiosk.

"What are you doing?" the German said at last. "You don't have to shut down because of me."

"I am not closing because of you, Your Honor," Mr. Yiannis said, less belligerently now, "I am going over there and talk to my friend and tell him how sorry I am for taking four of his chairs. And do you know what he is going to say to me?"

The boy shook his head.

"He is going to tell me that he understands because he himself is a shark. But, you know something?" he said. "He is the only one of us who is not a shark."

And paying no further attention to the German, Yiannis limped over to the cafenion.

Later that same morning, Nico Andreades left his family's hillside home and made his way down to the sidewalk Cafenion Hellas for a cup of coffee. Since he no longer had any money, Nico had to get his coffee on credit and hope that Spyros had some errand or a sweeping job for him to do to pay him back. By now the crowd had dispersed and the old man had carried most of the small marble-top tables outside to wash. White apron tied around his flat stomach, arms folded across his hollow chest, Spyros watched through the dense, light rain as Nico crossed Kastela Plaza and entered the cafenion.

"Good morning, Spyros."

"Good morning to you."

Nico brushed the rainwater from his arms and mopped his forehead before seating himself at the table by the large glass window.

"Coffee?"

"I have no money, Spyros."

"I know," Old Spyros said and headed for the small stove in the back corner of the cafenion. "There's plenty of work today."

"All right then." Nico cleared the window with the steam of his breath, and looked down the street leading to the beach of Turkolimano harbor, five hundred and fifty yards away, where all the shining yachts had moored before the war.

"How is your family?" Spyros asked as he brought the coffee.

. Nico shook his head. "I don't know, Spyros—they're all coughing their heads off."

"Did you get them a doctor?"

"Where in hell am I going to find a doctor?" Nico said, embarrassed. "I have no job. No money. No food. Those doctors who haven't left the city are too busy; besides, before they agree to see anyone they make sure he can pay. How in hell can I pay? They tell me to take my family out to the country." Nico took a sip of coffee. "How do I do that? What do I tell them? Mother, Taki, Katina, get up from your beds because we're going to the country? They can't even stand."

"Goddamit, goddamit, and more goddamit," Spyros said, slapping his fist into the palm of his hand. "A jewel of a man your father was. Back from America with money, marries a girl, has three children and enough money in the bank to retire. He had everything planned, he once told me. And he had, you know that? And all of a sudden the man has nothing. His money is no good . . . no wonder he died. Goddamn this war." Spyros had no money, either, real money, gold, not the inflationary paper drachmas or the German occupation mark. The only reason Spyros could remain open for business was that he wasn't paying rent. No one in Athens or Piraeus was paying rent anymore. No authority could make them pay. They just refused and the owners couldn't evict them.

Old Spyros kept open every day from dawn to curfew because of a lifelong habit he had learned at sea: early to bed and up before the sun. Spyros had only himself to support, and even so was barely scraping along from the profits of the roasted, finely ground garbanzo beans that may have looked like coffee but bore no other resemblance to the cotton-thick, steamy, lusty scented, chestnut-brown, mercury-heavy nectar that was real Greek coffee. Spyros watched Nico stare into the demitasse filled with make-believe beverage, and turned away.

Suddenly the old man's eyes came alive. Following his glance, Nico looked out the window, and there he was, walking with that jaunty stride he had developed, head high, acting as though he owned the world, as though the Germans weren't conducting a citywide manhunt for him —Petros! And he was well dressed, too, wearing what looked like a fairly new trenchcoat, with a wide-brimmed hat pulled low over his forehead as his only disguise. Leaping to his feet, Nico dashed out into the street.

The reunion was violent, the two young men embracing and pounding each other vigorously on the back. Then they stood apart and grinned at each other.

Nico's smile was a little self-conscious. "Well," he said, and paused for a moment. There was so much to say he didn't know where to begin. "Well—"

"That's my Nico," said Petros. "Ever the orator." Laughing, he took his friend's arm and guided him into the cafenion.

"You're looking the same as always. Better," Nico said as they went to his table. "How can you manage to look so well, dress so well, in times like these?"

"I'm a magician," Petros said in a stage whisper. "I have the ability to create illusions. Ah, Captain Spyros! How have you been since last I saw you?" He shook the old man's hand and winked.

Spyros couldn't help chuckling. "As well as could be expected of an old man, thank you." Shaking his head, he went to the back for three cups of coffee.

Nico regarded his friend in undisguised admiration. "Petros, Petros, let me look at you. You really outdid yourself the other day. The whole gang from the Olympics team was down at the docks with me, and we would have cheered out loud if it hadn't been for those Krauts with their automatic rifles. Nothing could have made them look more ridiculous, Petros. By now that story has spread, believe me, and you've made every man in the country proud he's a Greek."

Petros was faintly amused. "Is that why you think I did

it?" He clapped his friend on the shoulder. "The war hasn't changed you, I see. Still the boy patriot."

Nico looked at him in bewilderment. "Why else—"

Petros rubbed his thumb against his first two fingers. "I haven't collected yet on that deal, but I will."

Spyros returned with the coffee and pulled up a chair for himself.

Petros frowned. He had good reasons for not wanting the old man to hear certain things he intended to say. He turned to Nico. "I stopped off at your house before coming here in hopes I'd find you. Your family seems to be in pretty bad shape."

Nico squeezed his hands together helplessly. "I know. There isn't a thing I can do about it."

"Half the people in town are down with something, Nicholas: grippe, influenza, pneumonia, tuberculosis. Don't blame yourself for something you can't control."

"I'd do anything in the world to help them," he said passionately. "Anything."

Petros knew how deeply his family's illness must be hurting Nico. He was counting on that. Some of his fondest memories were the times he had spent at their home—they had been the closest thing to a family of his own he had ever had. He was particularly fond of Taki, Nico's kid brother, whom he had taught to catch a ball and once even let play with his stiletto. Now, more than ever, he felt confident Nico was his man. "As a matter of fact"—and he pulled his chair closer— "there may be a way you can help them after all. If my plans work out, you could get them whatever they need: food, medicine. . . ."

Nico's eyes sparkled; if anyone could help it was Petros. He grasped his arm. "You really mean it? You aren't teasing me?"

"I didn't get clothes like this by teasing, I can assure you. No, I'm completely serious." Petros looked at Spyros and hesitated. "Maybe it would be better if we went outside."

Nico seemed about to burst with impatience. "But it's raining. Why can't we talk here?"

"It's not the sort of thing everyone should hear—"

"Never mind," Spyros interrupted and got up. "I have to scrub the table tops anyway." He threw a burlap bag over his head and shoulders, and with sponge in hand, went out into the rain.

"We didn't have to do that," Nico said. "We hurt his feelings."

"What's done is done," Petros said, dismissing any concern as easily as he had dismissed the old man. He pushed his chair closer, and instinctively reached for his worrybeads. "I came looking for you, Nico, because I trust you more than anyone I know. If you decide not to go along with my proposal, I know you won't turn me in to the Germans, even though they'd pay a lot for the information. But if you agree, I know I can depend on you."

Was this the carefree, fun-loving Petros? In all the years he had known him Nico had never heard him speak so seriously. The only sound was the insistent clack of the black worrybeads.

"I'm working with the British, Nico."

Nico whistled softly and quickly turned to see if anyone was within earshot. "I see why you wanted to keep Spyros out of it," he said.

Petros nodded and put the beads away. Then carefully he outlined what was happening in the war, the war outside Piraeus, the war beyond Greece. He told Nico that the British were on the defensive all across North Africa, as Rommel's mechanized forces pushed onward. But the Afrika Korps was helpless without fuel and supplies, which, Petros said, brought the war right back home to Piraeus. "Piraeus is becoming a major supply center and staging area for the Nazis," Petros told Nico. "And if you need proof, just look at those three tankers in the gulf."

Nico stared at his friend in bewilderment. Petros working for the British. . . . Piraeus, his Piraeus, playing a major part in the war. . . . How did Petros fit into something so huge and important? It was too much for him to

125

assimilate all at once. "What are you suggesting?" he said weakly. "What are you saying?"

Patiently Petros explained that he and his new associates intended to destroy ships, trains, supply depots. "And we'll hit hard, fast," Petros finished.

It was too much. It was too impossible. One minute Nico was embracing an old friend whom he hadn't seen for ages, and the next he was calmly discussing sabotage on a scale so vast. . . .

"You mean blow everything up?"

"Exactly," said Petros.

"The tankers?" said Nico, struggling to understand.

"That's just what I mean," said Petros. "An attack is planned for late tonight."

There was a long silence, broken only by the sound of a Reichswehr troop carrier rumbling through the plaza. Nico watched the truck until it vanished from sight. "What do you want me to do, sink the tankers all by myself?" He tried to speak facetiously, but his voice shook with emotion. He couldn't believe the words that were coming out of his mouth.

But this new Petros apparently had no time for such banter. "Of course not," he said, lowering his voice, "but it's always best to keep your biggest operations small, personal. That's why I've come to you, Nico. I want you to round up three teams. The finest swimmers you can find. Three swimmers to a team, one for each ship."

Eight crack swimmers—nine, including himself. Tonight? Petros certainly didn't believe in long preparations. But then, maybe that was why he was so successful. What had he said? "We'll hit hard, fast."

"You're the best swimmer in town," Petros went on, giving Nico no opportunity to comment, acting as though he took Nico's acceptance for granted, "so I want you to take charge of the whole operation. You'll swim out with one of the teams. I'll give you explosive devices for the ships, and your job will be to see that they're attached securely and that the teams get back safely."

"Wait a minute," Nico said and put his hand on Petros'

arm to stop him. "I don't know anything about explosives." Even as he said the words, he realized he had already made up his mind. He would do it! He would be glad to do it! His only concerns now were technical: How could it be done? Who could do it best?

Apparently Petros sensed his friend's excitement, for he said: "Do you really want to help out?"

"Yes, of course. You know I do. But where am I going to find eight volunteers willing to carry explosives?"

"Who said anything about volunteers?" Petros said. "This is not going to be done for free. Each and every one of the swimmers will be paid by me personally upon their return, ten pounds sterling in gold. And you, Nico, will get twenty pounds, half right now, if you agree to go along. The British don't care how much money they have to pay. All they want is to make sure those ships never reach African ports."

Nico felt like shouting. Twenty pounds! In gold! Here was the answer to everything. The country, a doctor, all the medicine his family needed. He wanted to kiss Petros and thank God for sending him at the right time.

Petros hitched his chair closer. "There is no danger involved with the explosives. If there was, Nico, do you think I'd ask you to do it? There's nothing to it. The explosives—limpets, they're called—work automatically. They're pre-set and snap on the hulls like magnets. I'll explain it all to you in detail when we meet tonight, but believe me, Nico, it's the easiest money you'll ever make."

But one thing still troubled Nico. Where would he find swimmers, strong enough, daring enough, to undertake such a dangerous mission?

Petros looked at him with a hard, evaluative expression. "Kids," he said.

The very thought sent chills through Nico. "What do you mean, Petros?"

"Just what I said—kids. Eleven-, twelve-, thirteen-year-old kids."

Nico's protest was cut off almost before it had begun. "I

127

know, I know," said Petros, "but what do you think this is—our water polo match? Use your head, Nico. Kids are smaller, they're quick in the water as fish, most of them swim as well as grown men. But the main reason is that kids that age want to prove they're men. They're so eager for adventure they'll overlook the risks."

Nico cast about for something hard and practical to say in objection, something that wouldn't cry out: How can you expose *kids* to such peril? Instead he said, "But won't the money change all that?"

"Not at all," Petros said. "If the proposal is sprung on them suddenly enough—and you'll barely have spoken to them before it's time to hit the water—they won't have a chance to think it over. Maybe they won't even realize the danger. But even if they do, the gold is the string and they'll dance like marionettes. No one in Piraeus today can afford to turn down an offer like that."

Nico felt chilled at the coldness of tone, the impersonality with which Petros could manipulate other men's— boys'—lives. Everything about their conversation was upsetting to him. What had happened to the Petros Zervas he once knew? Surely money, food, and clothes couldn't change a person so completely, yet here was someone who could look at fellow Greeks like an outsider—bluntly, coldbloodedly. Where was the man he had once loved— yes, worshiped—as a model to follow? But even as the thoughts tumbled through his head, Nico kept silent. This wasn't being proposed as a duty he owed his country—in which case he would have accepted immediately and proudly—it was a business deal, pure and simple. Well, if the gold was the string, he could dance as well as the next marionette.

"Well," said Petros. "What's your answer? Are you with me? I haven't much time. It's either yes or no."

The head of the Andreades family knew he had no choice. "I'll do it," he said in a voice so low it was barely audible.

Petros was delighted and, clapping him on the shoulder, told him the time and place for their meeting.

Nico nodded, then rose and started for the door without a word. Suddenly he halted. "Where's my money?"

Petros' loud, coarse laugh echoed through the empty cafenion. Taking a purse from an inner pocket, he counted out the bills and handed them to Nico. "That's more like it, boy," he said. "You're learning just like the rest of us."

Less than an hour later Nico returned to his family's apartment high on the hill, a cramped flat of four rooms into which they had moved after his father's death. The furniture, what remained of it, was plain and homely, the better pieces having been sold during the months of the occupation to buy food. The floors were bare, the walls cracked. Mrs. Andreades, who had spent thirty years married to an intellectual who had cared little about physical comforts, tried to pretend she was indifferent to her surroundings, but she hated the apartment. For her children's sake she kept silent; her chief concern was for Nico, who was remarkably like his father. Both men were idealists who cared little for their surroundings since they walked with their heads in the clouds.

The two sick children slept in one tiny bedroom, and Mrs. Andreades used the other. Nico was forced to sleep on a cot in the living room, but never complained, accepting the lack of privacy as his due. The kitchen was the only cheerful room in the house, but it, too, was sparsely furnished with a plain table and chairs, an old-fashioned stove, and a tiny icebox. The pots and pans that decorated the walls had been scrubbed until they gleamed, but they served as bitter reminders that their usefulness was over—no longer did they bubble and crackle with fragrant roasts and stews. Even common herbs such as oregano, a staple in Greek cooking, were gone from the shelves.

Mrs. Andreades, a gray, tired woman, sat dispiritedly at the kitchen table, wrapped in a heavy wool cloak to ward off the chill. Although she had said nothing to her family, she knew she could not conceal her illness much longer; that much was obvious from the involuntary shock that crossed the face of Petros Zervas, Nico's old friend, when she opened the door to him this morning. Petros had not seen her in years, and though he tried to mask his surprise at the way she looked, and even kissed her, he did not fool her. In fact, he never had fooled her in all the years she had known him. She never said anything about her suspicions to Nico, however, because Petros was her son's great friend.

She heard Nico's footsteps on the stairs and waited for his key in the lock, but instead of letting himself in he rapped outside. She opened the door to see him with arms filled with bundles, and pockets bulging. Striding past her, he dumped the packages on the kitchen table with a loud clatter.

"You found some work, Nico?"

"Watch, Mama." With the air of a conjurer performing tricks, he began to remove objects from the packages. "Flour. Olive oil. Rice. Sugar. Coffee, real coffee."

She stared at him, then at the food.

"That's just the beginning." His smile broadening at the pleasure he saw he was giving her, he began to unwrap more bundles. There were cans of American corned beef and stew, obviously purchased by some hoarder before the outbreak of the war, others of British soups and several jars of French-made preserves. He presented her with two loaves of bread, both fresh, and—her favorite—a large wedge of feta cheese.

Tears came to Mrs. Andreades' eyes, but she brushed them away angrily. Then, her mind still spinning, she looked at him more closely. "You haven't answered me, Nico."

He replied by hugging her and kissing the top of her head.

The sounds of their voices brought to the kitchen a girl in her early teens and a boy a year or two younger. Both were dressed in shabby nightclothes and were barefooted; their faces were waxen, their eyes huge in their pinched faces. They kept up a constant coughing.

130

"Taki, Katina," Nico said, enjoying a fresh moment of triumph, "your brother is a sorcerer!"

The children's eyes widened as they stared in disbelief at the mounds of food, and then both began to talk at once.

"Taki," Nico said to the boy, "I have something very special for you." From a pocket he took a small jar of wild strawberry jam which he placed on the table as though it were a precious object.

The boy swallowed hard.

"And for you, Katina," Nico said, "something to use as soon as you can go out." He handed the girl a small lipstick in a brass container.

Katina clutched it fiercely, as much out of gratitude for her brother's faith in her ultimate recovery as for the gift itself.

Nico watched his mother carefully cut several thin slices of bread, spread jam on them, and give them to Taki and Katina. The children ate in silence, and he was pleased to see they hadn't forgotten their manners. Even in their hunger, they did not bolt their food ravenously but confined themselves to small bites, savoring each mouthful.

"One more miracle, Mama," Nico said, and handed his mother a bottle filled with a dark powder.

She turned the bottle over in her hand, looking at it suspiciously.

"Cough medicine," Nico told her. "A half teaspoon to be mixed in a glass of water. Each of you takes two doses a day."

"Now I know you were stealing," Mrs. Andreades said, and the joy drained out of her.

"No, Mama, I went to the apothecary shop of Gaglios, and when I saw it was closed I threw pebbles against the windows of his apartment on the second floor until he let me in. He thought I'd come to beg, of course, but when he saw I was ready to pay him cash, he sold me the powder without a murmur. Just like that."

His mother stared at him, deeply troubled.

"And in a few days," he added proudly, "there will be more food, more medicine. And then I will take you all to the country."

Mrs. Andreades made no reply, and sat rigidly at the kitchen table, lips compressed, until the two younger children finished eating and she sent them back to bed. Then she turned to her eldest and spoke to him in the tone he remembered so well from childhood. "Now, Nicolaki," she commanded, "you will tell me."

His elation evaporated. Much as he hated to disobey his mother, he knew he could not tell her what had happened. "I saw Petros Zervas today," he began.

"I know. He was here earlier this morning, looking for you. He seems healthy," she said. "And very prosperous."

Nico went to the stove and began to prepare coffee; it helped him avoid her searching gaze.

"What is he doing these days?"

"These days," Nico said, "one doesn't ask too many questions."

"Well, I must say I'm not surprised. One thing about your friend Petros. He always was able to take care of himself."

"Yes," Nico said dryly. "Well, Petros has given me a job, Mama. He's paid me ten pounds sterling in advance."

She pulled herself to her feet and embraced him. "Why, that's wonderful, Nico! Our prayers have been answered."

"Yes, and he'll pay me another ten pounds when the job is done."

"For all that money, it must be a very important job."

"Oh, it is." Nico could offer no explanation, even though he knew she wanted one.

His mother's eyes narrowed. "Twenty pounds sterling is a fortune these days. For that amount of money Petros wants you to do something dishonest?"

"No, Mama," he said.

"What then?" she persisted.

"Now, Mama, I can't tell you any details. If something should happen and you're questioned, you know nothing. They have ways of forcing people to give them information."

"Why would the police ask questions about a man who is honest?" she demanded.

"I said nothing about the police," Nico said. "Besides, the only police in Piraeus these days are the Italians."

She drew in her breath. "Then it is the Germans who might come to me with questions."

"Enough, Mama. What I do—is for Greece," he said, but even as he spoke the words turned to ashes in his mouth. Thanks to Petros Zervas, he was no patriot but a cheap, grasping whore.

16

Trudi left headquarters at noon and spent a quiet afternoon in her penthouse apartment. But it had been far from restful. The encounter last night had left her in a turmoil. She felt uprooted, suddenly vulnerable, as certainties on which she had grown to depend, on which she had staked her life, had crumbled away. She was shocked at how easily they had fallen. Trudi Richter was surviving the war because she thought she had learned an unforgettable lesson. Never again, after the death of Kurt, would she permit herself to indulge her emotions. Acting without thinking, on impulse, might be fine for an idealistic young nurse, but it was suicidal for an Austrian deep in the enemy Nazi high command. Up to now, she believed she had been able to carry off her perilous role because it was natural for her to think before she acted, to examine possibilities before she made a decision, and never, never to let her feelings dictate to her mind. Yet last night, in the kitchen, she had behaved like some lovesick scullery

133

maid, all atwitter because some errand boy had stolen a kiss. Where was the reserve, where was the precious wall she had built with such care and patience just so that she could insulate herself, her *self,* from whatever circumstances required she do to stay alive? Petros had sensed the contradiction at once: "I thought you wanted to live!" It had scarcely overstated the consequences should she continue to see him.

She knew that if anything happened to her he wouldn't care. Why should he? He had gone so far as to tell her where he lived—as if to taunt her that if she wanted to see him, it was her affair.

Well, to hell with the blue-eyed Greek! She'd be damned if she'd crawl to any man. She *would* live, she'd rebuild those walls higher and stronger than ever before, and no man—no German, no Greek, no one!—would ever make her vulnerable again.

She was so exhausted after her sleepless night that she threw herself onto the couch and did not stir until early evening. She had just finished dinner when the door buzzer sounded, surprising her. She expected no company, and recognized neither of the blond, athletic young men standing on the threshold when she opened the door.

"Captain Müller and Lieutenant Graz, Gestapo," the elder of the pair said, and showed her his credentials.

A stab of fear shot through her, but she smiled and stepped aside to let them enter. "Would you care for some refreshments?"

"We're on duty," Müller said. His gaze took in every detail of the living room before he sat down. "We'd like to ask you a few questions, Fräulein Richter. We hope you can be of help to us."

"Of course." Trying to conceal her nervousness, she seated herself opposite them.

"We were wondering whether you happen to know why Colonel Schneider's car needed a full tank of gasoline this morning."

So that was it! Trudi forced herself to remain calm.

134

"Why ask me, Captain? The chauffeur takes care of details like that."

"But you drove the car yourself last night, didn't you?"

"Only from here to the headquarters compound," she said. "I shouldn't imagine even a car the size of the colonel's would consume much gas for so short a journey." Lieutenant Graz, who looked uncomfortable in civilian clothes, was transcribing every word, Trudi noted.

"According to the motor pool records, Hans Kleinschmidt, Colonel Schneider's driver, filled the car with gasoline yesterday afternoon and again this morning. He can't account for an almost empty tank. Can you, Fräulein?"

"I've just told you everything I know," she said.

"Of course," said the captain. "Then perhaps you can help me clarify another point. Two soldiers on bicycle patrol reported they saw the colonel's car parked in a back street near the headquarters compound a short time before your arrival last night. Could you tell us what you were doing in that street?"

Trudi contrived to look blank. "I wasn't doing anything. I was never there."

"Then you deny the report?"

"Of course. Or, I should say, there's nothing to deny. I drove straight to the colonel's house from here." Trudi kept her hands tightly clasped in her lap.

"The report goes on to say that a young man, thought to be a Greek, had been seen talking to someone in the colonel's car a moment before he led the patrol in a diversionary action. By the time the patrol returned, the colonel's car and its driver were gone."

"That must have been embarrassing for your soldiers," Trudi said innocently. She began to sense they were fishing, and her confidence started to return.

"That is true, but not as embarrassing as it will be for the person who was driving the colonel's car. Do you happen to know any young Greeks, Fräulein Richter?"

135

"My acquaintances," she snapped, "are restricted solely to officials—high officials—of the Third Reich!"

Captain Müller bowed his head slightly in acknowledgment. "Of course, Fräulein. Although in war, strange things happen, not always of our choosing. For example, there is a young fellow, a Greek, we are presently trying to locate. He killed a German soldier and his description roughly fits the man reported by the bicycle patrol. If you would be good enough to look at this—"

And Müller threw on the table between them an official bulletin.

Staring up at Trudi was the face of the man whose name she saw was Petros Zervas! The photograph obviously had been taken some years ago—Petros still looked like a boy—but though the hair was parted in the middle there was no mistaking the jawline, the nose—and especially the eyes.

Quickly Trudy scanned the poster. Chaplains . . . an icon . . . the orderly. And then, relief flooding through her, she saw the heading. Above Petros' photograph in bright red letters was the designation: "Deceased."

Angrily she brushed the bulletin aside. "You and your bicycle boys had better get together before you go around accusing innocent people. This young Greek of yours must be quite a fellow—to be alive at the very same moment you list him dead!" She rose. "Now, gentlemen, if you're quite finished."

"We make no accusations, Fräulein," Captain Müller said, obviously ill at ease.

"I should hope not. If you want a character reference regarding me, I suggest you speak to Lieutenant-Colonel Willy Streck of your own organization. As well as to Colonel Schneider."

"We came to Greece in Colonel Streck's command, Fräulein, and we are well aware of your—ah—close friendship with him." Müller clicked his heels, Lieutenant Graz followed his example, and both men marched to the door. "Forgive this intrusion," Müller said, and they left.

Trudi was so weak she leaned against the door until her pulse stopped racing and she could breathe normally. Then, gathering her strength, she hurried to the telephone and called Colonel Schneider.

"Wehrmacht headquarters, commandant's office," Brugger was crisply efficient, as always.

Trudi identified herself and asked to speak to the colonel.

"The navy has taken him on an inspection tour of the harbor tonight. Is something wrong, dear Fräulein Richter? You sound upset."

From Brugger's exaggerated concern, Trudi was certain she had been the one to alert the Gestapo. "Why, no," she said. "Should there be?"

The woman's tone changed. "Shall I ask the colonel to call you when he returns? It will be quite late."

"No, thank you. I'll speak to him tomorrow." Trudi hung up the telephone, leaned back on the bed, and pondered her predicament.

She herself appeared to be in the clear, but if the Gestapo was on the trail of the blue-eyed Greek—she still preferred to think of him that way instead of the new Petros Zervas—he had to be warned. She ran into her bedroom and rummaged through her dresser until she found the slip of paper on which she had copied down the address. Going to the phone book, she checked the map of Piraeus and then called the colonel's garage and told Hans to pick her up.

She changed into dark, inconspicuous clothes and was ready by the time the car arrived.

Hans listened perfunctorily to her explanation that she was restless and felt in the mood for a drive to Kastela. The limousine had barely pulled away from the apartment building, when he looked over his shoulder. "Begging the Fräulein's pardon, but the Gestapo is investigating the gasoline—"

"I know, Hans. I had a visit tonight."

"It is a pity we can make no more trips to a certain quarter of town," he said, and fell silent.

137

"A pity," Trudi agreed.

From time to time Trudi glanced out the rear window; finally, convinced she wasn't being followed, and noting they were approaching the sea, she told him to stop. She felt in the mood for walking.

Hans sounded startled. "Here? Alone?"

"Why not?" Trudi laughed. "Our patrols are everywhere, aren't they? I'll be quite safe, Hans. Why don't you take the rest of the night off?"

Lela would be delighted, he knew, and he swallowed hard.

When she insisted, he jumped out, opened the door for her, and saluted. "Good night, Hans," she said, and waited till he had driven off before setting out for the schoolhouse.

Seeing places and people from a moving car is one thing, but seeing them on foot and at close range is quite another. Trudi had accepted what she had seen of Piraeus: the men were thin, the women were thin, the children were thin—a characteristic of the Greek people, she thought. She had noticed that most of the people moved slowly and that the children never played in the streets as they did in Vienna. Perhaps that, too, was a local characteristic. In Germany most people's eyes were blue, in Piraeus, with one notable exception, they were black. Trudi had accepted their hostility because they were an occupied people who had lost their freedom.

But now Trudi saw people lying in the doorways, on the sidewalks; she saw young, skinny children sitting motionless on the sidewalks, backs against the wall. This she accepted. She heard women wailing, she saw a wagon come by, drawn by a wheezing horse, and the driver take a small bundle from a weeping woman and throw it into the wagon. This she accepted. Even when the driver picked up one of the children leaning against the wall, she accepted it. But when he threw the youngster on the wagon, she blinked her eyes and did not accept it.

She went up to the wagon for a closer look. Through a crack in the side she saw the face of a dead child staring

138

at her. Trudi went around back and looked inside. The small bundle the man had thrown in was a dead baby. The rest—dead men, women, and children. Trudi turned on the driver and at the top of her voice screamed: "Why?"

"Starvation," the man replied.

Trudi's eyes grew wide, her face paled, and her knees trembled beneath her. The emaciated woman with hollow cheeks and deepset eyes, the same woman who had given the small bundle to the man, asked if she would like a drink of water—she had some saved. Trudi studied her face, the black and hollow eyes that looked mean from a distance but at close range were really tender and soft. Only now it was Trudi's eyes that were hard and angry at the thought the woman had given her child away. Trudi looked at the wagon and then back at the woman again. Trudi was not accepting any more. And at that moment, more than anything in the world she wanted to be with Petros, to tell him she understood just a tiny bit of what he must feel every day, and to tell him how ashamed she was.

Keeping an eye out to make sure she was not being followed, she hurried toward the steep flight of steps leading to the schoolyard.

Something was afoot tonight, something very much out of the ordinary, Petros told himself as he returned to the abandoned school. The entire area was crawling with Germans, and he had to exercise extraordinary care to avoid them. The journey took twice as long as usual, but he negotiated it safely, and was relieved to find Old Spyros sound asleep in the storeroom.

He still had a few hours before it was time to meet Nico, so he sneaked up to the roof of the building, whose decorative stone urns gave him a perfect vantage point and ample concealment. There was no doubt about it; the Germans were everywhere tonight. He didn't understand: they didn't appear to be conducting a search, although they had set up several checkpoints, and sergeants were sending out patrols to march up and down the streets. It was impossible to determine whether they were waiting for someone or merely setting a trap for curfew violators. The latter was more likely; they were known to set up spot checks without warning in one part of the city or another, and the Greeks despised them for it.

Another ten minutes passed, and Petros' tension continued to mount. Five minutes later when the church bells announced eight o'clock, a truck carrying relief troops rolled up. Petros lifted his head and looked around quickly. It was then he caught sight of Trudi. She ran through the gate to the far end of the athletic field adjacent to the school, the spot Petros had indicated to help her find the school.

What was she doing here?

Slowly Petros looked down the street to see if anyone was following her, and saw a truck slow down in front of the gate and drop off three soldiers armed with machine pistols. Trudi, who heard the truck, crouched low. One soldier walked to the end of the field and turned the corner around which Trudi had just appeared.

Drawing his stiletto, Petros steadied himself.

From the roof Petros saw another soldier approach from the other direction.

Petros picked up a handful of gravel from the roof and threw it behind him. Trudi flattened against the wall, as the soldier warily reversed his steps.

Petros waited until the Germans had disappeared, then catapulted from the roof and landed on bare hands and feet on the street. Trudi saw him and started toward him at a run. He waved her across and into the schoolyard. She felt like burying her head in his shoulder, she was so relieved to see him.

Placing a finger to his lips, Petros led her inside to an empty classroom. He whispered he was unable to take her to the storeroom, because Spyros was sleeping there. "What's the reason for all the patrols?" he asked. "Are they looking for you?"

"I don't know," Trudi said, clinging tightly to his arm. "They may be looking for you."

Angrily he shook her free. "What do you mean by that?"

Bitterly she remembered her firm resolve never to get involved again, especially with him; yet from the moment the Gestapo had left her only thought had been to see him and warn him. Now she was vulnerable as ever—even more so. "It's a long story," she said, suddenly feeling weary. "The Gestapo knows about last night—"

"When I broke into headquarters?" he demanded.

"No, what I did. The—the gasoline. I denied it, of course," she hastened to add.

He snorted. "If they sent out troops every time a tankful of gasoline was stolen, they'd have to double the size of the army of occupation."

"They also suspect you may have had something to do with it," she went on. "I think I convinced them they were wrong, but I'm not sure."

Petros caught hold of her wrist. "Tell me everything that was said. Don't leave out one word."

He released her, but remained menacingly close as she repeated in detail the conversation with Captain Müller. "That's all there was to it," she said at last. "I don't believe they *know* anything about you. You fooled them completely, Petros Zervas."

Her words electrified him, and he turned on her savagely. "How do you know my name?"

The sheer animal quality of his voice terrified her. She thought he might strike her, so swift was his change in mood.

"They showed me a poster—"

"Tell me!"

"The Gestapo regularly prints a list," she said, her voice trembling, "names, details, photographs, complete dossiers on enemies of the Third Reich. After you stole that icon, they must have obtained your description from the chaplains and managed to identify you. Captain Müller showed me the special bulletin they printed on you."

"Well." He relaxed slightly, and actually looked pleased.

"Above your name," Trudi said, "they have printed 'Deceased.' "

Petros laughed, and it was obvious he was delighted. "So they think I'm dead." His eyes narrowed. "That can be useful."

"Yes, you were drowned with the icon," she said. "The photograph of you wasn't very good. Your hair was parted in the middle, and you looked so young."

"I remember that picture, and you're right. It was not good. It was made eight years ago, when I was seventeen, and our team won the national water polo championship."

With the easing of tension, all at once her legs felt like lead. "Is there someplace I can sit down?"

He pointed to the straight-backed chair behind the teacher's desk. "That's the best I can offer you."

Trudi perched on the desk itself and crossed her long legs. "Is this where you live?" she asked, looking around curiously.

"No," Petros lied. "But I sometimes find it convenient to meet people here." He looked at her, a trace of the old arrogance returning. "So you decided to pay me a return visit."

"I've already told you why I came," she said. "I wanted to warn you about the Gestapo."

"You don't really expect me to believe you went through streets infested with German military patrols just to warn me to be careful of the Germans—something I already know?"

"You can believe what you wish," Trudi said and started to rise.

"No, please." He came alongside and placed a detaining hand on her arm. "I'm just astonished, that's all."

She remained where she was, conscious of his hand still on her arm.

"I am not expressing myself very well," he went on.

142

"You see, not many people do me favors, but none like this. Why, you risked your life, do you know that?"

Trudi made no attempt to move away. "It was stupid of me to come here, I suppose. I can see that now. But I became panicky, and I wasn't thinking too clearly."

Petros shook his head. "I don't think that's the reason."

"No?" Trudi challenged him.

"No." He tilted her chin upward and slid his arms around her.

To her own astonishment she found herself responding to him even more hungrily than before, clinging to him, one hand pressed against the back of his head, exploring and caressing.

Petros fumbled with the buttons on her blouse, his hand moved inside and he started to tug gently at her brassiere.

Trudi stirred and shifted her position slightly.

He mistakenly thought she was trying to move away, and removed his hand. But he was too aroused to stop completely, and reaching for her knee, began to move up the smooth silk of her firm inner thigh.

She pushed him away and stood. "I am not some street girl," she said, and as Petros watched in excitement, she removed her blouse and skirt, unhooked her brassiere, and stepped out of her panties.

She faced him, nude except for garter belt and silk stockings. "When I give myself to a man I do so freely."

A glance confirmed the glory of her figure, the high, firm breasts, tiny waist, rounded hips, and long thighs and legs. He undressed quickly and again they embraced, their bodies touching, then pressing close before he lifted her in his arms and carried her to the long, rectangular desk.

"There is no other place," he said. "I'm sorry."

"No, my darling Greek," she whispered to him. "It doesn't matter."

143

He stretched her out gently on the hard, smooth wooden surface, and as their lips met they lost consciousness of their surroundings. They kissed and Petros' hand closed over a breast; Trudi responded instantly to his touch. She, too, began to explore, and Petros came alive immediately, expanding eagerly.

In unspoken accord they wanted to prolong the moment, but their mutual desire was too great. Trudi pulled Petros onto her, he entered, and neither of them moved. Then, unable to restrain themselves, gradually their thrusts became violent, primitive, as their passion engulfed them.

Trudi screamed softly, her fingernails raked Petros' back. Her release triggered his.

As their ardor subsided they remained locked together.

Petros looked down at her and stroked her cheek. "For a moment there," he said with a soft laugh, "I thought we'd alert all the patrols in the area."

She kissed him on the nose. "To say nothing of your friend in the other room."

Suddenly their desire flared again, sharply, insistently, but this time they savored it, gave it time and meaning to the very end, draining the last drops of joy.

Exhausted at last, they lay back on the desk, their bodies still damp, hearts pounding.

"That was very strange and wonderful," she said softly. "You are a remarkable man, Petros Zervas.'"

He reached in his jacket on the chair beside them. He lighted a strong, pungent Greek cigarette and offered Trudi a puff.

Ordinarily she didn't care for tobacco, but now she enjoyed the aroma.

"You may not believe this," she said into the darkness, "but it has been a long time since I have really made love. I almost had forgotten how fine it can be."

"I believe you," he said. He took a long pull from the cigarette; its tip glowed brightly in the dark. Already he

144

was planning the quickest way to get her through the German patrols; he was determined to meet Cunningham exactly on schedule.

17

They rode at anchor in the Gulf of Phaliron, three enormous Bulgarian tankers that resembled whales. Killer whales, because of the anti-aircraft and machine guns mounted on their decks. In time of peace the Greeks, who knew and loved ships, would have regarded the vessels with contempt, with the paint peeling from their rusting hulls, refuse littering their decks, a contempt, they would have been surprised to learn, that was shared by the fastidious German marines in olive drab who patrolled the decks, armed with automatic rifles. But to the people of Piraeus they represented something more: they were menacing symbols of evil.

The tankers, rising and falling in the gentle swell of the gulf, were ungainly as whales. Thirty years old, they were far past their prime and suffered from years of neglect. They had been resurrected to satisfy the Third Reich's insatiable demand for oil, the lifeblood of the mechanized forces that had conquered most of Europe.

The gentle but steady rain that had fallen all day partly obscured the tankers from the shore. The breeze was slight, but it blew from the north, and as always at this season of the year the Macedonian mountain wind was raw, biting. The *carabinieri* had no difficulty enforcing the curfew this night, and even in the poorest working-class districts few scavengers and food hunters were abroad. The whole of Piraeus seemed to have become a dark, uninviting gray that matched the leaden sky overhead. This was what the people of Piraeus called "suicide weather" when even the most optimistic citizens became depressed by the cold and dampness.

On the heights above the cliff a few bare branches moved idly, but the gulf seemed strangely deserted. A Greek fisherman had received a mysterious message, urging him not to leave his craft in the Gulf of Phaliron tonight, and had decided to tie up at one of the commercial docks. He was forced to pay for the privilege, an expense he could scarcely afford, but he knew better than to take unnecessary risks. Once he had docked his boat he hurried home; if there was going to be trouble he wanted no part of it.

The sailors who manned the German navy's gulf patrol boat were told by their lieutenant to prepare for minimum duty. On a clear night, there was always the possibility that some foolhardy Greeks might make trouble, but tonight no one was really worried. It made far better sense to the lieutenant to sit before a roaring fire in the main bar of what had been the Yacht Club and sip schnapps to ward off the chill.

No stars were showing, the sky seemed a solid, gray-black mass, but then thick, heavy clouds began moving in from the sea. Apparently the Macedonian wind blew at a lower level than the somewhat stiffer breeze above. The ugly clouds merged, separated slightly, and then came together again to form a single blanket.

The town was eerily still. The German patrols had long since dispersed, and the footsteps of a pair of Italian sentries could be heard for blocks. The roar of a staff car's engine echoed through the empty streets as the vehicle started off on its run to Athens.

In a small, natural cleft in the side of the cliff, a few feet above the surface of the water, small waves made a quiet lapping sound as they rose and fell against the shore. But the two men pressed against the rocks behind them failed to appreciate the soothing sound. Both wore heavy black sweaters, dark trenchcoats, and slouch hats; anyone who happened to spot them from a distance, which was unlikely, would assume they were members of the Gestapo. This was not accidental, and they took care not to draw attention to their movements. This required

146

great self-control, but they had been trained for their task and were proficient at it.

Even so, Major David Cunningham was surprised to realize he was not especially tense. A great deal was at stake tonight, including his own military future, but he took pride in his assessment of men and felt sure the Greek who was the key to the entire operation would not let him down. The beauty of their plan was its simplicity, a lesson Cunningham had learned from Brigadier Campbell. When utilizing the services of amateurs and volunteers, the old man had always stressed, always limit your mission to straightforward action, leave as little as possible to improvisation and interpretation.

Nothing could be clearer than the Greek's instructions: sink those ships.

A short distance from shore a small, nondescript fishing boat, whose owner apparently had not been advised to anchor elsewhere or perhaps had elected to ignore the warning, tugged at its water-soaked line. The Honorable Robert Ashley-Cole, executive officer for the Piraeus command of Section 6, British Military Intelligence, found himself counting the number of times the boat bobbed up and down in the course of sixty seconds. That way lay madness. He desperately wanted a cigarette, although he knew, of course, that smoking was out of the question.

He stole a glance at his superior officer, who stood beside him. Damn the Yank—so cool, unperturbed—he actually seemed to relish the danger. In an hour or so the fate of the tankers would be decided, the Piraeus mission would either have justified its existence or be recalled in dishonor, but the man in charge was acting as though he didn't have a care in the world.

Cunningham became aware of his subordinate's scrutiny. "Robert," he said pleasantly, "you might check the limpets again to make sure they're protected by the oilcloth."

Ashley-Cole, realizing the major was inventing a task to dispel his nervousness, managed an equally cool reply. "They're ready and waiting, sir," he said. By God, give

147

the devil his due; Brigadier Campbell certainly had selected the right commander for the Piraeus sector. Cunningham would not become rattled, no matter what might happen, which was especially important with so many amateurs taking part in the operation. Ashley-Cole would never forgive London for depending on Greek volunteers for such an important mission. For the sums they were paying they could have assigned Cunningham seasoned Royal Navy frogmen. No doubt the Greeks would be courageous enough but tonight of all nights Ashley-Cole longed for the support of men he understood, British sailors who were trained and predictable and reliable.

A third man materialized, seemingly out of nowhere.

Petros Zervas, also dressed in a dark trenchcoat and slouch hat, grinned at the Intelligence officers. He had turned up precisely at ten-forty P.M. as promised—a fact Cunningham confirmed by glancing at his watch. This was Petros' first truly major job, and he was clearly excited. "Do you have the limpets? Have any of my boys shown up yet? Is there anything you want me to do?" he asked in hoarse whispers.

Major Cunningham glowered at him. "When I want you to do something, Zervas, you'll be told."

Petros accepted the reprimand in silence. Nothing could curb his exuberance. He peered out across the water of the gulf at the Bulgarian tankers, and felt a sense of anticipation. Thanks to his efforts they would be sent to the bottom, and then let them talk to him with disrespect. Just let them try! This entire operation depended solely on him, and the sooner they admitted it, the better. He would charge them plenty for any future jobs and they'd pay willingly, knowing he was one man who delivered on schedule.

The lights of a German patrol car swung into view on the road above, and the three men flattened against the natural depression, bending into the shadows. None moved until the automobile, not slackening its speed, moved on and vanished as it turned inland into Piraeus.

Nico Andreades appeared as stealthily as Petros had. The two friends shook hands, embraced, and grinned at each other, brothers in danger.

Cunningham and Ashley-Cole pressed deeper into the shadows, and Petros made no attempt to present his friend to them. Cunningham had briefed him with great care, and as far as the eight young Greeks who would take part in the operation were concerned, Petros was in charge. It was a role that he eagerly accepted, and he knew that Cunningham would not interfere or call attention to himself unless something went drastically wrong. For the sake of the future of his Piraeus headquarters it was far better that Cunningham and Ashley-Cole remain anonymous. If any of the Greeks should fall into the hands of the Germans it would be difficult for the youths to identify British Intelligence officers they had never met.

A stone rolled down the side of the cliff.

Petros instantly drew his stiletto; Cunningham and Ashley-Cole reached for their pistols.

Two youngsters, one barely into his teens, appeared on the ledge.

Petros looked at Nico, who nodded affirmatively, and the knife vanished.

The other young Greeks showed up soon thereafter, arriving singly or in pairs. All were in high spirits, like children at recess, obviously eager to do the job for which they had volunteered. Nico twice had to caution them not to speak too loudly.

When the entire group had assembled, Petros gathered the youngsters around him and, speaking in a low but intense voice, made a brief, impassioned speech. They would be acting, he declared, for the glory of Greece and to free her people from Nazi bondage. The whole world would learn of their exploit tonight and would applaud them for it. Contrary to the lies being told by the Germans, the spirit of freedom and rebellion still burned fiercely among the people of Greece.

"The moment you come back," he concluded, "I'll pay

149

each of you the agreed fee of ten pounds sterling in cash. The money will warm you and help you forget the water is cold."

They laughed appreciatively.

Cunningham listened to Petros in admiration. The Greeks always had been unequaled as orators, and one thing about Zervas—he was a real bullshit artist. At first he was surprised when he saw the swimmers—they were nothing but kids! Still, it was too late now—he just hoped the Greek knew what he was doing and that they could be trusted on a mission of such importance.

Petros reached behind him and produced two large cans of heavy grease from the far side of a boulder. "After you undress," he said, "smear yourself with this. It stinks, but it will protect you from chills."

The young Greeks knew these waters at all seasons of the year and accepted his suggestion without discussion.

When they had finished plastering the grease on their faces, bodies, arms, and legs, Petros removed the oilcloth cover from the limpets and held one up for inspection. "This," he said, "is the explosive device you'll use. It has two straps, and you'll carry it on your back, looped over your shoulders." He demonstrated, using Nico as a model.

Nico was surprised at how light it was.

"It weighs only ten pounds," Petros said, "but don't let that fool you. It packs a tremendous punch."

Get on with it! silently urged Cunningham, but then curbed his impatience, reasoning that men who used the limpets had the right to know something about the device. Besides, it was Zervas' show.

"On one side," Petros said, illustrating, "you'll see a suction cup. Press the limpet against the side of the ship, and it will hold there like a magnet. Press gently but firmly, that's all you'll need to do." He demonstrated by pressing a limpet against the boulder, to which it clung until he removed it.

The boys were impressed.

"Make certain," Petros said, still speaking in a slow,

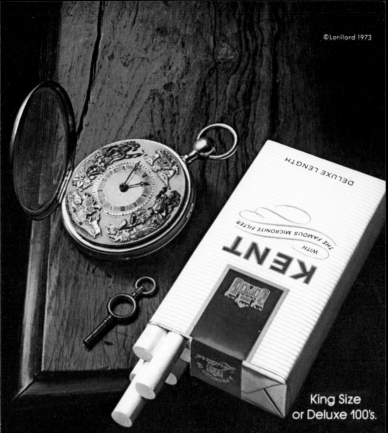

© Lorillard 1973

DELUXE LENGTH

WITH
THE FAMOUS MICRONITE FILTER

KENT

King Size
or Deluxe 100's.

Micronite filter.
Mild, smooth taste.
America's quality cigarette.
Kent.

Try the crisp, clean taste of Kent Menthol.

The only Menthol with the famous Micronite filter.

deliberate tone, "that you attach your limpet to the hull of the ship *below* the water line. It will work above the line, of course, but it was designed for maximum effectiveness underwater. Follow my directions, and I guarantee it will tear a hole five to ten feet in diameter in the side of the ship!"

"How is that possible?" one of the boys asked.

"Inside each limpet is a highly concentrated type of nitroglycerine. Just the tiniest amount is equal to several sticks of dynamite."

"What's to prevent my limpet from exploding while I'm swimming with it on my back?" one of the boys asked.

"What's the matter, Dimitri? Don't you trust me?" Petros' smile was reassuring. "You could carry it that way for a year, and you'd be safe. Absolutely nothing would happen. The limpet is a tremendously sophisticated weapon. It has a chemical fuse that is triggered only by metal. For instance, if I touched the suction cup to my wristwatch, that would start the chemical fuse burning." He held the limpet a fraction of an inch from his watch.

Cunningham frowned and silently cursed him. If the crazy Greek's hand shook or slipped, they'd have to get rid of that limpet in a hurry before it exploded and compromised the entire mission.

Petros' grin deepened. "Just remember, nothing happens until the suction cup touches metal."

Nico cleared his throat. "How long will the chemical fuse burn, Petros?"

"Forty-five minutes." Petros turned toward the British Intelligence officers in the shadows for confirmation. He saw Cunningham nod affirmatively.

"You'll have forty-five minutes to swim back here from your targets, dress, and leave the cliff before your tanker explodes," Petros said.

"More than enough time," Nico said. "It shouldn't take more than about twenty minutes to swim out and back."

"That's my estimate, too," Petros said. "As you can

see, this mission was planned by experts who have taken great precautions to insure your safety."

The youth who had asked the initial question laughed a trifle uncertainly. "I hope you're right."

Nico became indignant. "He wouldn't lie to us. He knows we're taking a big risk."

Petros clapped the boy on the shoulder. "I guarantee you'll be out of the water before the shock waves start rolling in from those tankers."

"You can depend on that," said Theodoros, captain of one of the swimming teams. "We'll swim faster than anybody you ever saw."

Everybody laughed.

Petros, crisp in spite of his amiability, divided the youths into three groups, one assigned to each tanker. He emphasized that Nico, who would head the group swimming to the farthest ship, would be in overall charge. The groups would leave on a staggered schedule, he said, with those swimming to the farthest ship starting first and the others following at three-minute intervals. In that way all would attach their limpets at approximately the same time.

Nico realized that his team would have the greatest distance to cover, both ways, but that was only fair. He and the two who would accompany him were the strongest and most accomplished swimmers.

"One man in each group attach your limpet near the prow, a second amidships, and the third at the stern," Petros said. "Remember, the tubs are loaded with oil, and the moment the explosions go off they'll ignite the fuel so the tankers won't stand a chance."

The boys smiled at each other.

"The most important thing to remember," he emphasized, "is that all of you must reach your targets simultaneously, which will reduce the chance of being spotted by the sentries on deck. When you swim back here, you should try to reach shore at about the same time, too, for the same reason. I needn't tell you to collect your clothes—and money—and leave the area as fast as you can. All hell will break loose when those tankers go up."

The swimmers responded with a burst of subdued, nervous laughter.

"If there are no more questions, let's start," Petros said. He distributed the limpets, which each boy donned, and then he checked to make certain they were securely attached. Everyone shook hands, including Petros and Nico. Both knew that of all the adventures they had shared in the past this was the greatest.

Then, motioning his two young companions to follow him, Nico slid into the water.

Petros looked at his watch and noted the time: it was 11:08 P.M.

The initial shock of the icy water was numbing, but Nico told himself it was no colder than the sea had been at this time of year on a hundred occasions when he had gone swimming for the sheer fun of it. Confidently, his strokes long and powerful, he plunged into the Gulf of Phaliron toward the three shapes that loomed up in the dark.

Petros flashed Cunningham a triumphant grin. He wanted the major to know that he had been given an exceptionally difficult assignment on short notice, and had managed it without a hitch.

Cunningham made no acknowledgment. The mission was just under way; he would reserve his congratulations for its successful conclusion.

As Nico swam, the water felt somewhat warmer and he could almost forget the cold. Once in the water, his earlier misgivings disappeared. This was a glorious night. He would strike a blow for Greece and be paid another ten pounds sterling after the mission was over. He had been wrong about Petros; he was a true friend.

At 11:11 P.M. the second group of swimmers slid into the water.

Ashley-Cole glanced up at the sky, then frowned. The clouds over the gulf seemed to be parting, which would make the swimmers plainly visible. But then another series of heavy clouds rolled in, sealing the break.

Cunningham remained silent, his face impassive. He was secretly pleased, although it was still far too early to tell what might happen, and he contented himself with watching the swimmers as they edged out into the gulf. Nobody, he thought, could swim as gracefully as Greeks who lived near the water. And these boys were better than most. In this, at least, Petros had chosen wisely.

Nico cut through the sea silently, rapidly, and the tankers began to grow clearer ahead of him. He could make out the bridge on one—no, two—ships. Then he caught sight of an armed man carrying a rifle, and he shivered involuntarily. This was no lark, but a grim assignment, and one slip would be fatal.

At 11:14 the last of the swimmers lowered themselves into the water and began to move in the direction of their target.

Petros looked at his watch, made some rapid calculations, and concluded that, if his estimate of the length of time it took to reach the tankers was correct, the limpets would be attached by approximately 11:35 P.M. The swimmers would reach land again by midnight at the latest, and everyone would leave the area long before 12:20 A.M., the time the explosions were set to blow apart the hulls of the Bulgarian ships. Very neat.

He had a desperate urge to talk, finding the continuing silence oppressive, but decided it was wiser to emulate the men for whom he was working. They had probably conducted dozens of such operations, he told himself, and he wanted to prove that he, too, could remain controlled under mounting pressure.

Cunningham stiffened when another German patrol car moved along the top of the cliff, and he hoped the swimmers would do nothing to call attention to themselves. The car slowed; the driver threw a lighted cigarette butt out his window. Cunningham heard it sizzle in the sea, and then the car picked up speed again and was gone.

Nico estimated he had covered approximately half the

distance to his target now; he was still breathing easily, his arms and legs felt strong, and he was filled with self-confidence. His two companions were keeping pace with him, and looking back over his shoulder, he could see the members of the second group far behind. So far, all was well.

Petros peered into the night. In the dark, with the steady rain, it was almost impossible to see anything. Those swimmers farthest from the shore were barely visible now, their dark heads blending with the water.

The members of the second group swam rapidly, its members instinctively staying close together.

The commander of the German navy harbor patrol drained his glass of schnapps, hauled himself to his feet, and extended his hands to the fire. Then he shrugged into his greatcoat, picked up his visored cap and gloves, and headed out into the raw night toward the berth where his crew awaited him. A quick swing around the harbor and gulf areas would take no more than thirty or forty minutes, and then he could go off duty for the night.

The youths in the third group of swimmers exercised less self-discipline than their comrades. Without realizing it they began to drift apart, and as the clouds parted Petros cursed them under his breath, willing them to unite. Eventually they became conscious of their error, and his relief was great when they began to move closer to each other. It was 11:23 now, he noted, so there wouldn't be too much longer to wait.

He wished he could celebrate with the Austrian girl, but it would be a serious error to go anywhere near her apartment tonight. The Gestapo would spread a real dragnet after this operation, so he had made careful plans, stocking supplies of food and liquor in the storeroom of the abandoned school. He would go there, and there he would remain until the furor lessened and he could take off for a few weeks in Athens. At least nothing would prevent him from consuming large quantities of ouzo in his private, solitary celebration.

Nico saw there were two guards on the deck of the

155

closest tanker, both of them German marines armed with automatic rifles. One stood near the bridge, as though rooted to the spot, and the others strolled around the deck, paying no attention to the Bulgarian sailors who appeared to be making the vessel ready for a daybreak sailing. That ship was too heavily populated for Nico's taste, so he gestured to his companions, indicating that a short detour around the vessel was in order. Then, to make doubly certain he remained unobserved, he took a deep breath and started to swim underwater.

The fine rain was growing sporadically heavier, reducing visibility and totally blocking all three groups of swimmers from the view of those standing on the stone ledge at the base of the cliff. But there were no gusts of wind, the breeze remaining steady and gentle, and Cunningham silently thanked M.I.-6's weather station in Turkey for selecting a perfect night for the mission. And Zervas was a liaison man beyond compare, a fact he intended to keep to himself. The bastard was cocky enough already, and would be impossible to handle if ever he realized he was indispensable. But he was worth all the extra trouble, no question about it.

Petros looked at his watch again, saw that it was now 11:33. At any moment now the swimmers should reach their targets. He was surprised to discover that in spite of the cold he was sweating, and instinctively took his string of black worrybeads from his pocket and began to stroke the smooth stones.

Cunningham saw what he was doing, and felt an odd sense of triumph. The damn Greek wasn't as fearless as he made out.

Nico bypassed the second tanker, which had swung partway around so he could see only its fantail, and headed straight for his own target, the most distant of the three ships. He took great care now not to splash or make any other sound. Exhilarated and excited, he still felt strong, and having come this far undetected, he was certain he and his comrades would succeed. In another thirty seconds he would reach his target, and again he swam

156

underwater, rising to the surface only a short distance from the hull.

Then, knowing he could not be seen from the deck directly above, he made his way rapidly toward the stern. A glance over his shoulder told him that his two companions were in position now, too. The tanker was as good as sunk.

Petros' eyes burned on his watch dial and saw the time was now 11:36. He wanted to call the fact to the attention of the British agents, but refrained, needing no one to remind him that sound carried clearly across water and that the mission was far from over.

Cunningham glanced at his watch, too, then took a small pair of powerful field glasses from a trenchcoat pocket and trained them on the tankers. It was too dark. For a moment he thought he could make out three tiny figures in the water, close to the farthest tanker, but he couldn't be certain. If he was right, they were in position—one at the waterline near the prow, another amidship, and the third close to the stern. The young Greek swimmers were carrying out their assignment with the precision of professionals.

Petros removed his hat to wipe away a film of perspiration, then settled it on his head again. By now the second group of swimmers should have reached their ship. It was 11:40 P.M. now, about five minutes behind schedule, but that was all right. On their return the swimmers would be aided by the tide, and should be able to reach the ledge no later than midnight.

Nico found a likely spot on the hull, and treading water, removed the limpet from his back. His fingers were colder than he had realized and the strap almost slipped from his grasp, but he grasped it fiercely, his heart and temples pounding. He waited a moment or two until he recovered, then lowered himself below the surface. Following Petros' directions, he pressed the explosive device against the metal, one of his feet momentarily touching the icy hull, too. Nico righted himself, and when he saw the limpet was securely fixed to the side of the ship, he rose to the surface and allowed himself the luxury of a few seconds' rest.

The limpet would not explode for three-quarters of an hour, which gave him ample time to reach land. He watched as one of his companions, then the other, completed their tasks. Staying close to the doomed tanker, he began his return journey. He could hear men talking on the deck above him, and although he could not understand what they were saying, he felt no alarm since their tone was conversational. So far he and his colleagues were undetected.

As his team began to swim back toward the land, with Nico bringing up the rear, he could see the figures of the second team attacking the next ship and he felt a surge of elation when he realized that they, too, were done. The boys were forgetting one phase of their instructions, however; in their desire to reach shore as rapidly as possible they were racing individually rather than in groups.

Nico realized they were too close to the tankers for him to call instructions, so he swam more rapidly, hoping to draw closer before he shouted.

Cunningham raised the field glasses and could just make out members of the last group. They evidently had already attached their explosive devices to the hull of the nearest tanker. Except for the possibility of the malfunction of the limpets—and he knew Cairo had checked them out thoroughly—the mission could not possibly fail now.

Petros needed no glasses to see the nearest tanker. All was under control, not one swimmer had made a single error, and the mission had been accomplished with brilliance and dispatch. It was 11:41 P.M. now, and by midnight the swimmers would be safe, just as he had predicted.

Cunningham lowered the glasses and made the "V" for victory sign with two fingers of his right hand. In another forty minutes the tankers would split apart, burn, and go to the bottom. Rommel would be deprived of the oil he so badly needed, and the Germans would realize, once and

158

for all, that their presence in Greece was being contested.

Nico counted the heads bobbing in the water before him, and was relieved to see eight. Everyone was safe, and the entire group was heading back toward land. He could not overtake them with the breaststroke, and the crawl might make too much noise and reveal his presence, so he pressed as hard as he could. Suddenly a warning pain shot through his left foot and traveled up the length of his calf. But in his desire to reach his companions and tell them to draw closer he ignored the sign, and a moment later his left leg pulled up beneath him.

The cramp was excruciating, driving everything else from Nico's mind, and he could barely refrain from crying out in pain. He was far too experienced a swimmer to become panicky, however, and he knew there was only one thing he could do. Methodically, acting with deliberation, he forced his leg into a straight position, then began to kick hard beneath the surface. For a time he seemed to have no success, but gradually the pain lessened and soon he was able to resume swimming.

By now he could see that his companions had gained on him substantially, and he knew that even if he used the crawl he probably could not overtake them before they reached land. Well, they had done spectacularly, he thought, and no one could blame them if their formation wasn't as precise as it might have been.

It was 11:45, and Cunningham felt he could begin to relax at last. He had already given Zervas the money to pay the swimmers; he and Ashley-Cole would depart as soon as he knew for certain that the men would reach the ledge and were safe. He would be able to hear the explosions from anywhere in Piraeus; no sense in jeopardizing the Intelligence operation by sticking around until every last Greek was ashore. For all he knew the kids would be so excited they'd bring the entire German army down on them. Besides, Zervas was being paid plenty.

Cunningham had handled his end of the operation, let the Greek take care of his.

The roar of a patrol boat engine suddenly shattered the quiet, and the three men at the base of the cliff froze. A powerful searchlight stabbed through the dark night, and the German patrol boat shot out of the small yacht harbor into the gulf, its bright searchlight playing over the water as it started on its rounds.

Cunningham had taken care to eliminate the Greek fishing boats, but German patrol boats were beyond his control. He had planned the mission with such a possibility in mind and had routed the swimmers away from the normal patrol area. Still, he found the steady droning of the engine unsettling.

The young swimmers were even more disturbed. Knowing nothing about German patrols they reacted to the unexpected by losing their heads. One or two abandoned the silent breaststroke for the much faster Australian crawl, and in a matter of moments all eight were using it, kicking up a boiling wake, even though the patrol boat was nowhere near them.

Petros, seeing their froth, kneaded his worrybeads rapidly. "Control them, Nico," he muttered under his breath.

But Nico had fallen so far behind his comrades that he could not halt their forward surge without calling out to them, which would have been suicidal with the patrol boat within earshot. He could only continue to swim steadily toward his goal, hoping that the Germans in the boat would not happen to turn their spotlight in his direction.

Suddenly a tremendous explosion cracked the air. One of the limpets attached to the farthest tanker exploded, and a moment later the entire ship went up. Although neither the British agents nor the Greeks had realized it, that vessel's holds were filled not with oil but with highly volatile, refined gasoline, and the limpet's detonation triggered an even greater holocaust. A deafening roar drowned all other sounds, the thunder blast lighting the gulf, the Hill of Kastela, and the better part of the Piraeus waterfront.

Within seconds the tanker disintegrated, and chunks of metal, dismembered bodies, and debris of all kinds flew high in the air, then plunged into the sea. A huge wall of angry, orange-yellow fire boiled skyward.

Within moments the blast was repeated on the second and third tankers, one of which was carrying large quantities of ammunition on its decks. Detonation after detonation reverberated across the harbor.

The sea churned, waves of searing air spread in every direction, the ground trembled, and the stunned trio standing on the little ledge thought the entire cliff would tumble and fall on them.

Burning oil spread out from the ships, but the worst of the inferno was concentrated in the immediate vicinity of what had been the three tankers. The wind, sucked into the vacuum, whistled menacingly as it was drawn toward the conflagration.

The flames leaped higher, emitting huge, foul-smelling clouds of heavy, black smoke. The flames were so bright it was impossible to look directly into the heart of the glaring mass.

Debris, twisted and charred, and cinders, still burning fiercely, hissed and bubbled as they struck the water.

Petros, horrified and dazed, automatically glanced at his wristwatch. The limpets had exploded a mere fifteen minutes after they had been attached to the tankers. The British agent—goddamn him to hell—had promised him, *promised* him, the swimmers would have plenty of time, three quarters of an hour, to reach the shore safely. He stood there, paralyzed with shock, as the explosions erupted around him.

Cunningham checked his watch, too, and immediately understood what had happened. Cairo had been taking no unnecessary chances and had lied to him and Ashley-Cole as well as the young Greeks whose lives were now in such grave jeopardy. Brigadier Campbell had known that fifteen minutes would sound too chancy—no one would agree to undertake the mission under those conditions—so he had blandly told Cunningham there was three-quarters of an hour leeway. Campbell had one concern and one concern only—the success of the mission. Afraid that the strange objects might be spotted from the decks of the ships or that someone on board might pick out the swimmers in the water and guess their intent, he had timed the devices to detonate a full half hour earlier. The high command in Cairo did not place high value on human lives, especially those of young Greek volunteer frogmen.

Nico was frightened. The concussions hurt his sides and back, his neck felt as though it was being twisted from his body, and the roar made his ears ache. Whistling drops of water pelted the back of his head and neck, and falling cinders stung his flesh. A rolling swell of the suddenly agitated sea lifted him high onto its crest and pushed him forward, only to pull him back roughly into the foaming trough that already smelled strongly of oil.

The Wehrmacht captain who was the night duty officer of the shore patrol studied the spectacle through his binoculars, and all at once saw several thrashing figures being drawn toward shore. He shouted an order, and five machine-gun crews raced with their weapons toward that section of the waterfront.

The eight young swimmers, still in a state of shock, barely managed to keep afloat in the mountainous, angry sea. For a few moments they had no idea what was happening to them, but gradually it dawned on them that the tide was drawing them toward the inner shore, away from the relative safety of the ledge. They exerted all their remaining strength in an attempt to pull back on course, but their feeble efforts were no match for the power of the aroused sea.

Petros, stunned into immobility could only cry: "My God! They don't have a chance! It's bright as day now!"

Cunningham caught him by the shoulder and pulled him back into the shadow of the huge boulder. All at once Petros seemed to recognize him, and his hatred and frustration burst free. He threw himself on Cunningham, screaming: "Murderer! Murderer!" Ashley-Cole slipped

162

behind him and dropped him with a chop of his revolver butt.

With a sudden whooping, the siren of the patrol boat echoed across the water. The boat chewed up a massive wave and swung in a wide circle, its searchlight piercing the water for the raiders.

Nico was sucked beneath the water. He stopped struggling, and by the time he rose to the surface his senses were restored. He treaded water as he tried to analyze his situation. His comrades, trapped by the tide, were being drawn closer and closer to the shore, and he could dimly make out troops in gray-green Wehrmacht uniforms hastily mounting their machine guns. The boys didn't have a chance, and he was overwhelmed by a hatred for the man he had once called his best friend.

May God damn your soul and may you rot forever in hell, Petros Zervas. You betrayed me. You betrayed us all. You gave me your solemn word that we'd have plenty of time to escape back to land. But you lied. For the sake of British gold you're sending your friends to their certain death.

The Wehrmacht captain watched the writhing, frantically struggling figures in the water being drawn inexorably closer by the tide, and bided his time. "Number one and number two guns," he ordered at last, "fire!"

The machine guns opened up on the two young swimmers in the lead. One half-rose out of the water, flinging his hands high into the air, before he toppled backward into the crest of an oncoming wave and floated brokenly. His companion slumped beneath the surface, then stretched lazily and floated face downward in a spreading, crimson pool.

Petros slowly dragged himself to his knees. He was weeping hysterically. He kept mumbling, "Got to do something . . . got to help them . . . help Nico. . . ."

Cunningham's strong hand detained him. "Easy, Zervas," he said. "There's nothing we can do, there's nothing anyone can do."

The oily smoke drifted toward the city, making breathing difficult. Cases of ammunition were still exploding on the derelict tankers, sending showers of steel fragments high into the air, the detonations echoing against the cliff.

The patrol boat's spotlight flashed across a dark figure in the water, passed by, then doubled back. A frantic swimmer was pinned full in the glare. He turned pleading eyes toward the patrol boat. The lieutenant took his time. He waited until he was almost on top of the boy before giving the command to fire. The water danced as the bullets peppered the target.

Nico was choking with rage as he watched his comrades helplessly being slaughtered, but then realized that his own situation was no less precarious. His cramp had saved him, forcing him to fall far behind, but he would need all his strength and cunning to survive. And he wanted to live. More than anything else he wanted to live long enough to take his revenge on Petros Zervas. For Theodoros, for Dimitri, for the other young boys. And for Nico.

The machine guns from shore fired another burst, and two more swimmers disappeared from sight.

The fire reached the aft hold on the second tanker, and fresh waves of flames boiled upward toward the thick clouds that covered the whole of the Piraeus waterfront like a shroud.

The body of one of the dead swimmers drifted close to the ledge and it was all Cunningham could do to keep Petros from leaping into the water after it.

Only one of the boys still survived, and the Germans toyed with him, waiting until he reached the shallow water near the shore. He struggled to his feet, and as he staggered through the waist-high water to the land, three machine guns spoke simultaneously and his body twisted wildly as he dropped.

Cunningham looked at Petros glowering in silence at the water, now illuminated by the patrol boat's searchlight. "Don't be so goddamn stupid, Zervas," he said sharply. "I'm sorry we've lost those men, but nobody could have

164

helped them. And we've got to live long enough to do more jobs. Tonight is only the beginning."

Tears glistened on Petros' cheeks. He appeared not to have heard a word.

"All right, boy, go ahead," Cunningham said, and gestured in the direction of the Wehrmacht captain, who was carefully scrutinizing the sea through his binoculars. "But the Germans won't shoot you. Not yet. They'll recognize you, and they'll take you alive. For very special treatment. Because they've got you on a very special list, which you seem to have forgotten."

Petros fell back against the boulder, shuddering violently. He was helpless and knew it, trapped by the British as well as by the Germans.

The heat of the fires burned the air, but the water was still cold, viciously cold, and Nico knew he could not stay alive in it much longer. If he swam any closer to the shore, he would be sure to run into the patrol boat, and if he tried for the ledge the shore patrol would get him.

His only hope was if the Germans believed everyone was dead.

He rested briefly in the troughs between the high waves that shielded him from the sight of the Germans on the shore, and as he hung there in momentary suspension, he prayed silently. Then slowly, painfully, he began to inch toward the rocks to his left. There was so much carnage in the surf that, if God continued to protect him, he might reach land safely.

BOOK II

JUNE, 1942

18

Piraeus, Aeschylus' jewel in the crown of Athens, was a badly tarnished bauble, dulled by more than fourteen months of German occupation. Physically there was little change in her appearance: the buildings on the cliffs still gleamed dazzling white as they looked out over the blue sea; the plain stretching toward the capital contentedly baked in the sun; grapes on their vines and vegetables in their gardens were tended with the care only a starving people can lavish on every precious morsel of food.

Piraeus had endured other occupations, but none—not those of the Romans or the Crusaders or the Turks—had been so harsh and cruel. The Germans had deliberately set out to destroy Piraeus' soul, but the patriots who suffered in sullen silence knew something the Germans could never understand: the Greek spirit was uncrushable. When the opportune moment came, her strength, her heritage of freedom, would reassert itself and she would prove Aeschylus was right, that she was immortal.

But that moment certainly was not at hand. All over the free world, the Germans and their allies, the Japanese, were winning new victories. Perhaps the swastika and the rising sun *were* destined to fly from every flagpole on earth; perhaps the Third Reich *would* endure for a thousand years. Boasts once regarded as the dreams of madmen had become reality, and the nightmare civilized men dreaded now had come to pass.

Much of the continent of Europe was occupied by the German and Italian armies. Adolf Hitler's columns were mopping up the last vestiges of Russian resistance on the way to the oil fields of Caucasus.

On the continent of Asia, the Japanese had taken Rangoon, the Andaman Islands in the Bay of Bengal, the Philippine Islands, had captured Lashio and the Burma Road, and had cut the supply line to China.

On the continent of North America, the Japanese had captured Attu and Kiska in the Aleutian Islands.

On the continent of Africa, Erwin Rommel and his Afrika Korps had neutralized the shores of the South Mediterranean, won Libya, and were successfully executing "Operation Aïda"—the drive toward the Nile. They were already deep inside Egypt, well on their way to the Suez Canal. From there they planned to turn north and close the pincers on the Russian oil fields from the south.

In southeastern Europe, in occupied Greece, a fleet of twenty-three ships, plus escort, was assembled in Piraeus to carry three German divisions across the Mediterranean to the Libyan port of Derna to support Rommel's Afrika Korps. To celebrate the event, Benito Mussolini, the Italian dictator, had returned from an inspection tour of the desert battlefields to personally welcome the German reinforcements when they arrived at Derna.

General Rommel, promoted to Field Marshal by Adolf Hitler after his armies had taken Tobruk and Bardia, followed hard on these victories by striking swiftly, entering Egypt and taking the city of Mersa Matruh, only 260 kilometers from Alexandria.

Rommel's "Operation Aïda" had been spectacularly successful, but his mechanized divisions had paid a high price for victory. To cross the Nile and capture the Suez Canal Rommel needed reinforcements and supplies— promised by Hitler himself. And indeed these troops and supplies would have reached Africa but for one complication. On June 16 the small Island of Malta that sits in the middle of the Mediterranean Sea had been reactivated by the British. In the past two weeks and in spite of heavy German air bombardments, 75 percent of all Axis ships carrying supplies and men to North Africa had been sunk by the British navy and air force. With the Italian ports rendered temporarily useless for supplying Africa, the Germans moved their point of embarkation to the eastern ports of Greece.

Anticipating the safe arrival of his reinforcements at

Derna, the Desert Fox pressed east toward El Alamein and south toward the pyramids at Tel el Giza on the outskirts of Cairo.

In Piraeus, the early summer rain had stopped and the clouds cleared away. The sun, slowly gliding into the sea, cast its last rays on the masts of the Italian destroyers. The heavy spill from the afternoon downpour gushed along the streets; dried-out acacia and pepper-tree leaves sailed down the gutters to the waterfront. On the docks, underneath heavy cranes, the German trucks and empty personnel carriers formed a single file for an orderly return to their motor pools.

The day-long embarkation of German troops was coming to an end. Most of Rommel's replacements, along with forty tanks, ammunition, water, gasoline, and food, were now aboard the twenty-three cargo ships. It was a short haul to the African port of Derna and the ships were crammed above deck and below. In spite of the heated objections of their captains, the seven Italian destroyer escorts had each taken on additional German troops. More men for Rommel, the harbor commander had said. Besides, what difference would it make? No engagement was contemplated; Mussolini's destroyers would simply escort the convoy through the safe waters of the Ionian and Aegean seas and on to Derna. There Il Duce himself would be waiting to congratulate them.

19

Nico Andreades watched the painfully thin longshoremen advance toward the gate to be searched as the afternoon shift checked in. Mechanically, the German guards ran their hands from neck to arms, along the chest to the waist, from crotch to ankle, then, with a pat on the shoulder, they waved the longshoremen on. The Germans searched the outgoing men for stolen food and the incoming for explosives.

At twenty-five, Nico was the only member of the Andreades family who was still alive. The terrible winter of starvation and sickness had taken Katina, then Mama. Now Taki was gone, too, dear little Taki, who had depended on his big brother and now was dead. Watching him slip away, standing by helplessly, had been torture far worse than anything the Germans could have imposed.

The deaths of his family had done strange things to Nico, things he himself was unable to understand. On one hand he felt only black hatred for everything and everyone. All alone in this oversized cemetery, he hated the Greeks as much as the Germans. He hated the sea, the night, the day, the land itself. He hated the dead in the streets and the day he was born. And for a time he wanted to die, too.

He was troubled by a racking cough that left him gasping for breath and in a curious anesthetized state. Soon he would be dead and his body dumped in the death cart and taken to the common burial ground, where Mama and Katina and so many others had preceded him, deposited with only the raw earth of Greece as their eternal blanket. But now that Taki had been taken from him and he had only himself to worry about, he began to feel a new will to live. He wanted to live at least long enough to do something for his people, something to preserve his own immortal soul.

The old Church of Saint Speridon cast long shadows over the benches in the park. The occupants, those with strength enough to follow the sun, were slowly shuffling away. The weak remained, huddled in their threadbare garments, clinging to the last rays of light.

"Hey, mister." A ragged girl, no more than ten years old was staring up at him. "My mother is sick, and we are hungry."

"Who isn't? Get out of here." He looked up at the clock on Saint Speridon. It was time. . . .

. . . Time for the hungry to come out, time for the zombies' promenade. They would fill the streets, the park, the alleys, walking silently, with a slight bounce, hands in front of them, unmindful of each other's presence. The German patrols, recognizing the signs, let them alone, left them to their empty dreams.

"Please, sir," the young girl repeated. "My name is Elena. Please help me."

The streets were filled with beggar children. "I told you to get the hell out of here," Nico snapped. The ragged girl wiped her runny nose with a raglike handkerchief and started away. She was used to rebuffs.

"Hey, come back here," Nico said. "Who do you think you are, coming around bothering people like this?"

"My mother sent me," she said defensively.

"You mean your mother sent you here to find me?"

"She told me to go out and find somebody."

She looked pathetic enough, as did everyone else; but Nico was sure she was as selfish, too, and in spite of himself began to bait her. "Didn't I see you running around bothering people last week? You were skin and bones then."

"So? . . ."

"How come you're all bloated now?"

She wrapped her arms around her belly protectively. "So I gained a few pounds. Some people from a farm came to our house and fed me. It doesn't mean a thing," she said, shaking her head. "Doesn't mean anything at all."

"I think it means something—"

"You won't scare me . . ." she said, as tears started to break loose.

"So you know."

"Up you . . ." she shouted, banging her left hand over her right arm, jamming her fist up in the air. "Up your . . . your . . . your ass, you big monkey."

Nico looked down at the small defiant creature. She knew the truth—that she was going to die—but at that age such a truth was unacceptable. Nor should she accept

173

the fact that those with food would not share it with her, so they would live and she would die.

The pounding on Nico's chest stopped and he felt the girl's arms around his waist. She clung there, staring at Nico's bare feet. Nico put his arm around the girl's back and started to caress her long, black hair.

"Elena, my little girl," Nico said, "we are all going to die. You, your mother—"

"My mother is not going to die," the girl said calmly. "She's already dead."

He nodded. "It's all like some bad dream."

"A dream?"

Nico looked around until he saw a woman with a load of wood on her back approaching a bench in the park. "See that woman going through the pockets of those people lying on the benches?"

She nodded. "She takes their shoes off too," she added.

"Yes, and takes their shoes off. Well, Elena, those people are dead or about to die. Now do you really believe things like that could happen if this weren't a dream?" he asked, the anger mounting inside him. "People go home and call the doctor if they are sick, they just don't lie on a bench and die. And people just don't go around and take their shoes off like that. . . ." He put his hand under her chin and squeezed it tightly. "It's a dream. Do you understand?"

"I don't know," she said.

"It's a bad, bad dream," he assured her.

The sun had gone down beyond the mountains; the gray melancholy of Piraeus had begun. Nico held the girl tight against him as the chill of the summer breeze cut through their weakened bodies.

"Where are you going to sleep tonight?" Elena whispered.

"Oh, over there," he said uncomfortably. "Over there in the auditorium's basement, I guess."

"Would you take me with you?"

"No," he said automatically.

174

"If we are friends, why not?"

"Look, kid," Nico said and pushed the girl away, "why have you all of a sudden decided I'm your friend?"

"If you take me with you," she said rapidly, pointing to his bare feet, "I'll get you some shoes."

Nico looked away quickly.

The girl tugged at Nico's shirt. "The shoes will be just right for you."

Suddenly he turned on her. "Haven't you understood a word I've said? Why don't you go bother someone else, and leave me alone? What good will shoes do me when I'm dead?"

Elena looked up at him and then, with deliberate emphasis, shook her head.

She had no right to feel so certain, and Nico was annoyed. "Why not?" he demanded.

"Because you don't want to die."

"What makes you so sure?"

"I can see it in your eyes. That's why I picked you—instead of one of them." Her wave included everyone—the pedestrians, the woman going from bench to bench removing articles of clothing, the Greek woman coming down the street, clinging to the arm of the lurching German.

"Have some more ouzo, Hans. It'll keep you warm. Ouzo is good for you."

"Ouzo is good, Lela, ja." Hans tilted back the bottle and took a long pull.

"That's right, Hans. And as soon as we get home, I'll cook you a fine dinner."

The little girl's eyes were fixed with preoccupation on Nico's face; she didn't hear Lela's words. But Nico did. Suddenly the blood shot into his face, and he burst forward.

Lela never had a chance, nor did Hans. All they saw was a skinny man, arms outstretched, lunge out of the darkness. His stiff, hooklike fingers closed around Lela's neck, squeezing tight. Lela gasped and dropped to her knees as she tried to pull Nico's wrists apart. Hans, recovering at last, swung the ouzo bottle viciously, breaking it just above the hairline on Nico's forehead. Blood spurted across Nico's face.

Elena, still not aware of what was happening, started to yell at the top of her voice for everyone to stop; but at the sight of Nico's bloody face she threw herself on Hans and beat her fists against his leg. Kicking her aside, Hans spun Nico around with a force that sent him flying across the sidewalk and crashing against a wall. Lela flopped to the ground.

Hans squatted alongside her and inspected her torn throat, all the while keeping a wary eye on Nico. Lela was gasping for air and Hans helped her to a sitting position. She started to cry.

"You'll be all right, Lela. But don't cry, not now. Not yet. I want you to see what I do to that Greek over here."

Nico was back on his feet, resting against the wall to support himself.

"No, Hans, forget him," Lela said, rising to her feet and dusting off her skirt. "Let's get out of here."

"Not yet," Hans said. "I'm not finished here."

"Please . . ." Lela begged. "Can't you see he's crazy?"

"I'll kill him. Don't you want me to kill him? He tried to kill you, didn't he?" Hans started forward but Lela held his arm.

"Please . . ." she begged, hanging on as Hans tried to break loose. "Please don't touch this man, Hans, I beg you." Her eyes began to fill again. Perplexed, Hans looked from her over to Nico.

"Tell me," he said in a low voice, "do you know this man?"

She raised her voice. "Of course not. I never saw him before. I don't know what got into him coming at me like that . . . that's the honest truth," she said and made the sign of the cross.

"Are you sure, Lela?" Hans asked suspiciously. "You

mean you really don't know why this man tried to kill you?"

"No, honey," she said, holding him close and trying to smile. "Let's forget about him and go home." Lela lengthened her stride to pass Nico as quickly as possible.

"Hey, Kraut!" Nico shouted.

"Ja. . . ?" Hans said, coming to a halt.

"How dumb can you get, Kraut?" Nico said.

Hans started for the Greek, but Lela begged him to keep walking. He shrugged; if Lela didn't care. . . . Over his shoulder Hans called back goodnaturedly: "Sure, sure, everybody's a dumb Kraut. Ja. . . ."

"She's a whore, Kraut . . . don't you know that?"

Lela had not lived on the streets for nothing. She had understood Nico's attack, she tried to pass it off, but now she had no other choice.

"Shut him up, Hans," she said fiercely. "Shut him up right now." She started to push him toward Nico. "Now he's insulting you too and trying to start trouble all over again."

Hans looked questioningly at Lela. "He said 'whore'?"

"Yes, that's what I said, Kraut. A whore. Ask anyone . . ." Nico said.

"Hans . . ." cried Lela, drowning out Nico's words. "If you won't do it, I'll shut him up myself." She rushed up to Nico. "Shut up, you. . . ." She screamed and started to beat him with her fists.

He blinked at her. "You don't believe it, Kraut?"

"Shut up . . . shut up . . . shut up . . ." she cried hysterically and continued to pound him.

"All right, Kraut. Then I'll show you." And he tore Lela's blouse open to the waist.

The woman shrieked more in surprise than shame, as she stood bared to the waist. Then she quickly pulled her torn clothes over herself and fell on him with new fury, one hand raking his head, the other holding herself together. "He attacked me," she screamed to Hans. "You saw what he did. You heard what he said. Liar!" She scratched him, beat his face, his shoulders. "You pig, you liar!"

But Nico remained motionless, not raising a hand to protect himself. All he could see was that stretch of bare skin, and over and over he kept saying: "It's gone. What have you done, Lela?"

Lela screamed louder to silence him, now using both hands to tear at him, mindless of the gaping blouse and the man who cringed before her naked flesh.

"Where's Petros? What happened to us?" he said dumbly. "What have you done to us?"

Hans looked on with a mixture of admiration and refused to strike back. He let her have her way a moment more, and then, dragging Lela aside, let out a wild cry and smashed his hobnailed boot into Nico's back.

Nico folded at the knees as he toppled over and found himself on the sidewalk.

"Dumb Kraut, ja?" Hans said, staring down at him. "Well, here's one Kraut that's not so dumb." Then, angrily pulling Lela behind him, he marched down the street.

The little girl ran over to Nico. "Did he hurt you?"

"No," Nick replied, placing his hand over his kidney where Hans' boot had torn through his shirt. He started to laugh. "Either his spikes weren't sharp or I've run dry." He stretched out his legs on the sidewalk.

The little girl turned and started to walk away. Nico followed her with his eyes until she disappeared. An empty truck convoy turned into the street, sped past, spraying water from the deep puddle of rain. Nico saw but didn't recognize the figure of the man waiting at the corner for the convoy to pass. Suddenly his eyes widened, trying to make out whether the figure standing so close was the person he thought it was. But by the time he got to his feet the last truck had passed and the man was gone.

20

The June weather in Cairo was suffocating; the Citadel trapped the heat and tempers were frayed. But none was as strained as that of Brigadier Ian Campbell as he stalked out of the office of the General Officer Commanding, the Commander-in-Chief, Middle East Theater of Operations.

The brigadier's boots clattered on the stone floor of the ancient fortress, and his scowl deepened as he climbed to the third floor, where he absently returned the salute of the sentry on guard outside the Intelligence division. He called into the open door of his deputy, Wing Commander Ross, and told him to come into his office.

"I've just had a chat with the G. O. C. and the chief of staff," Campbell said, throwing a folder marked *Most Secret* onto his desk. "It was quite a harrowing session, to put it mildly. I showed the old man Cunningham's recent reports on the German buildup in Piraeus. Troops, ships, large quantities of supplies, munitions—all of it obviously intended for Rommel." He paused for a moment, threw himself into his swivel chair, which groaned beneath his weight.

"What a barrage of questions. How many troops? Precise numbers, mind you. What units, and what armor? A breakdown of munitions and supplies. On and on it went, and what he didn't ask, the chief of staff did."

The wing commander looked sympathetic.

"I tried to make it clear that we don't communicate with Cunningham on an open wire, and all we know is that three divisions, plus support troops, are set to embark from Piraeus. In twenty-three ships. 'Are you sure of the total number, Campbell?' he asked me. How in hell can we be sure? For all we know, a half dozen more ships, another division, might show up in Piraeus tonight!"

Ross thought it prudent not to point out that the theater

commander expected his Intelligence people to know such details. He also realized that Campbell's outburst had been caused by something more significant than a grilling by the theater commander. "What does the G.O.C. want?"

Campbell vigorously dug the caked tobacco from the briar bowl of his pipe. "M.I.-6 has been directed to destroy the entire German convoy—ships, men, munitions, armor, supplies—everything. And before they can leave the Piraeus harbor."

Wing Commander Ross whistled under his breath. "But, Ian, that could be any time. Cunningham's last report suggested a possible sailing date of early tomorrow morning. That's pretty short notice, even for him."

"Don't you think I know that," snapped Campbell. "Of course, Cunningham has only himself to blame. He made quite a reputation for himself when he blew up those tankers last winter. And his information feed has been first-rate. Even so. . . ." Campbell's voice drifted, and shaking his head, he began to stuff a fresh pipe.

"Couldn't they have decided all this before, so that we could make adequate preparations?"

"And tip off the Germans?" Campbell shook his head. "No, we had to wait to the very last minute. Besides, with the pounding Malta's been taking, headquarters had only so much support available. They wanted to make absolutely sure before they committed it to us. But now that they have, we have to get cracking."

Ross looked up at him, startled. "You aren't suggesting what I think you're suggesting—"

"We go in tonight, Pudge. An air strike drawing on all available forces from every air base within flying distance—Malta, Cyprus, Port Said, Beirut."

"But that's a major effort!" Ross exclaimed.

"The old man has given us blanket authority to call on any combat unit we may need. They'll be placed under our direct command."

"Two squadrons of B-17 bombers arrived from the States the other day," Ross said tentatively. "But the crews are fresh from training at Randolph Field, in Texas. They've had no combat experience."

"A deficiency," the brigadier said with a short laugh, "that will soon be corrected in the skies over Piraeus."

But Ross looked troubled. "Can't we postpone it until daylight? You know we're virtually helpless at night. We'll have to come in low, beneath the firing range of the ack-ack, even lower if there's heavy weather. We can put it off to dawn and still have plenty of time—"

Campbell shook his head. "Even if we were sure of the Jerries' hour of departure, and we're not, a daylight operation would be much more hazardous. German anti-aircraft installations are too strong, and from what Cunningham has told us, their gunners are too damned accurate. Dammit, Pudge, I know everything you say is true. We can't go in by day because we'll get blasted and we can't go in by night because we can't see what we're bombing. That's why as soon as Cunningham laid it out for me a few days back, I told him his first order of business was to find some way to pinpoint the harbor so that when the attack order came—and I knew it was only a question of when—we *would* be able to see what we were bombing."

"And did he?"

"He has a complete set of beacon signals ready to go whenever we give the word. From what he says, they'll be better than a seeing-eye dog to lead us dead on target."

"I hope he's right," Ross said wryly, "because we'll certainly be coming in blind." He thought a moment. "Ashcroft will want to command this mission himself, and I'll fly with him."

At the brigadier's objection, he smiled. "Not to worry, Ian, we were classmates at Sandhurst and we've been to two flying schools together. Ashcroft won't mind."

"I will," Campbell said. "One look at the scope of the operation should tell you that. No, you're needed right here, Pudge. I require an experienced airman to coordinate all the angles of this strike. And you'll have your

181

hands full. Good thing those B-17's have been serviced and staffed. We barely have time for a briefing as it is."

"In that case, I'd better get on it straight away."

"Oh, Pudge."

Ross had already started out the door, and turned. "Yes, sir?"

"I know how much you must have wanted to fly this one."

"Yes, sir," said Ross.

"But there are two men absolutely indispensable to the success of this mission," Campbell said. "You're one of them."

Ross smiled. "If I know Cunningham, he'd be delighted to be spared the honor of being the other."

21

Colonel Schneider pulled apart the double blackout curtains of the Port Authorities Building and stepped outside. He looked up at the sky. It was the worst weather imaginable. He wanted clouds, heavy clouds. He wanted haze, mist, fog—anything. But thanks to the cool sirocco breeze blowing in from the south, all he saw were a few clouds—and a full moon.

The moon seemed to light up the harbor for miles. And Schneider, who was responsible for all troop movements and security inside the port area, was sure he could make out his patrols clear across the port; but he knew that on the night before a mission the mind can play tricks. Still he was worried. He had twenty-three ships and seven destroyers just sitting there, loaded and helpless, a perfect target for a British attack. And all because some idiot had picked the morning after a full moon to set sail.

He knew the culprit—Rear Admiral von Widdemer, the navy commander, had overruled his suggestion that the loaded ships leave the harbor immediately and at least moor in the Gulf of Phaliron, three miles east of the port and just the other side of the Kastela, until the convoy was ready to move. But the admiral, with his Prussian attention to military precision, had insisted the convoy remain intact until loading was completed, and for that purpose the harbor was ideal. Schneider didn't press the point. He knew that navigating so many ships through the breakwater was a difficult maneuver, demanding enough to require each ship be assigned its own Greek pilot; for that reason nighttime departure, which would have presented Schneider with much less of a problem, was always out of the question. Well, in spite of command stupidities, he would not rest easy until he saw the last ship past the mine cables and out the Straits of Salamis.

Johann Schneider ran his hand through his close-cropped graying hair. He was in his fifties with only a hint of a paunch; his bearing was erect, his manner crisp, and he wore his uniform with flair. He enjoyed nothing more than being mistaken for a Prussian aristocrat, but he couldn't fool real Prussians like von Widdemer, the hereditary rulers of the Wehrmacht hierarchy. They knew he was a soft Bavarian, the product of a middle-class mercantile background. He had been slated for obscure retirement when the war broke out; with the shortage of senior officers, he had been promoted and given the military command of Piraeus.

Although his authority was always subject to the approval of his superior in Athens, General von Schlichter, Schneider now had power, influence, and prestige. Though he realized he probably never would attain the rank of general officer, he would be a man of substance when he retired, respected by his neighbors in the Bavarian town where his father had been a storekeeper. Until that hopefully distant time he was relishing life as he had imagined it when he entered the Wehrmacht as a cadet. Those were the days between the wars when Germany, forbidden to build a standing army, had to disguise the very existence of military academies. As commandant of Piraeus, he had authority, more money than he had ever

183

known, luxuries beyond his dreams and a lovely young Austrian mistress, who helped him forget his stupid, overweight wife at home with her two grown, obese daughters, who would never marry. And he had no intention of jeopardizing all this because of the ineptitude of a Prussian admiral.

Schneider returned inside just as von Widdemer was bidding farewell to the captains of the Italian, German, Bulgarian, and Rumanian vessels that made up the convoy. Reminding them he would see them shortly at the dance at the Palace Hotel, he told the colonel he wanted a word with him.

Schneider always hated it when superiors used that tone with him.

"My successes are not accidental," the admiral began. "They always are solidly based on the laws of probability. For example, it would seem most improbable if the British were unaware of the convoy we're assembling to reinforce Field Marshal Rommel."

Schneider smiled. "The British are fully informed," he said. "Our communications people have picked up a number of wireless messages to Cairo in the past forty-eight hours."

"Indeed? And where are they?"

"They haven't been decoded yet, Admiral," Schneider said without apology. "They're evidently using a new code. We've forwarded the communications to Berlin, and our own staff is working on them here. In the meantime, I have detailed men to locate the sending set."

The furrows in von Widdemer's forehead deepened. "The navy," he said icily, "remembers the destruction of three tankers in the Piraeus harbor last December. I hope the army has not forgotten that incident."

Schneider nodded. "It was an embarrassment to us as well as to you. But you may also recall, Admiral, that within minutes after the explosion we did away with the gang of saboteurs who committed the crime."

"It would be more than an embarrassment if anything were to prevent this convoy from reaching Rommel," the admiral said. "The Führer himself has charged me with the responsibility of seeing this operation to a successful conclusion."

"Nothing can go wrong," Schneider said. "Every precaution has been taken. All Greeks have been barred from the port area, which has been placed off limits. Anyone who tries to enter must have a pass personally signed by me. The harbor has been mined. And every crate, every package, every piece of cargo being loaded on board the ships is being thoroughly inspected for explosives. The Wehrmacht is taking no chances."

Von Widdemer made no attempt to conceal his exasperation. "But, Schneider, if the British already know our plans they cannot afford to miss this opportunity."

"We realize it," Schneider said complacently. "And we are ready for them. Anti-aircraft gunners are at their stations, and all stations are on full alert. And blackout precautions are being strictly enforced in the unlikely event the British attempt a night strike. All signal battalions have been instructed not to switch on their searchlights in the event they hear planes overhead. Even our decoy beacons have been ordered blacked out. The British will have no way of knowing when, or whether, they are over the port."

"On a clear night, Colonel? Under a full moon?"

"Scheduling the sailing at this time of month is unfortunate, Admiral, but that decision was not mine. It was made by the navy, I believe."

The Piraeus commandant spoke the truth, and the admiral had no reply. The departure date of the convoy could not be delayed now that the Führer had personally promised Rommel his reinforcements.

Schneider could not help pressing his advantage. "The Wehrmacht is well aware that the convoy will be vulnerable, and so we have taken additional steps to make it impossible for a British raid to succeed, even on a clear night."

The admiral looked at him with interest.

"General von Schlichter has sent me one of the most

ingenious machines ever developed by the Third Reich. It produces smoke, in great volume. Two such machines would be sufficient to blanket the entire Piraeus harbor from invading aircraft, but to be on the safe side we ordered four. They had been emplaced, and like the anti-aircraft batteries, the crews have received their instructions."

The army appeared to be well enough prepared, but the admiral could not rid himself of a nagging worry. No less an authority than Admiral Canaris, head of all German Military Intelligence, had warned him that the British Intelligence command in Cairo was not to be underestimated, and there was every reason to believe they had infiltrated some of their top agents into Greece. If so, that probably meant they were right here in Piraeus, watching the Germans' every move, and planning some way to stop the convoy.

Yet General von Schlichter had seemed unconcerned, too, when the admiral had discussed his fears with him yesterday, and von Schlichter, unlike this bureaucrat Schneider, was an exceptionally able officer. Well, all the admiral could hope was that the general knew of additional precautions the Wehrmacht was taking, even behind the back of the Piraeus command. Although he was no admirer of Heinrich Himmler, who was becoming the most powerful man in the Third Reich, this was one time when von Widdemer would have welcomed the intervention of the Gestapo. Perhaps that was what General von Schlichter had meant yesterday when he had said, "Stop worrying. Your convoy is going to receive the best of all possible care."

22

Major Cunningham had provided Petros Zervas with false identity papers, the best Cairo could prepare, and a full disguise. The former Petros accepted but not the latter. He had his own disguise, and if ever he were to put it to the test, tonight was the night. During the day it was almost impossible to imitate a zombie successfully. At night you had a better chance, depending on how far you could keep from German patrols and how strong your nerves were when they scrutinized you.

Assuming his zombie's stance, dressed in an overcoat a few sizes too large to make him look emaciated, Petros shuffled by Saint Speridon's Church and passed the guard at the gate without causing suspicion. Tonight was the night he was born for. Tonight, on Kastela Hill, all the preparations of a lifetime would be tested. Nothing must stand in his way—nothing! Ahead three Germans blocked his path. They inspected him closely, ran their hands in front of his face, but Petros' eyes remained focused at a distance. The soldiers had heard about such people, and one of them poked his finger against Petros' chest. When there was no reaction, he pointed him toward an alley and gave him a shove.

Careful to maintain his measured pace, Petros made his way down the alley. Suddenly the night reverberated with the sound of crashing trash cans and loud cursing. Petros stopped, undecided whether to risk the main street with its danger of patrols, but finally decided to continue down the alley and take his chances with whatever lay ahead.

Nico Andreades had gone through half a dozen trash cans, neatly stacked outside the German mess hall by Greek volunteer kitchen help. As each came up empty, Nico would hurl it aside and reach for the next. The cans had been picked clean. Even so, Nico kept burrowing through them, one by one, in hopes some morsel, some leaving, somehow had been overlooked.

At the sight of the approaching figure shuffling forward in the persistent slow pace of the zombie, he dropped the can he had raised over his head, letting it crash and come to a noisy rolling stop against the corrugated metal back door of a shop. He strode into the middle of the alley and at the top of his voice warned off the intruder:

"You there, keep away. There's nothing here to eat, nothing for a creature like you. Keep away, do you hear me?"

Petros lengthened his stride even as he felt the cool beads of perspiration on his forehead. If the Germans hadn't heard the crash of the cans, they couldn't help but hear the man now. Petros couldn't run and he couldn't continue; he was in the middle of a block and the Germans could approach from either side.

"I warn you, don't come any closer," shouted Nico. "If you're looking for food you won't find any here."

They weren't human, these creatures; they belonged in the bad dream of the little girl. He backed up to the door of the vacant shop, and his voice echoed against the bare walls and ceiling: "This is my final warning. Keep away or you'll be sorry."

The figure kept coming.

The shouting made Petros feel as if his head was inside a ringing bell. The desire to escape this rolling sound tightened his nerves. He sprang forward and, clamping his left hand tight over the man's mouth and his right around his waist, he carried him through the door and dropped him inside the empty shop.

The alley was silent. No bootsteps could be heard. Petros reached into his coat lining and out came his stiletto. The metallic snap echoed from the bare walls of the shop, and Nico knew.

"This is the one time I could kill you without regret," Petros whispered.

Nico pointed to the hand that covered his mouth, but Petros did not remove it.

"This is the night I was born for." Petros' voice rose above a whisper. "All these years, I've lived for this night and nobody is going to get in my way. Understand?"

Nico pried Petros' fingers away and this time Petros released him. Nico crawled to the window as Petros watched him, stiletto in full view.

"Petros . . ." Nico said, "Petros." And the tears started to cut through the dry blood on his face. "Kill me if you want, I don't care. But before you do, you must tell me what happened."

Petros knew what was coming and said nothing.

"It's not for me. It's for the others. The others who are gone now and who won't rest in peace until they know." He wiped away the tears, leaving a blur of red on his cheeks. "You and your English friends were supposed to be waiting for us. Where in God's name did you go? You said we had plenty of time. What happened? Petros, they were only kids. Twelve- and thirteen-year-old kids. All of them had a chance to make it through this war. They were young, strong. . . . Why in hell did we find Germans waiting for us instead of you? Why? . . ."

Nico spat tears from his mouth. "Petros, the reason I'm not a ghost is that I was too slow. The others pulled ahead of me, and they got it instead of me. They went out there because they trusted me. I told them I trusted you but the ships blew up early. Why? Petros, I want the truth."

What could he say? That he tried to swim out to them? That the mines blew up prematurely? That he didn't know, that even Cunningham said he didn't know? How could he expect Nico to believe him, when he himself still wasn't sure exactly what happened?

"I went out there for you too," Nico was saying. "Not just for your gold."

The empty store was silent; gone were the owner, the customers, the dried fish, cheese, rice, lottery tickets, and plenty of wine. He could remember the prices from childhood. One drachma for a lottery ticket. One drachma for a pound of cheese. Two drachmas for a bottle of retsina. . . .

How much for a life? Nothing. Life cost nothing at all.

Petros kept one ear cocked to the street. He still didn't know what to say to Nico. How could he explain that Nico had been the only one who could do the job, the sort of job that did not care about friendship, or even life, a job that had to be done at all costs. Petros and Cunningham had a job to do. Their job was not to protect friends, their job was to destroy enemies. How do you measure a few lives against a ship carrying ammunition enough to kill thousands? Very simple arithmetic. Cunningham had solved the problem easily.

"Did you ever look for me after I blew up your ship?" Nico was asking. "The next day or the day after?"

"We heard what had happened to you. We didn't see any reason to look around."

Suddenly Nico said: "How much money do you have, Petros?"

So that was it! Petros found this new tack easier to handle. "What's that to you?"

"Don't you pay the people you send out and who come back alive?"

"Yes," said Petros carefully. "If they come back alive and we're able to find them."

"Well," Nico said, straightening up, "I contracted to do a job and I think I should get paid for it."

Petros laughed. "Surely you don't think I carry such amounts around with me."

"I want to get paid."

"And so you shall, my friend. Tomorrow I promise you will get paid in full."

"You are not saying this to keep me from yelling and bringing back the Germans, are you?"

"You worked for it. You did the job for us . . . what more is there to say? I know you need the money."

"Do you mind if I tag along? Because I'd hate to get betrayed again. I'm not the kind who would go for that twice—you should know me by now—I was your friend."

"I've always been your friend, Nico."

"Friend?" Nico cried. "Since when did you dump your friends in the water for fish bait? No, you aren't my friend, Petros. I'm just someone to use—well, you used me and now you'll pay me not only my share but the share of those you and I betrayed. My friend"—he spat out the word—"I can read your mind. You have only one choice left. Kill me now or be prepared to have me follow you until Judas pays off Judas."

"A few minutes ago I had a choice, but not now." Petros smiled bitterly and pressed the stiletto's slim blade against the windowpane, making it disappear inside its ivory handle. "Nico Andreades, long ago fate rolled the dice for us and we became friends. We had regard for one another and there was no leader. You had your likes and I had mine—different likes in many ways. You had a family, I never had a family. I don't know my name; they just picked someone in the orphanage, accused him, and gave me his name. He was convenient. I felt the way to be loved was to become important, so I became important and I was loved because I was the leader. I loved and respected no one because any one of them, at any time, could take my place and I would again be a nobody. And this is when you came into my life. I was not afraid of you and I opened up to you . . . my fears, my ambitions . . . all this we had, Nico. Now you tell me I've changed."

"You have changed!" Nico cried.

Petros shook his head. "No, you're the one who has changed. Look at you. You're not my friend now, you are a beggar. I'm not your friend now because you fell into the trap you think I set for you. It was unfortunate you had to see eight kids drown in their own blood, kids who were probably friends and who had done this thing just for fun, the way you and I would have done it at their age. I cried for you and the kids. But Nico, I want you to know that for what I did to you and to them . . . and whatever responsibility I may have for their death . . . I am not and I will not plead guilty. I lost no one in this war because I had no one to lose. I had one friend, you, and I've lost you. And I look around me and what do I see, Nico? I see friends friends no longer . . . families families no longer . . . kids growing old overnight . . . innocent girls turning into whores . . . and seeing all this, my friend I won't plead guilty, I can't plead guilty to what I did or what I'm going to do. For the lives I helped take I am not guilty . . . for sending you out there I am not guilty . . . and looking at you now I pity the man I respected and still I feel no guilt. If I had killed you with my own hands a few minutes ago I would have felt no guilt now, and if I should find it necessary to kill you, Nico, or anyone else, you can be sure I will not feel guilty, because I, Petros Zervas, have no choice left."

Nico tried to understand his friend's attempt to justify his ruthlessness. Petros spoke in generalities, Nico in specifics. Petros saw mountains, Nico saw pebbles. "Who in hell gave you the right to become judge and chief executioner?"

"I see what people have become," Petros said. "I know that a terrible evil is running wild and either you stop it yourself or you send others to do it. True, a certain number will die, but someone . . . someone is going to make it."

"After the eight kids and God knows how many others?"

"After the eight, ten, or twenty. There's no morality left now, only numbers. Arithmetic is all that counts. You and I and all the others are numbers on a slate that can be added or subtracted. You and I and the others . . . a few numbers—and how they love to subtract."

"You are not God, Petros Zervas. If you are out for revenge, go kill your own Nazis, Fascists, or whoever you blame and accuse. But you have no right to wipe innocent people off your slate with this arithmetic of yours just to serve your own purposes."

Petros felt a sudden need to try to make himself clear to Nico. "It is not I who wipe numbers off the slate. I am offering the chance to end this insanity of man. Why should people no longer live as human beings, why must they suffer, why must they die? Listen carefully and you'll hear all the voices asking one simple question: 'Why?' "

Nico said nothing, for he had nothing to say. He thought of Taki. He thought of the little girl. He thought of his friend who was no longer his friend.

The empty shop was silent but Petros could not hear Nico. Nico did not say the word. He moved his lips but he did not say it aloud: "Why?"

23

An insistent rapping sounded at the door to Trudi's apartment. How many times had she told the sentry downstairs to announce her visitors? The only exception was Johann, but tonight he was at the Yacht Club preparing for the farewell party for the convoy commanders. She was late getting ready herself; irritatedly she snapped on the lights and opened the door to the last person in the world she wanted to see at this or any moment. Wearing the insignia of a lieutenant-colonel on his black Gestapo uniform, a sardonic smile on his face, was Willy Streck.

Streck was short and slender; and in civilian attire—if one did not look carefully—he seemed insignificant. His dark hair was long, in obvious disregard of the standards of the Wehrmacht, but carefully combed. His uniform was freshly pressed, his boots gleamed, his fingernails were manicured, and he was doused with his favorite French cologne. His eyes were unusually steady, and few people were able to withstand his unblinking gaze for more than a moment or two. He habitually wore glasses set in heavy tortoise-shell rather than the steel frames that were Wehrmacht issue. Behind those glasses the pale, clear eyes never expanded or contracted, never revealed inner thoughts or feelings, even when he laughed or was irritated. "Heil Hitler," he said laconically.

"Heil Hitler." Trudi forced a smile, habit causing her to echo his private joke, but inside she felt the sudden panic well up in her. Of all the men she had ever known, Willy alone could inspire such instant, overpowering, unthinking fear.

Streck carefully closed the door behind him, then took her into his arms and kissed her deeply. Trudi tried to simulate equal longing. He was not the type who would be pleased to discover his advances were unwelcome.

"You appear well, Trudi *liebschen,*" he said almost impersonally, as he released her. "Permit me to look at you."

She led him into the living room, and old habits returning automatically, she pirouetted like a model for his inspection. At one time she had thought Willy needed the reassurance of a beautiful girl, but she had gradually learned not to guess at his motives; whatever his reasons, it was always wise to humor him.

"Positively radiant," he said. "And you have gained no weight, I see. Don't tell me Schneider keeps you on the same starvation rations he does his Greeks?" He laughed at his own joke.

"You know me, Willy," she said. "I eat and I eat but I can't seem to put on a pound." She knew he liked his women slender. He hadn't changed physically, either; and he still brandished that same polite, slightly condescending smile. She asked when he had arrived in Piraeus.

"I flew to Athens this noon. Yesterday I was in Berlin where I had a brief meeting with the Führer himself; last night I spent in your lovely Vienna, lovelier than ever under the Third Reich, and now—I am here."

She inclined her head in congratulations. Certainly he was acquainted with Hitler; and Himmler, she knew, regarded him as one of his most promising lieutenants. The influence Willy exerted was vast—and growing.

"I telephoned a little earlier, but you didn't answer," he continued. "I knew you wouldn't be out long, since your Colonel Schneider is a very busy fellow tonight, so I decided to come over and surprise you myself."

Trudi felt herself tense. A rush of memories returned—the forgotten fear that grew to terror whenever she had dared to do anything on her own—Willy liked to keep her on a tight leash, and she had never known when or whether he was keeping her under observation. The mere possibility that he might know of her present activities made her blood run cold.

"Well, you certainly succeeded in surprising me," she said with a light laugh. "Johann didn't say a word about you coming. Can I get you a drink?"

"He didn't know. Coffee only, if it's no trouble."

She knew he was working; Willy never touched liquor in any form, not even beer, when on duty. She went off to the kitchen to put up the coffee, and while there tried to get herself under control. There was no reason for apprehension. Willy didn't fly from Berlin to Piraeus just to check up on her.

He was sitting in an easy chair when she returned, his legs extended and resting on the heels of his boots. "Where *did* you spend the evening, *liebschen?*" As nearly as she could judge, it was an idle question.

Still, Trudi knew she had to remain on her guard. His seemingly casual questions could quickly become searching, and it would be child's play for him to wrest the truth from her. "What can one do in Piraeus?" she parried. "The coffee in the cafés is frightful. You must try it, just for the experience. They make it from pistachio nuts, I hear. And of course they no longer serve food."

He listened without comment.

Trudi knew she was jabbering, and warned herself not to appear anxious. "In my position one has few friends." She shrugged prettily. "So what is there for me to do? I stay home, and for an exciting change I take solitary walks, avoiding the Greeks, and then come home."

"Don't tell me you haven't been able to find a young Wehrmacht officer to offer you companionship and conversation? After all, what Schneider doesn't know won't hurt him."

"Really, Willy!"

"The Wehrmacht must be getting as soft as they say—which is why more and more responsibility is falling to the Gestapo. Why, in my day a young officer would risk everything for a brief liaison with a colonel's lady, especially one as exciting as you, *liebschen*. One look into those lovely, green eyes, and any man, any real man, would be lost."

Was he merely teasing her, or baiting her for some more sinister purpose? "I am faithful to Johann, just as I was to you, Willy," she said evenly.

Streck smiled but made no comment.

Trudi returned to the kitchen for the strong, black coffee she knew he liked. Even as she poured it, her hand refused to stop shaking. It was the worst time in the world for him to turn up in her life. She had too much to hide, and he was too shrewd, too persistent, as many underground operatives had learned to their regret. And if they couldn't escape from Willy, how in the world could she hope to?

She had an overwhelming urge to flee, as she placed the cup on the table beside him.

"Is it permissible to tell what brings you to Piraeus?" she asked, "or is it a secret matter?" He had rarely discussed his work with her, and actually she was just as happy not to know any details.

Willy stirred, and for the first time spoke in other than a lazy drawl. "The General Staff has been nervous about the operation we've been mounting here."

For a moment she didn't quite know what he meant. Streck saw her expression and laughed. "Really, *liebschen,* you never fail to amaze me. No one else in the whole of Greece could be unaware of the fact that we are sending a convoy of troops and supplies to Rommel."

"Oh, that," Trudi said.

"That, as you put it, and the annoying fact that the Greeks have begun to put together an underground organization, and they're getting help—more help than a great many people realize, including your friend Schneider—from the British. There are certain key Greek saboteurs—

and while we don't know who they are, we will. It's only a question of time."

"And that's why you're here, Willy?"

"Rommel has an urgent need for these troops and supplies."

Trudi assumed that meant yes.

Streck smiled. "They've sent the foxhound after the fox."

The fear she had felt growing ever since he first appeared crested, and carefully she lowered herself into a chair.

So his visit wasn't accidental! The foxhound was hot on the scent of its prey, and if she knew Willy, the chase would be short, efficient, and merciless. No fox was any match for this foxhound.

Especially Petros Zervas. . . .

For a long time after the incident with the tankers last winter she had not seen a trace of Petros. She didn't know whether he was alive or dead. The Germans still listed him as "deceased," and this time, for all she knew, it might be true. Security had intensified all along the port of Piraeus ever since the raid, and even if Petros had survived Trudi knew he would not be fool enough to risk being seen around the city. She had tried—how she had tried!—to erase him from her thoughts, her feelings, but for once her will could not be controlled. She kept seeing him—physically *seeing* him: his hands, his mouth, those remarkable eyes—she felt him about her like an invisible presence. One month went by, two, but instead of disappearing the obsession grew. She became irritable, nervous. Even Johann noticed it, but passed it off as heightened concern for his growing responsibilities. She had never felt anything like this before—it was as if she was anticipating his appearance wherever she went, in the most unlikely places. Every time she went to the kitchen in German headquarters. On street corners in Piraeus. She even manufactured some excuse for Hans to drive her past the empty schoolhouse, but the place looked completely deserted.

Then one night, shortly after Johann had left her apartment to return to headquarters, she parted the drapes leading to her little balcony and saw a dark shape on the far side of the glass move. It was the figure of a man.

He came closer to the glass and she recognized the blue-eyed Greek.

"Are you mad, hiding out there? Do you know what the sentries would do if they saw you? What are you doing here anyway? Where have you been all this time?"

As she unlocked the door her questions came thick and fast, and all at once she found herself crying. She wanted to throw herself into his arms but he just stood there, grinning at her like some idiot boy.

"Don't you know the building is guarded by armed sentries?" she said, caught up in this inane conversation and unable to stop.

His grin only widened.

"The only Greeks allowed inside must have special passes signed by the military police."

He walked over to her, and raised her chin until she was looking into those deep blue eyes. "Did anyone ever tell you you talked too much," he said, and lowered his lips to hers.

It was as though he had never left; no, this time it was stronger, deeper. The days, the empty nights with Johann, were obscenities. She realized she had been marking time until the Greek would come back, until the Greek must come back—

Afterward she saw him out the way he came in—by the balcony. "That's the secret," he said with a laugh. "You need passes to get into the building. But not to get out."

One minute he was there, and the next gone. She stared over the balcony, but the night was too dark for her to see clearly. She thought she caught a glimpse of a shadowy figure on the fourth floor, then on the third. After that she could not make him out at all. The man had a genius for making himself invisible.

Since then she had seen him often, but on an irregular basis and usually in the storeroom of the empty school, which he continued to make his headquarters when in Piraeus. At her insistence he no longer came to the apartment, as the dangers were too great and she would be ruined if they were ever discovered together there, although Trudi knew that Petros meant serious trouble for her, no matter where they met. Once he had taken her to a secret hideaway, as he called it, atop Kastela Hill. There he had told her a fantastic story about a whore named Lela and how she had initiated an impossible number of young boys into manhood. It was like so many of his tales—pure fabrication, with himself as hero, of course. But she had to admit the view from his hideaway was magnificent, with the city and port spread out below— and it was a perfect spot for young lovers.

And she felt young with him. Not since she was a mere girl had she imagined such complete abandon. Even now, hours later, and here in the same room with Willy Streck, she could still feel his presence from their afternoon together. She could always tell when he was about to undertake some dangerous mission; excitement sharpened and intensified his desire for her, and this afternoon he had taken her in his arms so hungrily, with near desperation, she trembled for his safety. Trudi never failed to be astounded at the fervor with which she responded to him. At first she attributed it to an understandable reaction to the cold, mechanical advances of Johann Schneider; she was a desirable, normal young woman, with healthy, unsatisfied desires. But she knew it was more than that. It was as if the two met naked in soul as well as body; they became one in their wild, free—totally free—outpouring of emotion. With Petros she felt vibrant, adolescently eager to experience everything, try anything. Forgotten was all caution, all self-protection (what had happened to that wall?); in those unreal moments, when she felt more herself than ever before, she became totally vulnerable, totally his.

This afternoon she had responded to his demands with

an urgency of her own, matching his soaring passion, his savagery—sinking her nails deep into his shoulder, gripping him to her fiercely as he drove into her body, the muscles of his back and thighs bunching and releasing.

Suddenly, as she felt a great scream about to well through her body, Petros stopped.

She opened her eyes to see his face above hers, his eyes gleaming.

"Today is the day I was born for!" he cried, triumphantly. It was as if he were some stranger lost in a wild secret climax of his own. She tried to pull him back to her, but he looked down at her with distant eyes and all at once began speaking in a tone she had never heard him use before, saying things he knew she never wanted to hear—

Did she have any idea who he really was? Petros Zervas, her blue-eyed Greek, did she have even the faintest notion of what he had done? To say nothing of what he was going to do? She knew him only as a black-marketeer, pilfering gasoline. Gasoline! What would she say to sabotage? What would she say if he told her that he, Petros Zervas, had masterminded the sinking of those three tankers last winter? He had rounded up the young Greek swimmers; he had supplied them with limpets to do the job!

She tried to burrow into his shoulder, to drown out the sound of his voice. He had always kept his activities to himself; she had never heard him talk like this. He seemed remote, transfixed by his own power. She had known many dangerous men—God knows, one of the most dangerous was here in this very room—but none had frightened her as much as this wild-eyed Greek.

But everything was only the buildup, he was saying, for tonight. Oh yes, he had laughed, he knew all about the convoy to North Africa. He rattled off the number of ships, their nationality, the scheduled time of departure tomorrow morning. Only they would never make it—he had a plan to stop them! Tonight, from his secret hideaway on Kastela Hill, Petros Zervas would make sure the convoy never set sail.

She wanted to stop her ears—she had got through the war by *not* knowing things, by *not* listening to the military secrets that made up the daily fabric of Johann's and Willy's lives.

The thickness began to ease in Petros' voice. His eyes softened as he stroked her damp body. In spite of herself— even after his frightening display of anger—Trudi found herself responding to his caress. Dear God, what kind of animal was she? And softly, persuasively, as his hands roamed her body, his voice purred on. He was talking about Kastela Hill—did she remember the night they spent in the hideaway? Did she remember how the whole of Piraeus lay at her feet? He kept stroking Trudi, stroking her face, her neck, her shoulders, the soft blonde down of her arm, which like tender grass rose involuntarily under his caressing fingers.

Well, tonight from their hideaway, he said, kissing her breasts, sending great chills through her body, he was going to destroy the German convoy. He alone had devised the means to seal their doom. What a blow for the Germans! What a blow to Rommel! It could change the war! And tonight, after the job was done, he wanted her to join him at the hideaway and see for herself. He would be waiting for her, waiting to show her how he, Petros Zervas, had destroyed a German fleet singlehandedly.

Even as she lay gasping under him, she searched his eyes, trying to make out whether he was serious; whether —if he succeeded was something else again—he really did plan some action against the convoy. Wild as he sounded, some of the things he said had the ring of truth. She still could remember the way Johann had arrived at her apartment an hour late the night of the tanker sinkings. Wearily he had dropped on the couch and for a long time remained silent. For once even her sensuality failed to arouse him. And then slowly he began to talk. He had tried to seek some consolation in the rapidity with which they had executed the saboteurs—children, Schneider kept repeating in a shocked voice; how can you fight an enemy that will sacrifice its own children? But though he hung the young corpses in Koral Square as a grim lesson to the Greeks, he never had discovered what kind of explosives were used or how they were employed. The destruction had been complete, leaving no clues. Yet what had Petros called them—limpets? And obviously he seemed to know other details of the sinkings.

Good God, what if Petros were telling the truth! What if he *had* been responsible for destroying the tankers? And what if he really did intend to stop the convoy tonight? One thing she knew for certain: under no circumstances was she about to join him on Kastela Hill. If what he said was true the last person she wanted to see tonight—or any night—was Petros Zervas.

Now, hearing Willy's words, she felt a cold dread. With Willy after Petros, all was lost. What would happen to her when he caught the blue-eyed Greek? Would he talk? Would she talk if the situation were reversed?

She looked up to hear Willy still speaking.

"I've been put in charge of counterintelligence for the reinforcement convoy. I'll cross to North Africa with the troops and deliver them personally to Rommel."

—And suddenly Trudi knew what she must do! She couldn't take a chance. Dangerous as it was, calling attention to herself as it would, tonight was one night she must get away from Piraeus. If what Petros had said was true, and he planned some attack, it would have to take place before morning. God knows what could happen . . . with the wild Greek . . . with Willy on the loose . . . with the biggest fleet ever to assemble in this tiny Greek port. Anything could happen, anything could go wrong. But most of all she sensed that everything she had struggled and schemed and sacrificed to preserve—her safety, her life itself—she was in danger of losing if she remained behind. This night let fate be kind to Trudi. Let foxhound and fox, Germans and British and Greeks, destroy themselves if they had a mind to. She, at least, would be sure she was out of danger, and far, far away.

"Trudi, my dear, what's wrong?" said Willy, putting down his coffee and coming over to her. "You're so pale."

He reached for her hand. "Why, your fingers are cold as ice." He smiled. "I must say I'm somewhat flattered at your concern for my safety, but there's nothing to fear, I assure you. A short sea voyage, and in a few days I'll be back and then we will have more time to spend together. How does that sound to you, my dear?"

She smiled absently, using his solicitousness as an excuse to gather her wits. I *must* get away tonight! After the dance, I must come up with some excuse. Maybe I can get Hans to drive me to Athens. I can stay in Athens until I know whether it's safe to return—

"Perhaps I can even arrange to have Schneider sent on a field inspection trip for a few days."

No! The adrenaline was working: her mind was suddenly clear. She must not be left alone with Willy. She shook her head quickly, perhaps too quickly.

Streck was somewhat annoyed. "Perhaps you should reconsider. You may be interested to know that your Schneider is under considerable pressure not to repeat the blunder he committed with those tankers last winter. I shall tell you something in confidence, *liebschen*. If your colonel fails to provide the convoy with the proper protection, I shall have him sent into retirement and put someone I trust in his place. Much has happened since you and I last saw each other. The highest authorities listen to us now—not the Wehrmacht."

But Trudi didn't have the strength, cunning, or courage for a new liaison with Willy. There were already two men in her life, and she couldn't handle a third as well, even if that third were an ordinary man. But the truth was that Willy simply could not be handled at all. Besides, as soon as he discovered that his mistress had been sleeping with a Greek, a common Greek (and Willy would learn it somehow, she was absolutely certain of it)—her mind refused to imagine what would happen.

She had to take a firm stand now, right now, before things drifted too far. Trying not to lean on the arm of the chair she rose to her feet. "I would not be pleased if Johann were sent away on an inspection trip, Willy. In fact," she marveled at her daring, but she had no choice, "I'm afraid I would have to tell Johann of your proposal."

He stared at her incredulously for a moment, and then his peal of deep laughter filled the room. "Trudi, Trudi, you *are* the complete innocent. But so refreshing. I can't remember when anyone has had the nerve to threaten me." He stood and gazed hard at her, his eyes still revealing nothing. "Do you know, you only make yourself all the more attractive to me, so that I am determined to see you again."

Trudi dug her fingernails into the palms of her hands to maintain her control.

"Our little reunion will be perfect," Streck said. "With caviar from Russia, champagne from France, Bavarian liver dumplings, Polish ham. And," he gave her a correct bow, "the most delectable of Austrian women."

Maybe she could find some way in Athens never to have to return here.

"You seem to have forgotten the months we spent together, *liebschen*. Your lack of response surprises me."

"I'll never forget them, Willy," she said sincerely, for her meaning was not the same as his. "When we were together, you were my only lover. You gave me to Johann, and now I owe him the same loyalty that I gave to you."

"Your faithfulness is inspiring." He picked up his cap with the gold-encrusted peak, and glanced at his watch. "Like your Colonel Schneider I have a busy night ahead of me. I had hoped we might celebrate a little reunion before I go back to my labors, but that is not to be."

"I'm sorry, Willy," Trudi said. "But I'm sure you understand."

"Oh, I do, *liebschen*. I understand far more than you know. Heil Hitler!" He raised his arm in the stiff Nazi salute, and departed.

Trudi hurried to the phone.

Ilse Brugger seated herself at Colonel Schneider's desk and lit up one of the little cigars Hilde regularly sent her from Munich. It was quiet and deserted here in the headquarters villa, in welcome contrast to the confusion and discomfort of their temporary offices in the Yacht Club. Like everyone else at headquarters she had been working without respite for forty-eight hours, and now while everyone else was celebrating at the farewell party at the Palace Hotel she would attend to some last-minute details and get some sleep. She'd need it; tomorrow would be a long day, with the convoy scheduled to sail before noon.

Maybe after the convoy had reached Rommel, and Operation Aïda was successfully underway, she could steal a short leave. A week with Hilde would be a wonderful change after the dreary life of this godforsaken Greek port.

The phone rang. Surprised that anyone would be calling headquarters when everyone was at the Yacht Club, she picked up the receiver.

"Why, Fräulein Trudi. I thought you were at the Palace entertaining our brave convoy commanders."

"I'm just about to leave, Ilse, but I'm trying to find Hans. Do you have any idea where he might be?"

"Hans? Hardly." Brugger laughed. "He's off duty tonight because the colonel needs him tomorrow. I suppose we could try all the taverns. Or perhaps the brothels might be better in his case. Why, Trudi, is something wrong?"

"I need a car tonight."

"Of course. Someone should be coming at any moment to take you to the party."

"Not now," Trudi said. "I need it later. It's extremely urgent."

Brugger sat up in her chair and carefully stubbed out her cigar. "But isn't that most unusual, Fräulein? Can't it wait until morning?"

"I must go tonight," insisted the voice over the phone. "If I can't get Hans, I'll just have to drive myself."

"But I can't possibly find a car at this hour. Besides"—and here Brugger automatically lowered her voice—"with the convoy scheduled to depart, every vehicle is spoken for."

"I'm sure you can arrange it, Ilse. It's vital."

"I see," said Brugger, scribbling something on a pad of paper. "I assume Colonel Schneider knows of this sudden excursion?"

"Colonel Schneider has nothing to do with this." Trudi's voice was sharp. "But he will if you don't get me transportation!"

"But Trudi," Brugger said soothingly, "you know that without his authorization, especially on such short notice and on something so irregular—"

Brugger heard Trudi's sigh of exasperation. "Very well, Ilse, I suppose I do owe you an explanation. Colonel Schneider doesn't know about this because I have to do something for someone else. Colonel Willy Streck."

Brugger ground the pencil into the pad. "Why didn't you say so in the first place?" she said, angry to have been put in this position. "What time do you want the car, Richter, and where?"

Long after hanging up, Brugger stared at the instrument. She lit another cigar and stubbed it out. Then reaching for the phone, she called Streck's office at the Gestapo.

"The colonel is presently away from the office," came the reply from headquarters.

"Well, as soon as he returns ask him to call Ilse Brugger in Colonel Schneider's office. Tell him it's most important."

"I want to show you something," said Nico, and told Petros to follow. They went down the dark alley toward the auditorium. As they approached the rear of the noisy Palace Hotel where the local German brass were giving a farewell party for the Africa-bound field grade officers, an accordion began to play "Lili Marlene." A few officers began to sing, then others joined in, and Nico halted to listen.

The fool didn't understand the first principles of self-preservation, Petros thought; under no circumstances did he want to be seen standing still, a sure sign to any passing German sentry that he was up to mischief. Why was he following Nico anyway?

The music seemed to soothe Nico somewhat; he appeared less agitated as he headed for the civic auditorium.

Petros walked more rapidly, and saw his friend disappear down the cellar steps. "Nico, wait!" he called after him softly. The steps were worn slippery by thousands of footsteps, the cellar was even darker, and Petros, unable to see, groped about, feeling his way by touching the damp stone wall.

"Nico. Where are you?" There was no answer from the darkness. "Nico, tonight could be the beginning of man's sanity, and I'm offering you a chance to share it with me."

It was an apology to his friend, the man who refused to answer but who was there in the darkness. "Nico, this could be my end tonight; tonight I may join the kids I killed. If so, I will tell them I had the right to take their lives just as I have the right to offer my own life tonight." Petros waited for a reply, but all he heard was the rhythmic sound of water dripping.

"Why don't you answer me, Nico? You asked me to answer your question. Well? . . . What more do you want me to say? Where are you, Nico Andreades?" He took two steps forward. "Are you there? If you are, why don't you speak? Nico, I'll tell you a great secret and then you'll understand. I have to guide the bombers over the port tonight. Do you hear, Nico? I will lead the way for the RAF to bomb all those ships in the harbor. The entire mission, the entire course of the war, depends on me, Petros Zervas. And I have offered to share this great victory with you. But I can't spend the rest of the night here trying to find you. I have a job to do. The port has to be destroyed tonight. Those Germans have to die tonight. Do you understand?" he asked louder, and came to a halt as his hands found a square cement post. "All right." In disgust he leaned against the post. "I haven't the time to play games. Where in the hell are you?" he shouted and searched around the post.

"I am right here," Nico's calm voice said from nearby. "I was making an old friend of yours presentable. Old friends must be presentable when they meet again." Petros heard Nico's footsteps coming closer.

"Stay where you are," Petros commanded. "What do you have there?"

"Come closer and see for yourself." Nico giggled. "Don't be afraid. I'm bringing an old friend of yours to say hello," he said and continued toward Petros.

They both saw each other's outline in the darkness.

"Shake hands with Taki," Nico said calmly.

Instinctively Petros reached toward the hand but recoiled with a gasp at the touch of the cool slippery object.

"You remember Taki," Nico said and struck a wooden match against the cement post.

Petros wondered whether he himself was going mad. Nico was holding his little brother in front of him and he was dead—the child's face was waxen yellow, the eyes open, the feet dangling.

"Yesterday I wanted to take him outside to be picked up," Nico was saying. "But he was the last of us to go and I am attached to him. He doesn't seem much now that

208

he's dead, but every time I try to take him outside I feel as if I am about to commit a sin. I loved him and he loved me. I've tried . . ." Nico said and his eyes filled with tears. "I've tried to take him outside, but now I love him more than ever. I try to keep away, but I keep coming right back here to stay with him, combing his hair, cleaning his face, talking to him . . . like when he was alive." He dropped the match. "How can you get rid of something you love?"

"I am sorry . . ." Petros mumbled.

"How can you be sorry?" Nico cried. "You never even had a dog that belonged to you."

"I knew Taki," Petros said, offended. "He was my friend. I am sorry, Nico."

"How can you say that, Petros, when you consider everything . . . arithmetic?" He spat the word.

Petros was too horrified to reply.

"Tonight," said Nico, speaking conversationally again, "tonight I am going to take Taki outside and give him away. And the more I think about giving him away the more I want to live."

"You should," Petros agreed.

"Yes, that's why I brought Taki down here . . . to live. There was food around. But somehow things didn't turn out right. I was too weak. . . ."

"Taki and you weren't the only ones; there are thousands starving to death."

"Yes . . ." Nico cried. ". . . yes, Petros. But not I. I was strong. I was strong until four months ago when I had to spend the freezing nights and days in the water in the cave behind the breakwater. Do you know that?" he yelled. "Pneumonia weakens you, Petros. You cough blood and that makes you weak. Do you know that?"

"Nico, I—"

"I blame you for the death of my family," Nico said. "I blame you for Taki's death, and I blame you for my condition. So, my friend, with the eighty pounds sterling you still owe me I shall leave the city, go to the country, and find myself a doctor. And when I'm well and strong again, Petros, I'm going to come back here, find you, and kill you."

"You're making it easy for me not to give you what is yours," Petros said.

"You will give it to me," Nico said and giggled again. "You don't know it but I am the only one who can prove you exist."

"And what is that supposed to mean?" Petros said irritably.

"That's right," he chuckled to himself. "I'm the only one left. All trace of you is gone now. Forever." He thought of Lela's smooth white skin and broke into fresh laughter. "You think you'll be remembered for this mission of yours—"

"I do!" said Petros proudly.

"But how is that possible?" asked Nico, his laughter stilling in wonderment, "when you have been wiped clean like that arithmetic slate of yours, by your acquaintances, your friends?"

Petros tried to humor him. "I hope you're not including yourself, Nico. I want us to be friends again."

"No," Nico said, and his voice became stronger. "You don't need my friendship anymore—or anybody else's. All your life you were liked. Admired. Envied, but never hated. Then the war came and you discovered a new game. You could now win by killing. Why do you kill, Petros?"

"Because—"

"No, let me tell you. You actually enjoy killing Germans. You do it because you think it wins you glory. You do it to satisfy yourself. You don't care about Greece, you've discovered adventure. All your talk—you don't give a damn about mankind."

Petros tried to interrupt, but Nico gave him no chance. "Your cause is nothing more than a game of hide and seek. But one day this is going to end. If the Germans win you will thrive, and if they lose you will be a hero. Heroes are loved, admired, envied . . . but never hated. But I will hate you. I will never forgive you."

Taki was growing heavy and Nico laid him against the post.

"Now," Nico said, "I want the gold you owe me as well as the gold you owe the others."

Even at this close distance Petros could not see Nico. He could only hear the voice which rang with the same assurance it had before the war. Suddenly Petros thought of the boy he knew before the war, the real Nico, with the strong, healthy body, his equal. And to the old Nico Petros spoke: "I don't have to give you anything. But just for old times' sake I will give you what is yours. I want to show you, Nico Andreades, that in spite of what you think of me now, in the end—and this is what I want to prove to you—in the end you will admit that you were wrong and I was right." Petros extended his hand. "Tomorrow?"

"Yes, I'll be here. I'll be waiting," Nico said.

The accordion at the Palace Hotel was playing "Lili Marlene" again. Nico Andreades felt tired and sat down next to his brother; he started to caress his cool small face.

Petros crossed the street with its empty fish and poultry shops and ducked under the low-hanging acacia branches. Their stocky thorns bit his face but he did not feel the sting; his thoughts were obsessed with the face of the dead child. The little boy had once laughed and shrieked at Petros to play with him, tease him; and Petros in turn had loved to play with Taki. And to see the one creature in his life so close to him dead—the child Petros used to fondle and admire for his straightforward innocence— unleashed a dangerous rage. It seemed impossible to believe children like Taki could die with no one to avenge them. What was he, thirteen, fourteen? Like the kids he had sent out to the tankers, he thought in sudden shock.

His fury mounted and he started toward the center of the plaza at a run. He ran past the glass-fronted florists' shops that divided the plaza and served as the border of the Italian motor pool. Petros ran blindly, aimlessly; he ran because there was nothing else for him to do.

He was two hundred meters from the Church of Saint Constantine when through the glass of the last shop he saw two Italian *carabinieri* slowly making their rounds at the motor pool. Damned Italians. Jackals who had been decisively whipped by the Greeks, and who now roamed Piraeus at the sufferance of their German masters. Nico had accused him of seeing war as a game, a game in which he sought personal glory. Well, who would care what happened here? Who would there be to witness his glory? He would prove to Nico—and, far more urgently, to himself—that he meant every word he said. He had no cause? He was fighting a personal war? He had never seen either of these Italians before, but they were the enemy and he would strike them down. And avenge Taki, a child who had starved and sickened and died because peacocks like the *carabinieri* had given them no chance to live.

With his stiletto tightly clenched in his right hand, the slim blade low and in front of him, he ran in a straight line. He was pleased to realize that the rage had subsided, replaced by the combination of tension and calm he always felt in moments of crisis.

The *carabinieri* turned the corner of the farthest florist's shop, halted, and raised their rifles to port arms. So far there was no change in their routine. Petros increased his speed, his stomach muscles tightening, his feet pounding silently on the cobblestones.

He was almost upon them when the Italians heard him and turned. For an instant they were stunned by the sight of the man hurtling toward them, and paused before bringing their rifles to their shoulders and firing.

That was just long enough. Petros rocketed between them, the sheer violence of his drive momentarily knocking them off balance as they tried to readjust and attack him with their bayonets. Their cumbersome weapons were difficult to maneuver easily, and Petros, who had gone into a crouch to present as small a target as possible, plunged his blade into the stomach of one Italian, then swiftly withdrew it and drove it deep into the other.

Rolling over and away from the pair as they staggered and fell, Petros regained his feet and saw that the elder, a man with graying hair, was begging for mercy. But where was the mercy shown to children like Taki Andreades? Feeling neither pity nor elation, Petros slashed the man's throat, stepping backward so his own clothes would not be spotted by blood.

The younger Italian struggled feebly, and Petros put him away with another blow to the stomach, and when that failed to finish the man, he slit his throat, too, before wiping his blade clean on the *carabinieri's* elegant uniform.

Gradually Taki's yellow face started to fade from Petros' mind, the anger began to clear, replaced by the fear that made him rise and run, this time for survival, for now he heard the gate sentry shouting the alarm and saw the slits of the blacked-out car headlights come alive as their motors started up.

Petros ran through the Church of Saint Constantine, up to the altar, and through a side door. He started for the Hill of Kastela. This was his territory, his world, and no one could catch him here.

He ran at top speed up the narrow, steep streets, dodging from one to the next, sweeping around corners, cutting through empty lots, and taking a dozen shortcuts that only someone who had played here as a boy could know. The knife was still in his hand, but he refused to interrupt his mad dash to put it away. Besides, he might need it yet.

He reached the western side of the pine grove and knew that in a moment he would be safe. But fifteen feet before he could touch the level ground ahead, his legs suddenly buckled and he collapsed onto the ground, sobbing for breath. He tried to crawl those fifteen feet, but his hands and knees refused to obey his will, and again he collapsed.

Never before had he failed so miserably. In the past he had sprinted far longer distances uphill without difficulty, but common sense told him not to struggle. He rolled onto his back on the rain-soaked grass, painfully spread his arms and legs, his temples pounding as he sucked in great quantities of the night air.

After a while he began to feel rested, and when he saw layers of dark clouds reaching toward the moon to blot it out, he wanted to laugh aloud. The Germans must be overjoyed, thinking that the sudden cloud cover would protect their convoy. But he knew better. He would beat them in spite of everything. No one would stop Petros Zervas. Not the Germans. Not the dead Italians. Not Nico. Not even dear little Taki. No one!

25

In spite of the hour the cafenion was doing a roaring business. The Germans imposed the curfew, but were under no obligation to observe it themselves, and the place was filled with Wehrmacht officers who had tired of the formal affair at the Palace Hotel. The outdoor tables were occupied by captains and higher ranks, the lieutenants took the remaining seats indoors, and between them they were running Old Spyros ragged.

"Kellner!" they shouted, banging their beer steins on the table. Normally Spyros closed early, but tonight he had remained open to serve the boisterous Germans. He appreciated the chance to make a little extra money— barely enough to buy bread, feta cheese, grapes, and figs, which kept him alive—but he had to pay the price for the extra business: these Nazi swine were treating the retired sea captain like dirt.

All the same, he tried to tell himself as he hurried from table to table, rarely stopping to wipe the sweat from his forehead, he was luckier than most. Poor Nico, who had lost his entire family and who was slowly starving to death, was too ashamed to beg from him, too ashamed to come to the cafenion anymore. As for Petros—

Spyros didn't like to think of him anymore. They met only on rare occasions now, although the old man continued to hide his Black Saint Nicholas in the storeroom of the abandoned school. What really bothered Spyros was his young friend's arrogance. Didn't he realize that when it came to arrogance, the Germans were truly the master race, and at any time could not only cut him down to size but end his life? Just like that. The old man remembered a Greek saying that had been popular during the long centuries of the country's occupation by the Turks: *Walk on eggs in the presence of your masters, but make certain the eggs are hard-boiled.*

One group of two majors and a captain, who sat at a corner table, received Spyros' special attention. They were attired in black uniforms, wore the death's head insignia, and were conscious of the fact that they were a special breed. The other officers knew it too, and occasionally cast an uneasy glance in their direction.

No matter what else Old Spyros was doing he kept an eye on the group, and so he was one of the first to see the chauffeur-driven staff car pull to a stop, the grandest vehicle ever to come to his humble cafenion, and out of it step a slender man with long, dark hair, unexpectedly attired in civilian clothes.

All at once the atmosphere was changed. The Gestapo officers jumped to their feet and stood at rigid attention. The other officers stopped talking and came to attention as well.

But it was more than the sudden quiet that astonished Spyros. It had never occurred to him that commissioned officers in the Wehrmacht could be afraid of any mortal human being. But it was clear that every last one of them dreaded the sight of the newcomer.

The black-uniformed majors and captain clicked their heels and raised their arms in stiff Nazi salutes. "Heil Hitler!"

"Heil Hitler," Willy Streck replied in his customary,

negligent manner, and accepted a chair ceremoniously offered him by the captain.

"We are honored, Colonel Streck," the senior major said, acting as a spokesman for the group. "Forgive us for not saluting sooner, but your clothes misled us for a moment, and we didn't recognize you until you got out of the car."

"I just changed," Streck said, obviously bored by the fawning attitude of his subordinates. "I find civilian attire more suitable for the job I have to do." He appeared to become aware of the silence for the first time, and his pale eyes swept the cafenion.

The Wehrmacht officers reacted as though a signal had been given, and all at once they began talking again, although in subdued tones.

Spyros had seen many men who exerted great power—he remembered one shipping magnate who virtually ruled the port of Piraeus—but none had inspired such fear. It was amazing to see combat commanders and staff officers reacting to him identically. Obviously he was connected with the Gestapo in some way, but that was enough for the old man to know. A Greek survived in an occupied country by minding his own business—and by making certain he showed deference to his conquerors.

Old Spyros hurried to his table.

The Gestapo captain began to fuss. *"Kellner,"* he said, "take the Herr Colonel's order, and bring him what he wishes without delay."

The newcomer sighed and glanced at the old man. Spyros nodded in acknowledgment, even though the man's eyes made him uneasy.

Streck smiled at the captain, but his eyes remained humorless and his voice cold. "When I appear to be a civilian, Schmidt," he said in German, "be good enough not to address me by rank."

The younger officer became flustered.

Streck turned to Spyros and spoke in precise unaccented Greek. "I want a pot of very hot, very black coffee. You received a small quantity of a special Vien-

216

nese brand early this evening in preparation for the arrival of a particular person. I am that person."

Spyros hurried off to the kitchen. None of the other officers were demanding service now, he noticed.

26

On the crest of Kastela Hill, near the whitewashed Church of the Prophet Elias, a high, rounded boulder huddled under the branches of a pine tree, the same low, far-reaching branches that, years before, had shielded Petros and Lela when she had made him and many other boys men. From the city and the homes below the boulder was half hidden; it led to a sharp drop hollowed out of the hill.

Before the war this small hollow had provided a secret lovers' hideaway. Before entering they first would have to check a white marble stone near the trunk of the pine tree. If it was crowned with some object—a rusty cannon ball, a pipe, a tin box—the couple would have to wait until the crown had been removed.

Over the years the crowns changed but the white marble stone remained, protecting the privacy of its lovers. During the occupation the crown was no longer needed; the secret hideaway hid no secrets—people had more important things than lovemaking on their minds. But tonight, as he had the night he had taken Trudi up here, before entering the hollow Petros searched under the pine tree for a crown. When he found the cast-iron fence spear, he set it on the white marble, not to make sure he wasn't disturbed—no one was coming up here after curfew—but out of respect for tradition.

Three days ago, on a map of Piraeus, he had drawn a rough arrowhead aiming at the port. The point was situated here, at the hideaway on Kastela Hill; the base cut across the center of the port, with each side extending a

217

kilometer inside the city. Last night he had told Cunningham to emplace the green lights where the lines of the arrowhead met.

Then he drew the shaft of the arrow and extended it twelve miles southwest, to the highest peak of the Island of Salamis, and with the help of two fishermen had set up two lights on the shaft of his arrow. He explained to them that at the sound of the British planes, they would turn on the lights. The Lancaster navigators would bring their planes to within five miles of the island, execute a slow thirty-degree turn northeast, while the lead Lancaster, the pathfinder, would break formation and, flying low to avoid anti-aircraft fire, head for the port. Once there he would drop a flare so the rest of the planes could peel off on their relay runs.

"That's where you come in," Cunningham had told Petros at their final briefing session three days ago. The ground operation had to be swift and precise. Over and over Cunningham had played Petros recordings of the British aircraft, the deep hum of their motors so different from the angry whine of the Messerschmitts. Everything depended on the sound of those motors, Cunningham told him. The raid was scheduled for 0300, but all sorts of things could go wrong. From the moment the pathfinder spotted the lights, corrected his bearings, and dropped the flares over the harbor, not more than five minutes must elapse. If the lights around the port could not be seen from the plane, the formations were ordered to fly past, make a wide turn over Athens, regroup over the water and start all over again. This would not only delay the operation but alert the anti-aircraft batteries dug in all over the outskirts of the city and Athens.

Petros had understood at once. The lights on Salamis would guide the bombers to Piraeus, and then it would be his turn. "I'll listen for the pathfinder, and when I hear it coming I'll turn my own light on and off, on and off."

"Right," Cunningham had said. "But there's one problem. The lights. Ideally your beacon should be distinctive in some way—in case the Germans are using decoy lights

218

to draw our people off target—something the pathfinder pilot can't miss. And, to protect you, something that can't be spotted from the ground."

Quickly Petros came up with a solution. He would mount his lights deep inside empty oil drums, which would protect them from view if approached from the side. As for the lights, they would be well diffused—giving off a weak glow instead of a bright beam that would pinpoint the operator in a blacked-out area—and he would make them green. "Nobody can possibly mistake them."

Cunningham chuckled. "Not a chance. They'll think it's the Irish army!"

The rest would be easy. The lead Lancaster would drop a bright flare to guide the five other Lancasters on its tail; the low-flying bombers would drop their load. Because the explosions would light up the harbor, succeeding waves, coming over the port at three-minute intervals, could fly in at much higher altitudes.

Petros had designed and assembled the lights two days ago and tried them out indoors, although not in the dark for fear the glow might give his secret away. In spite of the makeshift material he had used to soften their direct beam, he was certain his lights would be clearly seen from the sky.

Now Petros walked around his contraption, lifted the British raincoat he had used to cover it, and inspected it one last time. The device was extremely simple but his experience as an electrical engineer told him it should be effective for the five-minute period it was to be used. Petros had secured three round washtubs and extended them with twenty-five inches of sheet metal so they approximated the size of a large oil barrel. In the middle of the barrel, he had mounted six light sockets, above each of which he had soldered a tin reflector, shooting down. The barrel was painted black inside and out, but the bottom was coated with a thick blanket of raw cotton, which he had dyed green by sprinkling with dry powder.

When the bulbs were turned on they would shoot down into the cotton, which would turn a brilliant green deep inside the barrel with very little, if any, glow visible in the night sky. If everything worked properly, only the plane's crew directly overhead would be able to see the shining bottom of the washtub.

Petros walked up and down, staring at his invention, hoping his theories would prove correct when the time came. The success or failure of the raid, Cunningham had grudgingly conceded, would depend entirely on his lights. Covering his device with the raincoat again, he pulled himself on top of the boulder and looked down at the city below. It had life to the ear but not to the eye. The blackout was complete and only the firefly slits of the patrol cars were visible as they rounded the corner of the boulevard near the Italian motor pool.

Petros took a deep breath and was pleased to discover that he was not nervous. A good sign, he thought. He wondered about the men at the other two beacons. They were young, inexperienced. Would they stick by their lights? This wasn't like the night they'd destroyed the tankers. There was no action to occupy minds, no new challenges. This was just waiting, and waiting makes you begin to figure that the odds against you are piling up, and soon there are no odds left in your favor at all. Petros knew this. Would they be able to withstand waiting? Would they fall asleep? Would the sound of the air raid sirens frighten them into immobility so they forgot to turn on their lights?

He stretched out on top of the boulder, locked his hands around the back of his neck and let his eyes study the dark clouds in the moon's path.

The clock of Saint Speridon tolled the hour, and the ships' bells announced the end of one day and the beginning of another. It was midnight—twelve o'clock civilian time, 2400 hours German military time, and three hours before the scheduled destruction of the port of Piraeus. Things will turn out all right, he thought. Everything will

220

turn out as planned. With a little luck and a little help from the Black Saint Nicholas.

Black Saint Nicholas! He still had one more errand to do.

27

Nico reached out in the darkness and found his dead brother's face. It was moist from the drops of water falling from the stones and he wiped it dry with his hand. Then he knelt and kissed Taki. "I can't keep you any longer. I can keep the memory, Taki, but you are a substance without a spirit now." He lifted the small, rigid body and struggled to his feet. "Forgive me," he said and once again brought Taki's forehead to his lips.

He carried his dead brother up the steps to the sidewalk, where panting and short of breath, he held Taki in front of him and leaned against the wall to rest.

The only sounds came from the motor pool, where the Italians could be heard shouting excitedly that some killers had escaped. Nico wet his dry lips and searched for a spot to put his brother where he could be picked up early in the morning.

He saw an acacia tree at the corner and he carried him over, carefully letting his brother slip from his arms against the tree trunk.

He knelt over Taki, his voice strong and steady. "It was not easy for me to watch you sink little by little and to have nothing to give you. But there was nothing—no one had anything to give away. I couldn't find food for you, Taki, and because I was looking I wasn't there the night you needed me most. That's why you died alone. All by yourself." He put both hands over his brother's face. "Rest in peace, baby brother," he said, and started out for the basement again.

The silence and blackness of the basement made Nico

hesitate; it seemed to assume the sanctity of an empty chapel, filled with the knowing stares of a thousand icons. Nico took a deep breath, and dismissing the superstitious fear of his brother's hovering soul, slowly walked to the corner. He lay back on the newspapers and cardboards he used for a bed, trying to hide from his fears.

Why does it have to be tonight? he thought. Why do I suddenly fear death? Why am I afraid to close my eyes? Why do I have to crawl into bed and try to hold on when two hours ago I couldn't have cared if I died or not? Nico groaned and crawled along the wall. "Forgive me . . . everyone," Nico whispered. He found himself in a kneeling position, and suddenly wanted to pray.

"Help me, oh Lord . . . help me. Let me stay alive now that I have a chance," he murmured and put his hands in front of his face to hold back the tears. Nico had never cried for help before. He had seen people cry for help and he had pitied them.

"Please God . . . you have the rest of my family. Please give me another chance," Nico begged. "There is no one left." He raised his eyes to the ceiling. "Don't hold it against me that I turned to you so late. I am a religious man . . . you know that," he said and rose to his feet, started to walk slowly around his newspaper bed and the folded German blanket he and Taki had used for a cover. "I am sincere. I am not a pretender. . . ." But then the thought of dying sent him back against the wall. "Please don't do this to me . . ." he cried.

To relieve some of the horror, he struck a wooden match on the wall and lit the candle at the head of the cardboard bed. The light felt harsh on the eyes at first, but soon his fears calmed and he lay down on his bed, his eyes glued to the waterdrops above, trying to force himself into believing that he would live to see the morning. It was quiet. Nico turned over on his side and froze. His eyes caught a shadow moving along the basement toward the door.

"Hey. Hey, you," Nico called and wiped the tears from his eyes. "Come here, you," he added and raised himself to a sitting position. The shadow continued along the wall as if it hadn't heard. "Taki?" Nico whispered. "Taki . . . is that you, Taki?" He strained his eyes to cut through the dim background. "Whoever you might be"—he started to shout—"stop. I need to talk to you. Do you hear?" He rose slowly. "Petros, is that you? I thought you had a job to do. What are you doing here?" he asked, slowly advancing toward the creeping shadow. "Stop, damn you!"

The shadow came to a halt near the door. "Who are you?" he asked. "Why don't you answer me?"

And the shadow spoke: "Because you lied to me. This is not a dream."

"Oh. No . . ." Nico mumbled and closed his eyes.

"This is not a dream," said the shadow, extending two arms with a shoe dangling from each hand. "This is not a dream," the girl repeated. "This is real. I heard you. I heard everything you and that man said." She started toward Nico. "I came to give you these."

Nico opened his arms and the little girl walked into them.

"Here," Elena said. "My father used to wear them to church on Sundays. Tomorrow is Sunday. Would you take me to church tomorrow?"

Nico took the girl in his arms. "If I lied to you about the dreams, what makes you think I won't lie to you again? You don't want me to lie to you again, do you?"

"No," she said, shaking her head. "But I like promises. If you promise," she said and looked up at Nico.

"No," Nico said, "I can't do that."

"Why not?"

"I can't promise anything tonight. Yesterday I could, but not tonight."

"I promised shoes," she said. "Well, here they are. And I'm not asking you to give me anything. I only want you to put them on and take me to church . . . I heard you say prayers. . . ."

"I might say more before the night is over—if it ever is over," Nico whispered.

"You are scared," she said and started to press her small fingers against his spine.

"Aren't you?"

"Yes, a little. But I thought if I make believe all this is a bad dream, like you told me, there is nothing to be scared of." She rubbed Nico's back lovingly as though it belonged to one of her dolls.

"It will stop," she said. "You'll see. It can't go on like this," she added, trying to encourage Nico.

"No. It can't go on like this," echoed Nico.

"Ssssssh," she said and put her finger to his lips.

"It will go on," Nico said between his teeth.

"Please . . ." she begged.

"Goddamit. It will go on!"

"Please don't shout," she said quietly.

"All right," he said, lowering his voice. "I am going to promise you something."

"A true promise?"

"Yes, but it has a condition. You and I must be alive tomorrow."

"We will," the girl said. "You and I will."

"I'm going to come into some money tomorrow. Lots of money. If I'm still alive, you and I are going to the country and find the best doctors there are and they'll fatten us up again. What do you think of that?"

"I heard you talk to him. How can he give you the money when you want to kill him?" she asked.

"He will. I just know he will."

"Didn't he make that promise just to get rid of you?" She started to caress his black hair lovingly.

"You don't have to do that."

"What can I do for you then?" she asked.

"Just hope. Hope that you and I will be able to stay alive until morning. If we can do that our troubles will be half over."

"We'll make it."

"Just hope."

The candle was burning low and after a few last attempts to stay alive the wick drowned itself in the melted wax. Just before they fell asleep, a sudden thought occurred to Nico.

What if God had sent Elena to take the place of the departed Taki?

He wondered if he really was going mad.

28

The convoy captains assembled at the Yacht Club for a final briefing from Rear Admiral von Widdemer before returning to their ships. They were boisterous, still feeling the glow from the party, and as each of them sat with a pile of charts in front of him, they found it difficult not to talk among themselves while the admiral traced their route on a huge wall chart.

Colonel Johann Schneider was paying no attention, either. He was heartily sick of the convoy and the need to remain on duty around the clock. Even at the Palace Hotel he scarcely had a minute alone with Trudi. She had looked particularly lovely, and all the other officers had had a chance to dance with her, although Willy Streck, at least, left early on some mysterious errand.

Willy Streck! Bad enough Streck was Trudi's former lover, the man seemed to dog Schneider's steps. An officer spends his entire career in the Wehrmacht, climbing the ranks until he finally gets his command. And does a fine job of it, too, when along comes one of these Gestapo types, a subordinate at that, who acts as if he, not the colonel, was now running the operation.

Perhaps, when the convoy was safely on its way, Schneider would complain about Streck to General Jodl, chief of the general staff. In person in Berlin, of course, not on paper. Even an officer in far-off Greece knew enough to tread carefully when dealing with a senior Gestapo officer, even if he outranked him. Streck could leapfrog the Athens command and go direct to Himmler, while

Schneider was still wading through Wehrmacht channels.

So many problems pressed on Schneider's tired mind as he glanced around the room. In the days before the war this had been the Yacht Club's bar, and he had to admit the Greek shipping magnates of Piraeus certainly had known how to live well. The chairs of brass-studded red and black leather were deep and luxurious, and the butter-smooth leather must have cost a fortune. One could tell just by touching it, and the colonel stroked the arm of his chair appreciatively. Leather like this should be used to make boots for high-ranking officers. He resisted the temptation to imagine himself making love to Trudi in such a chair.

The tables scattered around the room were fashioned of highly polished, hand-wrought oak, no two identical; when the time came for him to leave Piraeus he would have one of them shipped to his home as a memento of his stay here. It would look very handsome in the study he planned to furnish for his retirement years. The Turkish rug on the floor was a work of art, but Schneider put it out of his mind. General von Schlichter had picked it for himself.

Heavy curtains framed the plate glass windows overlooking the gulf. They were made of the purest, heavy silk, and even a man who knew little about fabrics had to admire them. What a waste, Schneider thought, as he pictured Trudi in a voluptuously revealing gown made of the material.

An aide slipped into the room, and taking care not to interrupt the droning voice of the admiral, handed the colonel a thick sheaf of reports. Schneider allowed himself a satisfied smile. His command was functioning with precision and efficiency; these were up-to-the-minute reports on the state of the embarkation, on the men and material still to be loaded on the transports, on the exact location of every member of his command. His subordinates might regard him as a stickler, but only someone who lived by the rule book could demand that last ounce of energy from his men. To say nothing of looking forward to promotion. General von Schlichter had hinted as much when they had dined together the other evening. Yes, this war was the best thing that had ever happened to Johann Schneider.

The aide returned, earning a frown from Admiral von Widdemer, who stopped speaking for a moment. The young officer reddened as he handed his superior a slip of paper.

Schneider opened the folded note, which was brief and succinct: *May I see you at once?* It was signed, *W. Streck.*

Didn't the man ever sleep? He knew Streck—he believed the Gestapo took precedence, even over an admiral—and he didn't like to be kept waiting. With an apologetic nod to Admiral von Widdemer, he left the room.

The aide conducted Schneider to a smaller room on the same floor that had been used in prewar days for private parties. A large telephone switchboard and powerful wireless sending and receiving equipment had been set up in the little bar outside, and all units were manned by black-uniformed Gestapo troopers.

Sitting in the inner room, still dressed in civilian clothes, was Lieutenant-Colonel Streck. Schneider disapproved of the masquerade. The Wehrmacht believed its officers should be proud of their uniform and wear it at all times, but these Gestapo people insisted on regarding themselves as a breed apart, entitled to make their own rules.

A large map of Piraeus was pinned to a wall behind Streck; various other documents flanked him, along with a battery of telephones. He was speaking into one of them as the Wehrmacht commandant for Piraeus entered the room, and he half rose for an instant, in token respect to someone of higher rank, as he continued to engage in a low, earnest conversation.

Glancing at him, Schneider enjoyed a moment of ironic amusement. Streck liked to regard himself as something of a dandy, but tonight his suit was rumpled, his hair mussed, his eyes slightly bloodshot. The cuffs of his usually impeccable white shirt were soiled. Now Streck, too, knew how it felt to be working under severe pressure.

Even as Schneider seated himself in a red leather chair he was sorry he had come. He should have insisted Streck report to him in his own headquarters farther down the hall. After all, he was the senior officer; he deserved that mark of respect.

Willy Streck hung up the receiver and passed a hand over his face, but he was smiling as he turned to Schneider. "Thank you for coming, Colonel."

"Not at all, my dear Streck."

"I have some news of importance for you. We have broken a portion of the enemy's code. It seems the British are planning a major air strike on our convoy tonight."

Schneider sat up in his chair. "You are certain?"

"In matters of this sort we don't err, Colonel. The Gestapo can't afford to make mistakes."

Schneider nodded. "Well, we expected as much," he said, his confidence returning. "Yes, in fact, I am glad they are coming. We are ready for them. We can blanket Piraeus with smoke in minutes. The harbor is blacked out. The anti-aircraft are manned and ready. The raid is doomed to fail."

"Not this one, Colonel."

"What do you mean?"

"We decoded just enough to suggest that some kind of special lights have been set up in or around Piraeus to guide the enemy bombers to the harbor."

"You mean help from the ground?"

"That's precisely what I mean. As well as help perhaps closer at hand."

Streck was playing with him, like a cat with a mouse.

"The British may have found a traitor in our midst. Someone with friends in high places. The highest places, in fact." Schneider suddenly noticed an expression he had never seen on Streck's face—he looked deeply pained. Don't tell me the man can feel emotion!

228

"A few hours ago a car was ordered to take a certain individual to Athens. It seemed a most unusual request, at such a late hour. Almost as if this person had advance knowledge of the impending raid and was determined to get as far as possible from Piraeus before it occurred."

Schneider nodded.

"What called it to my attention was that she used my name to authorize the trip—a most unfortunate slip, and one someone would make only in a moment of desperation. Because, of course, I was informed at once and denied it completely."

"She?" asked Schneider, suddenly apprehensive.

"The automobile arrived as requested," Streck went on, "but instead of to Athens it took her to Gestapo headquarters. Right now some of my people are trying to ascertain whether the precise nature of the ground support is known to Fräulein Trudi Richter."

"Oh, my God." Schneider sagged into his chair. Streck flashed him an unexpected look of sympathy and busied himself with some work on his desk until the colonel had composed himself.

"I know, Johann," he said softly, "it caught me just as completely by surprise. And if it's any help, we're not absolutely certain she's involved, but under the circumstances we simply cannot afford to take any chances."

"Of course," said Schneider weakly. He wanted to protest, he wanted to *demand* Streck release the girl, but he knew it would be futile. Too much was at stake tonight. But why Streck—why hadn't Trudi turned to him?

Streck was asking a question. When he saw Schneider had not heard, he repeated it: "How long before we can get the ships underway?"

A telephone rang and Streck spoke into it softly. He nodded, looked over at the colonel questioningly, and then said something into the receiver and hung up.

"You mean our emergency plan?" The colonel seemed dazed, still unable to function.

Streck looked at him a moment, and then his voice cut

like ice. "Get hold of yourself, Schneider. I want to know just how soon you can start moving those ships out!"

"Well . . ." Schneider said, struggling to pull himself together. He looked at his watch. "The Greek pilots and the tugboat captains either are on board the transports or are due to be picked up shortly. I can dispatch the destroyer escorts in fifteen minutes."

"To hell with the destroyers! If I know the Italians, at the first hint of a raid they'll head straight to sea. What about the troops?"

Schneider quickly flipped through his reports. "Most of the men already have been loaded, as provided for under our emergency plan, to simplify the morning departure. Of course, if you are concerned about the raid, we could have them disembarked and moved to a safer spot outside the immediate port area."

"Those men aren't going anywhere!" snapped Streck. "Now is as good a time as any to tell you, Colonel. I am under orders from the Führer himself to get those reinforcements to Rommel as scheduled. And if it costs some of those replacements and ships out there, even if it means your life and mine, I intend to meet that schedule and get that convoy to Africa."

"And so you shall, Colonel!" said Schneider sharply.

"There is only one way," Streck said. "We have to locate those lights before the British do. I must ask you to send every man you can spare to hunt down those signal beacons. They must be found and put out of commission!"

"It is as good as done," said Schneider. "I shall dispatch as many teams as necessary."

Streck rose and saw him to the door. At the threshold, he pressed Schneider's arm for a moment. "I am very sorry about Trudi," he said and then headed back to the ringing phones.

"Connect me with the airport in Tatoi," he said to the operator. "First priority."

He drummed with a pencil on the edge of the desk

until he was connected with his party. "Colonel von Hellsdorf? Streck. You remember that plane you were telling me about yesterday in Athens? How soon can you get it into the air?"

29

The plaza appeared deserted, the news kiosk had been shuttered for the night and the doors of the cafenion were closed and locked. But as Petros had anticipated, a light was still shining in back.

He moved to the rear of the cafenion and peered through the open window. Old Spyros, his face a fatigued gray, was standing at the sink, painstakingly washing up the dishes left by his German customers. In spite of his weariness the old man had lost none of his dignity, Petros was proud to see. His shoulders were stooped, the lines in his face were deep and his body sagged, yet still he was a man of imposing stature.

Climbing through the open window, Petros advanced to within a few feet of the old man before clearing his throat.

Spyros was so startled he dropped the glass he was drying, shattering it on the floor. "I should have known it was you," he said in annoyance. "The only man in Piraeus who ignores the curfew. Don't you know the Germans will shoot you if they find you?"

Petros' laugh indicated his opinion of German sentries. "I wanted to see you," he said.

The old man was still annoyed. Didn't he realize that only thirty minutes before the place had been filled with German officers? Suppose one of them had left something behind, and returned for it? A young, healthy Greek who was abroad at this hour—particularly these days—would be handed over to the Gestapo for intensive questioning. "Maybe you don't know it," the old man said, "but the

Germans are very nervous about this big convoy of theirs."

Petros could not hide the light of humor in his eyes. That fact, he said, had called itself to his attention.

Still grumbling, Spyros began to clean up the broken glass, and was surprised when Petros took the broom and dustpan from him. The boy wanted something, he warned himself.

Petros made small talk, accepted a cup of good German coffee as a reward for his labors, and began to chat idly about the changes in Piraeus since his last visit. He had been sorry to learn of the death of Nicholas Andreades' family, but Nico himself would be all right now, Petros would see to it.

Spyros suspected that anything Petros did for Nico had a substantial price tag, but he kept his thoughts to himself. There was enough hostility already; all he wanted was tranquility.

Petros continued to talk, and as he sipped his coffee he lighted a cigarette. The old man noted that it was Turkish, a brand that was scarce and impossibly expensive these days. Obviously Petros was doing all right for himself.

Still speaking casually, Petros mentioned the excitement caused by the presence of so many Germans in town. The port hadn't been so crowded since the beginning of the occupation.

Spyros replied curtly that he paid no attention to the activities in the port. If he was healthy, it was because he was careful to mind his own business.

"I'd think those ships would fascinate a sea captain," Petros said. "There are Bulgarians, Italians, Germans, Albanians—ships flying a half dozen different flags."

The old man lifted his coffee cup to his mouth but said nothing. Petros got up slowly and went to the front of Spyros' establishment and scanned the plaza. There were no patrols in sight. Petros was nervous and Spyros knew it.

"How did it go today . . . did you make some good money?" Petros asked.

Spyros sipped at his coffee. Petros is in trouble and is priming himself to talk. "What's eating you?" Old Spyros asked. "Girl trouble?"

Slowly Petros went behind Spyros' counter. He did not speak on the way; he looked at the floor tiles so thoughtfully Spyros thought he was counting them.

The silence made Spyros uneasy.

"No girl trouble," Petros said finally, and pouring some water into a glass he sat down across from Spyros. "Not for me, at least. You know Tripanis, Sotiros Tripanis?"

"The best ship's pilot, second to none," the old man said.

"Better than you?"

"For his age, he is good . . . well, after I quit the sea and started piloting ships in and out of the port. . . . No . . ." Spyros said thoughtfully, "for a thirty-year-old man I would say that he is very good. Let's say that if I were piloting today, Tripanis and I could have been neck and neck."

"He's dead."

Spyros' face tightened and he kicked a chair across the room. "Goddamit," he said. "I just saw him with his wife and kids the other day." He stood up and pointed toward the veranda. "They were out there talking to me. Poor, poor woman, poor kids," he said, shaking his head. "How in the name of Christ did he die?"

"They found him stabbed to death. There is talk about another woman's friend—"

"No. Not Tripanis," Spyros said and refused to listen. "I worked with the man for three years and I know. He was not the type."

"Sit down," Petros said. Something in Petros' voice made the old man sink slowly onto his chair.

"I don't know who killed Tripanis or the reason for his death," Petros said. "But the terrible part of it is that he is dead."

233

"Poor boy, poor woman," Spyros continued with his thought. "Do you know his family?"

"No, I only knew Tripanis."

Petros lied. Only the night before, he had abducted Tripanis' family from their home in Piraeus and locked them in a basement in Athens while he made a simple request. At first Tripanis refused, but when he realized his family's lives depended on his cooperation, he changed his mind. Unfortunately, word of his willingness to go along with the scheme was never conveyed to Petros' men. When he left Petros, they thought he was on his way to the Gestapo to betray Zervas and they stabbed him in the street.

"Tripanis was going to do a job tonight," Petros said.

Spyros did not ask what it was, and the silence was long and uncomfortable.

"Tripanis was going to wreck the convoy commodore's ship," he said at last.

Old Spyros turned toward Petros with a hard, unbelieving stare.

"Yes," said Petros. "He was."

"If what you tell me is true," Old Spyros said slowly, as his eyes started to go wild with anger, "if Tripanis was going to wreck a ship . . . I wish he would rot in hell and his ever-living soul suffer forever."

It was the first time the old man had ever cursed a human so severely, especially one who was dead, a family man, a close friend, a brother of the sea. Spyros got up and Petros noticed tears in the old man's eyes.

"Tripanis was going to wreck the ship for his country," Petros said, swallowing. "Tripanis was not going to betray his trust as a captain," he explained slowly. *"Salvatore Spoleno* is an enemy ship!"

"No man has the right to wreck a ship. No man," Spyros said. His wrinkles looked deeper and his lower lip quivered. "A ship is helpless as a newborn infant, and it is up to the captain to nurse her and guide her, and love her and give her life and strength. And no goddamn man has the right to hurt an innocent infant and a captain's second

234

soul. No man!" he added with disgust and, nodding to himself, flopped back on his chair. "A captain of a ship sees no flags and no enemy. What he sees is the pride and joy of another human being, and no man, no man alive, has the right to take that beauty from him."

Petros leaned back on his chair and closed his eyes. He understood the old man and his love for another captain's ship, his love for Tripanis' family, his love for Tripanis himself; but the clashing contradictions staggered the old man, leaving him helpless as one of his beloved ships adrift in the open seas. "Goddamn war," Spyros mumbled.

Petros told him what Tripanis was going to do and explained the plan for the raid. He told him that the port was going to be hit sometime before three o'clock in the morning, that the ships were going to be sunk. But Petros knew the Germans. They were clever, they were unpredictable. One smell of trouble and all plans could change—they might decide to embark earlier, and if they did they wouldn't be around for the RAF strike. In that event, if somehow the Germans decided to take the ships out earlier, Tripanis had agreed to ram the ship on the breakwater and seal off the port. For the plan to work Petros had to know there was a trusted pilot on the Italian commodore's ship, the ship scheduled to leave the port first. Now Tripanis was dead and his plan was as good as doomed.

"Leave me alone," the old man mumbled and started for the front door.

Petros leaped up and sat the old man on the chair again.

"What do you want me to do?" he asked helplessly.

Petros pulled a folded batch of papers from his pocket and laid them on the table. The top page was a revision of the German command's ship departure orders and Petros pointed to Spyros Kanares' name, typed in capitals, next to the name of the ship, *Salvatore Spoleno*.

"No," Old Spyros mumbled again.

"I took my life and the lives of my operatives in my

235

hands to dig into the pilots' files and bring yours out. And now the only thing you can say is no?"

"Give me a gun to kill Germans. . . . I'll go kill Schneider for you. . . . Give me a stick of dynamite to blow up a train, but don't you ever ask me to do that, Petros." He begged the boy. "I never wrecked a ship in my life and it is not decent to ask me to do that sort of thing now. . . . I am an old man! Have some respect for my age!"

"There'll be a German vehicle coming any minute to take you to the port," Petros said. "The Germans'll be here soon, and I have to have your word. I have to know that if it's necessary you will ram the ship into the breakwater."

"The Germans are not going to find me here." Spyros rose.

"You are scared," Petros cried.

"I am not afraid for my life," he said with dignity.

"You are the only one left. Goddamn you," he said and shook the old man violently. "Leave the love of ships to those Greeks you are going to save, old man."

"You have no right to ask that from me, Petros Zervas."

Petros' lips drew tight. "You're like all the rest. You and your saint. That was just talk. Cheap talk. He's living there, rotting in a dusty storeroom, while you tremble for your safety. Make him proud of you!"

"He's proud of the fact that for forty years I sailed my ships safely and never lost a life," Spyros said.

Petros' laugh was savage.

"It is a sacred principle!"

"I would think that a man of your age and experience would know something fundamental," Petros said flatly. "Something that everyone in this world must learn sooner or later. There are times when circumstances force us to act *against* our real principles."

For the first time an expression of doubt crept into Spyros' eyes.

"All of us must give up our principles at one time or another," Petros persisted. *"To live.* Well, I risked my life

236

to save your Black Saint Nicholas for you. Now I call on you to repay that debt."

The old man tried to speak.

Petros put a gentle hand on his arm. "Hear me out. Not for me. I ask nothing of you for me. Repay the debt—by striking a great blow for Greece!"

"Take my life," Spyros said.

"I don't want your life."

"Petros," Spyros begged.

Petros shook the old man's shoulders lightly as if to wake him. "Look at yourself. Your proud body, bending over and making coffee for your enemy . . . to please your conquerors. . . . What's happening to you, old man? Where is the respect you are talking about? Old man. . . ." Petros spoke softly, "Stand up. Go out on your feet. Be free, mister."

The German weapons carrier came to a squealing stop outside, and Petros crouched behind the counter.

"Tonight may be the last night of our lives and I want to kiss you," Petros said from behind the counter. "If I don't see you again, old man . . . peace in life and peace in death."

The old man shook his proud head and then stepped forward to open the door for the Germans.

Yes, he was Spyros Kanares, the pilot, yes, he was going with them. But before they could take him to the port, he first had a stop to make.

30

In the port area, all around the docks, on the breakwater, in the railroad yards, in the open fields and parks, at the airports at Tatoi and Kalamaki and on the rooftops of buildings the alerted anti-aircraft battery personnel uncovered their guns, lined up their ammunition and waited for instructions.

Those manning the searchlights trimmed their arc lamps with new carbons and started the generators.

In the German motor pools, the personnel carriers, the sedans, the trucks, the armored cars, and all weapons carriers were dispatched at once to the barracks at the foot of the Kastela Hill and to the Naval Cadet School near the mouth of the port.

At the Greek fire stations and in the garage of the German firefighting detachments, the personnel mounted their engines and waited.

On telephoned orders from Colonel Schneider the dispatcher checked with the motor pool to make sure the fuel trucks were at the gasoline depot, filling their tanks with diesel oil for the tugboats.

The clouds continued to drift in from the west. They hung over Attica and under the moon.

Major David Cunningham was restless, and after spending a short time in his study on the second floor of the modest Piraeus house, he climbed to the roof. The cloud overhead was heavy, the night dark, and a feeling of impotent rage welled up in him. This was German weather, no two ways about it, and the gathering mist which promised rain before morning would make matters worse.

But the weather couldn't be helped; the bombers had to get through. There was simply no choice. This mission would justify the long months he had lived as an undercover agent in Greece, would prove whether the British really could function when the chips were down. By now the RAF squadrons should be in the air, heading from airfields in Cyprus, Port Said, Beirut, and Malta toward their rendezvous. And in a matter of hours, the battle for North Africa would be won or lost.

One way or the other, the American knew, his own service here was coming to an end. He wasn't sorry. In fact, he was damned lucky the Gestapo hadn't caught up with him yet, and if he survived the night he knew they'd redouble their efforts to locate him. It was inconceivable they hadn't learned there was a British wireless operating

238

in the area, and it would just be a matter of time—and precious little of it—before they zeroed in on him. By then, with luck, he'd be gone.

Ashley-Cole and Sergeant Peters would be sent back to England, where they'd be given an easy assignment training future agents, and they deserved the respite. As for himself, Cunningham knew what was in store. He would be promoted, probably given a desk job in Cairo in Campbell's section. And good-bye to all hope of any transfer to the United States Army. The brigadier would double-talk, exercise the steely charm that was the hallmark of the British gentleman, and would hang on to him until the war's end.

But first he had a big job to do—get through the night. He knew every member of the British Intelligence team in Piraeus was in place. But what about Zervas and the other Greeks? He wasn't too worried about the two fishermen on the Island of Salamis; they seemed reliable and could be counted on to signal the approach of the RAF. His main concern, his only real concern as always, was Zervas. The Greek was getting cockier every day. To date he had delivered as he said he would, no denying that. The scheme for the beacons—first-rate—he doubted if the signal corps could have cooked up a better solution. But just because the success of the operation did depend so largely on Zervas, Cunningham was worried. The stakes were too high. No one should be that indispensable—especially someone so unpredictable. Cunningham knew the Greek was out for whatever he could get. Not that he blamed him. What really drove that home was the night he had followed Petros to the schoolyard and saw him with the Austrian girl. What in hell was a beautiful woman like that doing with someone like Petros Zervas.

The next time he'd seen Zervas he asked him. Had he gone crazy? Didn't he have more sense than to play around with Schneider's woman? Why didn't he just walk up to headquarters and turn himself in? If he wanted to throw away his life, that was all right with Cunningham, but right now they had a job to do. Why didn't he find himself a nice, safe Greek girl and keep out of trouble?

"You mean, like Maria Asprou, the one who turned me in in Athens?" he said with a sly grin.

"You know what I mean, Zervas." And Cunningham wondered at the heat in his voice.

"I think I do," said Petros, smiling.

"What's that supposed to mean?"

Petros looked at Cunningham with those clear blue eyes. "Just that I'm good enough to die for you but not good enough to sleep with a woman you'd give anything for. Anything."

A truck careened past Cunningham's house, followed by a semi-trailer loaded with supplies. What the hell was going on? He snapped up his binoculars and vaguely through the darkness made out the port throbbing to life. The sound of a motorboat cut through the night, then the deep-throated roar of a patrol boat.

What's going on? Had they changed plans? Were they trying to move out the convoy before morning? Tonight?

Cunningham dropped the glasses and raced downstairs to fire off a message to Cairo.

Wing Commanders Ross and Ashcroft, the latter in flight coveralls with his helmet on a nearby table, both wearing pistols, hovered over the air signals officer in charge of what looked like a huge switchboard. Three airmen in headphones were seated at a console, and as they received wireless messages they scribbled a few words on scratchpads and handed them to their superior.

"The Malta squadrons are in the air," announced the air signals officer.

Ross scowled and glanced at his wristwatch. "What's delaying them in Beirut?" he demanded. "Do they expect everyone else to circle over Cyprus forever while we wait for them?"

He snatched the headphones from one of the seated

airmen and reached for a microphone. "Connect me with Beirut!"

The startled airman swiftly obeyed.

"Ross here," the wing commander said coldly. "Let me speak to Harris."

The connection was made at once.

"I hope I'm not disturbing your supper," Ross said scathingly, speaking into the microphone in a low, soft voice.

The officer in Beirut made some reply.

"Goddamit!" Ross said, "our schedule called for you to be in the air three minutes and thirty seconds ago. If you're having trouble with two of your aircraft, scrap them! Fly without them! We've just got word the Jerries have moved up their timetable. If we could, we'd advance our attack accordingly, but it's too late for that. But one thing I can tell you—the whole bloody operation can't wait until your mechanics have repaired some leaking petrol lines. I'll expect you over the rendezvous area on time, and if you aren't there I'll skin you alive. Personally." He removed the headphone set and handed it to the uncomfortable airman.

An aide near the door watched the flight commander expectantly. Ashcroft did not disappoint him. "Give the order for action stations," he said. "I will lead the flight to the rendezvous. We'll fly at eighteen thousand feet, and I'll expect all aircraft to maintain combat patterns all the way."

"Very good, sir." The aide left the room, and in a moment his voice could be heard bawling the orders over a loudspeaker system.

Wing Commander Ross went to a desk, opened a drawer, and poured some brandy into two paper cups. Handing one to his colleague, he raised his in a toast.

Ashcroft shuddered slightly as the brandy went down.

Ross watched enviously as Ashcroft clamped his flight helmet on his head. "Good luck to all of you, George—and good hunting."

241

31

Ordinarily Spyros would have enjoyed feeling free to move about Piraeus at night; it reminded him of the old days when he set out to sea. But tonight he was setting out on a mission that went against everything he had ever believed in all the decades he had been a captain.

The Germans pulled up to the abandoned school. He let himself in the gate, hurried across the yard, and made his way down the dark, airless corridors to the storeroom.

There, in a corner under a pile of rags, was his Black Saint Nicholas.

Tenderly picking up his icon, he stared at it for a long time, blinking away the tears that came to his eyes. He was ashamed enough of what he was doing tonight without involving his Saint Nicholas. But he had no choice.

Under no circumstances would he set foot on a ship, any ship, unless Saint Nicholas accompanied him.

Gripping the icon so tightly that his knuckles turned white, the old man returned to the weapons carrier. The Germans looked at him, at the icon, and then at each other. But the look on Spyros' face was fierce and serene at the same time. The Germans said nothing as they drove off to the waterfront and the waiting fleet.

As he rocked back and forth on the hard seat of the truck, cradling Saint Nicholas, the old man wondered if Petros Zervas would ever understand his deep sense of degradation. The Petros Zervas of old, perhaps. But this new Petros Zervas, with all his talk of repaying a debt by striking a blow for Greece, never. Spyros knew better, and he was sure the Black Saint Nicholas knew it, too. He could not look the icon in the face.

What Petros never would understand is that a man who had lived honorably every day of his long life paid his debts. There was no other way. And he *was* indebted to

Petros, who had rescued the Black Saint Nicholas for him—and made himself a permanent outcast as a result. Not only that, but Petros had nursed him back to health when he would have died of starvation and illness.

No, there was no alternative. *The debt had to be paid.* Not to Greece, but to Petros Zervas.

If nothing else, the Wehrmacht was commendably thorough, but tonight of all nights Willy Streck wished they would act with speed. He studied the detailed map of Piraeus laid out before him.

Schneider had sent out twenty patrols to search for the enemy signal lights. More than one hundred men conducting an intensive hunt for an object that, by definition, had to be fairly large and cumbersome; but so far they had reported nothing.

If the Gestapo in Athens had had any men to spare Streck would have commandeered them, but since Berlin regarded it as a secondary theater of war, Athens was understaffed. Streck had already brought every available man to Piraeus.

Berlin was aware of the difficulties he faced, he had seen to that, but at the same time he knew that Himmler would hold him personally responsible if the British managed to penetrate the German defenses and attack the convoy. Streck was proud of his reputation as an officer who didn't know the meaning of failure, who could ferret out an enemy's intentions before the enemy knew them himself. Streck had been decorated by the Führer personally for his exceptional work in Austria, Czechoslovakia, France, and the Low Countries.

Very well. If Berlin was counting on him, he had no intention of letting Berlin down. He still had a few tricks up his sleeve, and now, right now, was the time to employ them. He couldn't afford to sit around and wait for Schneider's troops; one way or another he'd have to attend to the job himself.

The hell of it was that he needed more cleverness and a

243

ruthless approach to the problem; at this moment he needed luck, too.

He reached for the telephone and asked to be connected with Colonel von Hellsdorf at Tatoi Airport.

"Von Hellsdorf? How long before I can expect the plane over the port?"

"It will be at least forty minutes, Colonel. We were lucky we could even start it. Do you know that we had to use five crash-landed Lancasters just to make the fuselage and wings?"

"I'm sure it is a mechanical miracle," Streck said dryly, "but the sooner we get it into the air, the sooner we'll find those signal lights."

"We are fully aware of the urgency of the mission, Colonel," von Hellsdorf said.

"Fine. Just let me know the moment our decoy is ready to make its approach and I'll turn on all the air raid sirens." Streck chuckled. "That should give the British a real surprise."

On top of Kastela Hill, Petros Zervas covered himself with the raincoat, knelt against the boulder, and lit a match to check his watch. One-thirty. A half hour to go. He smiled, blew out the match, and buried it in the wet pine needles. The moment the German listening posts heard the British planes over Pelopónnesos they would sound the alarm, and within ten to fifteen minutes the mellow tone of the Lancaster engines would be heard over the Province of Attica. Even if the sudden commotion below indicated that Schneider had decided to clear the port early, the port and all the ships in it were doomed—Petros Zervas had seen to that.

Not even Cunningham knew this part of the scheme. Petros' plan was unfolding as surely as time itself and two o'clock was the magic hour. As the lead ship of the convoy, *Salvatore Spoleno,* reached the fifty-meter-wide entrance to the port, the Greek pilot would inexplicably increase his speed. He would cut sharply to starboard and accidentally ram the ship's bow into the end of the

244

western breakwater. Petros had calculated that if the ship did not sink or block the channel, it would take the tugboats at least a full hour to pry it free. By then the RAF would have begun its attack.

Petros tried to peer down to the harbor but the night was too dark. He imagined how it must look from the air—an unbroken sea of black, with no landmarks, no targets. Yes, he thought to himself, if it weren't for him, the British never would be able to make their bombing run tonight. If it weren't for him, there would be no way of stopping all those men and munitions from reaching Field Marshal Rommel. Once this night was over, Petros Zervas, a nobody, would demand full recognition for his achievements. He'd see to that.

Meanwhile, he could only remain at his post and wait, for as long as it took the British warplanes to reach Piraeus. Petros wished he could see what was happening down in the harbor. He wondered if Spyros had arrived at the ship. He wondered if his two assistants were standing by their beacons. It was all in the lap of the gods. He lay back under the pine tree on top of the hill, breathed in deeply. This was the night he was born for, and before it had ended, his lifelong dreams would come true.

32

The room at the end of the corridor was no ordinary chamber. The lights were dim, two small blue bulbs providing the only illumination, the bare walls and ceiling had been sound-proofed, and thick, black, double black-out drapes covered the windows. In a far corner a piercing bright spotlight illuminated a strange-looking object, which at first glance resembled a dentist's chair. But unlike anything in a dentist's office, it was crisscrossed with thick body straps and a strong leather head strap. They were cutting cruelly into the naked body of Trudi Richter.

Against the wall was a glass case filled with surgical instruments, hypodermic needles, and a variety of other equipment that Trudi recognized from her days as an operating room nurse. In spite of her determination to show no fear from the moment the two young Gestapo officers in civilian clothes had picked her up at her apartment and brought her here, her eyes, the only portion of her body still able to move, kept wandering to those merciless steel implements and she felt the terror rise inside her. Then the spotlight was turned on, and she found herself walled in by a small pool of hard, intense light, so bright that she could make out nothing beyond its perimeter.

"Fräulein Richter," a harsh voice was saying, "this is your last chance. Why did you suddenly decide you wanted to take a midnight ride to Athens?"

Trudi began to tremble, but clamped her jaws together to contain her fright. "I told you before and tell you now. It was at the request of Colonel Streck."

"So you stick to that ridiculous story. Very well, then. We know about the signal lights. We know about the raid. We know you know about the raid, which is why you tried to save your pretty skin. Now who is out there waiting to guide the British planes? Where are they?"

The room was cold, but Trudi was bathed in perspiration. So far she had been subjected only to questions. But when they saw she would not answer—she had to cling to her alibi until Willy decided to repudiate it—her ordeal would really begin. Would they rape her before they tortured her? Could she stand the pain?

The voice was ugly as it said, "Richter, there is very little time. We are trying to spare you."

Desperately she cast about for something to confess, anything to postpone the terror that was only moments away. But what could she say? That there was a plan to sink the convoy? They knew that already. That Petros was involved and was hiding at this very moment in the

246

spot the two of them had made love? Maybe, later when the pain was unbearable, she would have to tell them, but she would hold that to the very last. That admission would seal her fate, would *prove* she was a traitor; otherwise, how would she know? If she could only hold out, perhaps Johann would get word of the interrogation and take pity on her. Or Willy, for whatever devious reasons of his own, would back up her story.

"Now traitor. Talk!"

Trudi's throat felt so raw and sore she didn't think she could speak even if she had something to say.

A face appeared silhouetted in the bright pool of light. She could make out none of its features. "We regret that you won't help us," the voice said, the tone indicating it was she who would suffer regret.

Trudi's terror was so great that the first time they touched her, she believed she would lose consciousness. Please God, make it happen quickly, so she wouldn't know what they were doing to her.

Suddenly the spotlight was turned off, and the room returned to ordinary illumination.

The girl's eyeballs smarted. Tears ran down her face as she blinked again and again, trying to accustom herself to the change in lighting. At last she could make out the two Gestapo men, who were looking at her from the far side of the room.

Their faces were expressionless, showing no emotion.

They said something she could not hear. One of them shrugged, then pressed a buzzer that sounded in the corridor outside.

The door opened and with horror and revulsion Trudi saw Ilse Brugger come into the room.

33

The German pilot of the decoy British Lancaster made a wide turn over the water and headed for the Island of Aegina, thirty kilometers southwest of Piraeus, designated as the start of his flight path for the port. The roar of its engines gave off a distinctive basso hum, and anyone hearing the sound had the feeling that the huge airplane was struggling to stay aloft and maintain flight speed. Even the RAF who flew it regularly shared that sensation, although they knew better. Actually, the Lancaster was last of a breed, a huge, ungainly craft, with engines far more powerful than necessary. Soon it would be replaced by sleeker, faster planes, bombers that could maneuver with far greater ease, but until then it still ruled the skies.

The air raid sirens groaned as they came alive, their moans rising in pitch as well as intensity. They rose to piercing screams, fell away to growls, and then soared again, higher. The sound drilled walls, jarred people out of sleep, and sent them scurrying for their survival holes in the ground. The tense silence hanging over Attica was shattered, and in Piraeus, in Athens, and in the countryside men and women ran to safety.

On the ships of the convoy the soldiers who lined the decks glanced uneasily at each other, straining their ears for another sound, the roar of the engines. They alone had nowhere to hide.

At the airfield every available Messerschmitt and Fokker was airborne in minutes. The fighter pilots realized they might not play a decisive role in the battle ahead—the sky was too dark, they would have to climb high above the clouds, high above the British bombers coming in low. But a slight shift in the wind and conditions could change all that instantly; the clouds could be swept away, and the British invaders could be revealed below, like so many helpless gooney birds, ripe for the kill.

The harbor commander gave the order, and the smoke machines began pumping. As the thick white clouds crept over the port, the Italian destroyers, racing for the waters south of Turkolimano, started their smoke generators, too.

Schneider strapped on his steel vest, settled his helmet on his head, and, picking up his binoculars, headed for the roof of the Yacht Club. His place during the raid was at his desk, to be sure, receiving reports and coordinating the various activities that would result in the complete rout of the British. But there was ample time for that. He had worked hard and he deserved a treat, the sight of the Lancasters roaring to their slaughter.

Major David Cunningham heard the sirens, checked his watch, and joined Lieutenant Ashley-Cole and Sergeant Peters. "Guess they got my message and decided to move up the operation," he said. "Don't open the line to Cairo until the Lancasters have actually dropped their loads. If the Gestapo hasn't already put a solid tracer on us, it won't be long. So we have no chatter to spare."

Spyros Kanares paid no attention to the sound of the sirens, and, ignoring the Italian officers on the *Salvatore Spoleno,* he busied himself affixing his Black Saint Nicholas to the protected rear of the bridge. He could not and would not sail unless his beloved icon was in place, and he prayed to the saint to forgive him for what he intended to do.

The rise and fall of the air raid alarm awakened Nico and Elena. Nico wanted to run to the docks, to watch the Germans dying, to finish off the wounded with his own hands. But she guessed his intentions and clung to him tightly. She had found someone to protect her, to look after her, and she had no intention of letting him slip away.

Petros Zervas heard the sirens, and, bewildered, he checked his watch. The muscles of his stomach tightened in anticipation. Damn Cunningham—somehow he had got word to Cairo of the German pullout, and the RAF had moved up its strike. There went his brilliant plan to seal off the port; the British would be overhead before Spyros could even get started. . . . He looked down at the harbor; pitch-black. It all still depended on him. Carefully, to permit no last-minute error, he removed the covering from his signal light and awaited the approach of the lone pathfinder plane.

To the ears of his two volunteers, the sirens sounded like the blaring of trumpets. They connected the leads to their batteries, aimed their lights toward the Island of Salamis, and waited.

The German pilot of the British bomber banked slowly over the water of the Saronic Gulf. The coastline was a gray-black smudge below as he made his run, barely visible against the dark water. Even the heights of Kastela Hill were indistinguishable, and the houses of Piraeus, the homes and churches, the public buildings, the barracks of the Germans, and the waterfront docks and warehouses, all were obscured by the night. No sign of the fleet of merchant ships and their naval escorts could be glimpsed from above. All seemed serene, deserted; only because the flight crew knew they were above Piraeus did they realize there was a city below.

They flew by instrument, and when they reached the plain of Attica beyond the city limits they began the turn that took them over Athens. Then they headed out to sea again. Neither over the land nor over the water could anything be seen below; the aircraft seemed suspended in a great void of blackness. The steady, droning roar of its engines was a whisper in space.

The maneuver was repeated a second time, then a third as the Lancaster moved back and forth, flying south past the Island of Salamis, then heading north again and passing over the suburbs of Athens before it headed back in the opposite direction.

On the third leg of its flight, the Lancaster headed a little farther out to sea, then started back toward the land.

As it sailed over the dark smudge that was Salamis, suddenly a tiny light winked below, followed by a second one.

Moments later, as the aircraft crossed the mainland, three faint green glows blinked on and off, on and off, directly below. By making a triangulation, the crew could see an arrow that pointed straight at the harbor—and the waiting target of the fleet below.

The navigator plotted each beacon on his map, and the Lancaster, its mission completed, headed back toward Tatoi. The Salamis lights snuffed out, the green glow on the mainland faded away, and murky blackness once again enveloped Piraeus.

34

The searing pains were only part of Trudi's torment. The realization that her torture was being inflicted by Ilse Brugger made her degradation complete. She strained against the leather straps, she could no longer hear the sound of her own sobs, much less the screams that ripped the last of her breath from her lungs. But she had passed the point of ultimate suffering: from now on, no matter what Brugger did to her body, her mind and her soul were free.

Trudi was winning the insane battle, she knew, because it was the only victory left to her. In this moment of supreme trial she was proving she had endurance, even if she lacked strength and courage. Her will was pitted against Brugger's and she would triumph.

All at once the pain stopped and Trudi heard voices, as though from a great distance. One seemed familiar, and by concentrating on it she finally realized that Willy Streck was speaking. His voice was low, but she knew that tone of absolute command, and those who disobeyed it defied him at their peril. So Willy had come to try his superior skills on the body he had known so intimately. Well, let him. He would find that even he had lost the power to hurt her.

A door opened, then closed.

Trudi felt a cool, wet cloth placed on her forehead, and a moment later the straps that held her to the chair were unbuckled. A supporting hand was placed beneath her back and she was helped to a sitting position.

She opened her eyes, managed at last to focus, and saw that she was alone in the torture chamber with Willy. He was regarding her with concern and offering her a glass of water and a capsule.

"A painkiller," he said as she examined it. "Take it. You'll feel better."

Willy gave her an opportunity to compose herself, then helped her from the chair and tenderly half-carried her to a washbasin.

There, with his help, she cleaned the blood and filth from her body. Gradually, as she recovered her senses, she wondered why Willy was being kind to her. He knew her story was false, and was not the sort to permit personal considerations to interfere with professional duty. Or was he really so fond of her that just this once. . . ? For a moment, she dared hope that seeing her in this predicament had affected him. Then she knew she really must be in worse condition than she had realized to entertain such delusions. No, he was probably softening her for the kill, that would be Willy's style.

He opened a silver flask and handed it to her. She sniffed a first-rate cognac and took a deep swallow, then another. The wrenching pains that wracked her body were beginning to subside, thanks to the capsule; the brandy steadied her and she could breathe a little more easily. But she warned herself to be careful; she knew this was when Willy was his most dangerous. She had seen too many people, lulled by his sudden affability, let down their guard to their eternal regret.

She realized that she was naked, but that was nothing after what she had just been through. Besides, Willy had seen her nude too many times for her to feel any false sense of modesty in his presence.

Streck must have realized what she was thinking, for silently he handed her her clothes. She dressed slowly, her body seeming to regain strength increasingly, until by the time she opened her handbag, took out a lipstick, and applied it, her trembling had all but stopped.

"Nobody told me what was happening," Streck said. "I was busy and couldn't be reached. I came here as soon as I heard."

Trudi took her time running a comb through her long hair. "Why did you bother to come at all, Willy?" she asked at last.

Streck looked more like himself as he smiled ironically. "I don't make war on women," he said. "Besides, as you may remember, I never employ physical torture."

It was true; he always claimed torture was the mark of an inferior man; he found he could get better results by other means. "I suppose you've heard the charges against me," said Trudi.

"You were tense, frightened. We all are. Only a fool could fail to realize it was dangerous to remain in Piraeus tonight." He shrugged. "You may be many things, Trudi, but you're not a fool. What you did was perfectly natural. I might have done the same in your case. You told a harmless lie, to try to save yourself. It's a pity you didn't ask me yourself, because I would have happily provided you with a car and driver. I only regret it did not occur to me to save you the trouble, to say nothing of this—" He indicated the room, a distasteful expression on his face.

It was almost too much to hope, that she could actually deceive Willy, but she bowed her head gratefully.

"It is all too ridiculous," Streck said, "you a traitor to the Third Reich! There will be an investigation after we return from North Africa, and the mere fact that the ships safely reach their destination will be important in clearing you. But just to make certain," he added, his smile broadening, "I'll take charge of the investigation myself."

253

That smile did not fool Trudi; she had seen it too often. Willy would be merciless if he ever discovered what she had done. Thank God she had not talked under torture. For a moment she felt a new surge of optimism. No one had established that she knew about Petros. No one had suggested she *knew* details of the raid. But it was difficult to believe her ordeal had come to an end. "So you'll send me to prison until you come back from Africa," she said.

Streck laughed aloud. "Hardly. Our jails are filled with real enemies, Trudi *liebschen*. We have no room there for you. Besides, you'll be here when I return. Where else would you go?"

And suddenly the full horror of her situation struck her. Where else *would* she go? She was a prisoner, whether in jail or not. It had been preposterous for her to believe that after tonight she might be safe. Willy could never afford to let her escape. She had committed the unpardonable sin: she, who had once been an intimate of his, had cast a shadow over his career. Yes, he would conduct her investigation, but he would see to it that she never lived long enough to testify. Or that if she did, she would be put through such torment she would welcome the simple-minded savagery of Ilse Brugger.

A telephone rang and Streck answered. "Von Hellsdorf! Yes, I told them to put you through wherever I was. What—" he listened carefully, and began writing down notes in a leather notebook. "Fine! Splendid. So our little ruse worked? Air raid and all? Our decoy plane is in the air? Excellent! How soon do you expect it over Piraeus? Splendid. Congratulations. And congratulate the pilot."

He hung up and turned to her with a smile. "What a pity that call couldn't have come just a short while earlier. Then none of this would have been necessary. It seems the matter of the saboteurs has been disposed of. My men are rounding them up now. So if you'll excuse me, my colleagues and I still have a night's work ahead of us." He opened the door for her, then walked with her down the corridor, his arm around her waist. "You're free to leave. And again, my apologies for the unfortunate excesses of some of my zealous associates. I will see you as soon as I return from Africa. Until then, look out for yourself."

"Oh, I will, Willy," she said. *I will!*

35

The Italian destroyers plunged north at twenty knots into the deep Gulf of Phaliron. When the ships reached a point in line with the Zacharias villa, with a mile of land between them and the port, they made a sharp turn south at full speed, and turned on the smoke generators.

The thick white smoke crept like some solid cloud over the water toward land; but as it reached the shore and the foothill of Kastela, it broke apart and drifted through the streets of the city, seeping through the cracks in windows and doors into the homes. The destroyers were too far from port for the smoke to be effective, but the Italians continued to grind out their smoke. Soon the streets around Kastela, the empty lots and the long, high stairways, were filled with a low-hanging chemical fog that began to creep up the cobblestoned streets toward the pine grove. To avoid the oily smell and possible suffocation, the people poured out from basements and air raid shelters and climbed to the roofs of their homes, whatever high spot they could find. When the children began to choke, the women screamed, cursing the British for resorting to chemical warfare. The men who had fought in the war tried to explain, but the women wanted only to sweep up their children and run—but where? Their city below seemed drowned in a viscous white flood.

Colonel Schneider, setting up headquarters in the Port Authority Building, already had executed some preliminary changes in sailing plans. He gave his permission for the

255

ship captains near the eastern docks to pull in their lines; since the wind was with them, they could try to drift into the turning basin and get out of the harbor on their own. Admiral von Widdemer countermanded this order on the grounds that they were single-screw ships. In a narrow channel with the ebb tide on its way, the port would be jammed with drifting ships within minutes.

Schneider conceded he might have a point, but suggested the pilots double or triple their normal speed so that the channel could be cleared completely within sixty minutes. The admiral compromised on ordering an increase in speed from standard low to half speed.

Schneider received a report that the captain of a Bulgarian vessel, terrified at the thought of so much ammunition aboard, had requested permission to leave the harbor. He said he had done it before, even without tugs. Why not? Schneider thought, it would be one less ship to worry about.

The admiral disagreed. "We will not deviate from the order of departure. The commodore's flagship leads the convoy, and then ships as called for in the schedule. The Bulgarian will wait his turn like everyone else."

"But he's near the mouth of the port already," protested Schneider. "I think he can do it, and what he says makes sense."

"He hasn't done it with a thousand troops on deck," snapped von Widdemer. "They are all over the hatch covers, on the cargo in the holds below, which is loaded with ammunition as ballast. I'm making you personally responsible, Colonel, to make sure he doesn't pull in a moment before he is scheduled to do so."

Lieutenant-Colonel Willy Streck waited until Trudi had walked past the gate of the German headquarters compound, and then began to follow her.

Streck had good cause to feel pleased with himself. The decoy bomber had proved beyond doubt that there *were* British agents in the area. A platoon of his own men already had been dispatched to Salamis, and the signal lights there should be destroyed at any moment.

Two other beacons were being tracked down; but the bomber crew had been unable to pinpoint exactly the light here in Piraeus. So he elected to follow a far simpler course. It had been stupid to let Ilse Brugger torture Trudi; anyone who knew the girl would realize she would say nothing. But honey caught more flies than vinegar, and once Trudi realized her predicament, that her fate was sealed if she remained with the Germans, she would head directly for her one remaining protector, the man who in all probability was in charge of the third Piraeus signal light. Especially now that she had news of vital importance to trade—that his capture was imminent—which is why Streck had left specific orders for von Hellsdorf to phone him in the torture room.

A half dozen of his own men, all heavily armed beneath their trenchcoats, trailed behind him. Once he snuffed out the signal lights the British would be helpless, blind men unable to find their target in the dark; their raid would fail and Rommel would get his convoy. All because Willy Streck understood the heart and mind of a stupid wench who had gambled her good fortune, her life, against the might of the Third Reich.

36

At the edge of the grove behind the boulder, Petros Zervas covered himself with his raincoat and again struck a match to check the time. Two-fifteen. Somehow the pathfinder had failed to see the lights. But how?

At the sound of its motors he had blinked the light slowly. Fearful that the destroyers' smoke, which now hung over Kastela Hill, had masked the beam, he moved the searchlight to the top of the boulder and began to make desperate sweeps of the sky. He followed the plane over the port, anticipating the flare that would light up the port. But the sky remained black. At the sound of the motors directly overhead, Petros blinked the beacon wildly and, cursing the British, picked it up and aimed the beam after the plane. The pine trees in the grove turned green. Defying all earlier precautions, he swept his light on the grove a few more times, but the aircraft could be heard heading for Athens.

Petros began to scream and swung the light around and down the hillside, daring all to see it. He called the British blind bastards. Dazed, he placed the light down on the boulder again. When he realized the switch was still on, he turned off the light and waited. The British armada was out there, waiting. He's going to make another pass; he's got to make another pass.

I cannot fail, the plan is perfect. The second time around the pathfinder will have to see my light; and in his mind Petros began to imagine ships afire, explosions, he could hear the screams of the wounded. The smoke about him rose higher, its acrid smell bringing tears to his eyes, but he reassured himself that even if the smoke should engulf his light, the observer in the aircraft would be able to see its glow. "I cannot fail," Petros said.

The officer in charge of the search units for the beacon on Acte Peninsula brought his cars to a stop on the ridge. Like Petros, the beacon operator was walking around his light, disgusted with the British. The smoke from the Italian destroyers had not yet crept past the peninsula, and the youngster left his post to walk over to the sea and investigate the smell. When he could see and feel the smoke closing in around him, he ran back to his light, and carried the batteries to higher ground near the Wall of Themistocles. Damn the smoke! It would diffuse his beam, making it visible from the ground. He cursed aloud. The Germans heard him, and crouching low, crossed the rise of the ancient wall. The finger-snap of an agent who had tripped over the batteries brought them to a sudden stop. The Germans knelt and waited. Soon the mumbling youngster appeared, carrying the huge light beacon on his shoulders. As he set it on the ground, the nearest German ordered him to put up his hands. He heard footsteps closing in all around him and broke away and ran toward the smoke. The Germans fired a long burst and he fell to his knees, his hands clutching vainly for the protective blanket of thick white smoke.

Trudi Richter leaned on the guard rail at the bottom of the steps leading to Kastela Hill. Her stomach was heaving, her throat throbbed and her heart pounded against her chest.

She wrapped her arms around the concrete block, pressed against it and let her head drop forward. She took quick short breaths. As her body grew calmer, releasing the tight control she had maintained during the torture, sobs began to shake her, and she wept without stop. Finally she caught her breath.

Exhausted, she looked up at the long flight of steps to the street above. Just beyond the fishermen's tarpaper shacks, where the rain-carved trails finished their downhill runs as they cascaded out of the pine grove, it was only a short distance to Petros' hideaway. Her legs felt somewhat stronger.

Willy Streck confidently narrowed the gap between him and Trudi. The foolish girl had never once looked back, and it was plain she had no idea she was being followed. Streck had no intention of losing her on the dark Piraeus streets. Even as he glanced over his shoulder to make sure his men were close behind, he knew it was unnecessary. They were professionals and, like Streck, knew their business.

What worried him now was that the British might be arriving over the port at any time. Time was passing and with it his margin of safety was narrowing rapidly. But he had no way of forcing Trudi to increase her pace without frightening her; all she had to realize was that she was being trailed; and instead of leading him to the man he wanted, the man with the lights, she would go off on a wild goose chase.

Trudi began to climb a steep, narrow stairway of white-washed stones between tall houses that appeared suspended in space, and Streck pushed forward until he was only fifteen meters behind her. He could barely keep his quarry in sight; the stairs were crowded with Greeks, men and women who had forsaken the safety of their homes for a view of the harbor when the fireworks started.

He lengthened his pace to keep Trudi in sight.

A number of the Greeks soon realized that she was being followed, and several of them spoke to her, pointing down the stairs behind her. Streck cursed under his breath as the girl turned back to look without breaking her pace, and he turned against the wall so she could not see him. Luckily, the very Greeks who had identified the dark trenchcoats and slouch hats worn by Streck and his men as Gestapo uniforms themselves blocked Trudi's view of her pursuers. She hurried on.

He could tell by occasional glimpses of her legs that she was bone-weary, that only determination to reach her goal made it possible for her to keep going. And small wonder. Ilse Brugger had been far rougher on her than a trained Gestapo officer; if the interrogation had been handled properly, Trudi would have talked an hour earlier and the man Streck was seeking would be dead.

But no matter. Trudi couldn't keep climbing these steps forever.

A burly Greek on the stairs blocked Streck's path, but soon learned better. Streck drew an automatic pistol from a shoulder holster, and one glimpse was enough for the man to draw back against the wall and let Willy pass.

But the sight of the weapon aroused the hostility of the crowd. Not that Streck himself minded, but his subordinates, lacking his ability to depersonalize the hatred of the crowd and feeling hemmed in on all sides drew their own automatic pistols. No one dared move against five armed members of the dread Gestapo and the people shrank before Streck as he made his way after the poor girl dragging herself up the stairs.

For he had suddenly realized Trudi's destination. Of course! She was headed for some place high on the Hill of Kastela. Common sense indicated that a signal light would be emplaced on or near the highest point in Piraeus.

Certain he was closing in on his prey, he signaled his men to put his plan into operation.

All available Gestapo men were to surround the hill and begin to climb from different directions. A full company of Wehrmacht troops borrowed from Colonel Schneider supplemented his forces. Speed was essential, and all operatives were to abandon any other projects at once. It was imperative that the signal light be knocked out of commission before the Royal Air Force began its runs.

Organization and order were the real secrets of his success, and if he performed seeming miracles it was because he commanded men who obeyed him instantly and without question. As he mounted the remaining steps he knew that his men were already on the move.

The enemy agent or agents, Streck told himself, were as good as dead right now.

Colonel Schneider also recognized the fact that a British attack could be expected at any time now. When he realized the air raid alarm had been a device of some kind to confuse the enemy, and when no attack followed the probe of a single British plane, he sent word for the aircraft to return to base but ordered the smoke machines to step up their output.

The oily fog soon became so dense that even from the Port Authority Building it became impossible to see the transports. The smoke screen was a complete tactical success.

Petros grew desperate as the thick clouds blanketed the crest of Kastela Hill. Even though for some unaccountable reason the British pathfinder had not led in the bombers, he was certain by now the British squadrons must be very near Piraeus and possibly were circling somewhere over the Mediterranean, waiting to zero in on their targets.

Petros stared at his beacon, and after a moment of hesitation knew what had to be done. Reaching inside the tub, he broke off the tin reflectors, exposing the light bulbs. This would send his signal straight up into the sky rather than down toward the bottom of the can. His beacon would be that much stronger, although he realized it would make it easier for the Germans to spot.

But that was a risk he was prepared to take. By the time the German artillery found his range, the light would be extinguished and he would be gone. Even if the chemical fog became thicker, it would no longer matter. His beacon was now strong enough so that its glow would penetrate the oily clouds and be visible to the British pilots above.

The chemical fog completely blanketed the harbor, and on the bridge of the Italian destroyer *Salvatore Spoleno* it was impossible to see more than a few feet. Spyros Kanares, holding a handkerchief over his face, welcomed the smoke. It isolated him, making him feel he was alone in the world as he wrestled with the terrible problem that had been thrust on him.

He could hear the self-assured voice of Petros Zervas cutting through the fog:

"You and your saint. Talk, cheap talk. Make him proud of you!"

Spyros moved closer to his icon and touched it, hoping it would give him strength and courage. But the wood felt cold and hard, unyielding and alien beneath his fingertips. Never had he felt so old and tired, so unsure of himself.

"You are afraid, old man."

I'm not afraid, Spyros thought. I've lived long and seen so much that it won't matter if I die tonight. I have no reason to live. I was once a proud captain who wouldn't allow a scratch on my hull, but tonight I'm supposed to wreck this beautiful ship, this innocent ship. It's an indecent act that goes against every principle I've ever held.

"All of us must give up our principles at one time or another."

The old man felt ill, and leaned against the bulkhead for support.

The disembodied voice became harsher:

"I risked my life to save your Black Saint Nicholas. Now I call on you to repay that debt."

The boy had become as evil as the Germans he was fighting. Spyros felt sick at heart at the thought that war could make such a change in the character of a sweet human being.

The voice mercilessly slashed through the thick fog:

"What's happening to you, old man? Go out on your feet. Be free, mister."

The boy had been wrong to say such a thing, dead wrong. Something had happened to make him believe he was no longer bound by the laws of men. His immortal soul was in danger. That was the real problem, Spyros thought. Not whether he obeyed the boy and created havoc in the harbor, or whether he ignored him and guided the convoy safely out to sea—what really mattered was what could an old, tired man do to save a boy's immortal soul?

37

The low-hanging smoke on the eastern slope of the Hill of Kastela swept forward suddenly, aided by a strong gust of wind, and seemed to swallow up the entire area, including Trudi, Willy Streck, and his men. She picked her way across the wet grass, the smoke causing her eyes to stream and making it even more difficult for her to see. But her hearing became more acute, and all at once she thought she heard footsteps behind her.

A sudden terror assailed her, and she knew, with dreadful certainty, why Willy had released her. He had understood her even better than she had known herself; and he had freed her, knowing she would lead him to Petros. And that was precisely what she was doing.

But it was too late now to turn back, to seek some other destination. Her mind told her to flee, to turn aside, but she'd had to call on the last reserves of strength just for this final stretch, and she was too weak to go elsewhere. She wondered if she could reach Petros' hiding place on foot or would have to crawl.

Just to make sure her imagination was not playing tricks on her, she halted. The footsteps stopped, too. Her worst fears were confirmed.

Fear froze Trudi to the spot. Then it occurred to her that as long as she remained motionless she was safe. And so was Petros. It was such a relief to rest here, unmoving, not calling on her tired legs to drag her forward again. She felt an overpowering urge to stretch out on the cool, wet grass. But she knew once she lay down it might be impossible for her to rise again.

Willy Streck, waiting sixteen yards behind Trudi, curbed his impatience. It was possible she realized at last that she was being followed and was seeking some means of escape, but there was none. Streck smiled humorlessly.

According to reports from his radio man, his own men were moving cautiously up the hill. And for once Schneider had responded to a request with alacrity. The Wehrmacht company had split in half and were climbing from two directions. The platoon leaders had reported they were nearing the crest, and Streck waited a little longer before passing along the order for them to halt.

An eerie silence settled over the top of the Hill of Kastela as no one moved. But Petros Zervas, unaware that he was the central figure in a drama being played out directly below him, crouched beside his homemade beacon, bewildered that the British still hadn't appeared. Where were those bombers, in God's name? Had something gone wrong?

He tried to calm himself. If necessary, he would remain

here for the rest of the night and would be ready whenever the Royal Air Force came. He wished he had some idea what was happening in the harbor below, but the combination of the dark night and the chemical fog made it impossible for him to distinguish the outlines of even one of the many ships. Were they still there? For all he knew, they had started out to sea; if so, it was all up to Spyros. Would the old man do as he had been told? Petros cursed his blindness, his impotence.

Fear suddenly gave Trudi renewed strength. It occurred to her that Willy could creep up behind her while she stood here, and she knew what would happen to her if she fell into his hands again. She would rather be dead than be forced to return to the Gestapo torture chamber, and this time Willy would be in charge.

Petros would know what to do. He was the most clever and resourceful man she had ever known. If she could only reach him, he would protect her, he would find some way for them to get free. Bending down, she slipped off her shoes and started forward again, carrying them in one hand. Even she could scarcely hear her footsteps now, and she could only hope that Willy, or whoever he had sent after her, wouldn't hear them, either.

Reaching the top, she stood uncertainly for a moment or two. Then, through the swirling mists, she caught a glimpse of the solid masonry of the Church of the Prophet Elias to her right. Sure of her bearings now, she began to run with all her might toward the tiny, secret hideaway where Petros would be waiting.

The girl might have escaped unnoticed, but Willy Streck was a trained agent and he picked up the faint sounds of her feet as they touched the grass. On his signal the Gestapo agents, the two columns of Wehrmacht troops, resumed their climb to the crest of the Hill of Kastela.

But this time he had erred. The sound of boots thudding on the wet ground drowned out the much fainter noise of Trudi's light steps. He reached the level ground, taking a few indecisive steps to his right, then doubling back to his left.

The Gestapo agents understood precisely what was at stake in this manhunt, but the Wehrmacht troops, not as well briefed, realized only that an enemy of the Third Reich was to be taken dead or alive. The members of the first platoon to reach the crest caught a glimpse of a figure in civilian clothes, and raised their automatic rifles to their shoulders.

Streck, sensing the danger, shouted an order to halt.

The sound of the rifle fire drowned his cry.

A half dozen more bullets slammed into him, toppling him backward onto the ground. But he did not die immediately. Willy Streck was a man of iron will, and he literally willed himself to live. Long enough to tell these Wehrmacht farm boys they had made one of the most tragic blunders of the war.

He opened his mouth to speak, but no words came. He tried again, but in this final moment of his life he could utter no sound.

The men who had shot him thought him already dead.

And so Willy Streck, lieutenant-colonel of the Gestapo, intimate of Himmler and friend of the top members of the Nazi hierarchy, died on the muddy side of a lonely hill in a drab Greek town. It was small wonder that an expression of stunned incredulity replaced his habitual sardonic mask.

The bursts of gunfire increased Trudi's sense of panic, and, casting aside all effort to throw off her pursuers, she ran as fast as she could toward the secret hideaway. Reaching its rim, she threw her arms around the lovely white marble, and sobbing wildly slid down the incline into the hollow of soft, wet earth.

Petros, who had jumped to his feet and then crouched low at the sound of gunfire, saw the body hurtling toward him. As the figure grazed against him, he lunged forward.

"Petros!"

The stiletto blade dug into the ground above Trudi's head.

"Trudi! It's too early. The planes haven't come yet!"

Sprawled on the ground, shaking with fear and relief, the girl began to babble incoherently. The British plane is being flown by Germans . . . they know about the beacon . . . they've got us surrounded.

Petros shook her by the shoulders. "Who's got us surrounded?" he demanded harshly.

"I don't know," she said, and started to cry. "The Germans. The Gestapo. They are all over. They were after me, and you."

"Why?" Petros leaned over her. "How?"

Trudi sobbed aloud and could not continue. She reached up for Petros but he slapped her arms on the ground.

"How many of them are out there?"

"I don't know." She sobbed.

Petros did not wait for an answer. Thrusting her out of his way, he climbed onto the boulder. He could hear the Germans talking below, and from their voices estimated they were fifteen to twenty meters away. They seemed to have halted.

"Hold your positions and hold your fire," he could hear an officer order, as the word passed from soldier to soldier. Petros listened intently; the voices were coming from every direction.

"Listen," he said, climbing down from the boulder. "Either they're going to wait for more troops to close the ring around us, or they'll try to find us with the men they have. But in this smoke they can't see a thing." A soldier cursed loudly nearby. He leaned close to her. "I'm getting out of here! Are you coming along?"

Their faces were close together, but on this darkest of nights, with the man-made fog swirling around them, Trudi could barely see Petros. Was it her imagination—he didn't look like the same man at all. He had a haunted expression, his eyes were wild. Worst of all, his mouth was drawn in a thin cruel line. She stared at him, scarcely able to believe her ears. There was no alternative, didn't he know that? Either she went with him—or waited here for inevitable capture and death. Surely he wasn't seriously suggesting she remain behind? She realized that her presence would slow him down, that his chance of making a successful escape would be far better if he made the attempt alone. But without him she had no hope at all. And he had to know it.

Yes! Yes! Trudi answered fiercely, and then realized she hadn't spoken. "I am coming with you," she said.

"Then follow me, keep your mouth shut, and do precisely as I tell you." He climbed to the level ground above them. Trudi followed, her muscles aching painfully, and froze when a German a few feet away coughed.

Petros, holding his stiletto tightly gripped in his right hand, pressed Trudi on the shoulder with his left and indicated they should remain very still.

"All right, men," an officer called. "We're moving up."

Trudi felt that she and Petros were trapped, that all was lost. But when she looked over at him she realized he was actually enjoying their predicament. A gleam had returned to his eyes, a half-smile creased his lips. He was accepting an impossible challenge, relishing it! He gestured that they would retreat to the hollow. He went first, helping her down the slope so she could negotiate it silently.

No sooner were they settled than the Germans began to advance.

An officer ordered his men to advance carefully. A soldier, coughing, started to climb toward Petros and Trudi.

Petros turned toward the coughing soldier and waited.

Trudi tried to crawl back to level ground, but the mud and grass gave under the pressure of her weight. Petros reached up and grabbed her ankle; she tried to pull free, but his grip became tighter and she understood he wanted her to remain still.

The approaching soldier coughed again. Petros' fingers gripped the stiletto and his heels dug into the mud until he reached solid soil.

The soldier spat on the ground and was about to take another step when Petros reached out, pulled the man forward and thrust the stiletto into his stomach.

The wounded man coughed loudly. Petros spun him around, covered his mouth and slipped the stiletto under his chin and into the brain.

"Halt," the officer called.

The German to Petros' left waited for the command to be passed along. "Brandt?" he called, and started to advance toward Petros.

Petros coughed hard in reply. His left hand was balancing Brandt's body so it would not slide, as he gave Trudi the German's rifle with the other.

"Where in hell are you, Brandt?"

Petros coughed louder while he unbuckled the soldier's bayonet sheath. He continued to cough and after a few more times it became hollower.

The officer lowered his voice as he ordered a cautious advance. The soldier was so close Petros could hear his heavy footsteps.

"Come on, Brandt," he said, coming closer. "Krueger, I think Brandt is sick."

The soldier had come close enough to see what he thought was Brandt, leaning against the boulder, the sheath of the bayonet propping up his head. Petros coughed softly. He spat on the ground in imitation of Brandt. It was so dark and the smoke was so thick Petros could make out only the outline of the German soldier.

"Are you all right, Brandt?" the man asked again.

Petros mumbled, and started to cough again.

"We're moving forward," he said in a hoarse whisper. "As soon as you can, move up and fill in to my left. Understand?" And he moved on.

Petros waited until his shadow was swallowed up by the smoke, and then took the rifle from Trudi and with the other hand grabbed her wrist. This was their chance. Through the hole in the line, he started downhill and she followed. When they reached the line of perimeter, they slowed down but by now the smoke was so thick it was impossible to see anything.

Coughing repeatedly, holding Trudi close to him, he made his way through the line until he reached the first cobblestone street.

Trudi could scarcely believe it. They were safe, at least for the moment. Petros' quick thinking had enabled them to escape certain capture at the crest of Kastela. Now perhaps they could lose themselves in Piraeus.

Her sudden joy cooled as she looked over at him. He was staring down at the port, where long shadows of the fleet could be seen in the harbor. "They're still there," he whispered. "I can still do it!" Hugging the whitewashed walls of the city, he dragged Trudi behind him as he hurried into town.

38

The double blast of ships' whistles echoed through the streets of Piraeus, signaling the order for the convoy to clear the port.

Spyros instructed the captain of the *Salvatore Spoleno* to cast off all lines. "The orders are to proceed at half speed," he said, unbelievingly. "And the ships are to close in at three hundred meters. This is unheard of, Captain."

"I know," replied Antonio Forno. "But as the convoy commandant, I want to make sure my ship gets out safely. I don't care how closely the rest follow."

Spyros shrugged. "As you wish. Slow astern, both

tugs," he ordered. The tugs replied with blasts of their whistles and began to pull the ship from the dock.

Spyros called out for the after tug to stop, but the German infantrymen lining the decks began to cheer their departure so loudly his voice could not be heard.

Spyros appealed for silence to the captain, who sent word for the German liaison officer to come to the bridge. The German gave one bark into his microphone and all sounds ceased.

Spyros' voice seemed uncommonly loud as he repeated his order.

As the forward tug began to pull around the ship's bow, Spyros saw two other ships swing into the channel. Suddenly he feared for Petros' plan: if they reached the breakwater before he did, the boy's strategy would fail.

"They are out of position. We have to pull ahead of them," he told Forno, and called down to the engine room to start engines. Immediately the ship shook from the grinding of the shaft. The after tug nudged the stern of the *Salvatore Spoleno* in line with the port's entrance.

The old man spotted the directional lights on the breakwater, and ordered the after tug to stop. He glanced at both sides of the ship, his eyes narrowing as they had in the old days.

"Cast off both tugs." The tug lines splashed into the water and two short whistle blasts from the tugboats indicated the transport was free.

Spyros strained in the blackness to see the breakwater lights. His ship was drifting too heavily to port, and quickly he ordered the helmsman to correct course.

He joined the captain, but he had eyes only for the other ships. Spyros nodded to himself and ordered the ship to proceed at half speed.

When the ship was pushing six knots, Spyros knew it was time to edge toward the breakwater. For a moment the old man hesitated, tried to weigh his promise to Petros against his duty as a seaman. The lights of the breakwater ahead were growing brighter; Spyros had to make a decision. He ordered the helmsman to turn right five degrees rudder.

Suddenly Spyros' eyes widened as he caught sight of the Bulgarian ship, its stern swinging into the channel. "Full speed ahead!" he barked. If an accident happens now, he thought, it will be blamed on the confusion.

"Full speed ahead," the helmsman replied, hesitantly bringing his hand forward.

The extra rings from the engine room startled the Italian captain. He spun around, ran to the helm, and pushed the handle back to half speed. "What are you doing?" he shouted. "Trying to wreck my ship?"

Spyros did not reply, merely pointing to the fast-closing Bulgarian. The captain saw the stern drifting inexorably into the channel on the ebb tide as Spyros shouted: "Full speed ahead!"

Again the helmsman hesitated and looked at his captain, who nodded in agreement.

The light on the right breakwater was bright and on the left dim. Spyros corrected the bearing, and the captain, thinking his pilot was compensating for currents, joined them at the helm.

"Steady as you go," Spyros said as the ship started to pass the Bulgarian freighter.

The Bulgarian gave an angry whistle blast, and with a shake of his head Forno returned to one side of the wheelhouse. He considered apologizing to the pilot but decided to wait; after all, they were only three hundred and fifty meters from the spot where he could reclaim control of his ship.

Spyros' eyes were fixed on the lights ahead. He was unaware of the captain, the Bulgarian ship's whistle blasts, the singing of the German soldiers, the steady tremor of the engine below. His mind had returned to thoughts of home, of his plaza, as it had been before the war. He saw youngsters running and playing, he saw his friends, his customers smiling, he heard the housewives noisily bargaining with the food peddlers; he saw life as life should be. He saw Nico Andreades, his sister and brother, Taki, his old friend Andreades and his wife walking their offspring proudly to church. Spyros kicked the side of the wheelhouse, and he rubbed the wrinkled skin on the back of his neck. Where is the noise of life? Where are the people? he thought, his mind at the Kastela Plaza. The people are gone, the noise of the children is gone. The peddlers are gone . . . gone. . . . Spyros filled his lungs with the air of the sea.

"Forgive me, ship," Spyros murmured. Involuntarily he glanced at his Black Saint Nicholas. Mutely it stared back at him. "Left five degrees rudder."

"Left five degrees rudder."

The captain looked out in alarm. The ship was pushing ten knots and the lights on the breakwater were approaching fast.

Spyros glanced behind him and saw the Bulgarian ship coming on at half speed astern.

"He should be shot," Forno cried. "Captains like him should be shot."

With its engine at full speed, the *Salvatore Spoleno* closed in on the breakwater rapidly. The entire transport vibrated as its propeller dug into the water, splashing the oily water halfway up the ship's side, spraying the German replacements who were hanging over the guard rail watching the disappearing waterfront buildings and the Bulgarian ship they were leaving behind.

Spyros could see the shape of the breakwater loom ahead, the anti-aircraft guns lined on its concrete top, the silhouetted gun crews standing by. Behind steamed the coast-guard tender pulling back the anti-submarine net.

Spyros gauged the distance to the concrete block ahead. He had given no orders to the helmsman for the last hundred meters to be certain his next order would be executed instantly. The ship was slightly off course, which was just the way he wanted it. The ebb tide was dragging the ship along, and any last-minute decision by the captain would work against him, for they were deep in the channel now and vulnerable to any current.

One hundred twenty meters from the cement breakwater. "Steady as you go," Spyros said in a low calm voice.

"Steady as you go," the helmsman replied, keeping his eyes on the compass.

One hundred meters.

The captain took off his cap and wiped his perspiring forehead. He stared at the boulders placed as reinforcements along the sides of the breakwater.

"Steady as you go," repeated the helmsman, glancing first ahead and then back to the compass.

Ninety meters.

"Right fifteen degrees rudder," Spyros said calmly.

"Right fifteen degrees rudder," the helmsman replied, lulled by Spyros' calm.

Suddenly the captain came alive. His ship was heading for the boulders at full speed.

"Full astern! Full astern!" the captain shouted.

That was precisely the order Spyros was hoping for. With the tide going out and the propeller pushing the water to the starboard, the ship would veer to port, not astern. The engineers below, who had never in their career executed such a sudden change of direction, hesitated in confusion and then reversed the propeller's pitch just as the ship's bow crashed on the boulders, breaking the forward plates below the waterline.

The captain cried out even as he was hurled to the deck. The bow of the *Salvatore Spoleno* was hanging on the boulders while the tide and the opposite push of the propellor pivoted the stern of the ship like some giant seesaw.

Antonio Forno braced for the crash of the stern into the opposite breakwater that would seal off the port. It was too late to avoid the catastrophe. "All engines stop," he cried, as the ship, carried by the ebb tide, continued on its unchanging course.

The captain grabbed the steam whistle and tugged at it frantically.

Then he saw the Bulgarian approaching them broadside. "We are going to be rammed," he shouted as the black shape closed in at forty meters.

He kept blowing short blasts on the whistle, and the Bulgarian replied in kind, although he, too, was unable to control his ship. His engines were stopped but the ship was being swept by the tide.

Captain Forno, blasting on the whistle, suddenly released the cord as the Bulgarian ship nudged his side. The two ships ground together.

Spyros, feeling very old and fatigued, raised his hands in surrender. The captain slapped his face and told him he was under arrest.

39

At 2:31 the squadrons of the Royal Air Force armada converged at their rendezvous high over the Mediterranean near the island of Kithira, and moving into combat formation, turned north and headed toward Piraeus. Wing Commander Ashcroft was worried about their prospects but kept his pessimism to himself. Yet everyone could see that weather conditions were unfavorable: clouds were heavy, and the ceiling had dropped too low for a bomber run. Even if the pathfinder plane picked up the signals of British agents in Salamis and Piraeus, the armada would have to rely upon instrument flying. Visual bombing was out.

As the heavy Lancasters and B-17's lumbered northward, Ashcroft clung to one small hope. This part of the Mediterranean was known for radical changes in weather, and there was always the chance skies would clear before they reached their target area.

Ashcroft imposed a strict radio silence on all aircraft during the final phase of the run, and his pilots knew what was expected of them in the event of engine trouble or other mishaps. A crippled aircraft would drop out of formation, report its defection to no one, and head for the nearest British base. Every pilot and crew member knew what was at stake tonight. Veterans who had flown on thirty combat missions and greenhorns who were going into battle for the first time realized that before dawn the delicate balance of the war could be tipped decisively, one way or the other.

Conditions in the Piraeus harbor were chaotic in spite of the efforts of Admiral von Widdemer, Colonel Schneider, and their aides. The crippled Italian transport blocked the channel, and the tugs were hampered in their attempt to clear the port entrance by the foundering Bulgarian vessel. When the damage was determined too severe for the ship to make the run to North Africa, the order was given to remove all troops and supplies and distribute them throughout the fleet. It was essential that everything possible be salvaged for Field Marshal Rommel.

"Stand clear!" men shouted, as the sickening sounds of metal grinding against metal were heard in the harbor.

Colonel Schneider, on strict telephone instructions from General von Schlichter in Athens, kept his smoke generators busy, pouring the thick oily compound into the air. The smoke reddened the eyes of the troops on the decks, the masters and their mates, making them choke and gasp for breath, but everyone recognized the need to maintain the heavy smoke cover. If the British bombers appeared before the channel was cleared, the convoy would be helpless.

Finally the admiral sent the word Athens was waiting to hear. He estimated that the convoy would be able to move out to sea in approximately thirty minutes.

40

Petros Zervas saw the sudden opportunity and seized it. As he and Trudi neared a corner in the heart of the city, a German sentry unsuspectingly crossed in front of them. Petros thrust his stiletto deep into the man's throat, killing him instantly.

Dragging the body into a small garden, he quickly shed his civilian clothes, flung them at the base of a small lemon tree, and donned his victim's Wehrmacht uniform. He slipped the soldier's pistol into his belt, picked up Brandt's rifle and bayonet, and all at once his face took on a savage expression. As Trudi watched in horror, he turned on the dead German and jabbed the bayonet again and again into the body.

Trudi, shocked at his contorted face, touched him lightly on the shoulder to bring him out of his frenzy. He wheeled toward her, and for an instant she thought he might ram the bayonet into her, too. The moment passed, his face cleared and he laughed aloud, a boyish laugh that was bright and confident.

She had watched the man change as he changed into the Wehrmacht uniform, and when he took her by the hand to lead her out of the garden she could have been following Willy Streck. Trudi did exactly as Petros commanded. His indifference to her earlier ordeal, the exhausting uphill run, his brutal impersonality, all confused her. The smoke was too dense for her to see him; he guided her by his voice alone. But even that had changed; it was sharp, cutting—the voice of a man who would let nothing, no one, get in his way.

She broke the long silence to ask where they were going. Her memories were sharp and painful, and she knew the Gestapo would not rest until the two fugitives were captured.

Petros, deep in thought, made no reply.

The girl repeated her question.

"I can still do it," he said as if she had not spoken.

She stared at him, not understanding.

"The British are depending on me to guide them," he said brusquely. "If I can't do it one way, I'll find another."

Trudi felt sick. Hadn't there been enough bloodshed for one night? Petros was as obsessed as Willy Streck. "Haven't you done enough?" she asked wearily, and even as she spoke she knew that he was impelled by an inner demon that would not permit him to stop. He was beyond her reach now, beyond anyone or anything other than the forces that were driving him. He wouldn't be satisfied until he destroyed himself—and God knew how many others.

They were close to the center of the city, and she had no idea where he was taking her. Suddenly he halted so abruptly she fell against him. Trudi clung to him, her head tucked against his back. She felt the immediate excitement as their bodies met, and knew that in spite of everything her need for him was as great as ever. She was tired, she wanted to quit, but she did not speak. She wanted to live. She had done all she could. Now. Let us quit now, she thought, and squeezed against him. All is lost.

The all-clear sirens rose to a steady scream, and the people began to pour from the basements to return to their beds.

Soon the street was full of citizens. Many were loudly commenting on the failure of the raid, while some could be seen making the sign of the cross for having been spared. A woman with a coughing child hurried uphill and Petros flattened against the wall to let her pass. She bumped against him and the child began to cough louder. She saw the uniform and began to hit him with her fists, shouting "Murderer!"

Petros tried to push her aside but she kept hitting him. Two other women tried to pull her off.

"Get the hell off me," Petros growled, and dragging

278

Trudi headed into the middle of a crowd. The people drew back at the crack of his boots on the cobblestones, and those too slow or too weak were shoved out of his way. The uniform, the steel helmet, the tight-fitting jacket and leather belt gave him a new sense of authority, a new sense of power. He could see the harbor clogged with transports filled with men. I can do it! he reassured himself. I can still do it.

He swung away from the main thoroughfare and threaded through a maze of narrow, twisting alleys. The long walk was becoming a nightmare for the frightened Trudi. She could sense the violence in him; this man beside her, this stranger, wouldn't be satisfied until he had committed some terrible act of violence.

Petros opened the rear door of the Church of Saint Constantine, and Trudi welcomed its sanctuary as they entered the cavernous building. It was quiet and peaceful here under the high Byzantine domes; but they kept going.

He led her into the plaza, where the abandoned florists' shops stood, and then suddenly turned into another narrow alleyway.

She could stand it no longer. "What are you doing, Petros? What remains to be done?" She leaned against a wall and then slid to the ground, wrapping her arms protectively around her knees. Trudi knew Petros was acting out of desperation, searching for some impossible scheme, some wild success, anything to justify their deaths. "Failure is human too, Petros. Defeat is human . . . you must accept it."

Petros refused to acknowledge her words. Failure. Defeat. Hadn't he already proved he was not bound by human weaknesses? To men like him a rope never ends so long as it can be knotted to another rope; another link always can be added to a chain. Determination knows no limits. Petros looked down at Trudi and realized that she was one of the weak, one of the parasites who live off the strong. The weak are the masses, figures who allow themselves to be marked on a blackboard, to be multiplied and subtracted at a stroke of the chalk.

Petros tightened the strap of the helmet under his chin. "Any minute they are going to be overhead," he mumbled to himself. "I know there is a way. There must be a way."

The generator halfway across the plaza was belching smoke. The chemical mixture, which was lighter than the destroyers' smoke, rose into the air and then drifted with the wind in a thick cloud toward the port. Petros pulled Trudi to her feet, heard the sputtering motors of the other generators cutting through the still of night, and realized that his hopes were dimming rapidly.

"Let's go," he ordered.

Trudi started forward, and when they were inside the smoke Petros took her wrist and began to run. They sprinted across the street in front of the auditorium and dashed down the steps to the basement.

He pulled Trudi inside. "Nico?" he whispered.

There was no answer.

"Nico," Petros cried. "Goddamit, where are you?" He walked around the cement column and stopped in the middle of the basement.

Elena saw the German uniform and tensed in fright. Nico, seeing this, quietly told her he was a Greek, the one who had promised the money. At once she relaxed. "Maybe he has the gold," she whispered. "Please, don't make him angry at you."

Nico put his hand over the girl's mouth and listened to the footsteps. He was trying to identify the other person. "Please speak to him," she whispered again. "He promised you he would bring it here."

But Nico knew Petros Zervas. His voice was not that of a man with the payroll. His was the wheedling voice of a man asking for help.

"Nico?" Petros called again in growing desperation. "Where are you? I know you are here." He snapped on the lighter. The flame blinded him and Trudi and he raised it over his head. The shadows of the concrete posts trembled against the walls as Petros scanned the basement for his friend.

"Nico?" He raised the lighter higher but could see nothing. Nico and the little girl were hidden in the shadow of a foundation post.

"Who is Nico?" Trudi asked.

"A friend," Petros said and snapped off the lighter. "A friend of mine."

"And he lives here?"

"Yes," he said, dragging her through the puddles. "He chases the smell of food, like the rest of them down here. You've seen them," he said in disgust. "NICO!" The name ricocheted off the ceiling and walls. "He's probably out there somewhere cringing in the dark." He straightened his helmet. "Well, I'll do it without him. Let's go."

Nico Andreades smiled but the young girl's body tightened with fury. Her breath came short. Where was the man who had promised her life instead of the dream, who had offered her hope and a full belly instead of death on the wagon? She had been a fool to believe him! She leapt to her feet and ran blindly across the basement.

"Hey . . ." she called out. "Nico was asleep and he couldn't hear you. But he's awake now. . . ."

Petros pushed past her. "Nico," he yelled. "Where are you?"

"What do you want from me, Zervas?"

Petros began to walk toward the voice. The young girl took Trudi by the hand and pulled her after her.

"I don't want anything from you, Nico," he said, and snapped on the light again.

"What do you need from me then?" Nico's face was cold, his eyes hard.

Petros returned the lighter to his pocket. "Listen," he said, kneeling down in the dark beside his friend, "I don't need you myself. We are needed by the sacred soil we were born on." He cut off Nico's protest. "No, Nico, hear me out. We are needed by the innocent who will die from starvation. We are needed to destroy all those on the ships out there," he said, pointing in the direction of the port

281

with his rifle. "We can't let those ships break out, don't you understand?"

"I understand!" Nico cried. "I understand that if you had any decency left, you would stick that thing in your ear and squeeze the trigger."

"Let's not discuss that again," Petros said. His voice became harsh. "I had everything set to turn those ships into firewood. They set a trap for me——"

"The only thing I want to hear is the jingle of yellow coins falling into my palm."

The young girl walked closer and smiled in anticipation.

"I don't have it," Petros said.

"Hey, you. You promised," she said. "I heard you with my own ears promising the gold." She started to cry silently.

Trudi wrapped her arm around the girl. "Please don't cry," she whispered.

"Why?" Nico said. "Why don't you have it? The gold is mine, Petros."

"Not quite, my friend. There's still one more job to do."

The girl began to shake, and Trudi pressed her against her body to deaden the biting voice of this man she had never met. The little girl buried her face against her, as Trudi stroked her back with one hand and with the other caressed her unkempt hair.

"I've risked my life once," Nico said. "No one can ask me to do it again."

"Nothing can save you, Nico. You are a walking corpse; there is no hope for you or the girl," Petros said matter-of-factly. "When was the last time you had a meal? Hey? One good meal . . . half a meal now would kill you, Nico." Petros waited for an answer. "I am offering you the chance to do something before you die. To do something to be remembered for. How many people get that chance, Nico? Think of the mortals left here on earth. Here is your moment to give them a little air to breathe, a little freedom."

Nico did not answer. His eyes were shut and his mind yearned for the tranquility of death. He was suddenly tired of life, tired of seeing others struggle to live. He thought of the little girl. He thought of Taki. Perhaps it is better that way, he thought.

"Nico," Petros was saying, "what does the next minute matter, or a year or two, or twenty, when it comes to that? Think back and it only takes an instant to see yourself as a kid in short pants. Live, and what do you have to look forward to? Minutes? Hours? What's important is what you do with the time you have left. What will you do?"

"What will I do?" Nico asked dazedly. "When I tried to do something I lost all those dear to me." He began to cry. "What do you want me to do, Petros? Tell me how I can do something for the mortals on earth. Tell me how to make the seconds count."

The sound of a single plane droned overhead.

Petros looked up in excitement. "The pathfinder! They'll make one pass and then they'll come around again."

"What shall I do, Petros?" Nico asked, struggling to his feet.

"Follow me," Petros said. "There is no time to waste. We have to get into the emergency powerhouse by the port. We'll light up the harbor from end to end."

The others stared at him in amazement. Trudi was the first to find her voice.

"You really do want to kill yourself, then," she said softly. "You realize, of course, that a company of Wehrmacht troops guards the power station."

Petros looked at her as if she were raising some minor technicality. "In case you've forgotten, I worked there myself before the war. I know the entire installation better than anyone else in Piraeus." He turned to Nico. "Let's go."

The little girl rushed forward. "Take me with you, Nico."

"No!" Trudi shouted the word.

"No?" asked Petros in surprise.

"I am not going to let you take her," she said in sudden fury. "I'm not going to let her sacrifice herself for your wild dreams of immortality. Unlike you, Petros, I value life. The minutes, the hours, and years you scorn matter to me. As they do to these mortals you speak of so grandly, so impersonally. You talk of doing something to be remembered for, but your methods are no different from those you say you hate. Well, you can destroy yourself and your friend here, but the girl stays with me."

Petros snapped on the lighter and saw Trudi and the girl staring at him. Trudi's eyes were narrowed, the young girl's wide and moist. Petros tried to speak but instead his lips formed a crooked smile. With the barrel of his rifle he tipped up his helmet so she could see him better. The smile faded and his expression turned hard.

"Very well," he said at last, "save yourself. Take the girl and wait for us at the school. My British contact—the man I work for—will send someone to pick us up there later. He's promised to sneak me out of Greece after the raid. I suppose a few more passengers won't matter." He snapped off the lighter. "Let's go, Nico."

"Who is she?" Nico whispered as they started for the door.

"A whore," said Petros. "Just another weak fucking whore."

When Trudi and the child were alone, Trudi reached around until she found the candle she had seen earlier. She lit it.

"I'm going with them," Elena said.

Trudi shook her head.

"I am!" The little girl started after the men.

Trudi caught hold of her thin wrist and pulled her back. "Stop fighting me," Trudi said. "You're going to stay with me."

"Let me go!" Elena struggled ineffectively as she tried to break the woman's hold. "Nico needs me. So does your husband—"

"He isn't my husband."

"But he and Nico are going to save Greece!"

"Petros and your friend Nico," Trudi said quietly, "are going to die."

Elena covered her ears. "I won't listen to you! I heard what Petros said. You are the German whore! What right do you have to—"

"I have the right to live," Trudi said, her voice becoming stronger. "And if I do nothing else worthwhile in this world, I'm going to see that you have the same right."

"You can't stop me—"

"I have stopped you," Trudi interrupted. "Now, listen to me, little girl. Yes, I'm the German whore, as you call me. Do you want to become like me?"

"No!"

"Then pay attention to what I say." Trudi sat down, dragging the still struggling child down to the pallet with her. "What Petros is doing is insane, and I've had enough of insanity. Even if he lives through the night—and the odds are one thousand to one against him—he'll be killed tomorrow. Or the next day. He'll keep going until he destroys himself—and the world around him. Can you understand that?"

The little girl shook her head and began to weep.

"Surely you can understand that." Trudi paused and peered at the little girl in the light of the flickering candle. "What are you doing here alone?" she said. "Where are your mother and father?"

Elena sobbed louder.

Trudi held her close. "I know, I know, but at least *you're* still alive," Trudi said. "You've survived. And you'll still be alive next month, next year—if you're smart and tough and shrewd. If you look out for yourself."

Elena looked up at her through her tears. "I never knew a woman so cruel."

"Cruel?" She considered the word. "Yes, I suppose you could say that. But I don't really ask for much. Just the right to live—every hour, every day. And not as a privilege, not as a favor. But as a *right*."

The child had stopped fighting and was listening, the sobs coming slower now.

"If I must," Trudi said, "I'll sell myself to a man. The price I pay is cheap enough. Because what I do with him doesn't touch me. What matters is that *I survive*. I've seen enough of death and misery and hell. If I'm forced to compromise, I'll compromise. So, no matter what happens to anyone else—to madmen like Petros Zervas—I intend to *survive*. And if you want, I'll see that you survive, too."

Elena said nothing. Then, slowly, tentatively, she extended a small, grubby hand.

Trudi took it, and together in silence, two refugees from the violence of violent men, they set out for the schoolhouse.

41

The smoke drifted over the waterfront in a thick mass. The port, the ships, the silos and cranes, the entire southern part of the city were swallowed in its paste; from above it seemed as if the rain clouds hugged the earth. The British aircraft turned south for the Island of Salamis and then north again, seeking the lights for their bombing run.

It was 2:57 A.M. and quiet at the emergency powerhouse. In the temporary barracks no one paid any attention to the commotion in the harbor. Most of the troops were asleep, and the sentries were just about to change shifts. The replacement generator operator hauled himself out of his bunk and went off to the latrine before going on duty.

It was time for the officer of the day to make rounds. The sentries along the barbed-wire fence and the guard at the gate saluted him, and the lieutenant automatically raised his hand to his visor in response. Even though it contained only the auxiliary power supply—two portable generators powered by fuel to provide the port with current in an emergency—the compound was defended like a fortress. It was surrounded by a stone wall nine feet high, with heavy barbed wire coiled on the top, and the gate was made of corrugated steel. Two machine guns, each with a three-man crew, were emplaced behind sandbags on a concrete terrace above the officer-of-the-day's quarters. Light anti-aircraft guns were mounted at opposite ends of the terrace to repel any possible low-level aircraft attempts on the port.

But at that moment the installation was in danger of a different attack. Petros Zervas and Nico Andreades had made their way silently through the back alleys to the power station, which was located only a stone's throw from the northeastern end of the main port.

There they paused, and Nico spoke for the first time since they had left the basement of the auditorium.

"If you get out of this alive and I don't," he said, "I want you to look after Elena for me. The little girl."

Petros nodded reassuringly. He wondered why Nico was staring at him in such a peculiar way. Something was wrong with him—had starvation finally driven him off his head? Well, he wouldn't be the first. So long as he was still able to help, nothing else mattered.

"Keep my money, I don't care," Nico was saying, "but I want you to spend some of it on the kid. I want her to be comfortable for a few days. And it will only be for a few days. You saw her," Nico said. He squeezed the arm of this man he had called a friend: the man whose talents and courage he admired until Petros had betrayed his friendship and condemned his family to the slow death of starvation. "You've got to promise me, Petros, and this is one promise you have to keep. I don't want her to die all alone like my brother."

"I promise," Petros said, and gestured for silence. They began to creep along the power station wall, halting as

287

they drew near the gate and heard the scrape of a sentry's boots on the cobblestones.

The timing of their attack, Petros figured, would have to be perfect. At the sound of approaching airplanes they would switch on the generators and turn the port into the greatest beacon of them all. But first they had to get inside.

From the port they could hear the sound of motor launches, an occasional, angry shout and the distant throbbing of engines. It was impossible to determine whether the Germans had opened the channel yet, and Petros could only hope Spyros still blocked the entrance. At least he had done his part in that vital operation.

A glance at Nico told him that his friend was badly frightened. Well, why not; Petros wasn't any too calm himself. These last seconds were the most difficult.

Faintly, somewhere in the distance, they could hear a steady humming sound. Perhaps it was only a motor launch in the outer portion of the port, and both of them listened intently. The sound faded, then grew stronger again, and Petros knew the time had come. In another few minutes the British armada should sweep over Piraeus.

He nodded, and Nico leaned against the gate, braced himself as Petros climbed onto his shoulders and reached for the top of the gate, the only part of the perimeter unprotected by barbed wire.

Petros hauled himself to the top. Directly below him was the sentry.

The roar of British aircraft became more distinct, and the sentry raised his head.

At that instant Petros jumped, landing on the soldier before he could cry out, sending him sprawling onto his back. The butt of Petros' pistol smashed into the German's face, dazing him, and strong fingers closed over his throat. He thrashed for several seconds, then lay still.

Petros leaped to his feet, unbolted the gate, and, handing the sentry's automatic to Nico, paused just long enough to gather up a cluster of hand grenades.

From then on the plan was simple. Nico would provide cover for him while he made his way to the building that housed the generators. He started in the general direction of the plant, but the night was so dark and the smoke so thick he had to move cautiously.

Nico darted to the far side of a parked personnel carrier, intending to use it as a shield, and froze when he felt rather than saw movement only a few feet away.

"Halder?" a German called nervously from behind the vehicle. "Is that you?"

Nico edged along the side of the carrier, then headed toward the compound's air raid shelter. Petros kept moving in the opposite direction where the generators were housed.

"Halt!" called the aroused German. "Halt and identify yourself!"

Two men opened the trap door of the air raid shelter to investigate, and Nico flattened against a wall. In the dark Petros tripped on some concrete steps and fell.

"Alarm!" the sentry shouted.

Nico aimed at the voice and squeezed the trigger. The automatic crackled and he saw the soldier fall to the gravel.

In the light of the flashes Petros found the door to the generator plant. He leaped up the steps and was inside before the soldiers in the shelter, drawn by Nico's fire, could swing their weapons toward the open door. Nico unscrewed the end of the grenade, pulled the cord, and dropped it inside the shelter. The grenade blasted the trap door and sent it flying, as Nico dove through the open door behind Petros. The Germans above opened fire with their fifty-calibers.

"Petros," Nico cried, and turned to see the ashen-faced lieutenant aiming a Luger at him. He had jerked aside so the German would miss when he heard the bark of a pistol. The lieutenant's arms flew back, his knees buckled and he crashed to the floor.

"In here, Nico!" Petros shouted as he flung open the door to the generator room. The operator, eyes wide with fear, clapped his hands over his head in surrender. Petros jabbed the muzzle of his weapon into the man's stomach. "Are you the only one here?"

"Yes," the man cried. "Please. I am not armed."

Petros squeezed the trigger and the force of the explosion lifted the operator off his feet and dashed him against the small generator. Petros pushed him aside, and the body fell to the floor.

Nico picked up the lieutenant's Luger and crawled to the hall. "Stay there and cover me," Petros said.

The Germans directed the fifty-calibers on the middle of the compound. The exploding shells, the hiss of flying gravel, the whistle of the ricocheting metal sounded like a thundering echo chamber. Nico pressed his palms against his ears, flinching with every blast.

Petros started the smaller generator and pulled out the throttle slowly in order not to flood the motor. As the generator responded, he pushed on the main switch to activate the master panel and set the voltage at 115. Then he ran to the larger generator.

Outside, the fifty-calibers halted suddenly. "Put up that damn ladder," a voice called from above.

There was no answer. Instead one of the soldiers advanced into the center of the compound and pumped round after round into the office; broken glass and splinters crashed against the ceiling and walls. When he heard the large generator cough to a start, he turned on the corrugated door next to the personnel carrier.

"Hold your fire," the young soldier screamed from above.

"Where's that ladder?" another voice called from the terrace.

Petros gunned the motor of the large generator just as the ladder hit the top of the parapet. Immediately bullets from the compound cut into the corrugated metal door and bounced from wall to ceiling; they clanged against the generators.

Nico saw several Germans at the far end of the hall, stripping the rifle rack. He withdrew, armed a hand grenade, and pitched it down the slippery tiles. Nico ducked back inside just before the explosion rattled the building.

When he stuck out his head again, he saw some Germans trying to rise to their feet. Firing two long bursts he stepped into the hall, disregarding the firing outside, and dropped them before they could get out of range.

"Nico! They are mounting a machine gun out there," Petros said, pointing to the corrugated door.

Crouching low, Nico rolled up the door just high enough to crawl under and slip into the compound. He saw the Germans mounting a fifty-caliber machine gun on the front of the personnel carrier. Creeping under the truck, he tossed his last grenade and ducked behind the rear wheel. There was a flash and a sharp vibrating blast, and the gunner on the terrace began to spray the entire compound in hopes of hitting the intruder.

Suddenly he heard running footsteps and men shouting orders. The fifty-caliber fired a few bursts and then the gunner paused to listen.

Overhead the British pathfinder flew past and Nico stared out into the dark port, waiting for Petros to throw on the floodlights. Petros had told him that once the pathfinder had dropped its flare, a wave of planes carrying incendiaries would set the ships afire. That was the time to shine on all the lights, but the only flashes Nico saw came from the rifles of three Germans running toward him.

Nico sprayed bullets in their direction until the clip was empty. The Germans fell to the ground, two of them dead, the survivor continuing to fire. Nico changed clips and fired. All became quiet again.

Nico waited for the second wave of planes flying toward Athens.

By now German headquarters had sent truckloads of patrols to support the power station. When the anti-aircraft crew heard they were coming, one of the crewmen trained his weapon on the gate and began to fire continuously, hoping to keep the attackers inside the compound.

Nico anticipated a pause, but the gunner seemed determined to turn the metal gate into a colander. Half a block away, behind the Church of Saint Speridon, German reinforcements scrambled out of their vehicles, while those patrols that had already surrounded the building broke ranks to let the infantry through.

Nico ran to the corner of the building and scanned the entire western port area. Not a floodlight could he see, and by now he could no longer pick out a sound in the sky.

All he heard were boots running toward the building and officers ordering their men to advance.

"Petros," he shouted into the open window of the generator room. "Turn the lights on!"

The German patrols across the street fired at the sound of his voice, then stopped to let the infantry move into position. The slow barking of the machine gun spat bullets steadily.

Nico tried to listen for the planes between the short pauses of the gun, but when he heard nothing he ducked inside to check on Petros.

"What in hell are you doing here?" Nico shouted. He saw Petros leaning over the dead German officer in the corridor. "The planes are gone."

Petros pulled a ring of keys from the officer's neck and ran back into the generator room.

Nico followed him. "What's taking so long? They've got us surrounded. The planes are gone. We've failed."

"They are still up there," Petros reassured him, as he worked the key into a red lock. "I told you there would be a three-minute pause before the next pass." He threw the clamp on the floor. "Get out there and hold them back."

Nico's eyes narrowed with anger. He hesitated by the door and then, sliding a fresh magazine into the chamber of his weapon, started out again. He heard rushing footsteps and realized that the Germans were moving the machine gun away from the fuel drums that serviced the generators, for fear of a possible explosion.

Petros opened the door. "They'll be flying in any second now."

Nico did not answer. Was that the hum of aircraft in the sky?

He ran to the door and looked out. "Now!" Nico shouted. "The planes are coming! Turn them on, Petros. Turn on the lights!"

"I heard," Petros shouted and activated the control of the small generator. "Watch," he said, and threw on the switch of the large generator.

Suddenly it was bright as day. From one end of the breakwater to the other, the floodlights, the buoy lights, the utility lights on the warehouse walls, the crane lights, the coal depot lights, and the lights over the railroad tracks burst forth in dazzling brightness. The thick smoke was transformed into a huge white cloud. The sounds of the port—the steam horns of the ships, the tugs, the rifle fire—stilled under the sudden explosion of light.

Petros brought up the voltage meter as high as it would go, the lights doubled their brilliance, and the pulsating glow of smoke burst into a lustrous dome. He held the lights at the sustained high voltage.

The fifty-caliber swung around to knock out the lights, while the patrols fired through the corrugated door and windows, pelting the walls of the compound. Petros and Nico, who had scooped up fresh ammunition and grenades from the hall and positioned themselves inside the power room away from the trajectory of the bullets, were firing machine pistols freely now. When one stopped to reload, the other would lob grenades at the German replacements. But both were intent on the anticipated whine of the British bombs.

The first wave of planes flew by and reported back the astonishing sight below. Wing Commander Ashcroft, suspecting the possibility of some elaborate deception, ordered the second wave to fly low to investigate closer; but when German searchlight beams started to sweep the sky and the anti-aircraft batteries opened up, he gave the long-awaited order, "Bombs away!"

293

The bombardiers released the heavy bombs along with thousands of small, deadly incendiaries.

Suddenly all rifle fire outside the power house ceased; the Germans fell flat on the ground and only the thuds of flak from the anti-aircraft guns broke the lull.

The troops heard the dread whistle of bomb fins cutting a path in the sky, and then the cavalcade of heavy bombs plunged into the water. They ripped apart the ships, scattering the cranes on the western docks like toys that thundered down their tracks, crashed against the walls of buildings, and collapsed into the sea. The exploding bombs sent tons of coal hurtling into the air like rocks, splattering the city and the port. Two ships splintered at the seams with such force that men, equipment, superstructure, and chunks of deck catapulted high into the air. Those replacements who survived hung onto the debris. When magnesium incendiaries tumbled out of the sky, burst into flames, and turned the decks into a white-hot furnace, the soldiers leaped over the side and tried to swim away. But the water around the burning ships became a boiling cauldron.

Twelve ships, the docks, the waterfront, and buildings one hundred meters deep into the city were afire. Now the entire area was choking in smoke; the leaping flames, fueled by the oily chemical smoke, ignited cotton bales, silos, lumber yards, the top floor of the port headquarters.

The bombardiers in the next group leveled their craft and released the bombs at channel center. The second salvo toppled the remaining cranes, demolished the entire row of warehouses on the west side, and set the remaining ones on fire. The anti-aircraft guns pounded as the bombers continued north breaking formation, they fanned out to confuse the searchlight batteries.

In the city flames leaped across the alleys from building to building, consuming everything. Fire engines raced to the fringes of the holocaust. Everyone who could do so headed for the center of the city, to get as far as possible from the fire.

The next RAF wave carried general-purpose bombs with delayed action fuses, and they released their loads over the length of the port. Only one ship was hit, but the bomb cut through the deck, penetrated the hull, and sent the vessel to the bottom like a stone. Two more bombs plowed into the park behind Saint Speridon's Church, where they exploded, but the church itself stood unhurt. Another cut a hole in the concrete roof of the power station, crashed through the stone wall, and rolled crazily to the far side of the street before it detonated.

Piraeus was brighter than it had ever been at midday. But the buildings were no longer pure white—they picked up the orange-yellow glow that pervaded the city. The colors flickered frighteningly with the flames.

Warehouses and schools, luxurious homes and scores of other buildings that had appeared as substantial and solid as the Hill of Kastela were reduced to shapeless rubble within seconds. The waterfront area was a twisted ruin, as one building after another shuddered under the falling missiles.

And yet, only a short distance away, houses and churches remained untouched, grape vines clung steadfastly to their makeshift arbors. Some thought the Angel of Death had decided to spare this portion of the city, not realizing that Piraeus was lit up so clearly that Wing Commander Ashcroft could not have asked for more favorable conditions to carry out precise, pinpoint bombing.

The entire port area was an inferno, and each succeeding wave of Lancasters and B-17's confirmed the results. The troop reinforcements, munitions, and supplies so desperately needed by Field Marshal Rommel would never reach North Africa.

42

At 3:38 A.M. the last wave of RAF bombers dropped its load, executed a slow turn, and headed back to sea. The air raid was over, but the devastation was so great in the port area of Piraeus that even the sirens that otherwise could have signaled the all-clear had been destroyed.

The disaster was complete. More than half the ships of the convoy had been sent to the bottom, and the remainder had been damaged, many severely. The warehouses, lumber yards, and other facilities of the port area had been smashed, and were still burning fiercely. It was impossible to estimate the number of troops killed and wounded.

All telephone lines were down, so reports of the destruction had to be sent to Athens by wireless, and even these were fragmentary, because of the confused state of the military structure in Piraeus. Admiral von Widdemer had perished when a bomb struck the bridge of the ship he commandeered to clear the port. The body of Colonel Johann Schneider was found by an injured aide a short distance from the mangled remains of what had been the anti-aircraft batteries. The senior surviving Wehrmacht officer of the Piraeus command was the quartermaster, a captain, who was half crazed by the bombing and was incompetent to deal with the situation. The ranking officer of what remained of the reinforcement division, a colonel, took temporary charge and informed Athens it would be many hours before he could restore even a semblance of order.

General von Schlichter proposed sending a support brigade from Athens, but held off at the suggestion of the colonel, who said that additional troops at this time would only add to the confusion. Besides, it was already too late to prevent looting. Once word reached the Greeks that the main German supply depot had been miraculously untouched, the residents of Piraeus descended on it by the hundreds to seize meat and bread, flour and rice, potatoes and vegetables, milk, butter, and cheese. Within minutes, or so it seemed, the larders of the supply depot were bare.

No one dared enter the port area until the fires had subsided; besides, the colonel reasoned there was virtually nothing of value left, and that there could be few survivors.

But, miraculously, some had emerged unscathed. In the generator room of the power station, Petros Zervas and Nico Andreades stared up at a jagged hole in the concrete ceiling and marveled that they were still alive. They were covered with grime and dust, and Nico, the first to stir, was dazed as he wiped the filth from his face. Not until later would he realize that of all places in the port area, the power station had been the safest possible refuge. The thick walls and ceiling, all made of reinforced concrete, had provided them with a perfect air raid shelter, and the one bomb to land in the compound had exploded elsewhere.

It was unbelievable but they were alive. Unhurt.

Nico hauled himself to a sitting position, and a few moments later Petros rose to his feet just as a flying oil drum exploded against the side of the building, spraying the wall with flaming gasoline. Petros picked up his automatic rifle and slipped out of the generator room. Idly Nico wondered whether he had decided to abandon him, but did not have the strength to follow. Nico heard a door slam behind him and spun around, raising the automatic at the same time. He was tired of killing, but if he was to die he wanted to take as many as possible with him.

Petros slipped inside, brandishing a bottle of schnapps that somehow had not been smashed. He took a deep drink and handed it to his friend. Nico enjoyed the delicious burning sensation as the liquor worked its way down.

Petros moistened his cracked lips, gave his friend a hand, and pulled him to his feet. He was grinning. Raising the bottle high, he proposed a toast: "To the beginning," and drank again.

Nico brushed himself off, picked up his pistol, and jammed it in his belt. To the beginning of what?

With the echo of the bombs still thundering in their ears, cautiously they made their way out of the generator room. Outside they realized they must be the only ones still alive. Bodies of German soldiers were scattered all over the yard, but there were no cries, no sounds. The ladder to the roof was still intact, and they climbed to the roof. Everywhere huge fires lighted the sky, and the two young men were stunned at the destruction that lay before them.

The fire was quickly spreading into the city and the air was heavy as lava. A ship exploded deep inside the port, sending a tidal wave rushing through the waterfront streets, carrying burning gasoline that set off new fires in its wake. The hot air smothered the smoke, kept it from breaking through the clouds; currents fanned it along the ground, spreading the fires swiftly.

The wind grew stronger, scooping up fireballs and hurling them deep into the city to start new fires. Nico was numbed by the spectacle. Piraeus was burning, transformed by man within a span of minutes, and the sight filled him with revulsion. The fires were spreading, consuming everything in their path, and the sickening stench of death was now mixed with the pungent smell of burning gasoline, wood, and oil. In spite of the great victory that he had helped bring about, Nico could feel no sense of joy, no elation, not even a sense of accomplishment. He was bewildered. He wanted to weep, but he had to choke back the tears.

Petros' harsh, triumphant laugh broke the silence. "Look, Nico, look what I did!" His exultant sweep of his arm took in the entire port. Climbing on top of the anti-aircraft sandbags, he shouted to the world, "Look, everybody. I did all this!"

Nico stared at him, aghast. My God! My dear God, he is gloating. The death, the destruction of ships, of homes, hospitals, innocent lives, they mean nothing to him at all.

The ammunition depots near the outer port blew up in a series of explosions that shook the earth. The rapid flashes produced a bright flickering in the sky, like some giant strobe light.

The first explosion knocked them both down. In the subsequent explosions Nico could see the face of his friend clearly. He was greedily absorbing every detail of the city, the port, the trembling earth. "Look what I did. I, Petros Zervas, who was born inside an orphanage and started life as nobody. Who will be able to forget me now? The Germans? The Italians? The British?"

The Greeks? Nico thought, whose lovely city has been destroyed?

Petros rose and helped Nico to his feet. The waters were receding from the city streets, carrying chunks of splintered ships, burning gasoline, the dead. A series of mines exploded, their blue flashes turning the yellow fires green on the ships, the coal docks, the warehouses. The wind grew stronger, bending tongues of flames downward to lick the streets. It was 3:45.

Petros suddenly turned to Nico. "This is only the beginning."

"You said that before." Nico felt his body trembling. "You burned down Piraeus . . . what's next, Athens?"

A delayed action bomb exploded deep inside a nearby mountain of coal, sending pellets like fireworks flying in all directions. In spite of the flying chunks Petros never ducked. Is he immune to fear? Nico asked himself. Or does he feel he has now become indestructible?

They heard voices coming from the dock, and saw three dazed soldiers trying to lift a wounded German officer into the sidecar of a motorcycle. Petros leveled his weapon, and with a few quick bursts killed them all.

Some air raid sirens, evidently undamaged in the outskirts of the city, began to give the all-clear signal. "That sound only reassures me that I will prevail, that I'll survive the struggles that lie ahead." He smiled. "To tell the

299

truth, Nico, I never thought I would live through this night. But now there is nothing to stop me." Taking Nico by the arm he attempted to direct him to the ladder. "Let's go, my friend. Cunningham is waiting for us."

Nico pulled away in horror. "What makes you think I want to go with you?"

"You have no other choice, Nicolaki," Petros said calmly, smiling. "You joined my cause when you agreed to come with me. I promised you'd do something to be remembered for. And you have! And it's only the beginning!"

Nico leaned over the sandbags as a sudden spasm of gagging hit his stomach. The sweat coursed through his body; once again he wished he were dead. He realized now that no one could tell what was inside the mind of Petros Zervas. Not man, not even God. Maybe he is right after all, Nico thought. Maybe I should join him . . . in whatever his cause might be. Why not, Nico told himself, what have I got to lose? He thought of poor Elena. Goddamit! Why not!

Nico inhaled deeply. He felt lighter. The sweat from his body was gone. Once again, he felt as he had before the war, like the tiger of Kastela Hill, like the shark of the Olympics water polo team.

Nico turned and found Petros waiting for him.

"I am glad," Petros said. "I needed you because with you it will be easier to carry on. We have to hurry if we want to pick up the girls and reach Anavissos before daylight. There'll be a submarine there."

A blast of thunder knocked them both off their feet. The burning transport in the middle of the port had exploded, sending twisted bulkhead plates, chunks of masts, German bodies, and fire high into the sky. The two friends waded through the foot-deep sea water on the roof to the parapet and looked out into the harbor. The flames burned brightly and they could see the remaining transports smashing against the other ships and against the docks. "There goes another one," Petros said, as he saw the Bulgarian transport break in half and sink.

Exposed behind it was the *Salvatore Spoleno*, still blocking the port, still clinging to the rocks of the breakwater. "Look, Nico," Petros cried. "Oh, you lovely old man. I love you, you saint of a man, and I promise that your name will become immortal."

Nico could see the transport blocking the port, he could make out a few figures running along its deck and jumping to the flat surface of the breakwaters.

He could not understand his friend, and Petros, sensing it, pointed at the transport. "Spyros Kanares, the first hero of our cause," he said.

"Spyros?"

"Yes. Our first hero." And he explained how he had coerced the old man into ramming the Italian transport on the rocks to close the port entrance and bottle up the fleet until the bombers arrived.

Nico went numb as he listened. "We have to go and get him out," he managed to say. "I can see people on board. He might still be alive."

Petros apparently thought Nico was making a joke and grinned.

"We have to go for him, Petros. We have to!"

Petros looked at him and saw he was serious. "Are you insane? There are delayed action bombs everywhere. Even if we wanted to, we could never get through the fire, the rubble. How would we get there?"

"The same way we are going to get out of here," Nico said.

"No, my friend. We haven't got time." Petros turned to go. "Come on."

"We must," Nico said, speaking quietly. "You had no right to force the old man to do this thing. You know how it must have hurt him. He did it for you, Petros. He went against everything he believed . . . he did it because he loved you." Nico paused. "If there's a chance to save him, we must. We owe this to him!"

"I owe him nothing," Petros said and started for the ladder.

"For years you told me he was like a father to you, the only man you ever respected."

Petros turned, grabbed Nico by the shirt, and pulled him close. "How dare you talk about respect! I went after his damned icon, didn't I? I risked my life for his piece of wood. Well, then, I have every right to ask for his life in return because his life belongs to me. I saved him and I gave him life."

"How can you talk like this?" cried Nico, the strange look in his eyes becoming more intense. "What happened to the Petros Zervas I once knew?"

"Look," Petros said impatiently, releasing his shirt, "the submarine is waiting for us."

"Then it will just have to wait. You can't let a man like Spyros just die out there on that ship."

"There's no choice," Petros said angrily.

"You owe it to him," Nico said, "and whether you like it or not, you're going to pay your debt to him."

Petros was exasperated. "To hell with Spyros! Are you coming or not? Make up your mind!"

Nico made no reply and followed Petros down the ladder to the street. He helped Petros pull up the German motorcycle, watched him pump it, start it, and all the while his face remained set in hard, unyielding lines.

Petros revved up the motor a few times and let it idle. "Get in," he ordered.

Nico did not move. "God . . . help me," he whispered to himself.

"Get in," Petros repeated, "we have to go."

"No, my friend," Nico said and drew the Luger he had taken from the body of the German lieutenant.

Petros gaped at him as the motorcycle engine died out.

"What do you think you are doing?" Petros asked, his eyes searching Nico's face. "I have to stay alive, I *have* to finish. . . ."

"You don't deserve to live any longer," Nico interrupted in a low, tense voice.

"You are not going to kill me," Petros warned, step-

302

ping off the cycle and onto the street. "You can't kill me. Not with all I still have ahead. I told you, this is only the beginning—" He started for the alley.

"You don't deserve to live, Petros Zervas." Nico watched Petros turning into the alley and cried out: "I execute you and I condemn your soul."

Petros stopped and turned around. He shook his head unbelievingly. "Spare me your lectures, Nico," he said roughly, "and get the hell into that sidecar. We have to go," he said and started back confidently.

Nico squeezed the trigger, and the pistol spurted flame. Petros clutched his side with both hands and slumped against the wall of the power station. He did not cry with pain and did not speak. His eyes brought Nico close.

"Stand up," Nico ordered.

Petros tried. "I can't," he said. "You are not going to kill me."

"You no longer have any regard for human life or dignity," Nico said. "You've lost your honor, your principles, your soul, Petros Zervas."

"Help me up."

"You hate all mankind, Petros Zervas."

And now Petros realized that Nico really was going to finish him. Slowly he reached into his pocket. "Let me live, Nico. Please, Nico, give me the chance. I know I can do it. At least let me try."

The click of the stiletto blade rang in the night. "Don't do it, my friend. Please don't do it. Not now," Petros said and smiled sincerely.

"May God rest your soul," Nico said and squeezed the trigger.

Petros was slammed against the wall as the bullets tore into him. His body tensed, and he slid down the wall of the power station. Nico knelt close to Petros. His friend's eyes were still alive. He opened his mouth to say something and Nico leaned over him.

"Peace, my friend. Peace forever," Petros said and his head fell back on the sidewalk.

"May God grant peace to your restless soul," Nico

303

whispered and rose. For a long moment he looked down at the body. He saw the stiletto slowly slip from Petros' lifeless fingers. Then he noticed Petros had something clutched in his other hand. Stuffing the black worrybeads into his pocket, Nico climbed on the motorcycle, kicked it over, and headed in the direction of the crippled Italian ship.

43

It was *haramata,* the time the Greeks call the dark dusk before daylight cracks its shell and breaks free from night. The clouds were still pressing low, but breaking up now, exposing the dark blue night sky. From the deserted beach of Anavissos, about twenty-five miles from Piraeus, the glow in the distance indicated that the fires set by the bombers were not going to be brought under control by man. They had to burn themselves out.

Two people stood on the sand beach looking out at the black outline of the submarine that had surfaced in the little cove. They watched as an inflated rubber boat was lowered into the water and two sailors of the Royal Navy began to row ashore.

Major David Cunningham glanced at the young woman beside him. She had been waiting when he sent the man to pick up Petros and even now, in spite of his weariness, he knew he wanted her. But as much more than a woman; she was familiar with the inner working of the Wehrmacht, the Gestapo, the whole German military apparatus.

Trudi Richter became aware of his scrutiny, and though exhausted she flashed him a provocative smile. "It is still dark, Major. Please, you promised. . . ."

The thought of deviating from schedule disturbed Cunningham, and he knew the rescue mission was timed to the split second. He studied his luminous watch, then glanced at the sky. It was not as dark as Trudi had suggested.

"Please . . ." Trudi whispered.

Cunningham knew what Trudi wanted him to do was foolhardy, but it had been a long time between women, especially one as stunning as Trudi. And even after the night's ordeal, the girl looked absolutely sensational. Maybe in this one case he could make a small exception. He walked over to a small sand dune behind which the little girl, wrapped in a blanket he had provided earlier, was lying in the base of a myrtle shrub. Elena's eyes were focused on the horizon.

The sailors stepped off the rubber raft and waded knee deep through the water to pick up Cunningham. But suddenly the major's ears were tuned to nearby Cape Sounion, where the sound of a Messerschmitt could be heard. It is either a returning night fighter, or it is making a reconnaissance of the damage of Piraeus, or it's patrolling the shores of Attica. But patrolling in the dark? There could be only one reason—"Get the girl!" he ordered Trudi.

Trudi hurried to obey, but Elena sprang from the blanket and ran up the dirt path.

"Come back here!" Cunningham cried.

"Please, mister," Elena broke in, "I know they'll come."

A British sailor with a tommygun under his arm approached Cunningham. "Can we be of assistance, sir?" He too had heard the sound of the plane.

"Get back to your fucking raft," Cunningham snapped.

Trudi seized the interruption to grasp the girl's hand and the two of them set out at a run. Cunningham's motion brought both sailors to his side. "Get the Kraut. I'll handle the kid."

From the submarine's conning tower, the commander suddenly made out the yellow light bouncing rapidly toward the beach. Instantly, the machinegunners trained on the headlights of the approaching motorcycle and waited for the command to fire. The commander tried to make out the figures on the beach. What in bloody hell is going on out there? he asked himself.

Still struggling weakly, Trudi was dragged into the raft by the sailors. Cunningham was about one hundred yards ahead, trying to talk some sense into Elena. He was not concerned with the motorcycle, because he knew that its riders had no chance to escape alive. But he was worried about the girl. He couldn't afford to leave her behind. She knew his name, his face, she knew he had Trudi, and much more. Cunningham cursed under his breath as he saw the submarine begin to move toward shore. It was too late to carry the girl to the raft. Either she came with him right now or he would have to kill her.

"Elena, please listen to me," he called softly. "They aren't coming, they are dead. Both of them. Petros and Nico are both dead."

The submarine commander lowered his field glasses. "Stand by to fire." The headlights had disappeared, but the commander assumed they would reappear any moment over the last ridge before the vehicle roared down to the beach. Still, he was not going to take any chances. His orders were to surface off the beach and pick up one M.I.-6 operative and a Greek. The signals flashed from his men indicated something had gone wrong and he was prepared to eliminate all living things on the beach to save his two men. He waited, but the headlights did not appear over the ridge as he had anticipated. He ordered the sub to come to a halt about four hundred and fifty yards from the beach.

The gray of dawn was slowly turning to light on the eastern horizon as the commander ordered his executive officer to retrieve his men. Two taps of light flashed from the sub tower.

The sailors relayed the message to Cunningham but he did not acknowledge it. He too had heard what Elena heard, and neither could understand.

The singer's voice was hoarse, off-key. Cunningham recognized the song the man was singing—it was a Greek revolutionary march of 1821, about a handful of patriots who took to the mountains to fight and free their land from the Turks. "Black is the night on the mountains," the voice sang beyond the ridge. "On the plains, the snow is falling. . . ." The words were clear and strong:

"But on the wilds . . ."

And now another voice joined in:

> ". . . and in the dark,
> On the side of the cliffs, the boulders
> And defiles, in the narrow paths
> The Greek sword is fighting for freedom.
> The Greek sword is fighting for freedom."

"Come on," the younger voice urged, "this is no time to rest."

"I am not tired," Old Spyros replied bravely.

"That's it . . . a few more steps and we'll be there," Nico said.

"Yes, a few more steps and we'll see the boy again. Petros, where are you? See who's come back to you," Old Spyros called out happily.

"He's waiting for us at the beach," Nico said, struggling to help Spyros over the ridge.

Cunningham picked up a signaling flare gun and fired it against a rock. The flame from the flare turned the cove magenta, and everything on the beach could be seen clearly from the sub . . . Cunningham's frantic arm signals . . . the two singing men limping down the path.

When Spyros and Nico saw the brilliant display, they started to sing again, but this time louder and with bravado.

> "Black is the night on the mountains
> On the plains the snow is falling
> But on the wilds and in the dark
> On the side of the steep cliffs and on the rocks

307

The crags and narrow passes
The Greek sword is fighting for freedom
The Greek is fighting and dying for freedom."

Old Spyros straightened up, even though the effort was painful.

"Come on, old man," Nico said, trying to keep Spyros on his feet, "show them who you are."

"My dear, dear God!" Trudi whispered, as the tears rolled unbidden down her cheeks.

Cunningham, the sailors, Trudi and the crew of the submarine watched in amazement as the two men, their faces black from the oily smoke, marched to the beach. A bloody handkerchief was wrapped around Spyros' forehead, and his weak eyes searched the sand.

"I don't see the boy," he said, trying to hold his battered body erect.

"Trust me," Nico said reassuringly, but Cunningham and Trudi both knew at once.

All at once Elena materialized in front of the oncoming Greeks. It was the first time in her young life she had known victory and she wanted to shout and let everyone know she had made them wait. Nico was there! She had saved him!

But Elena felt such a declaration of victory was inappropriate under the circumstances. Whispering, "The Greek sword is fighting for freedom," she walked downhill, stripping the ends from the myrtle-bush branches to make a path for the two Greeks.

Cunningham ordered the sailors to help Spyros and Nico aboard.

"Please don't," Trudi begged. "Don't you see what's happening?"

"Do as you were told," Cunningham snapped. "I haven't got time for Greek parades."

The dawn began to bring shapes to life; the clouds above were breaking up, exposing the blue sky.

Gently the sailors carried Elena and set her beside Trudi. Spyros whispered good morning to her, and Trudi, trying to hold back tears, smiled at this man she had never met, the old man Petros had loved so dearly.

Nico said nothing. He just stared at Trudi, his face and eyes communicating nothing. He scarcely seemed to notice that the raft had started to move.

Old Spyros closed his tired eyes and was already half asleep, relieved when Cunningham told him just to take it easy, that Petros was safely aboard the submarine.

"Where did you find the old man?" Cunningham asked Nico in a low voice.

"At the end of the breakwater. He was trying to get back on the bridge and save the ship he had crashed."

"Save the ship?"

"Yes!"

"An enemy ship?"

"Yes," Nico said. "It is something you and I will never understand. To men like the captain, a ship has blood, heart, and soul. When they are at the helm it is as if they have adopted an orphan, are controlling his destiny. Spyros, you know, is a diminutive for Speridon."

"What does a name have to do with all this?"

"Saint Speridon is the patron saint of orphans."

The slap of the oars echoed across the water. All at once a new sound was heard, a steady sound, the sharp clicking of worrybeads. At first no one noticed the black worrybeads in Nico's hands, for the clicks made a natural cadence with the strokes of the oars. Even Nico himself didn't realize that the black worrybeads were in his hands. He didn't remember reaching to get them out of his pocket.

In his semi-sleep, Old Spyros nodded, welcoming the rhythmic sound of the worrybeads. But there was something about the sound, something familiar. . . . His eyes wanted to make sure his ears were lying to him.

The old man opened his eyes and stared closely at the black worrybeads. His face went tight, his mouth hard, but he betrayed no other emotion. But when he spoke, his voice was slow, tired. "We lost him then. Saint Nicholas has left us, and Charon was cruel tonight. . . . He harvested the soul of the best."

He looked around the raft and nodded at every face. "He was the best," he said proudly and then turned to the sky and cried at the top of his voice: "Charon! I want you to know, Charon . . . it is not a soul you are ferrying, Charon. . . . It is the cream of youth and the best you harvested, Charon. You stole the life-giving nectar of Athena, Charon!"

Everyone's head on the raft was bowed except Cunningham's. He was looking at the old man; he couldn't turn away.

Spyros nodded to him. "My son is dead."

Cunningham nodded in return. He could say nothing. He could do nothing as he watched Old Spyros slide off the raft and slip into the water. Even then he made no move to stop him. The water was shallow, it reached to the old man's waist. Stumbling, wading into the sea, Spyros made his way toward the beach.

Silently Nico pressed Elena's hand. "Good luck, Elenaki," he said and kissed her cheek. "You know I have to look after him. He has no one. I am the only one."

The girl reached out but Nico had already slipped into the water after the old man.

Soon the sun came out of the Aegean Sea and its rays bathed the nearby Temple of Poseidon. The day promised to be fair, fair for everyone, weak or strong, friend or foe. It could have been another beautiful day for Petros Zervas.